Bluefeather stood up, staring around with a lot of curiosity. Soon he realized the voice was coming from above him. There, about thirty feet up on a pine limb, sat a lady in a long, exquisite dress with the waist pinched in like that of a gay nineties girl, but it was a fashion far older than that. Even from this low angle he could see her breasts pushed up and partly out. Her blond hair was piled and twisted on her head, causing Bluefeather to envision a royal ball. She smiled pleasingly and chattered down at him.

"Forgive me, but I can't understand your French."

"Oh, I'm so sorry," she said in clear English.

"So am I. It's a lovely language. I'm Bluefeather Fellini."

"I know. I've heard so much about you."

"Oh. I don't mean to be rude, but just who are you?"

"Why, I'm Nicole Vallier, ex-mistress of Emperor Napoleon."

"*The* Napoleon?"

"Of course. Bonaparte himself."

"Could I . . . I mean . . . well, what are you doing here—up there?"

"Ah, that bitch Josephine had me poisoned."

"Well, I'm sure sorry to hear . . . "

"No, no. Don't feel sorry for me. It was better than the guillotine."

"What I meant was . . . "

"Please don't fret yourself. I'm well placed here. You see, I'm Dancing Bear's assistant. In fact, I'm his substitute today. He sends his profound regrets, but he is overbooked. . . . "

BLUEFEATHER FELLINI

IN THE SACRED REALM

BLUE*f*EATHER

FELLINI

IN THE

SACRED REALM

MAX EVANS

BANTAM BOOKS
New York   Toronto   London   Sydney   Auckland

This edition contains the complete text
of the original hardcover edition.
NOT ONE WORD HAS BEEN OMITTED.

BLUEFEATHER FELLINI IN
THE SACRED REALM

A Bantam Book / published by arrangement
with the University Press of Colorado

PUBLISHING HISTORY
University Press of Colorado edition published 1994
Bantam edition / August 1995

ISBN 0-553-56540-0

Published simultaneously in the United States and Canada

Bantam Books are published by Bantam Books, a division of Bantam Doubleday Dell Publishing
Group, Inc. Its trademark, consisting of the words "Bantam Books" and the portrayal of a rooster,
is Registered in U.S. Patent and Trademark Office and in other countries. Marca Registrada.
Bantam Books, 1540 Broadway, New York, New York 10036.

PRINTED IN THE UNITED STATES OF AMERICA

OPM   10 9 8 7 6 5 4 3 2 1

One From the Heart

For

My wife, Pat, my number one critic, who also suffered safely through all those long decades of my taking notes, thinking and figuring on *Bluefeather Fellini*, and then the five and a half years of actually writing it down. My profound and everlasting thanks for surviving with me the roller coaster from poor to plenty over and over and—on occasion—actual degradation, as well as sharing the few glorious times of a treasured sense of accomplishment in our other stories.

For

Federico Fellini, the great director who taught me to feel the color, see the sound and hear the unsaid in such great films as *La Strada, La Dolce Vita*, and *8½*.

For

Burt Kennedy and Ed Honeck, who always kept the faith long past its due.

For

Those deeply loved and influential amigos and amigas who have gone on the "Long Adios," including my mother, Hazel, who taught me to read, and love it, before I started school. Wiley (Big Boy) Hittson, whose brief life of daring, courage, total loyalty and sudden shocking death by gunfire inspired my novel *The Hi Lo Country*. Luz Martinez, the "Santero" who followed me to Taos and carved cedarwood into permanent beauty and dignity. Woody Crumbo, the great pioneer Pottawatamie Indian artist, who became my artistic and spiritual mentor and whose spirit is in every chapter of this book. And finally to our little dog Foxy, who came to us as a stricken stray and stayed to love and be loved through the last, forever-long months while we sought the proper publishers of the words and feelings inside these covers.

MAX EVANS
Albuquerque, New Mexico

CONTENTS

PART ONE

~

ON THE TRAIL

OF THE GREAT SURPRISES

ONE

BLUEFEATHER PULLED THE ENVELOPES OUT OF THE mailbox as if they were a handful of glowing lava. Without daring to look at them, he unlocked the front door, entered the house and dropped them on the kitchen table as fast as he could remove his fingers from the repellent paper. He knew he would have to look at them later, but he needed time to gather up his waning courage. Bluefeather had used up a lot of his reserve bravery in recent infantry combat across Europe during World War II.

He started to open the refrigerator for a cold beer and then remembered that the electricity had been cut off a week ago. Bluefeather lifted a bottle of room-temperature beer out of a six-pack container, found the beer opener, jerked the cap off, took a swallow and walked out into the living room to cogitate.

He had just sat down and taken another swallow of his refreshment when he saw his guiding spirit, Dancing Bear, up on the ceiling, looking down, grinning like a hog cracking peach seeds.

Dancing Bear spoke first. "Hey, dear brudder, I'm glad to see your Indian blood overtaking your Italian half so you can see me again."

Bluefeather yelled, "Get down off that ceiling, you

crazy Indian, and lay some more of your cryptic advice on
me."

"I ain't on the ceiling. I'm sittin' on a tree limb."

"Your ass, you are."

"That's right. My ass it are."

Bluefeather took another big swallow of Schlitz, tightly
closed his dark brown eyes and rubbed his hand through
his black hair as if to get a new perspective on this whole
situation. He was in this mess because nearly all the gold
reserves he had mined before going to war had been
spent on good living, attending college and halfhearted
prospecting. Then he had willingly followed the legitimate
dreams of Dr. Godchuck and his Aunt Tulip through their
failed attempt to develop the medicinal values of the oil
of sage.

He did not regret these activities, but wondered where
he had lost sight of the strong advice his old mentor
Grinder had drummed into his head about always keeping
a home place secure and safe. After Dr. Godchuck and
Tulip left for the Amazon, Bluefeather had borrowed
from banks, mortgaging different things at different times
for different purposes, until now all was gone. The only
things left clear were his two beloved mules, and they
would probably be going next. How had it happened?
There had been plenty of caution signs, but he had simply
ignored them, and right now he was feeling some bitter-
ness and wanted to shift the blame somewhere else.

Maybe he had gone blind with his infatuation of red-
headed Marsha Korbell. The woman had begun to possess
his brain when she left him dangling, waiting for their
long-planned "proper" date in the lobby of La Fonda Hotel in Santa Fe. She had checked out without leaving a
note, and all his attempts to contact her at the eminently
powerful, wealthy Korbell estate had been rebuffed.

Maybe it was Dancing Bear's fault. Why hadn't his
guiding spirit guided him through all this properly? Why

had Dancing Bear taken the job of guiding if he didn't guide? Bluefeather felt a moment of resentment and a possible need for chastisement, but he remained speechless as he watched Dancing Bear climb off the invisible tree limb and float down, twisting slowly around until he landed on the floor in a sitting position with his legs tucked under him, saying, "Now, dear brudder, I ready to guide and help."

"Listen," Bluefeather said, "ever since you first showed up at Taos, I've been in trouble."

"That's true for sure. I probably wouldn't drop by at all if you were gettin' along good."

Bluefeather was getting increasingly puzzled. "What kind of a guiding spirit are you, anyway? All the others I've heard about were Indian chiefs or, at the lowest, a prince or princess of Tibet or ancient Egypt. Look at you in those ragged old buckskins. I bet the highest position you ever held was dog feeder. I have a powerful need for a Geronimo, a Crazy Horse or a Sitting Bull to help me out of this mess."

"Do not worry your head. Authority send me to other peoples lately. Mebbe fifteen or ten. Me, Dancing Bear, guides 'em all to happy hour. Now I catch up on my business. Got plenty time for you nowadays."

"Now cut out that Indian dialect. You're talking like you had never left the 'rez.' You mean to sit there and tell me that during the most difficult period of my life you've been guiding ten or fifteen other people?"

"That's just last week. Yessum, I do what Authority tell."

"Authority. Authority. Why doesn't he talk to me about this in person?"

"You not listening with ears open. I told you before, dear brudder, Authority busy, busy, busy person. People all over got plenty troubles. Plenty. This Indian see it around town and in the trees."

"Well, maybe I was asking too much, Bear. Sounds like you might have troubles of your own. I'm real sorry."

Bluefeather felt a little foolish. He hadn't been trying to call on Dancing Bear for a simple, friendly visit. No, he waited until he was about to lose everything he had. His own selfishness was also something to ponder on.

"Okay, Bear, you got any suggestions for right now?"

"Maybe you oughta think about white man's metals that cause you big problems."

"Yeah? Go on."

"Maybe you read little letters and do business with glass."

"Glass?"

"Glass. Yessum." Then Dancing Bear pointed to glass objects in the room—a glass ashtray, a bottle, a drinking glass, a windowpane. "Glass, uh-huh, glass."

Dancing Bear leapt up from the floor and started dancing in a circle around the room chanting, "Hay, yi yi, hay yi yi."

Bluefeather yelled, "Jesus H. Christmas Christ, can't you do anything but that buffalo dance?"

"How about Greek?"

"I've seen it before. I've . . ."

Dancing Bear did a "Zorba the Greek" right around the room and out through an unseen crack in the wall. Bluefeather could hear the zithers zinging all the way from Athens.

He shouted at the vanishing point, "You're no spirit guide. You're a cockeyed entertainment director."

He sat staring at the spot of Dancing Bear's disappearance. There were no thoughts of the dancing one right now, however. He was remembering something his father had told him long ago when he was growing up in the northeastern, coal-mining town of Raton, New Mexico: "You know, son, when I get the feeling I'm goofing up and can't find the reason in my mind, I start back a ways and write things down. It slows the head, and the problem will usually jump out at you."

The thought of his father, Valerio Fellini's, confident voice warmed him. Because Valerio was a "super" in the York Canyon coal mines, his words carried authority with everyone in the area, especially his young son, Blue-feather. So Bluefeather found a pencil, a sheet of paper and geared himself to write. He did not know exactly how far back to go so he started at the beginning.

Born Raton, New Mexico, to Valerio Fellini, son of a Sicilian immigrant, and Morning Star Martinez, daughter of a powerful Taos Pueblo shaman. Played with lots of Fellini cousins in Raton and in summer played with lots of Indian cousins at Taos Pueblo. Then went to school. Did good at studies because my parents read to me a lot and made me do my home-work. Liked baseball. Also a pretty good fighter. Fell in love with my fifth-grade teacher. What was her name? Leesa Curry, that was it. . . .

He stopped his note-taking and took another sip of the beer. It was not nearly as easy writing down his thoughts as his father had made it sound. His mind kept jumping back and forth like minds do. Well, he would have to concentrate all the harder.

Okay, he thought and wrote:

I was embarrassed a lot of the time because almost everyone thought I was pretty. The cure: insult my cousin Guiseppe "Hog's Head" Fontano (who was employed in Chicago as a "collector") when he came back to Raton for a visit. It worked. He changed my features all right. He gave me this scar on my nose and it did stop the "pretty" talk for awhile.

Bluefeather stopped and thought about the incident.
Hog's Head had obligingly whapped him in the face so
hard he had ricocheted around the room with blood
spurting from a beautiful split from one eyebrow all the
way down across his nose. Bluefeather thought it was perfect except that the family doctor had performed too fine
a job sewing it up. It had, however, accomplished its purpose, because it was permanent. Bluefeather rubbed
lightly at the scar. It gave him all kinds of signals, this thin
mark. When he was angry the scar burned. The greater
the anger, the hotter the burn. It gave other signs of his
emotions, when he could remember to feel. Even when
he was in love, it tingled like little electric needle stings.

He stopped daydreaming and starting writing again:

*Graduated high school. Worked as a "mucker" in
Trinidad, Colorado, coal mines. Mother was sad because I didn't go to college right then. But I was
promoted real quick. Family expected me to marry
Margaret Bertinoli. Might have, but met Grinder the
Gringo, the gold prospector. Told me great stories of
mines near Taos. He was a great man. Could chew
tobacco and drink beer at the same time with no
teeth. Great man. Followed him to Taos. Prospected.
Learned from old Grinder. He taught me much.
Taught me respect and love for mules. Taught me
much. Great man he was. Fell in love with Lorrie
Friedman.*

He paused and let thoughts of Lorrie race through his
mind. It all ended because of her mother. He liked and
respected her mother, Candi. She was a beautiful woman.
Talented. Rich. Strong-willed. But she made a mistake
with him—she tried to buy him. She did not need to. He
was sincerely in love with her daughter. Candi had offered
him whatever kind of business he wanted if he would

marry Lorrie and return to New York with them after the summer season in Taos was over. He was tempted but just couldn't do it.

He stopped the scenario, and began writing:

Left Lorrie. It hurt like hell to do it. Grandfather—shaman, elder of Bear Clan—and other elders took me to the sacred cave in Taos Mountain. Had the ceremony. My spirit guide, Dancing Bear, appeared. Got him for life, I guess. Left Taos. Went to Tonopah, Nevada, with beautiful dancing girl, Nancy. Learned to deal cards. Good woman. Fun in San Francisco. Had to leave. Killed man over poker game. Sorry for that. Me or him though. Left again with mules. Drifted back to Breen, Colorado.

Now he stopped, leaned back and reminisced. How could he think his current predicament was important after remembering Miss Mary and her elegant old mining engineer, Mozart-loving father, Ludwig? They were both buried in Breen. Ludwig on a hill near town and Miss Mary hidden for eternity in the tunnel she and Bluefeather had dug together with so much love. After her death, the great vein of gold they had found had become meaningless to him. He had left her there in the mine after covering her with pieces of their treasure. He had caved in the tunnel, hiding it so well that even a shaman of the highest order, much less ordinary gold seekers, could never find it. Ludwig had died because he was ready to do so. His beloved blue-eyed, sunset-haired daughter, Miss Mary, had died from a falling rock accidently dislodged off a bluff by Bluefeather's own foot.

He could not bring himself to pencil on past the lingering scent of Miss Mary and then the great war he had just returned from fighting. Nor did he need to write down anything about Dr. Merphyn Godchuck and Tulip

Everhaven. The mind imprint of the medical visionary was indelible. How could the vision dim of a man obsessed with the curative powers of the oil of sagebrush, who could dress in Scottish tweeds and carry a cane made from a bull's prick and always appear elegant? What manner of man could show the proof of his beliefs with his own seventy-four-years' skin looking like that of a healthy thirty-year-old? A rare man indeed, but they had failed to promote his patented formula somehow, even though Bluefeather had given the project quite a boost with a considerable amount of funding from his gold reserves. If only the wealthy and powerful Korbell had just come through with the needed financing. But then it was his own adopted daughter, Marsha, who had made the presentation. The same Marsha who had left Bluefeather in the paddocks. The why of her unexplained desertion and disappearance jarred Bluefeather back to the present. He was surprised he had grown to care that much for her in their few brief meetings.

Bluefeather shook away his thoughts long enough to read back through his notes. Nothing happened to hint at how he could solve his current difficulties. Even so, he did not feel it had been wasted time. He chugged down the rest of the beer and went in the kitchen to get another.

In spite of his natural fear of the pile of mail, he sat back down at the table, put aside his recent writings and picked up the letters, shuffling them like a large deck of cards. He dealt them out in a row into an oversized poker hand. He opened them in the sequence they had fallen. There would be no favorites today. He had already lost his Chevy Deluxe, and in just ten days he would lose his two-seat canvas-top jeep. The second envelope graciously explained that the bank had made every effort to help him save his adobe house and irrigated acreage. Since he had failed to respond to their repeated notices, they had no choice but to file foreclosure papers in two weeks and one day. Nothing surprising so far.

The third missive was something else. Bluefeather mused on the number three. Why was it that the third of anything seemed to move the cogs of the modern world most of the time? Was it ordained? Well, he might as well find out now. He opened the heavy, gold-embossed envelope.

The typewritten note was vibrating in his shaking hands like a mini earthquake. It was an invitation from Mr. Ricardo Korbell. Korbell! A car was coming to pick him up this afternoon at three. What had happened? Would Marsha be there? The questions came so fast that any possible answers were immediately lost.

Bluefeather looked at the envelope again. There was no stamp. No postmark. It had been hand delivered. Bluefeather looked at the clock on the table across the room. It said five after four—that, of course, being the exact instant the electricity had been cut off a week before. He grabbed the phone to dial for time. He listened to a dead nothing and placed the receiver back on the hook, feeling kinship with an orphan lamb in a cage full of mountain lions.

He hurried into the bathroom to shave and shower, but of course, the water had been cold for days. He grabbed his shaving equipment and his one clean suit from a closet, dashed outside to the jeep, started up and raced across the field to his neighbors, the Tranquilino Luceros.

He jammed on the brakes, grabbed up his shaving stuff and clothes and leapt out, heading for the front porch, just as Tranquilino stepped out to greet him.

"Hey, Tranc, what time is it? Can I use your shower? Where's Tina and the kids?"

Tranquilino followed him around, answering as best he could, with great liquid eyes asking questions from his heavy round face, his hands inside his bib overalls as if to keep his plentiful belly from tearing the threads loose.

"It is twenty minutes until three by the clock. Please use the shower. Tina and the kids have gone to the old woman Marquez to help with her granddaughter's wedding. I stay here to work in the garden when the sun is out of my eyes." He talked on about many things through the bathroom door, although Bluefeather could hear only parts of what he said.

Now he was as ready as he was ever going to be. He ran out by Tranquilino, slapping him on the shoulder. "Thanks, Tranc. Will you feed the mules for me this evening? I may be late."

He drove up in front of his house just as the long, dark blue limousine pulled into the driveway. It purred to a stop like a large metal cat with its motor still turning. There was no regular sound of the motor, only a low hum without vibrations of precision metal. There was a glare on the windshield, so the image of the driver was unclear. The machine seemed to study him with glazed eyes, making its own inanimate decision about the totality of his fate. He felt small and very alone as he stood motionless by the canvas-covered jeep, waiting.

The door on the driver's side swung open and a lady stepped out—a right keen lady. She was in a pale blue suit that matched her eyes, and the thick edges of autumn-colored hair blazed in the three o'clock sun. The orange orb had momentarily glazed his vision.

Bluefeather did not acknowledge the actuality of his jolted feelings. For just an instant, a paralyzing instant, he thought he was looking at a Miss Mary, only taller by about four inches.

Then she smiled—ah yes, she certainly did. She also spoke, although the words must have had some difficulty making their way through such a beam as that. It created considerable strain, but Bluefeather did hear her. It was Marsha. My God, it was Marsha Korbell, the deserter.

"Hello, Bluefeather Fellini."

"Marsha!"

"Mr. Korbell awaits your visit with much anticipation. Would you please get in?"

He got in. He was so stunned by her presence that he just sat immobile, speechless, as she drove away. There were things about these Korbells that called for momentary silence.

TWO

ORDINARILY, BLUEFEATHER WOULD HAVE ENJOYED THE ride up through the scattered piñon and cedars decorating the foothills. The mighty Sangre de Cristos dominated the horizon above, making the world seem very big. There was glass between him and Marsha, the driver. He did not use the intercom to speak, nor did she.

As they rounded a curve, the house was revealed. It was surrounded by a ten-foot-high adobe, concrete-plastered fence partly disguised in the trees. There was a huge iron gate ahead at the entrance, but it, too, was painted earth colors. The sight certainly jarred Blue-feather out of his comfortable musing, for it wasn't like any house he had ever seen before.

The first impression was of a medieval castle, but the lines of old-modern southwestern architecture dispelled this impact. The curvature and soft edges of the massive structure could only be adobe. It was multistoried like the Taos Pueblo main building, but faded back in more compact layers of levels. It exuded a sense of strength, permanence and, yes, power.

If Bluefeather had given any prior thought to it, this would be the kind of house Korbell, by his nature, would obviously occupy. One heard all the rumors of his financial manipulation. There was gossip, of course, that he was in oil, mining, manufacturing, arms shipments and on and on.

Bluefeather couldn't remember a single interview with the man in print or on radio. However, now and then, one would see a photo of him at some exclusive international gathering with several lovely ladies surrounding his imposing presence.

Bluefeather, using his mind-voice, said, *The son of a bitch is a mystery all right, and it was one created by his own choice.*

When Korbell had moved to the Southwest, the local papers, and some national ones, had simply stated—without giving reasons—that he had decided on this part of the world for his permanent home and hinted at the fact that everyone in the state would all be better for it. Personally, Bluefeather had paid little notice to the latter. It had been his minor experience that the move of big money always created that same initial reaction, even if it was later found that the wealth came to pour concrete over the hills and hide the natural horizon with all kinds of look-alike structures.

Bluefeather had been trying to quit smoking for over a year now, but he suddenly reached for his security pack in his coat pocket. He hesitantly put it back and wiped his suddenly dampened palms on the sides of his legs.

The great gate swung back in front of the limousine. Now, after entering the acres of compound, Bluefeather's practiced eye saw the hidden guard boxes on each side of the gate and scattered every hundred yards around the entire estate. He had no doubt that they were being watched with careful interest.

The security commander was a huge man with a deep scar angling like a steep mountain trail carved into his face. By their subtle gestures, Bluefeather could tell that the man and Marsha were somehow close. Then he re-

membered seeing her with him in the Cerrillos Bar south
of Santa Fe before they met.

She said, "That's Fontaine. You'll meet him someday.
Now, Blue, don't go into any fits or questions. Just calm
it all down and I promise you it will all come clear in the
future."

Well, he might as well play along with this plot, game
or whatever it was. What, really, did he have to lose?"

They drove upon a circular graveled driveway bordered
by arranged groupings of piñon, sagebrush, cacti, yucca
and other plants indigenous to the region. The limousine
stopped. My God, he was about to meet the man. His
brain turned into a cement mixer.

The lady opened the limousine door, waiting, still smiling.

"We're here."

Bluefeather exited, giving a weak thanks.

As they walked along toward the large antique doorway,
Marsha talked casually and comfortably, but he didn't remember a single sentence she uttered. He hoped he had
answered if questioned, but he didn't know for sure. The
door, like the front gate, swung open before they reached
it. Bluefeather truly expected a polished British butler to
greet them, but instead there stood another elegant
woman of indeterminate youth, smiling.

Marsha introduced him thusly; "Elena, this is Mr. Bluefeather Fellini."

Elena shook hands in a solid way and said, "It is so nice
you could come. Korbell is expecting you."

Bluefeather noticed she did not preface the name with
the usual "Mister."

"This way, Mr. Fellini."

Bluefeather followed, glancing back for Marsha, but she
was walking away down the long, tiled hallway without
having said another word. However, the vision moving
ahead of him was sufficient to hold the attention of a

lobotomized lizard. Elena's long, ballerina graceful legs floated under the flowing gown that intermittently clung to and outlined her entire body. The gown had Aztec designs of varied hues from top to bottom. Maybe Rembrandt could have given proper attention to these works of art clinging to her surfaces. Bluefeather could only think of the Great Spirit's art underneath.

She stopped at another large door, smiling as she opened it. Bluefeather was struck by the glowing whiteness of her skin and the delicate but strong chin under the slightly arced crimson lips that curled invitingly around teeth whiter even than her skin. Her hair was blue-black like the barrel of a new gun, with a large silver comb placed so that the long strands snaked around and over a shoulder, just reaching one of her slightly revealed breasts. Bluefeather had an urge to dive into the two pools of eyes that matched her hair and to swim straight to heaven, if he didn't drown first. What was wrong here? He was thinking like a beginning madman.

Then the man, Korbell, was walking across the room, smiling of course, as if he were meeting the Pope or a king, but it was just plain Bluefeather Fellini.

Elena said, with the purr of a little tiger, "Korbell, this is your Mr. Fellini."

"Ah, what a pleasure to meet you in person, Mr. Fellini. Of course, I've heard about you from Marsha." He grabbed Bluefeather's hand and gave it a shake that would have torn limbs from a great oak. He turned it loose just as swiftly as Bluefeather muttered, of all things, "Howdy, Mr. Korbell. It's sure good to meetcha."

"Korbell. I prefer just Korbell."

Bluefeather would never forget the last statement even though his present retention was being shattered like a dropped clay pot.

Korbell was at least a couple of inches taller than Bluefeather, probably six three, and as lean and tan as a tennis pro with Aegean Sea eyes and a long Sherlock Holmes nose over a wide, thin-lipped mouth. His hair was, to use an ancient description, shining silver, of course—it would have to be. His age, like Elena's, could not be determined. Bluefeather guessed it could be either side of fifty. Korbell, too, had the same perfect teeth that gleamed from the ladies' mouths. Bluefeather ran his tongue over his own rather common ivories and then figured that maybe he could get a recommendation to their dentist, if nothing else. To top it all off, Korbell wore a very casual umber smoking jacket.

"You've met Elena, my adopted wife?" Bluefeather's voice-mind clicked in again. *Horseshit and smothered onions,* he thought, *an adopted wife . . . he actually said that.*

Bluefeather swallowed and decided he had better just enjoy the show before he got lost in the mezzanine.

Elena vanished. Bluefeather was seated in a luxuriously soft chair as Korbell took a matching one to the right of him, angled so they could look at one another without twisting and both could comfortably gaze out a ten-foot picture window across miles of rolling hills rising through blue-hazed timber to barren, snow-covered peaks. Right magnificent.

"Well, now, Mr. Fellini, do you feel like a drink?"

"Blue. My friends mostly just call me Blue." He had to do something in self-defense. He added that he would be delighted to have a drink with him.

Another striking woman quietly appeared. In contrast to Elena, she had on a simple, tailored dress. Her brown hair was done up in a neat twist on top of her head. Bluefeather felt better when he saw that she had one tooth slightly out of line. She waited, smiling. After the introduction failed to come, Bluefeather heard her say, "Brandy?"

"Perfect," he answered, aiming to oblige where possible.

As she poured the drinks in a distant corner, Korbell looked at the boundless panorama, sighing contentedly, "What a perfect setting for our first meeting."

Bluefeather said, "Leonardo da Vinci would be honored."

Korbell chuckled slightly, adding, "Very good, Mr. Fellini. Very good, indeed."

Bluefeather thought, *The bastard has got me snake-charmed already. I'm almost ready to rise up out of a basket and start weaving to the music of his flute.*

The brown-haired lady came with a large tray holding the brandy and a box of Havana cigars. Bluefeather took the brandy and placed it on a hand-carved Spanish table next to his chair. The lady hesitated just a moment, so he took a cigar along with a gold-embossed match box. She served Korbell. Bluefeather waited. Korbell lifted his snifter. Bluefeather lifted his.

"To our potentially highly rewarding association."

"Whatever that might be."

Korbell gave his underplayed chuckle again, and they drank. It was very fine stuff. Bluefeather expected Korbell to speak of some exclusive, expensive brand name, but he was fooled again. Korbell lit his Havana. So did Bluefeather, wondering when the Philharmonic would enter.

"I do so like to mix business and pleasure, Mr. Fellini. More so all the time. Much more so." With that he reached down by his chair and picked up a flat leather folder, opened it and began to read. Bluefeather knew for sure now that the game had started. A change came over him. He was no longer overwhelmed. He knew a contest was beginning between the two of them. Overmatched? He might be, but he was prepared to challenge the odds. What, really, did he have to lose? He was ready. Excited.

Korbell read, muttering at first, "Now, uh-huh, yes. Born 1914, Raton, New Mexico; Italian father . . . mine foreman, now retired; Taos Indian Mother, has become a

fairly successful traditional water colorist of Indian art."
Korbell continued to read, "B-student, baseball and track
star in high school; assistant mill foreman before you were
twenty; became gold prospector; bought property and
moved to Corrales; went to war, Europe, three major
campaigns . . . aha awarded a Silver Star at Brest . . ."

Bluefeather swallowed some high-priced cigar smoke
and coughed out, "No, that's all wrong. It was a mistake.
I didn't deserve it . . . I swear . . ."

"I like modesty in its place, Mr. Fellini, but this is not
the place. I can fully read and understand a commenda-
tion. I was myself in the OSS for four years, you know?"

Then he read on briefly in silence. "I see you left the
School of Mines a few months before graduating . . . setting third in your class at the time. Oh, well, it's not my
concern why. I see you've hidden the fact that you did a
stint of mercury smuggling out of Mexico recently. Not
that it concerns me, but is that why you left school?"

Bluefeather had hidden the last even from himself.
There would be little he could hide from this man, so why
bother.

"Yes. That is why I left. I think you've already figured
that. At the time the mercury movement was faster than
a quarter horse track, and a hell of a lot more profitable."

"I see. The short-range profit motive overcame the
long-range solidity of a degree as a mining engineer."

"I've never witnessed any solidity in the mining game."

"Game. Game did you say? You might have been . . .
no, let's forget this part." Korbell shuffled the papers and
continued, "You did have a very successful early life considering the choices you made. You survived the Great
War in good shape and were building up your investment
property just outside Albuquerque. Then things started to
go to hell. What happened, Mr. Fellini? What in this
world happened?"

"Several markets broke, including mercury. I became jaded and careless, that's all. It won't last. I won't let it."

Korbell continued to read, "You were married briefly. Your wife, Mary O'Kelly, expired from a mining accident near Breen, Colorado. What, I pray, young man, was a woman doing mining?"

"She was very good at it. It was just a . . . a freak accident. I'd rather not speak of it again."

"As you wish. Forgive my impertinence, but I have to know certain things. Oh, oh, I almost overlooked this. You killed a man in Tonopah. Self-defense. That's good."

How could this man go on so casually about the major events in his life? He decided to fire back. "Before we go any further, I want to know why you turned down the presentation on Dr. Godchuck's sage oil. It could have stopped a lot of suffering. And Marsha said you thought it was a good deal."

Korbell looked up from the papers, smiled and said, "Maybe so, Mr. Fellini, but you see I have something that is far greater than that of the good doctor, and the time is now. You know, one may be fortunate enough to have great wealth, but it will not purchase him a single second more of his allotted time. I have things to be fulfilled and my hope is that you'll see your way clear to help." Then he returned to the reading. "Let's see, where was I . . . ? your father is now retired from the mines and your mother has become a successful watercolorist of Indian art. You phone her on the first Sunday of every month," Korbell was smiling so slightly that Bluefeather had to strain his 20/20 eyes to see it.

This last personal piece of information was just a little too much. Bluefeather was sure the man knew the brand of toothpaste he used. He decided to end the inquisition. "Well, it looks like you know how many times I fart each day. Let's cut the crap and get down to the deal."

"Deal?"

"Yeah, you said you needed my help. And I know you haven't invited me here for my scintillating conversation, have you?"

Korbell chuckled again, finished his brandy and relit the Havana. Bluefeather did likewise. Waiting.

"Forgive my intrusion into your personal life, but I have a delicate proposition to make you, and one needs to know with whom and what he is dealing. I hope you understand."

Bluefeather countered with, "How about another brandy?"

Korbell raised his right hand and said softly, "Nedra."

The brown-haired serving girl entered the scene from around a latticework and they soon had their brandy. She exited.

Korbell stood up, brandy in hand, and said, "Please come with me."

Bluefeather followed him, warming the amber liquid with the palm of his hand as he walked. They wound through a hallway down a curving iron stairway beneath the house. They went through another heavy, iron doorway that opened smoothly at Korbell's touch. Everything seemed to be machined perfectly around here. Everything.

Bluefeather followed him perhaps twenty steps to a like door. Korbell touched it as lightly as one might a frozen windowpane to test the cold. It swung silently open. They were in a vast wine cellar. Maybe it was average to Korbell, but it was mammoth to Bluefeather.

Korbell did not hesitate now, but strode purposefully past rows upon rows of worldly wines without even glancing at them. At last he turned and started down another aisle. Here he stopped by a tall, small-topped table that reached above their waists. He smiled around his teeth, white even in the dimly lighted cellar, and lifted his brandy to Bluefeather in a silent toast. He acted like he

was in a library full of sacred tomes. Their glasses touched
ever so lightly, making a ringing sound in the underground stillness.

Bluefeather followed Korbell's lead as he placed his
glass on the odd-sized table. With delicacy and practiced
skill, Korbell took a bottle from its resting place and very
carefully placed it upright on the table between the
brandy glasses and whispered, "Read."

Bluefeather bent down in the dim light, somehow
knowing not to touch the old bottle. He read aloud,
"Mouton Rothschild—1880." There was more fine print
that he could not make out in the poor light.

Korbell whispered now as if he stood before the open
casket of a dearly beloved, "That, Mr. Fellini, is one of
the great wines of the world. And just as important, it
pleases the palate like no other. The Rothschilds have
refused to sell me another. They value each bottle in the
thousands of dollars. Many thousands. It would do no
good to offer more. Each year, at the end of the grape
harvest, one—only one—bottle of this is opened in honor
of the eldest of this noble clan. It is a priceless product
to the Rothschilds, and to me. Do you understand?"

"I don't believe I do . . . unless . . . unless it is craving
something one cannot buy, can't have just for money."

"Ahhh, you are partially correct, but you see I can have
it . . . more Mouton '80 than even the Rothschilds have
left in their cellars."

Bluefeather could only stare at him.

"Mr. Fellini, have you heard of Joshua Tilton?"

"The famous mining man?"

"The same, indeed." Korbell explained, "Joshua Tilton
struck it very rich in mining between the two great world
wars. He built large homes all over the Southwest and
lavished friends with many, and varied, gifts. He was
known as an eccentric—mainly, I felt, because he spent

his wealth publicly and opulently on parties for renowned people from all over the world."

Bluefeather was aware that both Tilton and Korbell had become legends, even though their public approach to life appeared to be exactly opposite.

Korbell continued, "At the time Hitler invaded Poland, Tilton had become obsessed with the concept that the dictator would truly conquer the entire world. Tilton was reported to have gathered a great store of gold and silver bullion and hidden it in one of his mines. Great fortunes and many lives have been spent in a futile effort to find this treasure. If the reports were true, or if the treasure has been found, I've not been able to verify it."

He paused a moment, watching Bluefeather, his piercing eyes showing his enthrallment with the story and his curiosity at its effect on his visitor.

"Tilton's unsolved murder in a Silver City hotel during the height of the bombing of London only added to the mystery. It became a notorious incident since the head was missing from the body and has never been recovered. All the forces of the law were expended in a futile attempt to solve the case. Every lead, no matter how vague, was followed. They all petered out. Right now as we visit, someone, somewhere, is seeking the fabled fortune."

Bluefeather was aware that Tilton's bullion had become almost as famous as the lost Adam's diggings of the Superstition Mountains near Phoenix, Arizona. Elusive dreams or hard facts? The thing is, people wanted to believe in its existence, so they searched on and on.

Korbell sighed, looking at the Mouton '80 and spoke again, "I'm sure, Mr. Fellini, that your mind is racing with whirlwind thoughts of Tilton's lost bullion. Well . . . that is a strong rumor, but a rumor nevertheless, you see. But, a mostly unknown fact is that Tilton did hide sixty cases of Mouton '80. Sixty cases, Mr. Fellini! Do you realize what a treasure that truly is? Perhaps a million dollars' worth of Mouton. Maybe more. Who knows what the careful disclosure and handling of such a find would accrue. But, you see, that is not its true value, is it? Far from it. It would be like owning half interest with the French nation in the Mona Lisa. I have the old shipping and arrival bills, proving without a doubt that this wondrous shipment was delivered only a short time before Tilton's demise. The wine is here. Somewhere in finding distance."

Korbell was breathing like a milerunner at the tape. His eyes were staring through mountains. An obsession had possessed his being. Then Korbell recovered and got right down to real business. Real for Bluefeather at least. He informed Bluefeather that Tilton was certain to have secured the wine underground to keep an exact and constant temperature. Bluefeather was surprised by Korbell again when he admitted that the very cellar they now stood in had already been dug by Tilton and the foundations of the great house had already been poured and most of the walls laid at the time of his decapitation.

Korbell praised Tilton for his choice of this location and admitted that it was his exhaustive research on Tilton that had led him to this most perfect of all places to build his final and permanent residence.

Korbell explained that he and Tilton were of the same stand of timber; all that remained to be done was the finding and glorious consumption of their Mouton '80.

Now he led Bluefeather out of the expansive wine cellar and up to his sanctuary. It was a room almost as large as the cellar—a room hung with paintings of the old and new Taos masters: Sharps, Couses, Phillips, Berninghaus—the whole drove and more. There were the originals of world-famous Indian artists such as Woody Crumbo and R. C. Gorman's landscapes and varied styles of Andrew Dasburg, Howard Cook and Fremont Ellis. There were long shelves of southwestern titles from such

authors as Mable Dodge Luhan, Willa Cather, Oliver La
Farge and many, many others that Bluefeather recognized
at a glance. It was difficult for Bluefeather to listen to
more talk of lost bullion and wine when the mentors of
his mother's birthplace hung about the adobe castle as
casually as an old hunting dog.

Korbell forced him to return his attention to Tilton's
legacy. He showed him maps of all the mines in New
Mexico that Tilton had either owned, prospected or
leased, as well as the dates they had been opened, or
closed, or abandoned.

Then the deal was pitched. Korbell would pick up all
Bluefeather's overdue payments, thereby saving his home
and land, and pay him a generous retainer for six months,
renewable at Korbell's choice. If Bluefeather found the
wine, he would pay one-half its immediate market value.
He wanted the wine. Simple.

It did not take Bluefeather long to make up his mind.
He was on the verge of losing everything that had taken
so much real blood and love to accrue. It wasn't just the
monetary worth of his loss. It was old Grinder's advice
that was being downgraded. Anyway, he loved the Corrales place, his mules, his neighbors. The place had to go
on existing for those from the past. It hurt to think it
might not be there for some future ... future ... ? What
the hell! He might as well admit it. He had goofed. His
balls were in a red hot vise that was rapidly closing. Another thing that shot through his system with a surge was
Marsha. He would be with her, because she definitely was
part of this strange equation unfolding like the wings of
a giant butterfly. Without hesitation, Bluefeather gave
Korbell a powerful handshake. The act would indeed
change his life completely.

Korbell held Bluefeather's hand a moment, looking
through his forehead, and probably beyond, saying, "I ex-

pect the same dedication to our great cause from you that I myself have given and will continue to bestow. Do you totally understand me, Mr. Fellini?"

Mr. Fellini said, "I do." And he did.

"Fine. Fine. Now let us retire for cocktails and dinner."

THREE

THEY SAT ABOUT THE GREAT ROOM OF THEIR FIRST
meeting. Elena, Marsha, Korbell and Bluefeather talked
about current painters, potters and musicians of a local
bent. It was easy-flowing conversation with no interrupting or domination of the talk. Nedra served the drinks
and appetizers smoothly, without any wasted apologies or
fuss. Bluefeather felt it was an omen that he and Marsha
both asked for J.B. Scotch. The world was made of small
likes and dislikes.

The hiding sun was turning the snow-peaked mountains
watermelon pink. The Spaniards had long ago designated
this last light of day as *sangre de cristo*—blood of Christ.
The valleys and hills had already become part night with
misty blues and purples that made one think of long ago
and the possibility of eternity.

The mellowness of the booze and the relief from many
suffocating debts had put Bluefeather in a pleasant torpor.
They all seemed to sense that. Korbell, as well, was a
happy and relieved man. Marsha's eyes and rosy skin
beamed like summer sunspots. She sipped her drink casually, occasionally pushing a random strand of auburn
hair back from the side of her face, giving him looks that
he was sure had deep meaning. Of course, those looks

could only be special for him, no matter how brief. He was right. She *was* studying him, wondering how Korbell could trust him on such short acquaintance, even with all the prior information he had gathered and her own short acquaintance with him. Well, they would all soon know what his capabilities were.

As Marsha looked at Bluefeather's strong features again, she was embarrassed that she felt a quickening of breath. My God! She was feeling like a high school sophomore and praying it didn't show. She could not let him know that—not until she could explain, someday, why she had left him in Santa Fe without an answer.

Elena listened to whomever spoke with a rare raptness. As the natural outdoor light receded, her white skin again drew Bluefeather's gaze. Her large dark eyes fastened on him like those of a master hypnotist. He wondered for an instant if they had hypnotized him—this Korbell group.

No. The mountains, now becoming one with the sky, were real. The drink he held was real. He took a small, cool swallow to verify. He pushed his own thick, black hair across his scalp. It was his own head he was inside of, for sure. Well, whatever. A few hours back, he had arrived here with one leg hanging in space above a chasm of darkness, and now both feet were planted firmly on the Indian-rugged, tile floor. Solid. Even though he felt it unnecessary, he was certain he could elevate himself to the ceiling like Dancing Bear, on command.

At the instant of this thought, the aquarium of tropical fish that he had noticed in a far corner moved toward them. It slowly circled the entire group, stopping for a fraction of a moment in front of Bluefeather. The multicolored fish swam about in little liquid rainbows, nuzzling the bottom of the aquarium among pebbles and swaying vegetation. One large white fish looked arrogantly at Bluefeather a moment, knowing all. Then the aquarium settled down and moved on four little wheels to the great window and stopped. Bluefeather looked about—casually, he hoped—at the other faces. They had taken no notice at all; their current attention was on Korbell, who was expounding his admiration for Maria Martinez's San Ildefonso Pueblo pottery. Nedra, smiling, served as the aquarium now smoothly rose up and floated to its former place.

Bluefeather thought, *My God, how they all smile. Did rich and powerful people take smiling lessons, and . . . and ignore magic aquariums as if it happened to be their due?*

Bluefeather was confident that he had maintained his composure as Korbell spoke, "Ah, yes, Mr. Fellini. I forgot to apprise you of one more item. My adopted daughter, Marsha, will be your assistant on our little venture. I trust you will find that satisfactory, as she is extremely efficient in many fields."

Bluefeather looked at her teeth lined so perfectly back of her luscious lips and said, "If you say so, sir." This was one of the closest six or seven times in his life he had ever come to dying of both shocked surprise and pained pleasure.

Marsha controlled the jumbling and jangling of her nervous system, emitted a sigh of acceptance and nodded her head so casually it was almost imperceptible. Oddly, everyone in the room watched her minute indications of acceptance.

Dinner had been, to say the least, grand. The wine was of such a bouquet that the young guest wondered why in the holy hang-dogged hell a man ever needed to give a thought to Mouton '80. They had duck à l'orange that chewed and swallowed itself. There were many more courses, but Bluefeather blanked on what they were. There are only so many goodies a man can swallow at once without choking. He did not, however, resist when Korbell insisted that he stay the night. They all had brandies except the elegant, somehow aloof Nedra.

Bluefeather was happy when he was shown to his room with a bed big enough for a basketball team. He was wondering about the adopted wife, the adopted daughter and, no doubt, adopted serving girl as he pulled the silken covers over his shoulders.

He thought, *By God, maybe the obsessed bastard will adopt me, too*.

He was just trying to think of a single disadvantage to this as a coyote howled off toward the north, answered by one farther on, when he realized a figure stood silhouetted against the window, backlit by a rising moon. It was a female. No doubt about that at all. The scent of a subtle perfume from some faraway island wafted about and mixed with the Scotch, brandy and wild dreams in his head.

She crawled into bed beside him. He couldn't make out her features, nor did he have a chance, for her smooth, warm arms folded over and around him. Her breasts had his chest captured and enraptured.

He croaked out, "What are you doing here?"

The unrecognizable whisper came soft as the first breeze of autumn, just as her hands found him.

She whispered, "Well, the Orientals say there are one hundred and one ways."

Bluefeather lost count at six or seven.

Later he realized he was alone. One of the three adopted ladies had permissively raped him. It was too late to care. He was too lusciously tired to stay awake and ponder.

FOUR

BLUEFEATHER AND MARSHA WERE ON A WINDING, hilly highway, heading for the place of an old friend of his in the mountains of southern New Mexico. Willy Ruger and his sister, Flo, owned a ten-room log house on 160 acres of patented mining claims smack in the middle of a national forest. Zia Creek ran right through their property. It was also a central location to search for the mines on his benefactor's maps.

Long ago, during one—or maybe his very first—meeting with his spirit guide, Dancing Bear had prophesied to his young new client that he would have a life filled with wild adventures. Dancing Bear was right. It would all speed up like an idling motor suddenly thrust into full power. The trees along the promised quixotic trail had already begun to blur from his awesome and increasing velocity.

Korbell had come through swiftly with the funds and influence to get Bluefeather's messed-up world back in order: all back payments on the property were paid and the gas, water, electricity and phone had been reconnected. Bluefeather had hired Tranquilino to take care of the place any way he saw fit. He had even retrieved the three Patricino Barela and the two Luz Martinez wood carvings he had hocked to his insurance man. It had given him a grateful feeling of warmth to place them back in his living room alcove, where they belonged.

He was also pleased and surprised at Marsha's interest and practical suggestions when he had talked of the addition he planned for his house. She had figured out the right location for his new den. She also suggested a sliding glass door opening out onto a private patio. The enigma of the woman equalled that of the lost wine, but he held back any prying into her privacy, albeit with difficulty.

It was spring. The birds were flying about from tree to bush, trying to reach a satisfactory agreement on mating. Cattle moved about the land, chasing the tender green shoots that shoved their way up through the dead, brown remains of winter grass. The bulls were busy following the cows, sniffing, pawing, curling their upper lips, searching for the scent that signalled permission to mount the backs of mother cows whose new calves frolicked freely about with their faces white and new before the world had a chance to dirty them.

They entered the village of Meanwhile, New Mexico, population 240 people, forty cats and thirty dogs. The highway split the town in half. There was the usual mixture of adobe and slant-roofed, frame houses. The store buildings mostly still had old frontier fronts scattered along an erratic wooden sidewalk. A few pickup trucks and cars were parked at odd angles here and there. It was Saturday, so over half of them were in front of the Dos Amigos Bar.

"Hey, Marsha, do you like burritos?"

"Yes, especially the bean and beef with red chile."

"Well good. Ol' Dominguez makes the best in the whole world."

He bent the loaded jeep to a stop. They got out and entered the Dos Amigos. Before they got inside, they could hear the jukebox playing country songs. Old Dominguez spotted Bluefeather as soon as they sat down at the whiskey-, cigarette- and elbow-worn bar.

"Hey, Blue, where you been? Don't see you for months, maybe, huh?"

"Been dodging rocks, amigo."

"Don't see no knots on your head."

"They're all on the inside. Dominguez, this is Marsha."

"Happy to meets you, ma'am. What'll be your pleasures?"

"Bottle of Pabst Blue Ribbon for me. What about you, Marsha?"

"That will be fine for me, too."

They ordered two burritos and ate them sitting at the bar. Of course, it took three more bottles of beer and two more burritos before they could get their strength straightened out. Marsha put away the chile, beef and pinto beans wrapped in a homemade tortilla as if she had returned from a year in the Arctic. Bluefeather liked that.

The crowd kept gathering. Bluefeather had made the mistake of ordering a round for the house. The people of this land could smell a generous fool through a three-foot adobe wall and at least twenty miles' distance—if the wind was right. It was right, and about everybody in the whole county was showing up or sending a "rep."

Suddenly, all the old, musty cowboy prints, beer and cigarette signs, along with the comforting smell of a million spilled drinks and the sweat of miners, cowboys and social security retirees made the Dos Amigos the only place in the whole world there had ever been or ever would be. Eight bottles of beer might have helped some. However, Marsha had sipped only two. She was laughing and visiting with every awestruck habitué who approached. She fit right in.

Bluefeather was swiftly becoming very proud and kept sneaking looks at her in the backbar mirror. She was doing the same to him. She sat there on the bar stool in new jeans so tight he couldn't imagine how she had been able to tuck in her tan shirttail. The folded, turquoise blue scarf tied around her head looked like the crown of the most majestic queen who ever lived. Bluefeather thought all this, and then some.

He walked over to the jukebox and punched out two dollars' worth of tunes at random and asked Marsha to dance. She eased off the stool into his arms and wrapped lightly around him like a snake on a limb. Her chin fit right over his shoulder without any strain. Talk about floating; compared to Marsha all eagles and swans were amateurs. He was suddenly very proud of himself that he could control his agitation at her vanishing insult in Santa Fe. He would not bring it up verbally and would eradicate its existence from his mind. There was no other way he could handle both her and her father's deal.

By the time they finished three or four songs, two other couples had joined them on the dance floor. A whey-bellied miner was yelling every turn. The good times were rolling.

"Hey, Doming, another round for the house."

Since the place was nearly full now, Dominguez and his helper responded to the request with amazing rapidity.

Bluefeather looked at Marsha and asked, "Do you suppose Korbell will allow this party to go on our expense account?"

Marsha had a way of cocking her head to the side like a puppy and doubling the size of her big blues when asked a question. She made him feel that the fate of the galaxy depended on her giving an accurate answer. "I'm sure he wouldn't mind. He only expects results. He doesn't care at all how they come about."

"To Korbell," said Bluefeather, raising his bottle of beer. She anticipated and did the same.

"My God, she said, as if the end of the world had come

and passed before she had gotten a good look at it, "I forgot my Agatha Christie book."

"You read her?"

"I love her work. Is that anti-intellectual?"

"Not at all. I've got a copy of Jack London's *Call of the Wild* in my bedroll. I've read it ten times, I suppose, starting when I was twelve or fifteen years old. Anyway, I think Christie is one hell of an underrated psychologist and a jim-dandy maker of puzzles."

Marsha was pleased and started to express it in some way when Bluefeather turned definite attention to an old man just opening the front door.

Bluefeather saw eighty-year-old Dolby enter the bar with his permanent puzzled expression on his face. He was retired from politics—not that he had ever run for office. On the contrary, he had worked in second and third position for U.S. senators, land commissioners and mayors and as speech writer for most all of them. He had made few enemies, lived well and had lots of fun until early middle age, when he turned to private endeavors. The wizened old man was dressed just as cleanly as he was shaven. His little fedora was cocked to the side a tad, giving him a slightly rakish look. His comfortable grey suit had grown a little too large for him. His necktie fit his collar perfectly, but the collar hardly touched the wrinkled, scrawny neck. Dolby stopped at the end of the bar and started talking right off to Dominguez, ignoring the noise and activity around him.

"I never saw so many people as there was in town yesterday. I don't understand it. Yesterday was only Friday," Dolby said.

Dominguez answered patiently, "There was a funeral. Old man Mullins was buried."

Dolby left the end of the bar and headed for the only empty stool next to Bluefeather, muttering, "I meant to go to that funeral. Musta forgot."

"Howdy, Dolby. You're looking frisky."

Dolby totally ignored Bluefeather, struggling carefully onto the bar stool, still talking to himself. "Musta forgot." The old man held a wrestling match with his knobby old hands that ended in a draw.

He said simply to Dominguez, "Whiskey."

He took the glass of straight bourbon, held it toward the light, giving it a good looking at. He turned it up as if to down it all, but only took a tiny sip. Then he turned his little dark eyes, hidden back under two bushes of grey eyebrows, and said, "The moon'll be full next week. Then we can either plant our garden or all go mad and howl with the wolves." He waited a good thirty seconds and then said sadly, "Of course, our wolves are gone. All gone. But they'll return with the buffalo."

Bluefeather said, "I can't wait."

Marsha joined in, "Me either. I saw a pack in Canada last year . . . an entire pack . . . and there was more love between them than in all the romance novels ever written."

Bluefeather started to ask her about Canada, but Dolby was speaking again.

"I don't raise a garden anymore. Sherry does that. My part's eating it."

Everyone in Meanwhile knew Sherry—his young, Hardvard-educated, East African from Nairobi, Kenya—who had come to the village several years before, had moved in with Dolby and stayed.

Dominguez asked Dolby, "How's your ex-wife getting along with her new husband?" The question was not out of place, since this was her fifth marriage. She was over sixty years old, and her new husband was under forty. Dolby was either ignoring the bartender or thinking it over. He repositioned his fedora slightly and readjusted the knot in his tie. Then he said, "A woman's love is similar to lightning—it's just as likely to strike a shithouse as a castle."

Bluefeather said to Dolby, since he had been around politics most of his life, "Who is gonna be our next governor?"

The old man raised his whiskey glass to his lips with the same fierce gesture that a thirty-year alcoholic might and then took his tiny, little sip, barely wetting his tongue. Bluefeather was fascinated with this movement, reading into it such a thing as, he fools himself or others into believing he's had a big drink. It is a way to share the company of the bar—which, in effect, is Meanwhile's country club—without hangovers and little expense. Maybe, it might simply be for effect.

Dolby leaned over toward Bluefeather without turning his head. His little eyes strained sideways under the hedgerow eyebrows, however, and he said, "Beware of scare . dogs and ideologues."

Bluefeather decided that was all the conversation he was going to get about the governor's race and turned his full attention to Marsha, who was politely dancing with a big hay-baler. Bluefeather could see he was pulling her closer than she liked. He started to get up and cut in when she winked and smiled, signalling that it was all right.

She did not enjoy this creature one bit, but she didn't want to create any fuss their first night in the land of hunted treasure. It would not be fair to Korbell or Bluefeather. She kept looking over the hay-baler's shoulder at Bluefeather, wondering what he thought of her. There was something tender about him, but also a force of danger contained in his easygoing and flowing body and manner. She wanted to know more about him, but Korbell had taught her above all, patience, when it was needed.

Bluefeather went to the bathroom to unload about a gallon of beer. The horizontal urinal was plugged-up, looking like a dirty horse tank. A lot of it had overflowed onto the floor, but he couldn't wait for a plumber.

When he stepped out, he saw Marsha trying to sit back down at the bar and the hay-baler pulling and pawing at her. She jerked loose and threw a karate chop alongside his jawbone and the side of his neck in the same swift motion. He dropped like a sack of wet sand. Everyone, except Dominguez and Bluefeather, was yelling, clapping and enjoying the show. The hay person scrambled up with a confused expression. Just as he took a step toward Marsha, Bluefeather side-winded his rudeness. He flopped around and down on his face. Bluefeather could tell by the way he fell that he wouldn't have to kick him. This time the fallen one eased up with great caution and stood there rubbing at his twice-jarred jaw.

Bluefeather had learned from Stan Berkowitz, the mill foreman back at Breen, Colorado, that a smiling man might be holding a knife behind his back. But the hay-baler stuck out his hand, saying with much sincerity, "Dear, dear friends?"

They shook hands. He bought them all a drink—even Dolby, who refused to acknowledge it in any manner. Then he moved over to replenish the music.

Marsha said in a low, scolding voice, "I could have handled him."

"I believe you. Believe me, I believe you."

The secret of a successful evening at a country bar was not to leave too soon or too late. They finished their beers in a casual fashion. Bluefeather ordered up a case of Jim Beam as a peace offering for his friends Willy and Flo. They both liked sipping very brown whiskey.

Bluefeather paid up, giving Marsha the eyeball signal and receiving it in return. Bluefeather laid some money on the bar and yelled, "Drinks for the whole damn house." In the midst of loud, appreciative anticipation, the two of them escaped.

They loaded the whiskey and themselves into the jeep and backed it up. Bluefeather geared right down the highway out of town. Both were giggling like they had just graduated from first grade.

When the jeep had been coaxed to the right side of the road, Bluefeather said, "Hey, hon', crack a bottle of Willy's whiskey, will you, please?"

She did. Taking a light sip herself, she waited for a straight stretch of road before handing the bottle to him. Bluefeather was thinking that he might never know any more about Marsha than he did right now, but even so he was going to settle in on the fact that she was one hell of a woman.

Then it smacked him and he blurted out, "God uh mighty, I musta forgot! Old Dolby was Tilton's right hand, and was for a decade, right up until the night he was beheaded."

"That's interesting to know. Very." Marsha said, reaching to take the bottle back, "Do you mind sharing with your assistant?"

"Lord uh mighty no. You can have the whole bottle if you want it."

Bluefeather pulled over at the area's only motel. Got out and checked them into separate rooms. They both thought of the waste. One room. One bed. One view. That would have to do. Both acted as if they would always sleep apart. Both were already getting used to the scent of the other, but they also had been mentored into the dedication of business first. They tumbled in the covers an equal amount of time, trying to remember Korbell's mission assignment. It didn't work. They only thought of one another. Neither would have believed the mind-images of the other.

FIVE

THERE IT WAS. WILLY RUGER'S PLACE. THEY WERE TOP-
ping out over a relatively small timbered mountain. They
had seen nothing for about three miles of dirt road but a
few blue jays, two does and a fawn that had crossed the
road in front of them. Down in the valley they could see
the log house with its barn, corrals, a bunkhouse, pump-
house, chicken house, haystack and a garden area. It
looked like a small, secluded village. The meadow grass
was already becoming green, and Zia Creek sparkled its
eager, winding course a quarter of a mile west of the
house. The sage and scattered cacti slowly mixed with the
patches of timber bunched around rusty orange bluffs. On
to the west, everything fused and thinned as the desert
took over. To the north and east the timber thickened so
that only the mightiest of cliffs bulged their way through.
The mountains stair-stepped up, each higher and lighter
blue than the others. If one looked closely, piles of mine
tailings could be spotted from the old-time miners' attack
on the earth. They had looked and dug here, over a century, for dreams seldom found, and much quicker lost. In
a day or so the young couple would be doing the same.

Marsha clasped her hands together and held them to

her breasts, uttering, "My God, it is beautiful. It's too much."

Bluefeather suddenly felt right and comfortable and confused at being accompanied by such a saucy, knockout assistant.

The hound dogs came to greet them first, barking furiously, but with tails wagging. There was an old World War II jeep, a pickup and a sports car parked at random in front of the house. The last meant that Willy's niece, Sally, was home from school. Willy, Flo and the young Sally all came out on the porch as they pulled to a stop.

Marsha and Bluefeather got out of the jeep. There was much hugging and handshaking with everybody talking at once. Bluefeather introduced Marsha, and they all gave her welcoming hugs and handshakes.

Bluefeather asked Willy, "How're you getting along old pardner?"

"Grandy dandy. I went to bed last night with a lot on my mind, I got up this morning and my mind had vanished. I know not where."

Flo asked, "How was the drive out?"

Bluefeather grinned and continued the silly banter, "Just like a frog going to water, steady but by jerks."

Between all the greetings, the introduction of Marsha and vice versa, the petting and saying hello to the hounds, it took them a few minutes to break free and gather up the whiskey gift. When they finally got in the house, things settled down and the sporting activities made haste. It was the time for partying. Bounteous drinks were poured. Joyful toasts were made, and everyone bubbled.

Flo wanted to know if they were hungry. She had a venison roast in the oven. They all stalled at this, settling down to drink and get the necessary small talk done before the eating started—the way things should be when old friends, long apart, get together.

Red-faced Willy's upper body was built like a jeep. Between drinks, he constantly pushed the thin grey-blond hair back on his head. He was fifty years old, but in some ways he was younger, and some ways older. His powerful shoulders and arms were bent forward as if he were reaching for a heavy rock. He had done plenty of that, for sure. When he got up to move across the room for a drink, his log-looking legs broke into a little, short-stepped run. They did the same whether in the house or on a mountain.

Flo was built somewhat like her brother, except she reared back instead of forward to compensate a bit for the two heavy weights hanging from her chest. She had a small waist, considering the fullness of the rest of her, and caused one to think about old photographs of the gay nineties girls. Her weather-lined hands and arms showed all of her forty-six outdoor years, but her face was surprisingly soft. She had always worn a hat, any hat, to block the sun from her short brown hair and constantly thinking hazel eyes.

Sally? Well, Sally was five four and filled out about as perfect as one can get in eighteen years. There was more mischief than anything else exuding from a face that moved from pretty to petulant in an instant. She wore her dark brown hair in pigtails.

"Hey, guess what, Senor Bluefeather Fellini," Sally said, "I finally made it out of high school. There's the proof right there." She pointed to the framed diploma above the couch and cast him a deliberate, flirting glance that without any guessing said, "Look at me. I'm grown up, just like you."

Bluefeather couldn't help but look at her silent suggestions. Sally could see that he saw. She warmed and glowed like a new light bulb in a cool room.

Bluefeather said, "Ain't that just keen," stepping closer to her framed diploma where it hung on the wall. "Congratulations, Sally." That gave them another excuse for a toast. Bluefeather continued, "Going to college this fall?"

Sally looked at Bluefeather, then at her mother and uncle, hesitantly saying, "Well, it all depends."

Flo said, " 'Course she is. New Mexico State University over at Las Cruces."

Bluefeather knew that Flo really meant it, but he was also aware that they probably couldn't afford it. Well, that was another damned good reason to find the Mouton '80. At that thought, he asked Willy to show him around the place, since it had been quite awhile since he had been here. They got another glass of whiskey each and walked out. The women were visiting like wild ducks behind them.

Willy was very excited, even though he tried to appear calm during the "showing." He was mighty proud of his overhead gas tank, the new pumps and electric generator. He beamed like a kid on a pony when he showed Bluefeather the rebuilt smokehouse hung with dressed deer, elk and hog meat. He reared back like a fresh-bred rooster at the solid condition of all the outer buildings, but what really made him preen was the new phone booth on the back porch.

"I like my privacy when I talk on that damn public thing. I never had nobody call me with any good news on it yet. When they got that, they come in person."

The two friends sat down on a log by the woodpile, petted the hounds and got down to serious visiting. It came out that Willy had leased his Virginia Bell Mine down at Hillsboro for three years, but the lease payments had been dropped just this month. That explained both the money to do the improvements on the place and the hesitation in Sally's voice when she spoke of continuing her education. They didn't have any source of income except what Willy hustled from leasing his mines or doing day labor on other men's claims.

The hounds were slobbering with friendliness all over Bluefeather when he noticed one was missing. "Where's Ol' Red?"

The whiskey and the visiting temporarily lost its effect on Willy as he said, "Lion killed him. Ate him, too. Got three of our goats and a yearling heifer."

Bluefeather said, "Well, you got three dogs left—why can't you go get him?"

"Tried. That's when he killed Old Red. You know I really ain't much of a hunter, Blue, except for minerals. Just never had the touch."

"Don't worry, ol' pardner. We'll get him while I'm here."

"If he don't bother no more . . . maybe we oughta just let him . . ."

"He will. The pickings have been too easy."

"Well, I about . . ." and he shook his head at the ground.

Bluefeather just couldn't wait any longer to tell Willy about Korbell. Now seemed the appropriate time. When he had finished, he waited expectantly for an enthusiastic reply from his friend and confidante.

Willy didn't say anything. He picked up a stick and started whittling on it with his pocketknife.

Bluefeather ventured, "Seeing what a pitiful financial shape I was in, I didn't see where I had anything to lose."

Willy stopped whittling, closed and pocketed his knife, picked his glass off the log and drank what little was left in it and said, "Korbell? Well, shoot a monkey. Heard a lot of different things about Korbell. You might oughta use some extra caution with him. Sounds spooky to me."

Bluefeather felt a little bowknot tie itself inside his guts. "How do you mean, spooky?"

"Well, my pa knew Tilton some, and he dealt with Korbell some just before he died. He never could figure him out. One thing though . . . there's one thing for sure: papa did believe Tilton hid all that bullion somewhere down here. But wine? I never heard of no wine. Not never."

"Well, Willy, I gotta believe it. I saw the papers."

"Anybody can have papers faked."

"You're right, but then why would he put up all this time and money, sending his daughter along to watchdog me, if he didn't believe it himself?"

Willy grinned, "You got me there, Blue. Hellsfire, we'll get to lookin' for the wine startin' tomorrow. Right now I'm so thirsty I could drink mud."

"Here, have a swallow of mine. I want to know all about Sally's school plans."

"Well . . . she had six hundred dollars saved up to start, but that boyfriend of hers, Harvey Holt, from over at Las Cruces, done conned her out of it."

"What do you mean 'conned her'?"

"Oh, he had a sure bet on something that makes ten dollars to one in two months. Never happens, Blue. Hell, you know that. In the mining business we got 'em like Holt by the hundreds."

"Yeah. Well, what are we gonna do about it? Does she like him a lot?"

"Cain't tell. It's a lonesome country out here for a pretty young woman. He's an entrepreneur of the defecation of bulls." At Bluefeather's quick glance, Willy smiled shyly, saying, "I never thought that last line up. Heard old Dolby saying it." Then he got serious again. "But what I can tell you about Holt is, the son of a bitch laughs at ever' thing you say. Makes people think they're great comedians. He'll ha, ha, ha you right out of your bank account."

Bluefeather didn't like what his best friend had told him, but he could not think of the right reason to vocalize at the moment.

Willy started his little turkey trot toward the house. Bluefeather followed, feeling great again.

They had fun like people are born to do. Flo fed them delicious venison, baked potatoes with homemade butter, green beans she had put up from last year's garden and a peach pie almost as good as Mary's. Not quite though, for in Bluefeather's experienced opinion nothing was as good as Mary's had been. Nothing. They were full of drinks, food and that incredibly rare feeling shared with friends who don't care what you say, and even less what you do, except to join in.

Marsha acted like she had known these people as long as Bluefeather had. They felt the same about her. She told them about spending a year on a kibbutz in Israel and quoted an old rabbi she had admired. "Rabbi Sharut said that Goliath didn't have a chance against little David, with all his mighty muscles and outsized club, because David and his people were so long experienced hunting and fighting with slingshots, they had even killed lions with them. Why, poor Goliath was horribly overmatched. David might as well have been armed with a 30.06 rifle. Don't you see? Don't you see how history gets all turned around?"

Willy, who obviously had taken a shine to Marsha, agreed. "You're sure right about that, hon'. Look at the Billy the Kid legend. Thousands of stories and every one different, all swearing they're right. Why, the whole damn thing's a wild guess. There's things that happened during his time, and even mine, that's been told all wrong," and he launched into several examples.

Flo, sensing that he might have "whiskey tongue," interrupted cleverly, asking him to play the banjo. Willy forgot all about talking and put his mind to what really mattered, music and whiskey. Willy was adaptable.

He started out picking "Cotton-eyed Joe," "When the Saints Go Marching Home" and then went on to some real fast steppers.

Sally grabbed Bluefeather by the hand and pulled him

up to dance. She saw to it that their fronts were close. So close, it both pleased and embarrassed Bluefeather. He tried to be brave and enjoy it. She could feel that he did and wiggled even closer.

All the women danced with him. Bluefeather couldn't be too flattered by this since he was the only available dancing partner. He relished it just the same. It was still cool this time of year, but everyone was sweating. Bluefeather, being outnumbered three to one, was wetter than the rest. Flo and Sally literally rubbed their precious parts all over him. The longer the whiskey and music went on, the more active the rubbing. It became more disconcerting to Bluefeather. Marsha didn't hold back anything, but she didn't push herself forward enough so that a man could make a clear judgment of her attitude. Bluefeather Fellini was disconcerted. Then Marsha pulled loose from him and did a wild, whirling Israeli dance by herself with her long auburn air flowing out like a wind-whipped flag. She got a standing ovation and bowed accordingly.

Finally, Willy put his banjo down, emptied his whiskey glass and dogtrotted erratically toward his bedroom, saying, "Grandy dandy."

Sally tripped over the coffee table and just lay there comfortably on a bearskin rug. Bluefeather hoped she wasn't dreaming of Harvey Whats-his-name. Bluefeather and Flo gathered her up and led her to bed in the room where Flo slept.

Then Flo showed Marsha and Bluefeather to separate rooms. Flo said she didn't feel like going to bed yet. She had to clean up the kitchen first. Bluefeather knew she meant that, but he was also aware that she would probably stay up and drink and mess around the kitchen until dawn. He had seen her do just that, scores of times.

Marsha came out in a robe and volunteered to help, but Flo would not hear of it, insisting she'd had a long trip and needed rest.

There they were. Bluefeather wanted to grab Marsha and run her into his room, but he wasn't about to blow away his beloved place in Corrales just for a roll in the sheets. Not now, anyway. Maybe later he would blow up three counties for her. For now though . . . well, he would just go on aching like all frustrated youth. There was no way he could move toward her. He tried valiantly to convince himself that she had been the one who had crawled into bed with him the night he had spent at Korbell's— and lots of other things. He didn't know for sure. Anyway, he pulled himself back.

Flo said, "That's a very high-toned, regular lady, Blue. I hope you get along with her. She's what they call 'a jewel.' Understand?"

His heart did seven fast circles around his chest and he croaked out, "Yessum. I sure do. She likes you guys, too. I can tell."

"Good. Well, I just wanted you to know how much I like your new friend. I feel like she's ours, too, already."

That was all Flo said, right then. He waited. He waited some more, not moving his body purposely, although the surging blood moved parts of him. He went in and put on his robe and then slipped out into the hallway. He had decided that the only thing left in the universe that could give him the help he needed was some cool, fresh, mountain air.

He walked softly down the hallway and out on the porch. He had forgotten Flo, and almost everything, except Marsha. Flo was in the kitchen in her robe now, wiping off the cabinet. She spotted Bluefeather and motioned him to come inside. He had no choice. He tried to pull and hold the robe so she could not see his obvious problem. It did not work.

She poured him a drink, whispering, "Couldn't sleep, huh?"

He, being so suddenly sobered, took half the glass in one swallow saying, "Naw. I got a lot on my mind."

She reached down and grabbed him, saying. "I can see what you've got on your mind, Blue dear."

Without letting anything loose, she led him right out on the porch like a kid pulling a little red wagon. He went along for fear of bodily injury. Now she turned loose, as her robe fell apart too. There it was, the uppers big and inviting as bowls of ice cream, and the dark mount of Venus hairy as a black wolf pelt.

"I haven't been with a man since me and Crazy Dugan split."

"When was that?" Bluefeather foolishly gasped out.

"A year and six days and about three hours." Flo grabbed one of his hands and put it on her breast. The other she shoved between her legs.

"See?" She said.

He couldn't see, but he sure as all hell could feel. She sat down on the porch and spread her strong legs wide in the ready, aim, fire position.

Bluefeather hesitated perhaps a second, thinking what old Grinder the Gringo had once told him: "A hard-on ain't got no conscience."

Being momentarily weak-willed and out of control, he just dived right in, at the same time feeling that he was certainly young and healthy, so that left him nothing to be but kind and generous. It was quite a ride.

Flo bucked and wiggled, getting unfelt splinters in her rear. She moaned and hissed until Bluefeather got frightened and put his hand over her mouth. She clawed him in the back of the head until he felt like he had been half scalped and spurred her bare heels into his butt like a champion bronc rider.

She rasped out, "Find the pearl, honey darling. Find the pearl."

He must have found it, because he finally became conscious again. They were both unmoving now except for their struggling lungs. Bluefeather rolled off and barely clutched the edge of the porch before falling on the ground flat on his back.

A happy face soon gleamed dreamily down at him, saying, "You may not get on or off very pretty, darling, but you've sure got a pile-driving ass."

Bluefeather took a deep gulp of cool, mountain air and said, "Why, thank you, Flo."

The party was mostly over.

SIX

BLUEFEATHER AND WILLY WENT OVER THE MAPS UNTIL they became blurs to their searching eyes. Willy knew the location of most of the mines, as well as their history, but there were rumors of three old tunnels that even he had never located. Somehow, Korbell had come up with faded maps to the Commonwealth, the Dutch Joe and the Copper Star. Willy decided against taking the mules, because the trails were rough, but of no great distance.

They bumped, ground, twisted and jolted their way as far as the jeep could make it. It looked like a day's backpacking into the upper wilderness. Marsha stayed right in there, not complaining or even commenting. None of them did. The altitude and the steep climb, along with an intentionally subdued sense of possible discovery, took the chatter from their lungs.

They had lunch at about eight thousand feet. Up ahead a bit, they could see the first large stand of aspen. The greyish white bark of the trees stood out like battalions of daytime ghosts against the deep-shadowed undergrowth of the mountain. The tender, light green leaves trembled in the mountain breeze as if afflicted by a billion tiny frights a minute. To the west they could see over seventy miles across land fractured, eroded and wind-singed into sienna, burnt orange, vermilion and every hue of blue, violet and velvet-purple that the eye could stand to behold. Then the land rose again to form a whole hogbacked horizon even deeper blue than the sister sky.

Bluefeather felt Marsha absorbing the ageless message of this vastness, just as he was. He was pleased without being totally aware of why. There was a combination of intensity and serenity as she looked across the immense southwestern earth as if she were somehow absorbing it into her being. Her own coloring, silhouetted against the arced sky, seemed to match and meld with the Indiantrod, snake- and lizard-crawled, coyote- and bobcat-traversed, spread-out land.

Bluefeather was developing an ancient aching, longing, for her. He could no more explain it than he could the development of penguins or cosmic dust. For now he would struggle to not even try. Besides, she was probably a spy. Even so—forgetting Korbell—he wondered if it would make any difference if she were a Mata Hari. He doubted if it would change his unformed feeling for her at all.

Willy was standing, looking up the rock-choked canyon facing them. It was a bitching climb. The old burro trail to the mine had been washed out long ago, leaving jagged boulders and wind-fallen trees covering a big part of it. They moved on up, constantly clambering over, down and up again. They were sometimes on their hands and knees like awkward rock squirrels, but they must not stop now.

Bluefeather let Willy lead with Marsha in between them. Willy was older, slower, but a lot more knowledgeable in selecting the erratic trail. He maintained a slow but steady pace that would finally get them to their destination without killing them off. Sometimes, when the earth levelled slightly, he would break into his little trot.

No wonder Willy had lost two inches of height since he passed the forties. With the hundreds of climbs, with

packing equipment up the mountains, and with carrying
sample rocks down, over and over, it seemed a small miracle that he was more than four feet tall.

Not even the struggle of ascent nor the shortness of
high altitude breath could keep Bluefeather from taking
many glances at the rear view of a moving, twisting Marsha. There was a sensual grace about the movement of
her long legs over, under and around the hard rocks. He
couldn't help it. He wanted to roll her in the shade. The
extra breath he expelled at these many varied thoughts
caused his lungs to work harder than otherwise.

They were past nine thousand feet now, and all wondered if they were going to run out of mountain before
they found the mine. Then Willy and Bluefeather discovered pieces of green malachite copper. Marsha became
grade school excited at this and acted like she was on an
Easter egg hunt.

For just a few moments, she was a little girl back in
her past somewhere, ohing and ahing excitedly as she
found the scattered pieces of the vein. Then she regained
her necessary stoicism.

Suddenly, they all were side by side, an hour till sun-
down, staring at the mine entrance. They had found it. It
had an extensive waste pile with copper disseminated all
through it. Bluefeather guessed that the tunnel would be
over a thousand feet deep. The mountain had shed some
of its skin in a vain effort to hide the insult of the hole
dug into its guts.

There was only a small opening left at the top of the
tunnel. Bluefeather and Marsha wanted to go in right off,
but Willy wisely said it would be better to pitch camp,
gather wood and cook supper while they still had time
before dark. Willy was right, of course.

After the fire was going, Bluefeather and Marsha lay
back on their bedrolls, staring at the hypnotic fire, smelling the smoke and the venison Willy cooked in the skillet.

Bluefeather was more tired than he had realized. Marsha's eyelids drooped almost shut. Then she jerked her head up and strained her wondrous, blue eyes wide. She was a stayer. She had volunteered to cook, but Willy would not allow it. Cooking outdoors was one of his prides. At home, Flo and Sally were welcome to it, but up here it was his domain. He had thrown several wads of sourdough in the combination skillet and dutch oven to go with the venison. They ate till the wild meat and bread were all gone. Then he handed them a few dried apricots to wash down with big tins of hot coffee. They made a weak effort to visit. It did not work. They scoured the aluminum dishes by rubbing them with clean mountain dirt, finishing them off with a precious splash of water.

They crawled into their bedrolls and were asleep before they had time to hear the night birds sing or the coyotes call.

The morning comes early on top of mountains. The sun gets first shot there. Willy had gotten up at daylight and scouted around, finding springs that were actually the headwaters of Zia Creek. He remembered now that his father had brought him up here, from a different direction, when he was a kid, but the mine had been completely caved in back then. That at least meant the mine had been opened since Tilton's time, even though the tunnel had nearly filled again. There was a remote chance of discovery this day.

Bluefeather gathered some more wood while Marsha went to the cold spring to wash. She returned to the new fire, combing at her hair. Her face had paled from the cold water, but she appeared fresh and eager for the day's adventures.

They ate the sizzling bacon and biscuits ravenously and got their gear ready to enter the mine by the time the

sun had first touched the mesas on the desert floor so far
below.

Now Bluefeather took the lead, crawling in the opening
with his battery light. Marsha also had one. Willy carried
an old, open-flame carbide light to detect poison gas if it
was waiting silently, invisibly.

Willy and Marsha were right behind Bluefeather as he
moved the light about the tunnel. There was a small pool
of water in the overly large room in front of them. He
had seen this before so many times that it pained him.
The miners had found a profitable pocket of ore here and
had carved out the dangerously large room in front of
them. This was both greedy and foolish, because a cave-
in here would not only have risked the lives of the workers, but it could also have closed the mine, necessitating
digging another costly entrance. The stope went up about
thirty feet above them. Bluefeather checked it as closely
as possible with his light. It looked as if it would hold,
although there were two piles of smashed rocks that had
fallen to the tunnel floor at some time.

He led them around the edge of the pool. The lights
showed the water to be so clear that the gravels, some as
small as grains of sand, could be seen. The bits of oxidized
malachite, azurite and sulfide copper shined under the
water like a sultan's tomb. It was just as silent. It is not
known for sure why, but when people first speak in a mine
tunnel, they do so softly, as they would in a library or
church. Maybe being underground, at the mercy of a
pierced mountain with millions of tons of rocks hanging
above one's head, creates a more holy feeling than usual.

Bluefeather whispered, "Watch out for loose rock. The
idiots raped another mine."

Willy excused the old-timers, whispering back, "I can
understand why. They could only afford to haul high-
grade from this inaccessible bitch."

Marsha spoke softer even than the others, "I feel like we just walked through time into an old, old world."

Bluefeather eagerly answered, "You got it right, lady. The rock still in place here is way over thirty million years old and was first touched by humans less than a hundred years back."

They moved carefully on. Willy and Bluefeather tapped the walls with their prospector's picks, searching for a hollow sound that might reveal a hidden side drift. The deeper they moved the better the ore looked to Bluefeather. Beyond his initial resentment, he marvelled at the determination of the old-timers who had dug the tunnel for more than a thousand feet with crude hand tools, plunging for the heart of the noble mountain. The vein had a general strike northeast to southwest. It dipped to the southeast. It was in a porphyry and gneiss formation. Bluefeather knew this was good host rock for a large deposit of copper, but that was not what they were after. He almost laughed aloud when he remembered they were after wine. Wine.

They looked, too, for Tilton's metal of long ago, mined and melted and cooled into solid bars of bullion. As far as Bluefeather was concerned, the sixty cases of lost wine would do just fine. Any treasure would do, but gold. That had taken away his family—one yet unborn.

Korbell had hired him to find just the wine. Thinking of Korbell, Bluefeather inadvertently blurted out, "Don't know what we're supposed to do . . . what . . . how . . ."

The other two lights danced about nervously at the shock of his voice. Bluefeather felt like he had been caught pissing in the kitchen sink.

They had pecked at every foot of the tunnel on the way in. To the best of their judgment, the tunnel had not been altered. It was solid, natural rock all around. Anyway, it was frivolous to think they would find the cache on the first try. All felt a little let down, but then most everyone expects mountains to give too much too quickly. Mountains never let one know anything for sure. They only make one think so.

The three were about twenty paces from the face of the tunnel, on their way back out, when Bluefeather halted, hearing the haunting sound of an Indian flute. The others stopped, watching him, eyes wide. At first the sound came so softly that he thought it was emanating out of his head instead of into it. Then the sound swelled rapidly. Bluefeather wondered if he was the only one to hear it. His question was answered when he felt Marsha's hand grasp his upper arm for a fleeting moment.

Bluefeather turned around and shined his light back into the tunnel. Suddenly, the music stopped. There was a silence so profound that it seemed to have a singular existence, with its power being in its nonbeing. A small pebble fell from the ceiling to bounce on the tunnel floor, making a noise—to the only listeners—far beyond its true size. Then a larger one fell, and another. Then the face of the tunnel bulged out like a huge, stone balloon and shattered, sending large pieces of rock rolling forward. The bluish brown dust puffed forward from the rubble. A rumbling noise came from the tunnel and the bowels of the mountain like the mighty garbled voices of arguing giants. The entire face of the tunnel, the ceiling, and the hang and foot-walls started falling toward them.

Bluefeather grabbed Marsha and Willy, hurling them forward, screaming, "Run, dammit, run."

Bluefeather held himself back with great difficulty. The tunnel filled, and its crumbling, grinding fullness moved toward them like a stone tidal wave. The air forced out by the jumbled tons of rock filling the void blasted the dust forward, around and ahead of them. Bluefeather was choking, shouting at the other two, without knowing what he said. He could hear and feel the forces moving toward them like a herd of rampaging elephants on their heels.

Bluefeather reached out blindly with his wildly groping hands, pushing, dragging them toward the tunnel entrance. He had lost all sense of direction and constantly ricocheted off the walls. Somehow he could hear Marsha and Willy coughing even in the terrible roar, above his own rasping lungs. They were slowing, for he was having to manhandle them forward, cursing, cajoling more each instant. The dust was almost unbreathable now. He felt Marsha leaning, gasping, against a wall.

He screamed right at her ear, "Hold on!" He shoved her hands into the back of his belt and felt them tighten. They moved forward. It was all darkness. The noise and shaking of the tunnel was comparable to attending a ballet during an earthquake.

They stumbled over Willy, who had fallen to his knees. Bluefeather strained up as he lifted Willy. All three struggled on. They could feel the blasts of air on their backs growing stronger, which meant the tumbling rocky guts of the mountain were gaining on them, closing in, to form a multiple, unknown grave. So-called TIME was nonexistent, in the thousand-odd feet of the man-made wound in the now angry mountain.

The lights had long been lost. The absolute darkness was a fearsome thing, but the as-yet solid sidewalls ahead kept them moving, stumbling erratically forward. Bluefeather could sense Willy's strength leaving his powerful old body as his lungs closed down from the dust so thick they could have been buried in midair. He could also feel Marsha's weight dragging more as the belt almost cut off his circulation. If it would just hold. He felt his being becoming as cloudy as the tunnel dust, certain that he was entirely without air, breathing the boiling mass in and out with an effort that was ripping his lungs loose and turning his blood to cement.

All of a sudden, there was a numbness all over him—

the kind that must come when a person gives in to the false warmth of a blizzard and dies in comfort. It was a teasing temptation to be seduced by the pursuing rock. All he would have to do was fall with his comrades, and in four or five seconds there would be no more agonizing effort to breathe, to find light, to live. There would be no more pain. Nothing.

Just then, he felt light. Yes, it was there. The flicker of light that pushed through the small opening at the top of the tunnel was quickly suffused with the dust, but it was definitely there, a short distance ahead of them. With the tiny beam of beckoning sun, his lungs found more air. They were all three on their hands and knees, clawing across sharp-edged rocks up toward the shiny beacon from the beckoning outer world. The tunnel narrowed ahead of them and fell, roaring, like a thousand dueling lions behind them.

With the power-granting, adrenaline-charged force that comes when all of life is based on surviving a second, or a fraction thereof, Bluefeather grabbed Marsha and hurled her like a spear ahead of Willy. It was single file for them now.

Bluefeather pushed at Willy's scrambling feet, yelling a continuous chorus of "Go. Go. Go. Go."

He could feel the mountain's masonry falling after them, making a last desperate effort to devour their flailing bodies before they reached the outer surface of its epidermis to continue life.

"Go, Marsha, Go."

Bluefeather did not remember the last few feet to the exit. He did recall rolling joyfully down the bruising rock pile, once outside, as if playing on a feather bed. He turned and watched the inside of the mountain seal the crawlway so full that several fresh azurite specimens tumbled outside, rolling down a few feet before stopping.

All three were on their hands and knees again, coughing, spitting and coughing more. Finally, the spasms slowed and then quit. They lay back spent and limp as worn-out ropes. Bluefeather stared into the sky, trying to see beyond the blue. The sky moved back and forth and pulsated into violets and greens. It had holes and protrusions like the ground, or a cloud mass. He had just now, after thirty-odd years, learned to really see. One tiny, white cloud crossed his vision, slowly enlarging, growing by itself and then evaporating away to nothingness. He knew there was no such thing as nothing becoming nothing, so the cloud must simply have changed into another form.

The sky was the second most beautiful thing his agitated eyes had ever seen. The height of the mountain that had almost claimed them created a brisk, clean wind that refreshed their lungs and consequently their entire bodies. The first most beautiful thing on earth raised its head and turned to him speaking, "Would you care to discuss the stabilization of the world political situation, Blue?" Marsha gasped.

"Dearest Marsha," he coughed out, "it probably would be more appropriate than discussing religion. I'm afraid I've just used up my year's allotment of prayers."

It was hard for him to believe, but the Korbell clan smile radiated enchantingly from her dusty face like a second, white sun. "We wouldn't have made it without you, Blue."

"No. No, it took all three of us."

Willy let out a comforting sigh and said, "The price of metal just dropped today, but . . . it'll go back up in a week or two."

Then they all laughed at their silliness, which was standard, anyway, until they realized the shaking of their mirth was stirring their coughing again.

They rested a few minutes. Each one struggled to a sitting position, moving joints and limbs to test for dislocated or broken bones. There did not appear to be any, but they were a ragged, skinned and bruised threesome.

Willy said, pragmatically, "We've got to get off this mountain before the soreness sets in."

It was a tough decision to make, but he was absolutely right. Bluefeather stood, wobbling and held out his hand to Marsha.

She said, "Thanks, but I have to know if I can do it on my own." She did.

Willy made it, too. Then they started laughing and hugging one another again. The slightly hysterical fun was soon negated by another resounding spell of coughing. After that they drank deeply from their canteens, filled them again from the birthplace of Zia Creek, gathered and packed their gear and moved out, limping down the mountain, feeling like the sole survivors of the Hundred Years War.

When they came across a rare, smooth place, Willy would break into his little shuffling dogtrot as if nothing had happened. Something had though. They all three knew it. A warning? An event? Maybe. Maybe.

Willy and Bluefeather had climbed and struggled over a lot of mountains and deserts together before today, but now Marsha had joined them. They were bound together by the unbreakable bond that can only exist between humans who have successfully survived facing the spectre together. Beauty of the voice and flesh would eventually break, but not this. The reality of the thought made the young man's tired feet bounce like a whore's butt on a steel-spring mattress. Both thoughts were good. The mountain swiftly shrank.

SEVEN

WILLY WAS RIGHT ABOUT THE SORENESS AFFLICTING them. They limped around like they had entertained lions in the Roman Coliseum. Flo and Sally had little sympathy. What with keeping everyone fed, clothes washed, the log house clean, chickens, mules and hogs fed and watered, the garden weeded and watered, along with a few other chores, they were a mite busy. To be fair, Marsha pitched in and helped with the household chores. Willy's back was out. He couldn't do much but lie around in agony with his legs propped up.

Bluefeather was in the kitchen drying dishes for Sally.

"So, what kinda guy is this Harvey House, I've hearing so much about?"

"They told you already, huh? But the name is Holt. H.O.L.T. They don't like him, you know? You probably wouldn't either."

"That's not the point, little darling. Do you?"

"Well, I did, or at least I thought I did, but I'm gonna break it off. Old dumb me . . . it took me a year to find out what an asshole he really is. I'm gonna break it off the next time he phones."

"Have you told Willy and Flo that?"

"No, I don't want them to be too self-satisfied. When he 'no-shows' for a few weeks, they'll catch on."

"Poor ol' Harvey Wallbanger."

"Mr. Harvey Shit is more like it."

"Say, don't they teach you kids anything past four letters in school?"

"I learned to talk like that listening to you and Willy long ago, Blue dear."

Marsha and Flo were pulling the new weeds out of the tomato patch when the phone rang out on the porch. Since Sally had her hands in soapy water and Willy would never make it from the couch in time, Bluefeather answered. The connection was bad, but he finally figured out that it was Willy's lawyer calling from Las Cruces. He obviously thought he was talking to Willy. Bluefeather puzzled the pieces together from the static noise of the phone and surmised that the lease had now been dropped on Willy's Hillsboro silver mines.

Bluefeather muttered to himself, "Jesus H. Christmas Christ. I'd rather be kicked in the belly by a karate champion than tell these folks that news."

He stood there by the phone trying to figure how to give the message easily. He walked out and circled the jeep about three times. Before he thought about it, he lit up a forbidden cigarette. Being so weak-willed made him feel worse. He stomped and twisted the smoke out of sight in the earth.

"Sheeeit. I might as well just go in and get it over with." He walked inside and said, "Willy, I sure hate to tell you this."

Willy was propped up on a pillow now, sensing something coming down. When Bluefeather told him about the phone call, he simply said, "See? I told you nobody ever calls you with good news on them damn things. Hell, it's happened before, Blue. You know? You know as well as I do it'll happen again. We ain't gonna die from it."

"Yeah, I know. All right. But I'm just worried about you guys."

"Don't worry your head about it. Everything will be okay. You hear? We'll figure out something."

"You're damn right we'll figure out something, old pardner. We'll pull off this Korbell deal, I tell you. We'll find that fancy wine. And not only that, we've got nearly six months of full expenses paid ahead of us. Hellsfire, we never had that much time on a deal ever before."

"You got that gathered up right, Blue."

Bluefeather knew that inside the old man was hurting, but he sure wouldn't let it show. He went back to the kitchen to help Sally, but she had already finished putting the dishes away. He intended to make some light, clever remark, but she did not give him a chance.

"I heard."

"Well now, Sally . . ."

She turned her perky little face to him saying, "Look, Blue, I'm used to this kind of thing happening. My God, don't look so stricken. It's not the end. There are lots of things I can do in this cockeyed world besides being a veterinarian."

"I know you can, hon'. It's just that you'd be such a good one, and your mother and Willy wanted it so much for you."

She was wiping the sink and table dry with a sponge. She squeezed it out, put it down and stepped right up in front of him with her bold, firm little breasts barely touching him, put her hands on his shoulders, looked up and said, "Now, you listen to me, Bluefeather Fellini. I'm a big, little girl with a long way to go yet. You . . . you old folks just dig out your own skunks and quit worrying about me."

He hugged her up close and softly caressed her soft

brown hair, knowing she was false fronting with a lot of painful courage, but the warm, little body spun his thinking machinery around. She clung to him like a spider web. He decided to go fishing and cool off.

Bluefeather gathered up his gear and sneaked out the back door, heading for Zia Creek. He forgot about all the rock bruises as he made his way through the few head of cows and on across the open grassy meadow into the trees.

Chipmunks darted from rock to rock, chattering at him. A brown squirrel shimmied up a tree and peeked around the edge, observing the intruder. A magpie flashed swift glances of black and white feathers through the limbs, squawking to all the other inhabitants of the woods.

There was no way out of it, he had to deliver for Korbell . . . and therefore for Willy and Company. He felt a little bit foolish, but vowed to deliver that wine to the great man's cellar, no matter what he would have to do. A lot was at stake now. He could take care of Willy and Flo's payments on the home place for awhile, but it was about three months before Sally would have to prepare for college, if she was to make the first semester.

On the other hand, he did not really know if the wine existed, in spite of all the documents Korbell had shown him. At the same time, he couldn't figure what other use Korbell could possibly have for him. Was he making too much out of it? Maybe it really was just the wine. Somehow, though, he had the feeling of other invisible movements and plots.

Where did Marsha really fit in? She was beginning to obsess his thoughts. She was as much a mystery as her adopted father. Adopted? Hah. Well, no matter how much he had desired her, and that was considerably, he had been unable to bring himself to make any sort of move on her. It wasn't just bedding down with her, although that thought made the roots of his teeth ache and his blood turn to white-water rapids, but there was an indefinable aura about her that held him back. True, she had been capable and solid on every count, so far, just as Korbell had said. Bluefeather still had a feeling, though, that she was there just to watch him. He had unintentionally caught her giving him surreptitious glances, like a spy. But what for? Well, if the wine story was true, Korbell certainly would not want him skipping off to France with it. Still, he had to admit Marsha had been open and warm with all of them, fitting in better than blood kin.

He had learned little about her past and had even suppressed his curiosity, just as he had the lust for her body. It was difficult, maybe impossible, for him to let the fact surface that he wanted her for all time. This sort of thing had last happened to him at Breen. He wasn't sure he was "horse" enough to have something that precious destroyed again. He had always just moved right in and found out quickly. His unnatural reticence was puzzling.

Bluefeather unconsciously entered a private circle of trees and oak brush. He sat down in the thick grass, leaning back against a tree, enjoying the sun's blessings more than his thoughts.

Sally tiptoed into the opening. She had her own rod and reel. Very carefully she dropped the hook until it caught in Bluefeather's shirt. Then she easily, slowly reeled it in. He muttered something, but didn't awaken completely. Grinning, she sat down in front of him after removing the hook from his shirt and felt warm and melting as she stared at his—to her—perfect features. She could have shared this private time with him for years. She was as sure of that as all young women are at least once.

He awakened slowly, surprised that he had dozed off. There in front of him sat Sally with her legs crossed under her. If he remembered correctly, she had been wearing Levi's just a short time back. Now she had on a soft, cotton dress. She tucked the skirt into her crotch, which caused the hem to pull up, revealing a goodly portion of her smooth thighs.

"What are you doing out here?" he asked.

"Oh . . . a notion struck me back there in the kitchen that I wanted to go fishing with you. You're pretty when you sleep." She was grinning at him in a lopsided way. "Say, Blue, forgive me if you wish, but I'm going to get personal."

"Fire away."

"Are you getting it on with the redhead?"

"Boy! That's sure as hell personal all right. Where'd you learn to talk like that? Besides, her hair is auburn."

"Red, auburn, dark pink, what's the difference? You haven't answered my question."

"Well, it's none of your business, Sally, but, no, I'm not."

"What's the matter? You afraid you might blow your deal with Korbell?"

The night in Korbell's guest room when one of his adopted ladies had certainly adopted the wadding out of him flashed into Bluefeather's memory store again. Had it been Marsha?

When he did not answer immediately, Sally pushed forward with, "Go on, Blue. Admit you're stymied. I can tell you are wanting her. What's holding you back?"

"Okay. Okay. You're the psychologist. You tell me."

"I think you're really hung up on her, but afraid to admit it."

He had to agree that Sally might be right, but since he did not know for sure, he just plucked a stem of grass and started chewing on it.

Sally raised her legs up, holding her knees together. She constantly now spread them casually apart and back together in a nervous gesture. It was not consciously meant to tease him, but it was driving him a little mad and a little angry at both of them.

He could see all the way down her leg to her loose, flimsy panties before she closed them each time. He saw more than he thought he should, and looked away embarrassed. He was beginning to perspire and breathe heavier. His eyes returned to her. Then he raised his eyes to hers and the feeling that flowed back and forth between them was as old and new as birth.

She slowly spread her legs. Oddly, there was nothing lewd in her movement—just an eternal sensuality, an offering, a true gift.

He moved to her, and they lay in the grass, kissing, feeling, as the young of all earthly beings have always done, and always will. Ordained.

She rolled over on her back and turned her head to one side. Bluefeather did not remember her partial disrobing, but she had, because he was kissing her tight little breasts and feeling her dampness without any wearing apparel infringing.

He held back as long as he could. Then he moved. It wasn't all the way and it wasn't violent; more like the waves of a small lake lapping at the near shore. He felt her tiny convulsions under him and knew he must separate their bodies glued with the sweat of heavy courting. She knew instantly he was pulling away from her. She also knew that heavy petting was the most they would ever have together of physical love, but she couldn't help but feel thrilled that he was in pain doing so. Honor. Damn that honor. Too late.

Then she took his face in both her hands and looked him squarely in the eyes. "That was beautiful, Blue."

"Yes it was."

"I've got a confession to make."

He waited.

"I've watched you craving Marsha until it made me hot-

ter than frying grease . . . besides, I've been wanting you
for two or three years."

"Quit talking like that. My Lord, Sally, you'll get kicked
out of college before you even get started."

"I don't care. I'm only talking to you, my friend, my
amigo, my amico, my lost amour."

"That would have been the first?"

"Yep, numero uno."

"Oh, my God." His brain convulsed as he realized she
was still a virgin and he had almost taken her offer from
pure weakness of desire. Trying to be a decent fellow
often creates a terrible time of turmoil. He hurt worse
than he had after the mine had assaulted them. Then he
asked her, "Why me?"

"Why not you? I need to know about these things
someday, and you, my old and beloved friend, seemed to
be suffering."

"I wouldn't argue with that, even if I knew how—which
I don't."

"Good, now that's settled. Go on and enjoy your fishing."

"Oh no, little girl, not after what you put me through.
You're going with me, but I insist you fish the other side
of the creek." At her puzzled stare, he said, "It's the only
safe way. You can't get pregnant at that distance."

"You bastard," she said, hitting him in loving mockery
on the shoulder.

They fished until almost dark before they caught
enough for a meal. Their timing was off. It had been for
several hours.

EIGHT

BLUEFEATHER WAS FISHING ALONE THIS TIME. HIS LUCK was better. He was having a pretty good joust with the trout. He had banked six ten- to fourteen-inch rainbows and one ten-inch brown. There was a five-foot hole of water just before a curve in the creek, where he had fished a hundred times. It was circled by brush. He eased up, ducking low, and dropped the hooks loaded with fireball salmon eggs. The idea was not to be seen and to walk so lightly that the ground didn't vibrate and notify the fish of an alien presence.

Instantly, he felt the first tentative tug and he took it. He jerked the fish out shiny wet, flopping on the bank behind him. Bluefeather knew before the hooked fish broke the water that it was the biggest catch of the day. A sixteen-inch brown was as big a fish as the Zia Creek could support.

He was especially elated, because the wary browns were difficult to catch and highly prized in this part of the state. Besides, the size of the day's catch was enough for a good meal at the Ruger household today.

He removed the hook from the slick-spotted brown's throat and cleaned and gutted his entire catch, feeling a keen sense of accomplishment at having the privilege of supplying Flo's table with a fresh feast.

As he placed the trout in his creel, he heard a flute wafting a lovely melody across the creek. He knew at once: it was Dancing Bear sitting way up in the pine tree nearest the Zia, his head and arms moving in rhythm with the music. He played on as if Bluefeather didn't exist.

"Hey, Dancing Bear. Hey, it's me."

Dancing Bear went right on playing, ignoring his client's voice. Instantly, he was on a lower limb with his back still turned toward Bluefeather.

"You old bastard, that ain't any way to treat your humble subject."

Just that quickly, before Bluefeather finished the sentence, Dancing Bear sat right across from him on a cluster of boulders, smoking a peace pipe, making signs to the four winds and chanting noises that sounded like he had a croaking bullfrog for accompaniment. Maybe he did.

"Dear brudder," he said, "A very good morning at you."

"It isn't morning, Bear. Can't you tell it's late afternoon?"

"Cannot tell that thing. Time all the same over here."

"Where've you been? We damn near got killed in that copper tunnel."

"Chure. Chure. I play the music for you in the hole of the mountain."

"How . . . how the hell was I to know what you meant? People play music to sing and dance and make love by."

"You got to learn some of these days, for sure. Me, Mr. Dancing Bear, I only point the way. You got to go do the right thing by your ownself. That's the way it is. I have no say on that."

Bluefeather gritted his teeth, knotted his jaws and said, "I've told you please, please, don't use that confusing dialect. I can't understand it. You savvy?"

Dancing Bear's mouth smiled into a half-moon. He was

silent, motionless. Bluefeather threw his fishing pole on the ground and started to cross the creek. Bear raised a palm toward him as Bluefeather stopped, saying, "Just what kind of spirit guide are you anyway, speaking in riddles and mysteries to a poor mortal, leaving me alone to figure out all these complicated problems? You're the spirit guide after all. Well, let's have some simple, helpful guidance for a change. How about it, ol' pard? Huh? Huh?"

"I've got many business to do. I been here on the fourth level about a hunnert years. Gotta get more busy. Authority is expecting me to move up."

"Move up? What do you mean?"

"I think about seven more to go before Authority give me thousand year vacation. Some peoples make two, three levels at one jump. Me . . . Bear . . . I been here on this same level about a hunnert years."

"You said that already."

"Don't talk about Authority with voice like lion in steel trap."

"I didn't mean anything by it . . . it's just a manner of speaking. Hey, I'm sorry, Bear."

"Now that's a good thing to hear, dear brudder."

"Okay, all right. I've got a bunch of problems and you haven't been around when I needed you, that's all."

"I been aroun' some. You maybe so busy worryin' you not see me."

"Well, I can't go around looking up at tree limbs and ceilings for you all the time, or I'd trip over something and break my cockeyed neck. Now, you know all that, don't you?"

"Maybe so that's true what you say. Maybe it don't make any difference where I'm at the way you always lookin' at that red girl. You gonna fall and break something you love more'n your neck, you not careful.

Huh? Huh?" He imitated Bluefeather and let out a single continuous roar of mirth.

Bluefeather's chemicals were jumping around in his body to the point that his blood felt like it was simmering. It caused his mind-voice to click in. *That Indian guide is laughing at me so hard inside, he's having to hold his ribs to keep them from busting out of his body.* He could hear the laughter spewing out now like steam from a starting-up train. Not even a spirit guide could control such comicality. Bluefeather was embarrassed and checked himself to see if anything was hanging out of his trousers. He felt around to the rear. Everything seemed covered. This waggish wimp was laughing at him just for the fun of it. Making sport of him for no reason.

"You gonna fall and break . . . your . . ."

Bluefeather interrupted the happily teasing voice and whatever raffish thoughts were in Dancing Bear's head with, "Listen here, Bear. If I could sail around in the air like you do, I'd fly over there and stomp enough shit out of you to fertilize Texas . . . just for the fun of it, of course."

"Be mighty big job. Why not fertilize Rhode Island? Won't take near as long."

"Look. I don't need any more funnin' around with you. No more smart-ass cracks. I need some serious advice and help. You hear, Bear? Get serious. Now, come on . . . please . . . perty please."

"That red girl . . . she bother you all over, huh?"

"Well, except for her being an all-around good hand, I don't know much about her."

"Hah. Now you get close at truth. Maybe so you are afraid to know more."

"I'm not afraid of anything. Well, not much anyway."

"Hah, again. You know red girl pretty like rainbow over blue lake. Pretty like little fawn playin' on long green grass of meadow. Pretty like feathered arrow flyin' through air. Pretty like . . ."

"Awww, oh, buzzard droppings on a dead stick, cut out that whimsical crap. If you don't cooperate, I'm coming after you when I die."

"You are not ready to crash through and come over here with me, yet."

"Well, when I am, your heart may belong to Authority, but your ass is gonna belong to me. You hear, ol' friend?"

"I hear hot wind blowin' over garbage dump."

"What do you know about garbage dumps, anyway?"

"I see 'em all over the world where I go to help. I see about a hunnert thousand . . . and the whole world soon gonna be one big dump. How am I gonna help people clean up their lives if they're livin' in dirty dirt?"

"Well, I'll be a puking dog. If I haven't inherited an ecologist for a guiding spirit. Hey. Hey, Dancing Bear, do you belong to one of those fix-everything-up clubs?"

"No, we make clubs out of a sharp rock with stick tied on it with rawhide. Good for fighting, huntin' and . . ." Dancing Bear's hands were pantomiming the construction of a tomahawk.

Bluefeather realized that he must change the direction of the conversation. He couldn't force Dancing Bear into simple, clear statements. He didn't know how. "Well, Mr. Bear, what should I know about the red lady? You tell me."

"She let you know when she ready. Squaws always do that."

Bluefeather started to tell him Marsha was not a squaw and then decided that would be a waste.

"Marsha is so pleasant about everything—enjoys every little thing so much—and she's dedicated to our search. There is no way to tell what she is thinking."

"I say to you, dear brudder, you will know this thing when red lady slide on mountain."

"That's it? That's all the help I'm gonna get?"

"I tell plenty. Use the beans in your head."

"Bear, you . . . you're talking under water. All I'm getting is bubbles."

"That is right. See the idee?" he said with a pleased giggle.

Bluefeather truly appreciated Dancing Bear's use of his mentor, Grinder's, words, but he still couldn't catch the message he knew was there somewhere. It always was. Always.

"Then just tell me this. Is Korbell lying to me about Tilton's wine?"

"Korbell man, he talks circles in circles. Someday circle get so small it make a dot."

"Look here, I'm not asking for instant miracles. I've finally caught on that I'm gonna have to do most of this on my own. That's the way it's supposed to be. But why in hell can't you just give me a hint where the wine is? What would be wrong with that?"

"Wine. She somewhere north."

"North? That could be in Alaska. Let's narrow that down a bit. How far north from right here?" Bluefeather picked up a stick and made an X on the ground.

"Done told you. We got no hours, no minutes, where I am. Don't got no miles either."

"Ohhh Lord. Bear, you're giving me hemorrhoids."

"Sit in hot water, maybe three times a day, rub your behind with buffalo grease, don't lift anything heavy and . . ."

"God, oh please, God. Authority. Number One. Please, I beg you to put words in this Indian's mouth that a common earth man can understand. He's changed from an entertainment director into an M.D."

"It comes clear, when you are ready, dear brudder."

"Look, Bear, I do remember clearly that you said many answers would come at the place under trees where the water burns. Well, when is that coming about, anyway? Just a hint maybe."

Dancing Bear smiled softly now, his black eyes somehow wishful, but all he said was, "You wish I play flute for you?" The wooden flute appeared in his hands as he looked at Bluefeather expectantly.

"Not right now. Thanks, just the same."

The flute vanished.

"I don't suppose I've got anything to lose by asking you about Tilton's gold and silver bullion, and maybe who killed him, huh?"

"Me, Dancing Bear, don't know all these things you ask. I think that bullion is looked after by a brain with few thoughts."

"Well, thanks a lot, Bear. Thank you ver-r-r-y much. That's a big help." Bluefeather continued even more caustically, "Three-fourths of the world is without thoughts worthy of mention." Bluefeather realized that sarcasm was getting him nowhere. Dancing Bear was having a show of combined temperament and fun this day. So he decided to try other approaches. "Say, Bear, do you need a favor? Is there anything I can do down here to help you move on up?"

"Kind thought you have there, kiddo, but to tell you a truth, I sorta like it where I am. This dog-eater, gut-cleaning Indian likes to stay busy all the time. Same thing when I where you at. Indian no more lazy than white, black, brown, yellow people. I got no prejudice. That's why I get plenty work all the time."

Bluefeather mumbled and moaned low and to himself, "Now he's converted into a cockeyed sociologist. A damned do-gooder, a full-fledged integrator."

"Better you pray for yourself, Blue. I got more business than I can handle right here where I at."

"How're you gonna know when your time comes to move on?"

"Same like you, dear brudder, with red lady. All the same. See the idee? You got to be nice to a mule or they kick the beans out of your head and the crap out of your belly, but they haul big load for you just the same when you patient and kind. Understan', dear brudder?"

"Yeah, about as well as I understand the law of gravity. If I don't watch out, a ton of rocks will fall on my head, right?"

"See there. Like I told you. You gettin' many smarts." With that he jumped up chanting and started doing an eagle dance on the flat front of a boulder.

Bluefeather yelled, "Hey Bear, come on now and stop that dancing. There's a lot more I need to know."

Dancing Bear stopped, saying, "How 'bout Russian dance?"

Before Bluefeather could answer, Dancing Bear was squatting down, bouncing around and kicking one leg out after the other, shouting like a drunken cossack. Then he appeared across the canyon, carrying on the wild dance atop a bluff. He danced right out into the pure mountain air right over Bluefeather's head, whose mind-voice explained, *He's zooming out of sight again, like a fiery-ass rocket.*

Bluefeather picked up his fishing pole, his day's catch and headed toward the house for the fish fry. It didn't seem like there was much left this particular day. Bluefeather was convinced he heard a distant voice echoing from the heavens over and over, "See the idee?"

Was Grinder talking to him through Dancing Bear? He didn't know, but somewhere in the mad conversation there were some clues of truth for him. That he knew. He smiled. No matter how disconcerting Dancing Bear could be, he always felt better for having visited him. Much better. If he had thought further, he would have realized that was one hell of a gift by itself.

NINE

THEY WERE ALL MOSTLY HEALED UP NOW FROM THEIR copper tunnel experience except for Willy's back. He was making heroic efforts to disguise the fact.

Bluefeather had gone over Korbell's maps with Willy, pinning down the best approach to the Commonwealth and Dutch Joe lode tunnels. The mines were about a mile apart and had been driven into the opposite sides of the mountain. Bluefeather decided he would explore them both in one day if the old roads were passable for a four-wheel drive vehicle.

"Willy, in a couple more weeks you'll be ready to jump over the Dos Amigos Bar from a flatfooted start."

"Two weeks, hell. I could waltz all the way to Billings, Montana, right now." He jumped up from the sofa and started his little half-running shuffle across the living room. Just before he reached the door, his back locked and he fell facedown. Bluefeather had to help him up and assist him back to the couch. That took care of any protests Willy might have made about being left at home.

Flo was working in the garden and Marsha was helping Sally hang out the wash to dry.

"Marsha," Bluefeather said as casually as possible, "I'm going up and check out a couple of tunnels. Should be back by dark. Willy knows the location. If I'm not back by tomorrow noon you might come and see if I'm broke down."

Marsha said, "Oh good. We'll be finished here in just a minute. It won't take but a jiffy for me to get ready."

Bluefeather patiently tried to explain that these were safe open tunnels, and she might as well stay here and help around headquarters, where she was needed. She started to answer, but Bluefeather turned and walked toward the house to get his prospector's pick and lights. He had eaten a big breakfast and figured he could get by without any lunch. He was walking around in front of the house to his jeep when Marsha stepped right up in front of him, blocking his way.

"What do you think you're doing, anyway?" she confronted him.

"I told you. There's no use in two people going on a one-man job."

"You don't know. You may need help. Besides, I want to go."

"Look here. It's not that. I don't want you to . . . well, it's . . ."

"You made the deal knowing I was to be your assistant, Blue."

"That's right. So assistants do what they're told. That's what assisting means."

Her wondrous pearly skin was glowing so that the color almost matched that of her hair, and her eyes were speaking with sparks, "I'm going with you."

"Now look, if you're worried I might find something and hide it, then the deal is off."

She stared at him a moment before her face relaxed into her human-killing smile. "You're right. We've got to trust one another all the way. I'm sorry."

"It's okay. Hell, you're just as dedicated as I am when taking on a job. I like that."

"I like your liking it. Good hunting, Blue."

"You know now, don't you, Marsha, we have to find it for other reasons than Korbell?"

"Yes, I know. We must for Korbell and now, of course, for Willy's family, too. That is what you mean, isn't it?"

"Yes . . . yes." He moved slightly toward her, intending to give her a small hug and a kiss for a temporary good-bye, but she had read his intentions and so smoothly moved away toward the house that he couldn't be offended.

Bluefeather felt that he knew less and less about the "red" woman all the time, but for sure, she was as determined as a mountain goat in rutting season to succeed on their mission. She also had enough temper to start a forest fire even though she had clearly dampened it. So far, they had survived their first disagreement without rancor.

He drove until he could see the waste dump of the Commonwealth, but the rough, rutted road was blocked here from a landslide. He decided to walk on around the mountain to the Dutch Joe and save the nearer tunnel for last. After dealing with Marsha, the craggy terrain would be easy.

The tunnel still had fairly good timbers holding up the portal. He walked in with no trouble. The miners had been after gold here. In places the little grey-white quartz vein narrowed down to a thread and in other places widened to a foot. It was a good solid tunnel so far. He tapped one wall and the floor all the way in. He tested it all the way back out. The tunnel was solid. No secret rooms here.

He walked backward on the way out, however, watching and remembering like a mouse does a rattlesnake. Nothing happened and nothing of value was there. The walls were just like "the Authority" had made them.

He left this wasted dream and headed across the mountain to check out the Commonwealth. Nearing the highest

point, he would have to climb a granite formation turned
rotten. The surface was pulverized into billions of little
pebbles. This slowed and tired him considerably, because
he was constantly slipping back, having to hold his balance
with his hands.

He finally made the summit and started downhill over
a barren patch of granite. The gravel felt like he was walking on marbles. He moved sideways to slow his descent,
but even so, he fell down on one hand many times, bruising and cutting it.

There are selected sequences in life that it doesn't pay
to think at all. Marsha had come into his mind again. He
could see the entire woman and imagined he was feeling
over her body, smelling her feminine scent. At the very
moment she was opening her flesh and spirit to him, he
slipped, falling onto his back, sliding downward uncon-
trollably.

He was going full speed, digging at the earth with his
boot heels and clawing desperately at the pebbled earth
with the palm of one hand. He instinctively held onto his
battery light, desperately trying to protect it. It seemed
silly for sure. Here he was plummeting straight for hell
and was struggling to save a twenty-dollar light. His small
pick was safe as long as his belt held together. As he
gained velocity the gravel ripped at him even more. Then
he saw the sheer drop-off about forty yards ahead. He
grabbed with his free hand at a boulder that had fallen
from higher up. The futile attempt didn't even slow him
down. He was a goner.

Then there was flute music all around and through him.
He was instantly out of, and back behind, his physical
body, watching it from behind as it plunged forward to
its doom. His out-of-body spirit screamed ahead for his
physical body to grab a scrawny cedar tree near the edge
of the drop-off.

The music stopped and he was back inside himself

again. He grabbed at the tiny cedar and held. It bent, but didn't uproot or break. Bluefeather felt his arm and shoulder stretch out to the limit. His feet dangled over the precipice. He pulled himself up, straining mightily, still keeping one finger in the handle of the light. Then he sat up against a tree. He never knew how long he remained there absorbing the wonder of it all. Life. It was still his. It took all his reserves of courage—which he could have stuck in his ear with room for more—to crawl along the edge of the cliff. Inch by terrified inch, he moved until he came to a gentle slope leading right to the mine. He didn't dare walk down. He scooted on his ravaged feet and buttocks.

The Dutch Joe was caved a little here and there, but he made his wasted tests with no fear at all. The inside of the mountains had become safer than the outside. He reminded himself with his mind-voice, *You play by the mountain's rules or it will destroy you. Even then, it will occasionally remind you who is master by ripping some of your skin and jolting your liver loose.*

He eased down the old trail to his jeep, just beginning to feel the pain of the mountain's recent warning blows.

It was dark when he arrived back home. The three hounds came out to meet him without barking this time. He bent stiffly down to hug them as they gave his face a good washing.

Willy walked out to greet him as he stepped upon the porch. "How'd it go?"

"Fine, but fast. Real fast," he said as he walked in the open door past his friend.

"My God, Blue. What happened to your back?"

"I got the itch so bad I had to scratch it with a mountain." Then he thought to himself, *Well, at least I'm still able to keep up the traditional silly chatter with Willy,* just as his legs collapsed under him.

All three women surrounded him, commiserating

something pitiful. Marsha undid the single button left intact on his shirt and pulled the torn cloth from his body. She took charge, leading him to the bathroom, telling him to undress completely. He stripped.

She checked him out from floor to crown and pushed him into the shower while she rummaged in the medicine cabinet. Then she dried him off, patting the towel softly over all his body—all over. Then she put medicine on all the abrasions and followed that with an ointment as calmly as a registered nurse.

She yelled for Sally to get his bathrobe from the bunkhouse. Sally did, looking shyly away from his nudity, handing the robe to Marsha with her head turned.

Bluefeather thought this odd, considering she had already felt his nakedness.

Flo had been holding dinner for his arrival. She served it in a hurry now. As Willy poured him a big drink of bourbon, Bluefeather told them about the uncontrollable fall and how lucky he was to grab the lone tree. He left out the other incidents—the life-saving ones that came with the music of a flute.

After eating, he had one more shot of bourbon and headed for his room, saying, "I'll see you folks in the morning, raring to go."

"Grandy dandy," Willy said.

The soreness was coming on now, but he didn't mind. The privilege of being able to feel pain, or anything else, was what mattered. He lay on his belly, getting drowsy from the meal, the bourbon and the day's climbing, with a deep thankfulness for the bountiful blessings he had received over the last ten hours.

He was into the first drift of sleep when he sensed a presence on the bed beside him. A hand was tenderly rubbing the back of his neck. Somehow, he knew that this time it was Marsha. He turned over in the bed and reached for her, but she was up and to the door.

He could see her silhouette there as she stopped and turned back to him, saying softly, "You need sleep most of all now. You can tell me about the rest of it when—sometime when we're alone."

She was gone.

He rolled back over on his stomach, absorbed in a rare contentment. He slept. Deeply.

TEN

WILLY'S SORE BACK AND BLUEFEATHER'S ENTIRE BODY healed. They hit the mountains again. Marsha went along. They studied the maps even more carefully, blocking out where they had been and where they intended to go. They climbed and climbed, dug and dug, searching carefully every tunnel and drift. When they found a cave-in they either hand-dug it out or shored it up with timbers laboriously cut and braced.

They found a lot of minerals too. The deposits and veins were mostly of marginal value at current prices. Someday, if the people of the world survived, scarcity would make their unearthing of immense value. Under any situation, they were fine homes for bats, bears, lions and bobcats.

The mountains toughened the three in muscle and determination. They were a team now in top physical condition. Flo and Sally did not accompany them on these excursions. They stayed home and took care of the necessities. All five became very close from a hard-shared endeavor.

Bluefeather had not smoked in a month. Daily, he wondered about Dancing Bear's confusing prophecy that he would know when Marsha was ready to commit to him by sliding on a mountain. Very confusing. They had done a lot of that every day, and there had been no evidence of a mutual fulfillment to come. She remained her uncomplaining, hard working, cheerful, dedicated self. Yet there was a grey area she reserved, letting no one in—an enigma for sure, but a deep, tormenting mystery for Bluefeather. He tried not to let it interfere with their work, and almost succeeded.

Bluefeather often wandered off from campsite, trying to conjure up Dancing Bear. But he failed to appear. The flutes were silent.

Finally, the moment arrived when they checked out the last mine on Korbell's maps. It was late day in midsummer when the three confederates exited the last tunnel. There was still no trace of the rare Mouton '80.

They had a two-mile walk downhill to the jeep. They strode without speaking, feeling a sense of failure, even though Bluefeather knew the search was not over—not at all. He would just have to wait for the appropriate moment to bring it up again.

It was dark before they arrived at the campsite. Bluefeather had expected they would drive home, but Willy was already getting his equipment ready to cook. He and Marsha gathered wood. After the meal, they leaned back on their bedrolls, drinking coffee and staring at the fire.

The sensation of loss was tempered slightly by the knowledge that they had given their best. Bluefeather had no idea what the others truly felt. However, this was not good enough for him. But this stage of defeat had to be accepted by all three. It was the way of men and women who fooled with mountains.

A night bird called, and was answered. A coyote howled his ancient statement down below. Bluefeather stood up, listening hard as he had always done. He could not verbalize what the coyote told the sky, but he thrilled as if

he did. One thing he knew, the coyote had a message as
yet to be interpreted by humans.

When he sat back down, Marsha said, "You are fascinated by the coyote, aren't you?"

"Yeah. They are the greatest of survivors." He felt this
was an inadequate response, but couldn't gather another
at the moment.

The campfire flickered across her face, highlighting one
part and then another. Her blue eyes were dark now like
the depths of an ocean. The shimmering flame made her
hair appear to ripple and flow like molten bronze. God,
she was beautiful. At just that moment she represented
to Bluefeather all the mountains he had climbed, all the
dreams he had or would ever have, all the light and life
the sun granted. Somehow, he realized this tiny swift vision was related to a fresh-forming cloud and was part of
what the coyote sang.

Willy broke his inconstant reverie with, "You know, for
twenty years I didn't do anything but look at a mule's rear;
then I found a silver mine that paid for awhile. Not much,
you understand, but enough to start me looking all over
again when it petered out."

Bluefeather knew what he was trying to get at, so he
said, "We've got to think of other possibilities. Right now
I don't know what, but we have to."

Marsha contributed, "The wine is somewhere . . . we
just have to look harder, think harder."

Willy looked at her with deep admiration. "Ain't nothing impossible. Look at what old Bill Mundy up at Chama
did."

They waited.

"He ran down a healthy deer on foot, and killed it.
Don't too many people believe it, but I was there. You
see, we was out of ammunition and hungry. People do
strange things when it seems important enough to 'em.
Jimmy Bason over at Hillsboro killed five coons with one

shot. You see this coon, this old mama coon, had been tearing up his garden and stealing chicken eggs as well. Jimmy's hounds treed her on a fence post early one morning. He ran out with a .30-30 and took a shot at the coon. He damn near fainted when five coons fell off the fence dead. Four half-grown youngsters had been lined up on the fence straight behind her. So a feller is liable to pull off anything if he keeps on climbing. Ain't that so?"

Bluefeather could tell by the way Marsha slung her head that the "one-shot" story had made her uneasy as she said, "Sad. That is really sad. The mother coon was just trying to care for her babies. Now, that is really sad."

Willy replied before Bluefeather had to, "You're sure right about that, Marsha, but Jimmy was protectin' the food for his young'uns, too."

Bluefeather tried to change the subject. "You know, right now we haven't got a new direction—but somehow . . ."

Willy broke in with another of his off-base comments, "Everybody in the world is a treasure hunter, of some kind or other, but most don't seem to know what they're lookin' for . . . much less where. We're breakin' our butts lookin' for wine when we can get it at Dos Amigos for two or three dollars a bottle. Good stuff, too. Smart, ain't we?"

Marsha chuckled warmly at this. Bluefeather grinned wide enough to do justice to the Korbell family tradition and said in the Willy-Bluefeather "silly" tradition, "Hellsfire, in spite of rat turds in the gravy we have no choice but to go on looking."

Everyone unrolled their beds and crawled in, hoping for a revelatory dream.

ELEVEN

WILLY HAD NOTHING MUCH TO LOOK FORWARD TO NOW, except hiring out as a guide during hunting season. The marauding lion had already diminished his livestock by a third and his pack of hunting hounds by a fourth. For the last three days he had disappeared in his old jeep. Flo explained that he had a girlfriend over at Silver City, and she was sure he would be back soon. Bluefeather sure hoped so, because he had already reserved rooms in the only hotel at Meanwhile for the weekend.

The annual Founder's Day celebration was coming up. It was a big day for the town. Gold had been discovered there a hundred years back, and the citizens were combining the two celebrations. People would come from all over the Southwest, and a few would drift in from other parts of the country. It had been declared an annual, official state celebration.

Bluefeather was looking forward to it for a lot of reasons. First, he wanted to have a few drinks and relax. He also thought Flo and Sally deserved a chance to have some fun and maybe meet a couple of men. It was hard to extremes on women way out here. They all needed to clear the confused air and make decisions about what the next moves were going to be.

Bluefeather had called Charlie Waters in Santa Fe to invite him down to the festivities. Charlie was an old friend from Bluefeather's futile, mercury smuggling days and a bloodhound of a research man. When it came to running down records in courthouses, there was no better. Bluefeather didn't explain fully on the phone that he wanted Charlie to study all the building plans Tilton had ever had on his numerous homes and buildings. Bluefeather reasoned that the sixty cases of wine would have to be hidden under, or in, one of these structures, since the mine tunnels had turned up a blank. It was a chance they had to take so they could keep on legitimately earning the wages and expenses of Korbell's six-month commitment.

They penned up all the livestock at night while Willy was gone. He had insisted on this for weeks now. There was only a month left for Sally to register for college. Bluefeather's money draw from Korbell would keep them fed and the payments on the Ruger's home place paid until the minimum ran out. Then they would be in a mess if they didn't deliver the find. All except Marsha, of course, and yet, he felt she would also feel a great loss because of their shared closeness. However, she didn't have to worry about overdue bills, foreclosures and food. That was a difference of some dimensions.

It was the time for searching. Bluefeather slipped out into the woods, hoping Dancing Bear would choose to be found. It was one of those summer days when the air was sparkling and undulating like rivers in the sky. The blue jays flew about like tiny solidified pieces of firmament. The squirrels and chipmunks barked all around, holding a constantly moving convention. Insects buzzed and chirped, completing the symphony.

In a wild game trail, he saw the familiar arrowhead track of a lone coyote, and on the bank of the Zia Creek, he came upon the prints of the old killer lion. He could tell it was the one all right, and the reason he had chosen domestic instead of wild stock to kill was revealed. The size of the tracks indicated that he was a tom and that he was old. It took full maturity to develop a foot that big. His right hind foot print twisted out to the side more shallowly than the others. Bluefeather was sure he had been crippled by a bullet. If it had been a steel trap it would have shown part of his foot missing. He could no longer fill the demands of his stomach on elusive, wild meat. The initial burst of speed it took to accomplish this had mostly been taken away by his injury.

A few feet from where the lion had crossed the creek, Bluefeather saw the prints of a raccoon. They were unmistakable in their likeness to the handprints of a human baby and were similar to a bear cub's, only more delicate. Many creatures hunted and hid here. So did Bluefeather Fellini.

He listened for the music of the flute. It did not come. He tried to appear casual as his eyes searched the trees and boulders for Dancing Bear. He did not appear. He walked along the creek until he found a place he could cross by stepping on large rocks. He climbed up the opposite bank into a clearing, his mind straining a call out to his spirit guide. He was not connecting, so he sat down on a fallen log, lit a smoke, feeling guilty, but enjoying it for a moment—until in anger at his weakness he stubbed it out of sight in the forest floor.

He was in half-vision, making love to Marsha, when he heard the voice. It was unmistakably French. Since he knew only rudimentary phrases in the lovely language, he could not understand the entirety of the rapid-fire speech.

He stood up, staring around with a lot of curiosity. Soon he realized the voice was coming from above him. There, about thirty feet up on a pine limb, sat a lady in a long, exquisite dress with the waist pinched in like that of a gay nineties girl, but it was a fashion far older than that. Even from this low angle he could see her breasts pushed up and partly out. Her blond hair was piled and twisted on her head, causing Bluefeather to envision a royal ball.

She smiled pleasingly and chattered down at him under a thin, delicate nose. Her hazel eyes appeared to slant up and around her face like those of Korbell's adopted wife, Elena.

"Forgive me, but I can't understand your French."

"Oh, I'm so sorry," she said in clear English.

"So am I. It's a lovely language."

"Thank you, sir."

"I'm Bluefeather Fellini."

"I know. I've heard so much about you."

"Oh. I don't mean to be rude, but just who are you?"

"Why, I'm Nicole Vallier, ex-mistress of Emperor Napoleon."

"*The* Napoleon?"

"Of course. Bonaparte himself."

"Could I . . . I mean . . . well, what are you doing here—up there?"

"Ah, that bitch Josephine had me poisoned."

"Well, I'm sure sorry to hear . . ."

"No, no. Don't feel sorry for me. It was better than the guillotine."

"What I meant was . . ."

"Please don't fret yourself. I'm well placed here. You see, I'm Dancing Bear's assistant. In fact, I'm his substitute today. I hope I can be of some help to you, sir."

"Blue. Just call me Blue. Why didn't he come? Bear must know I need help. A lot of help. All of us around here need help desperately."

"Ah yes, he sends his profound regrets, but he is overbooked right now. He is in London to advise one of his subjects in danger of the gallows. Falsely accused of murder, I might add."

"Well, skunk shit and cherry blossoms."

"What's that you say?"

"Oh, nothing. Just a Willy Ruger slip. How many subjects does he have? Really have?"

"Now don't quote me, but at last count he was tending fifty-six souls."

"Fifty-six! No wonder he can't keep me properly posted."

"Oh that's not so many for one so skillful. Often he has many more than that, especially in times of major wars or great natural disasters. Occasionally, he has fewer. It varies according to the number who cross over."

"How long have you been, uh, where Bear is?"

She started counting on her fingers. "Let's see. About . . ."

"Never mind. I know when Napoleon hooked up with Josephine." Bluefeather had ascertained that Nicole wasn't heavily versed in mathematics. He still wanted a little more assurance of her position before he got into personal problems. "Why have you been on Bear's level so long?"

"That's a good question. You see, Blue, I've tried so hard, but . . . well, I just haven't been able to completely shed some of the . . . uh . . . earthly talents I was gifted with while in your world. These special talents were my true calling there, and old habits die hard—even over here."

"Would it be impertinent to ask what your specialities are?"

"Not at all. I've always been asked that."

"Well then?" He waited.

"Now just be patient. You'll see very soon."

"Well, okay. Have you got any messages for me from Bear?"

"Surely. That's why I'm here. Well, one of the reasons anyway. Dancing Bear said you should get close—very close—to a Mr. Dolby."

Bluefeather exclaimed, "The old man in Meanwhile, who worked with the mining mogul Tilton. That Dolby?"

"Monsieur Bear never gives me many details—mostly just messages to pass on."

"Well, I hope to Authority that's not all."

"No. No. Let me see. There was something else. Oh yes, he said the subterranean would give you many clues.

"The subterranean? Poodle poots and perfumed pee-pee. Don't tell me I'm gonna have to go plumb to hell to get any clear information."

"Oh, I don't think so. Monsieur Bear said you weren't ready for that trip yet."

"Well, thank goodness for that . . . but is that all?"

"Almost. Say, would you mind my coming down there? I'm afraid you're getting a crick in your neck."

Bluefeather's mind-voice cracked in: *The lady is right. My neck is beginning to swell.* She was right there in front of him before he ended the thought.

"Soon is now," she said softly and welded her spirit to his tight as a rocket seam.

They were now about eight feet in the air. Bluefeather looked down over her shoulder and saw that they were now about twenty feet up and gaining altitude. There wasn't a thing left to do but hang on. They floated on up, twisting in the pure, fresh mountain air until he had difficulty discerning which end was up. All the physical and spiritual action combined with the summer sun on his back made him forget the upcoming and all past winters. It was summer forever up here. Then he forgot everything.

They were descending now. There had been a period up there of blankness. What had they done? He'd probably never know, but something had occurred, because he was short of breath. Maybe that was from fear or . . . Oh well, like Agatha Christie and Shakespeare, said, "Old sins cast long shadows."

Then they were safely on the ground again. He kissed her some to be sure she knew how much he had appreciated the ascension.

Suddenly, he realized she had vanished. Bluefeather lay in the grass with the rest of the insects. He felt right at home.

TWELVE

THE DAY BEFORE THE "BIG DO" IN TOWN, WILLY CAME straggling home. He had a red-eyed, bowlegged hangover. He also appeared weak in the joints, and one could have smelled him through three feet of adobe wall.

Bluefeather said, "Welcome home, Uncle Willy. Can I get you a drink? Might as well keep going. Tomorrow's the big day in Meanwhile."

Flo wanted to know if she could feed him. He looked as if he needed nourishment.

"Been playin' so hard I forgot to eat. Broke myself of a bad and expensive habit. Ain't that grandy dandy?" He really meant he was too sick to eat, but would never admit it. He had a large, blue knot on his forehead. He rubbed at it tenderly and explained only to a degree, "If I could throw punches as accurately as I receive them, I'd be the boxing champion of the world."

Flo did not question or argue. That stage was long past. She just poured him a bourbon, saying, "Here, brother. This will take the curve out of your spine."

"Thanks, sis. I owe you my life." With that he did a crazy little jig, slipping on a Navajo rug and tripping across a footstool. He somehow shuffled around and made the near-fall part of the dance step. Bluefeather wondered what it was with these old men like Willy and Dancing Bear—always performing these one-man dances. Maybe they just wanted to be sure of the continued ability to move or maybe they continued celebrating life itself.

Willy threw his worn, old grey hat on the couch and plunked down by it. He still held his glass without having spilled a drop. In a couple of minutes there was nothing to spill.

"Ain't somebody gonna help me out? I'm havin' more fun than I can handle by myself. This goddamn fun is killin' me, in fact."

Bluefeather felt a vast and knowledgeable sympathy and agreed to help out. Marsha, always alert, got them each a drink and then all three women disappeared. Flo went off to finish hemming her new celebration dress. Marsha and Sally retired to wash and curl their hair.

Bluefeather lifted his glass in a toast. "Here's to the gods. May they forgive us our pleasurable sins."

"And for those we ain't committed yet."

They drank. Willy felt a mite better. He ran one shovel-hardened hand through his thinning, grey-blond hair and pointed his sunken eyes straight at Bluefeather.

"Have you come up with any new ideas, Blue?"

"Yep. A couple of wild ones as a matter of fact. Say, how long has that girl—what's her name—been with Dolby?"

"Sherry?"

"Yeah, that's her. Sherry."

"Oh, I'd say 'round eight or nine years—thereabouts. She's one of them real educated gals."

"Educated? How do you mean?"

"School educated. She's one of them anthropologists. Whatever the hell that's supposed to be. Got a Ph.D. in it."

"Well, I'll be damned if that isn't a weird one."

"Yeah, she looks after old Dolby like he knew the date of the second coming. Totally dedicated to him."

"Willy, I've got to ask you some questions about Dolby, and I sure hope you know the answers. Tell me all you know about Sherry. Do you think the old man confides in her?"

"Well, I tell you this much. He got beat up and threatened about something, so, he got a permit to carry a gun. Then a few months after Sherry showed up, some young buck did an ass-grabbing job on Sherry, and old Dolby shot his ear off. Don't nobody fool around with her anymore."

"That's understandable. Tell me, did your dad believe Dolby made off with Tilton's bullion that everyone has wondered about all these years?"

"He sure did. Yeah, he believed it for sure. If he knew the details though, he never mentioned them to me. I believe, for sure, I would have remembered it if he had. My dad thought Tilton was a genius."

"How's that?"

"Well, making money out of mines for one thing. 'Course everbody knows that. But there was other things. Tilton studied—or was involved somehow with science or history or something. Shit, I don't know, Blue."

"You're absolutely sure you never heard about that rare wine from anyone? Anyone at all?"

"Nope. Never. Folks around here have got plenty of interest in gold and silver, but only the winos and the church give a hoot about wine."

Bluefeather said then, "One more thing: what else do you know about Sherry besides her profession?"

"Well, not a whole lot, for sure. Talk is she was an orphan from Nairobi, Kenya. Accordin' to rumor, she's three-quarters Kenyan and a quarter French. Makes sense 'cause her adopted parents were French scientists working at Los Alamos."

"Thanks, Willy. We'll get it all tied together here before long." Bluefeather hesitated a moment, leaning toward Willy, saying with such dedication that Willy forgot to breathe for a moment. "Listen here, ol' pardner, we're gonna find that wine. You hear? I guarantee it. Somebody's gotta know something we need to know. Sixty-five cases takes up a lot of room and somebody, somewhere, remembers. Nothing is gonna stop us—no guns, no lies, no cleverness, is gonna stop us. Nothing."

Willy nodded his head in full agreement, adding, "Well, shoot a monkey."

Flo made a worried effort to get some food into Willy's dissipated body. He took about four tentative bites of the venison stew, piddled around with the peach cobbler and took off for bed without saying a word. Willy was in search of lost sleep.

Bluefeather sat at the table sipping his last drink while the ladies cleaned up after the meal. They all seemed to be talking at once and enjoying it. He didn't even attempt to hear anything specific as he drank and thought. As soon as Flo and Sally said their good-nights, Marsha poured herself a light drink and sat down at the kitchen table with Bluefeather. He was glad, having just enough of a buzz on that he didn't relish drinking alone.

She said, "I know you don't like to drink alone, so I'm going to have exactly two with you."

"Exactly? I don't know what that word means."

"Two. That's all. So you might as well make yours strong enough to compensate. Personally, I want to feel good tomorrow."

"You will. I'm gonna see to that." He hesitated. She waited, sensing that he wanted to talk other than about the weather. "Marsha, are you certain, without any doubt whatsoever, that the wine actually exists?"

"Yes. As certain as a human being can be about any- thing. Korbell is far too obsessed with it to be wasting his emotions. He doesn't waste things. He makes use of them or . . . discards them swiftly."

"That makes me feel better. If it exists, then we're gonna find it. Nothing on this earth can stop us. You know that don't you?"

"I know. I'm ready to work it as long as we shall breathe if that's what you and Korbell wish, and that seems to be an obvious truth."

Bluefeather whammed a fist into a palm, smiled in unison with Marsha and said, "Good. Good." He felt comfortable and full partners with her.

Then he told her about his talk with the hungover Willy. About Dolby and Tilton. She agreed that was the only lead they had going for them right now and that they should pursue it with full energy and dedication. Bluefeather knew she wasn't faking it just to make him feel good. She had already proven in many surprising ways that she was a sticker. He did make his drinks heavy and hers light as she had stipulated. He sure didn't want her to leave.

When she had emptied her second glass, he blurted out, "You know, don't you, Marsha, that I care for you very much?"

She cocked her head over in her puppy dog fashion and laid her big, blue lookers on him, saying softly as a baby's kiss, "Yes. Yes, I know you do. And . . . I feel the same about you."

"Then what in the whirling world is holding us back?"

"Nothing. We're just not ready yet."

"Jesus H. Christmas Christ, I'm as ready as a lit firecracker."

"I speak of the both of us, darling." She got up, walked around the table and kissed him on the cheek. Placing her fiery hair over his shoulder, she gave him a quick hug. The feel and scent of her essence thoroughly slammed extra blood into his temples and half closed his access to air.

Then she walked out of the kitchen, adding, "Would you please pen up the dogs? Willy forgot."

"Oh yeah. Sure. I'll take care of the dogs." He stumbled out into the night confusedly from having been kissed on the cheek by the woman he was rapidly becoming goofy over. The cheek. What a raging romance this had turned into. It was hard for him to accept how cowardly he had been in his approach. This woman made him feel like it was his first day at school and he was emperor of the universe at the same time.

He called the dogs with a smile in his voice, though. They came running, wagging their tails. Bluefeather wagged his all the way to the pen.

Willy felt so sick the next morning he declined the trip to town. They tried to get him an eye-opener, but he refused all offers of help, explaining that he couldn't leave the place alone when the killer lion might strike again.

THIRTEEN

ON FOUNDER'S DAY THE POPULATION OF MEANWHILE usually doubled, but tied to the gold strike celebration, it more than quadrupled. People came in every kind of vehicle, pickup trucks and cars, most pulling campers and trailers. The streets were lined with commercial stands of all kinds, selling and trading every sort of knickknack from homemade quilts to Indian jewelry. Other booths offered an assortment of foods—hamburgers, hot dogs, barbecued beef, chile, pancakes and eggs, and country gravy with sourdough biscuits.

Visitors came from all over the Southwest and other parts of the United States—businesspeople, government employees from Alamogordo, Los Alamos, Albuquerque and Santa Fe. There were artists, Indians, miners, cowboys and kids. Kids were running everywhere—yelling, dodging about among the grown-ups, the boys teasing the willing girls. Old acquaintances were renewed and new ones made. The teenagers moved about, trying to act older but glancing quickly and constantly about, measuring the opposite sex with a forced casualness.

The small-town parade was supposed to start at ten. Just as parades everywhere seem to be tardy, this one got moving at eleven A.M. There was an old stagecoach

pulled by four bay horses. Old-timers in fancy dress of
the period rode in it. A real, bearded prospector led a
mule with a pack on its back. Working cowboys, mixed
with western-dressed dudes, rode finely made quarter
horses. A team pulled a wagon with a country band playing in it. Various dances were done by a group of Santo
Domingo Pueblo Indians. Their colorful costumes made
wildly colored flashes as they turned. Children with their
pets followed the proverbial convertible hauling the day's
queen and her attendants—all in long formal dresses. The
audience quit shopping, visiting and drinking until the parade had passed, then resumed their choice of activity.

After the parade one could see long lines of people
waiting at the many food dispensaries. They knew eating
now was not only a pleasure but a necessity, for soon the
music, dancing and drinking would swiftly gather momen-
tum.

Bluefeather's group had watched the parade amid the
scores of handshakes and hellos to friends. They had a
twenty-minute wait to get the huge and juicy barbecue
sandwiches. It took about the same amount of time to eat
them and enter Dominguez's Dos Amigos Bar.

Bluefeather had been searching through the outdoor
crowd for Dolby or Charlie Waters. He had seen neither
out there. Now he spotted Charlie standing at the
crowded bar. Charlie grinned at them from a well-
chiseled face under thick crew-cut brown hair. His lips
pushed his cheeks up from the pressure of his smile so
that the brown eyes seemed as merry as those of a professional Santa Claus. He and Bluefeather could have
worn one another's clothes without alteration of any kind.

Bluefeather introduced him to the three women and
Charlie ordered them drinks all around. They had to wait
a spell for that too, but Marsha spotted a table being vacated and grabbed it while she could. They all sat down
at last with their first drink of the celebration.

So many local people were stopping by the table to visit with Flo and Sally that Bluefeather had a chance to talk to Charlie between introductions. The noise level was so high that he wasn't afraid of being overheard. If he had been able to pursue his hobby of blind-listening, the variety of pure thinking and feeling in this little town would have pleased him very much.

A table of loggers was discussing their jobs.

"My salary is so very damned small compared to what I do."

His friend settled the fate of a glass of beer, belched and replied, "The return on my expenditure of energy don't match my paycheck either."

A retired banker talked with a teacher of sociology. The banker said, "We do not need more voters. Half of the ones we have are functionally illiterate. We need fewer voters. Should make 'em all take tests to qualify like they do teachers and college entrants."

"Aw, hogwash, you'd wind up with a monarchy with that method."

"So what? I would make the politicians take a much harder test than the voters before they could even think of running for office."

Then a water well driller told a table of drinking buddies, "His mouth didn't fit his stupid face, so I rearranged it so that it did. He did look more natural when he got out of the hospital."

Then another voice added, "He dealt the cards slick as a fresh-laid egg. Sure enough, I got three deuces to his three aces. That's why you folks should buy me a drink. Soon as I start drawing aces, I'll start buying the treats."

An old rancher walked from the men's room, through the crowd, back to a table. He walked so stiffly he could have been a bunch of weathered boards nailed randomly together. After his wife died, he had sold his ranch and moved into town. He never would have done it, but he had finally got to the point that he was physically unable to mount a horse. In his youth, he had been six feet two, but the constant jamming of his bones by horses, one way or another, had left him at about five eleven.

His face was aimed toward the chair, his upper body a few degrees to the left and his lower body angled off to the right. One stiff elbow stuck out from his side, permanently positioned awry. His nose had been knocked sideways by the slinging head of a bronc. Instead of being flattened, the bridge was mashed thin and curved like the inner portion of a hay hook. His hips and tailbone were smashed and tilted under him from fifty years or more in the saddle. Only by watching his eyes could one tell his real direction—the rest of him moved at different angles. He finally got seated across from the university professor of history of the American West, to continue their conversation that the professor was instigating with much acuity.

The young professor, perhaps in his early forties, had authored a couple of books and several journal articles expounding to his readers his version of a world-famous time just past. He had a large balding head and the required beard, shoulders of a football tackle, hands of pianist and blue, curious eyes as active as baby brother's.

The battered cowboy sitting there in front of him was the perpetuation of the living past through his father and grandfather, all the way back to Juan de Onate and his horses. The two men were fated. The horseman was the end, and the professor was, he must be, the honest continuation. That was what he had studied, lived, loved and dedicated his life to. They were both privileged to have met at this exact moment in infinity. The professor must observe, teach, write and enshrine these truths with as much energy and commitment as the old horseman and his ancestors had lived them.

The professor spoke first, "Now, according to my research on . . ."

The old rancher, who had lived both the old and the beginning of the new West, raised a long, battered hand, "Whoa, there. I've been listening to you all day. Now you listen to me for a spell. The only true record of the cowboy comes from the skin of the human ass glued to the leather of a saddle for twenty or thirty miles a day for a long, long time. Horses have killed and crippled far more cowboys than all the lightning, snakebites, booze and bullets combined."

"How's that?" the professor urged him on.

"Well, first there's the gettin' tangled up in a rope tied to a thousand-pound bronc and getting jerked almost in half, or a bad dally around the horn after catching a big old steer and gettin' a thumb or some other finger jerked off. Then, of course, a lot of 'em were forced to ride their horse under a tree, where a posse or lawman tied one end of a rope to a limb and the other to their neck and then spooked the horse out from under them."

"But . . . but . . ."

"Just a damn minute, son. It's my turn, my turn before it's too late."

"I'm sorry . . . go on."

"Well, a lot of cowboys went to whatever reward they had coming, from getting knocked off, or thrown off, and hangin' a foot in a stirrup. Them horses sure enough resent a cowboy in that position. They'll run until they've batted his brains out against rocks, trees or posts. Sometimes they'll run through barbed wire and cut both of 'em to death. If all that don't get the job done, they're more than likely to kick the cowboy to jelly. When they fall by accident—ranch horses don't fall on purpose—they can mash a feller's guts flat as a stomped centipede or break him so's he'll never walk in the same direction at the same time ever again. Just like me. This I know, you see?"

"Well, yes, but there are other things I have found in my research, such as . . ."

"I ain't got time to listen to things that I don't know and you're not real sure about. The way I see it, perty soon now, pickup trucks will kill more cowboys than all the guns, crazy horses and other accidents combined."

The professor was both agitated and excited. He was taking mental notes right now, but he would sneak off and write them down later. He was too experienced to make obvious notes that might halt the natural flow of the old cowboy's wisdom. This conversation was also his work and life. He must not waste it.

" 'Course, you know, young man, that horses come in all sizes, colors, and dispositions. There are those beautiful paints, golden palominos, kingly blacks, noble bays, browns and chestnuts and sorrels so perty they'll melt a dude's heart just to gaze upon 'em. Those very creatures will do all I've told before and more, like run you under a limb trying to break your neck, slam you into a tree trying to crush your leg beyond repair. Sometimes by accident—sometimes on purpose. Young broncs, or spoiled horses, especially, like to buck you off onto piles of sharp-edged rocks, into mud holes and cactus. That's a specialty a lot of horses enjoy. There's been plenty of cowboys flat-ass bucked to death. Sometimes it took only a few minutes or months or years to die, but their innards never healed right, savvy?"

"History is as important as the future. I'm not going to back down on that, no matter how many of your truths you tell me," he slyly urged the rancher on.

"I'm not sure you fellers should be mixing the fun myth with the hard reality. You're gonna get everybody as confused as politicians."

"Exactly what do you mean by that?"

"If you can't figure it out for yourself, after what I just told you, then I ain't got the time to waste trying to explain it any better."

The professor was revising something in his head somewhere. He opened his mouth to speak, but the old ex-cowboy-rancher decided to finish his little say and then shut up about it.

"Now don't get me wrong, professor. I've loved some horses just like a man naturally loves some women, but I just wanted you to know a simple, broken-up truth before you go on writing down all this research again. Horses was it. There wouldn't have been no West without 'em, I don't reckon, not even in all those make-believe picture shows and books. They are a hell of a lot of fun, but I'm not sure they've got much to do with how it really is, or was, or what you been talkin' about. Hellsfire, for one thing, real dedicated, working cowboys was too poor to buy bullets to practice shooting. Mostly it was mind-sick, town dudes dressed up like cowboys, twisted-brain meanies and roundup quitters that learned to shoot. Now listen careful, these were the people who went around robbing banks, stagecoaches, trains and mostly shooting people in the back. Real working cowboys and their horses were way too tired to even think about racing all over the West committing these murderous fairy tales."

The old rancher was quiet a moment, looking way back. The young professor was quiet with him, honestly trying to feel where this real, old cowboy had been.

Then the rancher ordered them each another drink, grinned through seven scattered teeth the horses had spared him and said, raising his glass of brown whiskey, "You can count on one thing, though: cowboys do a lot of laughing when they get together, because they all know they've somehow survived being killed by horses. It was mostly those lovable horses that did 'em in, son. That's just the way it was."

"I've appreciated this enlightening conversation, but I'd like to . . ."

"We're done talkin'. Let's have some fun."

"I was just going to say that you surely told me . . . something all right."

"Yeah, I surely did."

Great and varied noises of this tiny portion of the West talked, laughed, danced, flirted and plotted, cascading around them like the incessant roaring of a waterfall.

Bluefeather did hear through the pulsating energy of sounds someone say, "Hey, ain't this the keenest day that ever was? I had a good breakfast, ain't in jail, and I'm already half-drunk and it's still six hours before closing time."

Then he thought he heard a sort of prayer. "Oh, great mystery in the sky, I am too insignificant for you to answer my personal prayers, but I beseech you to give approbation and save us all from these greedy, screaming, Bible-waving puppeteers."

Another voice finished, "A great big happy amen to that."

After considerable small talk, Bluefeather finally told Charlie what he wanted—plans to every house and building that Tilton had ever had anything to do with. It was Charlie's nature to enjoy any job he liked enough to take. He was fairly wiggling in anticipation of getting after this one. Bluefeather handed him an envelope containing enough cash to get the job done, if it was possible.

Charlie swallowed his drink and said, "I think I'll start at Silver City, where the killing took place. I might as well head over the mountains right now. I can get checked in tonight and begin when the courthouse opens in the morning. I got a camper on my pickup so it won't matter what time I get in." He said the words to Bluefeather while staring at Sally.

Bluefeather had seen Sally taking several quick, interested glances at Charlie, so he told his friend, "Charlie, you might as well stay here tonight. We might think of something else important to hunt. Anyway, we're having too much fun here at Meanwhile's unofficial country club."

As nearly always, Charlie was agreeable. "Well, since you put it so high-classed, I believe I will. The only way I could get in a real country club would be to buy it."

"Okay, that's settled."

Charlie raised his six feet up and headed for the juke-box. He wasn't going to waste any time starting the fun. He went about any job he did the same way. He was soon back, moving agilely through the crowd, and stuck his hand silently out to Sally. They were in each other's arms, around tables and out onto the dance floor, smooth as flying squirrels.

Bluefeather felt real good about that. He touched Marsha on the shoulder and said, "Our luck's beginning a run."

She raised her glass in a quick toast of agreement.

Harvey Dixon from Albuquerque, who owned two Mexican restaurants, sent them a round of drinks, then came over to say hello, asking Flo if she would care to dance. She did.

Bluefeather was glad again. Harvey Dixon was a go-getter about the age of Willy but without the wear and tear of climbing hundreds of mountains and swinging an ore pick uncountable thousands of times at hard rock.

Bluefeather was exulting. The three women he escorted were all so attractive. He was one proud ex–mining man. He looked at Marsha, grinning like he had just invented chocolate pudding, and said, "It's our turn now."

She gave him back that old magic Korbell adopted family smile and said, "Agreed." But, being the brilliant lady she was, she suggested they wait until one of the other couples sat back down, so they wouldn't lose their table.

"You're right there. This place is filling up like a church at a rich man's funeral."

"I like it here," she said. "I don't know when I've had more fun. Yes, I really like it here. You know, I feel right at home. I was raised near a little town about this size in the High Sierras, not too far northeast of Fresno, California."

Bluefeather was both amazed and honored that she had finally volunteered something about her life before she had been adopted by Korbell. That explained her knowledge of the outdoors and more. He felt so flattered that he made a circle with his hand to Carmelita, Dominguez's sister, denoting another round of drinks. She nodded an acknowledgment. Things were working.

As Harvey and Flo sat down, he led Marsha to dance. They did several. The music stopped as the machine automatically changed records. He unglued himself from Marsha with regrets, saying, "Boy, I hate to leave now, but I gotta go look for Dolby."

"I know."

She did, too. The fun was fine, but they had a chore, a big chore, that hadn't been taken care of.

FOURTEEN

BLUEFEATHER WALKED ALL OVER THE TWO-BLOCK-long main street. There was an old-time fiddler's band making music from long ago. The seniors were sashaying back and forth, feeling and loving the nostalgia of other times. Their times. Farther down the street a country rock band was blasting out for the younger blood, and they were shaking their bodies, swinging their arms and really getting after it. The conglomeration of different ages, colors and styles, mixed with the natural attitude of abandonment, was contagious.

It was extremely difficult for Bluefeather to concentrate on his mission. He walked the side streets and alleys looking for Dolby's collector's Bentley. It wasn't there. Maybe he didn't intend to show up at all. If not, it put Bluefeather in a poor position. He knew it would be far better if he ran into him accidentally. His move had to be ultrasmooth to get any information out of the crazy old man. Hundreds of others had tried before him, even using force, and had failed.

He walked on, looking.

Back in the Dos Amigos, a little middle-aged, sparkle-eyed man named Mac Brown introduced himself and asked Marsha to dance, saying, "It's okay, darlin', for you to dance with me. I'm Mac Brown. Blue won't mind at all. I've prospected, and got drunk and been in jail many times with ol' Blue."

She said, smiling with dangerous whiteness, "That's the best line for qualification I've heard in a month."

He was surprisingly agile and, though several inches shorter than she was, also surprisingly strong. He whirled her out and away and back again with a hand that held hers tight as set concrete.

Other dancers respected Mac, she observed, because they left them a larger space to dance in than the other couples. Then Mac, still holding her hand, dropped coins in the jukebox and punched up a lot of slow music. They needed less space now.

Marsha noticed that several local couples danced by them and scratched Mac in the middle of his back. He paid no mind at all, as if it was either his due or he had no feeling in that portion of his anatomy. Most of them smiled and said something to one another as they circled away.

Finally, she could take the curiosity no longer and asked him, "Why do those people keep scratching you on the back?"

"Oh, that. Well, that's a joke. A joke on me. They're just friends lettin' me know they remember."

"Would you care to share the joke with me, or is it none of my business?"

"Ah, you'd just be bored."

"I truly doubt that, and I am really curious. Anyway, you'll find that a friend of Bluefeather's is a friend and confidant of mine as well."

"Now that you put it that way, well . . . alrighty, I'll give it a try. You see, I used to be a workin' cowboy. Then I got me a little ranch of my own and married up with Norma Mae. She was a good wife and perty as six new kittens. She didn't much like me going off runnin' coyotes with hounds and lookin' for gold mines."

Marsha said, "Something must have been neglected among all those activities."

Mac beamed and fast two-stepped at her statement. "Now you're gettin' it, gal. I was neglectin' the ranch and Norma Mae, too. 'Course, I didn't realize it at the time."

"I guess that would be pretty good grounds for argument, Mac?"

"Yeah, but the truth is, it was more fightin' than arguing. She had a tendency to pick up things and hit me with 'em, and if she couldn't get close enough, she'd throw 'em. Things was always nervous and chipped 'round our outfit."

"Are you still married? Where is she?"

"Don't rightly know. You see, I'd been gone 'bout three months, up in the Gila region, and got drunk over at the S-Bar-X Saloon in Hillsboro on the way home. She was mad. I'm telling you, she was real mad." Mac danced on about ten whirls, receiving another unacknowledged scratch on his back, saying nothing.

Marsha said, "Well, go on. You can't quit on me right in the middle of the story." And she was serious. She just had to know how it ended.

"Yeah. Well, we got to cussin' at one another and the next thing I know she's comin' at me with a butcher knife. I jumped around her, trying to get to the door, when she stuck that damned knife in my back hard as she could. I'd reach . . ." he was demonstrating right on the dance floor, "with one arm over my shoulder, but I couldn't quite get a hand on it. Then I'd reach back and under, but I couldn't get hold of it that way, either. I was just standing there helpless with a knife in my back. She musta been studying that unreachable spot for years. All the time I was stumbling about screaming and trying to reach that knife, she was packin' her clothes. I musta looked like one of them magicians that's tryin' to get out of a straitjacket. Only I couldn't help myself. I started to beg her to pull the knife out, but instantly thought better of it."

"She just might have done it, Mac. What did you have to lose at that point?"

Mac stepped back from Marsha again, saying—swelling with indignation, "Lose? What did I have to lose? My head, I reckon. I'm sure she would have pulled it out and cut my dumb head off."

Marsha wanted to laugh at his description but choked it back admirably, not wishing to hurt Mac's feelings.

His little eyes enlarged along with his nostrils as he said, "By the time I got that damned butcher knife out, she had driven off in our pickup, taking what little money and prospecting gold I had, and vanished. Just disappeared like a coyote in thick brush. Never showed up nowhere again. Never. Musta gone foreign, I figure. Way off somewhere foreign."

"How did you get the knife out, Mac?"

"Oh, that."

Mac stopped dancing, walked over to the wall, turned his back to it and rubbed hard right and left. Right and left. Unbeknownst to him, his local friends had witnessed and recognized the show he was putting on for Marsha. He received an ovation of appreciation.

She had enjoyed his story and the dance. She gave his sore back a light scratching and one-hand massage. Then she told the old man, whom she had enjoyed so much and now strangely felt close to, as if he were an older version of Bluefeather, "Your back will never itch again."

He danced with her again, so slowly they came to a stop, as he said, "Danged if you ain't cured me, darlin'. Cain't feel a thang back there but staring eyes."

Then Mac held her close and she was both radiant and safe as her mind turned him into Bluefeather for a few moments. The jukebox was playing a popular song, "Tears on My Pillow." Somehow the misty mood of the music mellowed her body and her heart so that she constantly glanced over Mac's shoulder at the door for Bluefeather's return. Then she asked in a voice soft as a dropping feather, warm as a wool coat, "How long have you known Bluefeather?"

"Ohhh . . . let me think. Something like ten or twelve years. You get to know a man real quick when you work the desert or the high mountains with him."

"Yes. Yes, you certainly do . . ."

Mac was silent a moment, but being a man of deep, mostly hidden, feelings, he knew Marsha was sincerely casting a fishnet.

"I'll tell you true, and for barn rat sure, that man's as loyal to his friends as a loving mother is to her firstborn."

She was surprised how his words thrilled her and made her feel safe. There was no danger from Korbell or any of his adoptees. For that one moment, there had never been any wars in the history of the world; hateful jealousy and grinding greed were nonexistent. Just for that little moment, there was just Marsha and Bluefeather.

Then the music changed, but she didn't hear it. She stopped and leaned down, kissing Mac on the cheek, saying, "Thanks, friend of my friend. Thank you until there is no more."

Mac led her politely to the table, thanked her for the dances and wondered what she meant by the "until there is no more" stuff. He went to the men's room to cogitate. Marsha smiled after his healed back.

Bluefeather re-entered Dominguez's place and rejoined his group. He gave Marsha a tiny head signal out toward the dance floor. He wanted to let her know what had happened even though he had been unsuccessful. Other things were moving along as wished.

Charlie and Sally were holding hands, laughing and giggling at every statement they made, no matter how silly.

Harvey Dixon had one arm partially draped over Flo's back. They were both talking and enjoying themselves almost as much as Charlie and Sally. This was, at least for the moment, good enough for Bluefeather. He worried all the time about Flo and Sally's dedication to taking care of Willy, because he had done the same for them when Flo had been widowed. Just the same, it sure restricted their chances at a love life, living in such an isolated place.

Three couples that Bluefeather was slightly acquainted with sat at an adjoining table. Among them were Pearl and Bill Dozier. Pearl was an old friend of Flo's and yelled meaningless things at her now and then. She never stopped talking, whether she had listeners or not. She mouthed on about her garden, her dog, her kids; then she would repeat the same subjects. Her husband was a retired air force colonel, but he wasn't giving any commands here. He drank mostly in silence, giving a nod when one of the others tried to wedge in a sentence.

Suddenly, there was a crash. Bluefeather's instincts directed him to duck and whirl, leaping back ready to defend himself. The colonel had crash-dived to the barroom floor. There was a doctor from Las Cruces sitting at the bar. He gave Bill mouth-to-mouth resuscitation while Bluefeather pumped rhythmically on his breastbone, trying to revive him. Dominguez yelled for someone to get the emergency squad that was always present at these celebrations. They came and slipped an oxygen mask over the colonel's face. It was too late. His heart had evidently worn out from listening to Pearl's endless repetition of superficialities. She had actually talked him to death. It was slow murder and she would get away with it amid much sympathy and honor.

Some people led Pearl out of the room. She was screaming, over and over through her tears, "How could he do this to me?"

The whispered voice of tragedy witnessed washed

about the bar for a brief time; then everyone gradually returned to drinking and dancing.

Flo said, "Well, old Bill flew through five major campaigns without a scratch, and it only took Pearl three years to talk him to death. Gotta give her credit—she's still maintaining her average. That's about how long it took her to cash in her two previous husbands."

The empty table was taken up by three husky young men with two-day beards and soiled baseball caps. They were accompanied by a pretty, if unwashed, eighteen-year-old girl in very tight Levi's.

Carmelita was trying to clear their table so she could serve them. The largest, with a growing belly pushing his pale grey-checked shirt out over his belt, rubbed Carmelita's rear, saying with a shared grin of sleaze, "Lookee what we got here. A regular quarter horse mare. What time you goin' out to pasture tonight, Sugar Doll?"

Carmelita moved away, taking the dirty glasses without comment. His two companions made remarks just as dumb. When she returned with their beers, they chorused even more stupid utterances. If there was anything that could unlock Bluefeather's controlled anger it was some idiot making rude, suggestive remarks to waitresses. He had always felt they had a tough enough time serving people, standing up and running around, hour after hour, on their tired feet, without having to defend their private parts from some smart-ass, numb-headed, macho fool.

Every time they finished a beer, one of them would snap his fingers at Carmelita and yell, "Hey, you," like she was his personal slave.

Bluefeather figured they would probably leave a fifteen-cent tip. It was difficult indeed for him to keep his breathing down. He could feel the scar across his nose searing and the hairs itching on the back of his neck. His face was becoming flushed. He tried to cool himself by hoping some cowboys would take up Carmelita's case even though he craved to bash the Neanderthal skulls. Then, too, he and Marsha had fought with a similar dunce the last time they had been in here. He didn't want any trouble as long as there was a chance Dolby might show. At that thought he heard flute music. Indian flute music.

There in the middle of the dancing couples stood his spirit guide. At his stare, the flute disappeared and Dancing Bear indulged himself with an Irish jig even though it didn't fit the music.

Bluefeather excused himself as soon as Dancing Bear jigged to an outside circle. Bluefeather walked by and whispered for him to follow.

"We gotta talk."

They walked past the rest room and out the back door. There was no one out there to interrupt them but one drunk cowboy who was leaning up against the building by the palm of his hands, trying to keep from vomiting on his expensive Paul Bond boots.

Bluefeather held onto a cedar post holding up a drooping, barbed wire fence with one hand and relieved his kidneys.

Dancing Bear sat on top of an old gasoline barrel. "You know, dear brudder, old man Phillips, he tell me this. When he was young man he have to put his thang under the wire to keep from peeing in his face. Now when he get very old he have to drop his thang over the wire to keep from peein' in his boots." With that Dancing Bear started laughing and stood up on the barrel, holding up one leg in the stance of a Masai hunter.

"I haven't got time for your worn-out jokes, Bear. You've been playing around in London and Authority knows where else, while I've been in desperate need of help."

"That's for sure. But I send substitute with many messages. She give it to you? Huh? Huh?"

"She gave . . . well, let's put it this way. I couldn't figure out what she meant."

"Don't tell me this thing. Sometimes you smart boy. Sometimes you don't do so good."

"Good? By the almighty Authority, you tell me how."

Dancing Bear said, "Now don't get your bowels in uproarious condition. Things movin' along pretty good. I tell you this truth."

"I gotta admit some of the crazy things you tell me have come to pass. But they've only created more confusion. Korbell's not going to wait on me, or anyone else, forever."

"Korbell wait like horny buck for doe to tell when time she's right. Like that 'red' girl do it to you, huh? Ain't that about right, for sure."

Bluefeather felt like running back into the bar and drinking all the whiskey in Dominguez's place, but he was too confused to find the door. Instead, he said weakly, "I haven't figured out all I know about this world right here, much less the one you inhabit."

"No matter. I been 'round a hunnert years, maybe more, and I haven't learned but a . . ."

"Please, Bear. Please. I beg you like a little baby brother to help me right now. Just give me something solid to hang onto. Anything. All you've been doing is handing me pieces of broken limbs and shattered bottles."

"Sure as sun smile on morning dew, sure as mother's milk, sure as moon make ocean tides, sure as buffalo return, sure as the snow turn to rivers in the spring, sure as . . ."

Bluefeather's ears went numb. His head felt like the wheel of a windmill in a tornado. He felt for certain he had sunk into the earth up to his waist.

"Shut up!" he yelled. "Just shut up that poetic flea shit and tell me. Just plain tell me what to do. Oh, what did I ever do to deserve you?"

"You just lucky, I guess. All the time you white men hurry, hurry, hurry like rabbits making million baby rabbits. Then the coyotes, the bobcats, the mountain lions, they all come and eat 'em to pieces. Poor dumb rabbits. They got to jump on one another, hurry, hurry, before they all gone. Then . . ."

Bluefeather stumbled toward the bar.

"Wait one step, dear brudder." Bluefeather stopped without turning around and Dancing Bear said to his slightly humped up back, "That pretty Mexican waitress, Carmelita . . ."

"Carmelita?"

"Yes, her. She show you the way to where the moon don't have no chance to glow. That girl don't know she gonna do this for you, but, dear brudder, you watch what happen like one thousand eagles. Huh? Huh?"

Dancing Bear then leapt from the gasoline barrel to the top of an old shed and started yelling at the universe, doing an expert rainbow dance. Then he shouted at his subject, "You like Scottish fling?" He flung himself from the shed out into the crisp, mountain air. He did such an expertly executed dance that it would have made a real Scotsman rupture his bagpipe in awe.

Bluefeather walked past the drunk. He was now sitting down with his head back against the building and his still-clean boots shoved out in front.

"You need any help, old buddy?" Bluefeather asked him.

"Naw, I'll be ready to get after it again in just a minute."

Bluefeather entered the throbbing bar. It was the time of insanity. It would do nothing but improve until two o'clock in the morning.

Flo said, "We were just about to send the militia to look for you."

"They wouldn't have me."

Charlie said, "Hey, Blue, we were thinking about going somewhere to get something to eat. Dominguez is outa burritos already."

"You folks go ahead without me. I gotta wait here for somebody."

Marsha volunteered, "Tell you what, folks, Sally and I will go get something and bring it back here. Any idea what you would like?"

Harvey Dixon said, "Anything that's not talking."

Everyone left it up to them. Food was simply fuel now. Naturally, the table with the three scummy baseball caps and the soiled, but pretty, girl had to yell after two women as fine looking as Marsha and Sally. That was excusable for the moment. Those two women would have drawn a reaction from a mummy.

Harvey said, "You know what, Blue? I think I'm falling in love." He grabbed Flo around the shoulder and pulled her to him.

She liked it, but said, "Aw, shoot, he's just had enough drinks to start smelling roses in a cat box."

Bluefeather said, for no reason he could think of, "Watch out for him, Flo. An uncle of mine was going broke and he decided he'd slowly teach his dog not to eat. Soon as he got him trained, he died."

There they were just as one-track-minded and silly as all the other drunks in the world. Right now they were all thinking of the food to come.

Bluefeather decided he should ask Flo to dance. They did.

"You kinda got the itch for Harvey, haven't you gal?"

"We'll know about that by morning, Blue."

"Well, there's not a drove of people around that I'd recommend to a friend, but Harvey's about as right as you're likely to run across these days."

"He's a lot of fun anyway, but I wish Willy was here to share with us."

"Now you listen to me, Flo. Willy's just hungover and worried about a lot of things. Listen to your buddy Blue. Everything's gonna be honey and grapes before you know it."

"Okay, boss. If you say so."

"Guaran-goddamned-teed. I got it on high authority. We'll just stay hooked to the wagon even if the axle breaks."

Marsha and Sally returned with the food—green chile burritos and barbecued beef sandwiches. This would take care of them for the rest of the evening.

Bluefeather ordered another round of drinks from Carmelita. She served them from the side of the table so the sweat-stained idiots couldn't grab at her. Bluefeather must remember to watch her as Dancing Bear had insisted so adamantly. He did. Sure enough, she stopped at the bar to speak to someone. It was Dolby and his Kenyan lady, Sherry.

Bluefeather uttered, "Slapping thunder. It's Dolby."

He felt Marsha's hand on his arm, silently speaking to him. It was suggesting he take it calmly. It was a difficult chore for him to do, but his nerves quit jumping. The bar table inhabitants chattered on with reasonably intelligent conversation that could only come from comfortable company appreciating each other.

Then it happened, of course. One of the three cretins was trying to pull Sherry away from old Dolby onto the dance floor. He made the mistake of saying, "Come on, honey, your old daddy won't mind."

Sherry was trying to tug her arm free, looking helpless and angry at the same time. Dolby was slowly becoming aware of the intrusion. Bluefeather saw his hand start under his coat for the pistol.

There was no time now for thinking things over, being cool and all that. Everything Korbell was paying wages for, and he and his friends had been struggling for, was about to be blown away by one worthless half-wit. The strong lock that Bluefeather kept on his anger broke apart into powdered metal.

Bluefeather decided this had to be done instantly. He reared up and ran at the abuser of women, shoving a thumb and forefinger in each of his eyes. Then he kneed him forcefully in the groin. The baseball cap's lungs were partly paralyzed as he bent over, agonizing out a howl that denoted pain.

Bluefeather grabbed him by the top of his head and with both hands pushed down hard, bringing up his right knee to meet the descending face with much force. They met. A number of things on the victim's face squashed and the blood splattered about like water from a busted garden hose. He dropped. "Thunk."

Charlie had another "baseball cap" down and was pounding the dog piss out of him. The third one had poor Harvey on the floor doing the same to him. Bluefeather charged through the milling, yelling crowd to give his friend Harvey some relief. Marsha beat him to it. She had one knee in the assailant's back and was opening both of her arms wide and then whamming both palms against his ears. The third time she did this he fell off Harvey onto the floor, screaming, "I'm deaf. I'm deaf."

Bluefeather jerked him up and whammed him across the nose so hard he could feel the bones splinter. Now the whey-bellied "cap" was without proper hearing or smelling abilities. Charlie was trying to kick him blind to make his deserved punishment complete, but a throng of peacemakers were pulling him backward toward the bar, handing him refreshments to cool him off. The crowd's action was correct, for a change. Any more punishment would go unfelt and waste good partying time.

The defeated ones' little girl companion was about to faint, so Bluefeather handed her the only drink that hadn't been spilled.

"Here miss, try this."

She took it in shaking hands and said, "Thank you. I just met them today and I've been embarrassed ever since."

The Dos Amigos went through the after-fight bedlam of the law arriving, and the losers trying to fake breaking loose from restraining arms to fight some more. The officers talked to Dominguez, Carmelita, Sherry and a few others, then hauled the three "caps" away. One of them screamed back vengeance.

The place slowly returned to more peaceful drinking and dancing. The usual accompanying yells quieted for awhile. Their table was sent many complimentary drinks from other patrons. Some of them added that Bluefeather's bunch had saved them the trouble. The night was about normal for a hundred-year celebration: one dead colonel, three whipped smart-asses, several new romances in progress and old and new drunks dancing again.

Old Dolby was calmly sipping his drink, without having had to fire his pistol. Sherry was talking seriously into his ear. He would nod almost imperceptibly to her. Then a stool emptied next to Sherry and she put her purse on it, motioning Bluefeather to join them. Here it was. The main move. Indeed, for once—this once, when it counted the most—Dancing Bear had clearly guided him to the desperately needed connection. The success of the meeting would be entirely up to Bluefeather. By defending Sherry without hesitation, he had just earned the sudden trust of both Dolby and his lady.

Sherry moved over at his approach so that he would be sitting between them. He glanced back at Marsha as he sat down, shaking hands, and their eyes locked in space with understanding. These moments would be IT, one way or the other. They both knew it. Dolby was the only entrant left in their shell game. Unbeknownst to Bluefeather, he had just become the finalist in Dolby and Sherry's desperate search for a partner.

"Thank you, Mr. Fellini," Dolby said.

Bluefeather started to tell him to drop the mister, but Korbell had worn him out on that subject. "My pleasure, I assure you. They had been insulting Carmelita, too."

"We both thank you, Mr. Fellini," Sherry said.

"Please call me Blue," he felt free to suggest to her.

"Of course. At any rate we are deeply appreciative."

"Hey, it's just part of the celebration. Perfectly normal happening."

Dolby didn't look him directly in the eyes, but stared far away at some distant cloud bank or mesa. His mind seemed to be only partially here. Oddly, Sherry Rousset had that same expression of a knowledge that only the two of them could share. There was a vast loneliness emanating from these people as if they sat at a bar in some other world and time.

Bluefeather was struck again by the huge, black, shining, African eyes whose outer edges arched up around Sherry's head as if she had the peripheral vision of a chameleon. Her light, milk chocolate skin pulled over the cheekbones as tightly as little drums, but her full-lipped mouth had a hidden sadness about it.

Dolby's face, under the slight shade of his little fedora, showed lines that could have been etched by a linoleum cutter. He stared at the glass of whiskey in his bent, bony hands as if the ultimate answer of existence was being revealed in the amber lights flickering there. They were a couple out of context with this milling, sweating, laughing, celebrating little world around them.

Bluefeather thought of the larger world, of other cities in other nations. In his mind-pictures the couple was unique, no matter where he placed them.

"Do you visit?" Dolby asked in a whisper, turning his little eyes toward Bluefeather without moving his head.

It threw Bluefeather off, but he answered, "Yes. What do you have in mind?"

"The millenniums are less than seconds."

Bluefeather just simply did not know how to reply.

Sherry placed her hand gently on his forearm and spoke lowly, "Would you come to our house—alone?"

"Now?"

"If it would be at all convenient for you."

Dolby emptied the few drops of whiskey left in his glass and said, "The vassals and vessels are empty. It is the time of conceptions."

Sherry interjected, with only a trace of urging in her voice, but Bluefeather felt it quivering in her being, "If you could come now, please. He . . . he is ready at last."

Bluefeather nodded yes, went to his table saying, "Have fun, kids. I have to leave you for awhile."

Marsha reached out and took his hand, squeezing it with a soft strength that made him feel warm, calm, sure and just plain good.

FIFTEEN

SHERRY DROVE THE PERFECTLY TUNED BENTLEY ALONG the well-graded, graveled dirt road. Dolby sat in front with her. Both silently stared straight ahead. Bluefeather sat in the back, looking out at the sagebrush and yuccas. The foothills became larger, and the cedar and piñons began to thicken. In openings around curves he could see the mountains climbing in green, then blue layers, furred with spruce and pines.

They came to a huge fence and a guard post. There were two men in their seventies with rifles slung across their shoulders. They were in dark, loose uniforms. Without the belt and holsters for revolvers, their dress could have been taken for monks' robes. The age of the two, who pushed the buttons to swing open the huge electric gates, surprised Bluefeather. Behind them was a big guard house with a tower and dark portholes all around. There was no way of knowing how many guns there were here.

Bluefeather's recently jubilant mind was now somehow tilted out of kilter at the old men and their raiment. There, across a lush, heavily grassed valley, was the house nestled against the last big foothill at the base of the heavily timbered mountains. It was a huge, brown brick against the bluffs. Because of its low profile and the long, hexagonal sloping roofs, the compound of buildings blended into the background as if it had been carved there by a giant sculptor.

There was another artfully designed fence and guard gate nearer the house. It was perhaps twelve feet tall. Bluefeather was certain it was electrified. The fence had been painted in army camouflage colors and was hard to follow as it wove erratically through clusters of natural trees and vegetation. The guard house was even larger here. There were several old men and two elderly women dressed in the same unique warrior-monk uniforms.

One leaned over and spoke into Dolby's ear so softly that the words were indistinguishable. The car pulled across the cattle guard into the grounds area, where there were no lawns, just gravel and stone pathways winding through natural vegetation. A massive wood and iron-laced door opened and let them into a rock-fenced area that closely surrounded the entire house.

Sherry turned sharply to the right, into a huge garage that housed several jeeps, pickups, a new Buick Roadmaster and another Bentley. A couple of old men were slowly moving about, checking and cleaning the vehicles.

My God, Bluefeather's mind-voice elevated, *Dolby's got a combination old folk's home and senior citizen army here. Why? Why and more why?*

As they got out and entered the house from a doorway connected to the garage, Bluefeather saw a hallway perhaps twenty feet wide and eighty feet long, just like the one at Korbell's. It was even floored in a similarly colored design of Mexican tile. The paintings—some of which he instantly recognized as Taos masters—hung on the walls. There was one great difference: instead of being escorted in by Korbell's beautiful, adopted wife, Elena, two great danes and a mastiff were lined up, staring at them motionlessly from the end of the hallway.

Sherry gave a hand signal and they fell from formation

and came to meet them. Bluefeather was certain they would smell his fear and take three parts of him for play. They all gave him a slight touch of the muzzle.

Then Sherry said, "Hello guys. This is Mr. Fellini."

They wagged their tails now, fully smelling Bluefeather's legs and allowing him to touch their massive heads. They actually roughhoused a little with Sherry, but not enough to give up their dignity. Bluefeather was surprised that he wasn't surprised at them totally ignoring Dolby's existence except to circle him without looking or smelling.

They walked through an archway into a large living room full of old prints and dark walnut furniture. Great urns and brass objects were placed about. Bluefeather didn't have a chance to study the room's contents, but he got a feeling of ancient things residing here even though the main compound itself couldn't be over twenty-five or thirty years of age—at least it was new for the land of the vanished Anasazi and Mimbres Indian tribes.

Sherry smoothly led the way into the combination kitchen and sitting room area. Bluefeather sat in a modern, rounded chair. Dolby took his own matching one, as if from long habit. The dogs scattered about in a semicircle on Navajo rugs, lying heads up, watching, listening. For what? The young man did not know.

There were richly colored draperies hanging beside the huge picture window facing mountains to the north—just like Korbell's. All sorts of green living plants flourished in pots of many sizes around the room. In this room the paintings were much more modern than those in the hallway, done in broad and brightly colored strokes. They varied from barely recognizable figures—ghostly, religious, devilish, both delicate and deformed—to wild, almost unrecognizable, landscapes. Two long sets of bookshelves balanced the sitting room. One held leather-bound tomes that appeared scholarly, the other books of a more recent vintage. He couldn't read the titles from where he sat, but he had an almost irresistible urge to go and search for old, familiar names with which he had spent so many wondrous and adventurous hours. He kept control somehow, and yet he had this feeling of déjà vu, as if he were back in Korbell's mansion being set up again.

He looked out past a great landscape, over the small lake in the valley and felt another charge of electricity tingle all his skin. There were at least thirty gorgeous mules—some grazing, others turned head to rear, swatting flies from one another. A couple of younger ones raced about in a mock running fight. There were bays, browns and blacks along with one grey. They were so solidly fleshed, so sleek of hair, that he could tell they were exercised and fed to perfection. Well, that was one thing for sure he and Dolby had in common—the mules, man's most useful partner of the entire animal kingdom. There was so much he bubbled to ask and discuss that he had to grit his teeth to refrain. He was here for greater—if mostly unknown—purposes than discussing common likes and dislikes.

Sherry brought liver pâté and cheese wedges with little crackers and placed them on the coffee table between the two men.

"Now, what would you like to drink?"

Usually, the drinks would have been served first, but this turnaround seemed proper to Bluefeather here—now. He asked for Scotch and water. Dolby was served his usual glass of sipping whiskey. Sherry poured herself a rich, red burgundy wine.

They were all seated. Sherry raised her glass in a silent toast. Dolby raised his along with them, staring at the glass only. He seemed to see things in the lights and tiny bubbles that no one else could envision. Dolby took a tiny sip, moving his lips soundlessly. It was as if they should know his thoughts without the interference of words. Now the old man seemed to be staring across vast landscapes, looking for the fountain of truth.

Sherry sat a moment, slowly whirling her wine after the first sip. Her thick, black, minutely wavy hair picked up reflections of blue and brown as did her large, slanted eyes with the whites gleaming around them in contrast to her coloring. She was indeed striking. Her eyes penetrated the space beyond the strongly sculptured face and looked into Bluefeather's head. He felt as if she saw all the way through so that she could have computed the hairs on the back of his neck, if she so desired.

"You are searching for something, Mr. Fellini. Something very special?"

"Well—yes. Aren't we all hunting something we don't have?"

"Surely. But the rare few seek the difficult—the impossible. Impossible to most of us, I should say."

Bluefeather fished forward. "I've done a bit of gambling in my time—with cards, of course, but far beyond that."

"We're aware of that. That's why—among other reasons—we asked you to join us here."

Dolby mumbled, "The world cannot control all that is in it any more than it can the human mind."

Sherry glanced at him with obvious fondness and appeared to understand what he meant. Bluefeather admitted to himself that he sure as hell didn't. Lord, he was mixed up, what with the riddles of Dancing Bear and the unexplained, almost invisible, games of Korbell and now the incoherence of the seemingly senile, imponderable utterances of Dolby.

It was the time of decision. Sherry Rousset made it.

"Blue—I recall you wish to be called Blue—as Dolby said earlier, 'It is the time to move on.' We might as well start now. Right now. We have decided to put our trust in you with multiple, and what will at first be shocking, revelations. We're not going to ask for guarantees, either verbal or written, that you will keep faith. Faith is only as good as a person's heart and honor. We, as of now, accept yours. Let me add, however, that even if you keep it, and we believe you will, it could still lead to disastrous and momentous events. If you do not keep it," she paused a beat, "well, it will mean certain doom for many who do not deserve such a fate."

Bluefeather could not resist, not for a second, the promise of such unknown escapades. It was imbedded as deep in his blood as coyotes howling. Bluefeather Fellini was a natural-born yearner. He committed.

"Whatever it is, I will give you my best."

Sherry's face now softened a mite with a slight smile, "We, as you shall see, have waited a long, a very long time. Our waiting must come to its agonizing end now. Now," she repeated louder, looking at Dolby.

A metamorphosis took over the old man. He straightened. His pallid skin gained color. His eyes moved thoughts to their surface from hidden recesses. He finished his drink in a single swallow and stood up, suddenly animated, exuding the forces of life. For just a moment he looked into Bluefeather's dark eyes with his recessed blue ones. The old man's dry stare was as merciless as the gaze of a tiger hunting to feed her young. He must never forget this look, thought Bluefeather. Never!

Sherry rose now, saying, "Come then. We shall begin."

Dolby led the way, momentarily in charge. He pushed lightly on a shelved wall of Mimbres pottery. It moved back, opening into an empty concrete passage. He pushed on another wall—again not unlike Korbell. It swung back, then closed precisely, as they moved on down curving concrete stairways.

Bluefeather had felt, or believed he felt, a slight quivering. He even believed for a moment he could hear, but he wasn't certain, giant motors running somewhere. The curving stairway slope was long and gentle, and old Dolby negotiated it with confidence.

They circled many times, going deeper and deeper under the compound until they came to another wall of the same material. There were soft lights from indentations in the wall showing the way to it.

Dolby swung the wall open with another light push, and they were in a room possibly forty by eighty feet. At one end there were wheel handles of a large steel vault. Heavily reinforced file cabinets lined part of the room. There were tables filled with microscopes and all sorts of chemistry tubes and glasses. Several shelves were loaded with metal boxes of bones. Bluefeather could not, at a glance, tell what was skeletonized.

Sherry moved forward and slid a panel back over a narrow, heavily glassed window. She motioned Bluefeather to have a look. Down below was a large power plant humming the sound he had felt and heard. A couple of old men—as old as Dolby—sat on stools conversing, watching the machinery.

Sherry said, "We call our workers the Olders. You'll understand why later. This is our own private electrical plant fueled by our own thermal-powered wells. No one knows about this outside the compound. You'll see why this has been a requisite as we move you forward into the greater aspects of our installations and situations."

There was a film projector at one end and a pathway through the other items in the room to a large screen. There were six softly made chairs facing the screen.

Dolby pointed from one end of the great room to the other. "We could show you many astounding things here, but Sherry shall take you to see the real thing."

Sherry opened a gun rack—more like a small armory— which included automatic weapons, handguns, and hand grenades, even two flamethrowers and several rifles with grenade launcher attachments. She handed him an M-16 and a belt of cartridges. She placed a huge pair of binoculars around each of their necks.

She said, in a soldierly manner now, "We probably won't need the weapons today on so short a trip, but . . ." She picked up a battery light as big as a loaf of bread, saying, "We have lights installed for miles, but just in case." She shook the hand light, testing it. She pushed a file case on smooth rollers away from a wall and spun a combination lock behind it. Then, with a push the same as Dolby had used, a huge concrete and steel door three feet thick swung open with precision movement—soundlessly.

Dolby said, "Not past station C-One for now, Sherry. Understand?"

"Yes," was all she said, and they entered.

In the next few hours Bluefeather had a slight understanding of what Dancing Bear had meant about the subterranean and there being no time in his dimension. What he saw down below was so real, so very real, and so unreal, so believable and unbelievable, so unearthly, and yet more earthbound than he could have dreamed with the mind of Edgar Allan Poe.

Upon their return, they ran the film of the subterranean. Bluefeather remembered again that Dancing Bear had used the word more than once. He was in a state of exhilarated shock. The film had been such an addition, revealing wonders past—far on past—those he had just seen with his naked eyes.

Dolby finally slept as the last hour of the unimaginable reality of the documentary film unreeled. Sherry shut off the projector and, with that, Dolby awoke and sat up, staring again at Bluefeather. Waiting.

Bluefeather asked, "Why me?"

Dolby stated, matter-of-factly, "I'm not going to be here much longer—that's pretty obvious—and I need the assurance that Sherry, and the project I've given my life to, are safe from the greedy clutches of . . . an old adversary."

Bluefeather took a deep breath and said, "I'm honored, Mr. Dolby, to be part of your world—your world inside a world." And he was.

SIXTEEN

Back in the sitting room, Sherry Rousset served strong, aromatic Turkish coffee. They needed the caffeine jolt to hold on for the dawn assembling itself outside, painting away the night with sun rays brushing the northern peaks pink on their eastern tips and violet in the valleys. The outer world, the one that suddenly seemed commonplace, had made a complete circle during their short trip to the interior.

The coffee tasted good, but Bluefeather did not really need it to keep awake. He could literally feel the nerves of his entire body vibrating like a driven jackhammer.

"Well, folks, it will take me awhile to organize everything—since we can't hire any strangers. You'll have to trust my people just as you have me. My experience in the mines and World War II, the trips back and forth across the Mexican border, may be useful to us now."

Dolby spoke as alertly as an Olympian finalist, "Of course, Mr. Fellini. We are totally committed now. All of us. You make the necessary preparations. We shall comply and help you with all our physical, financial and mental resources."

Sherry looked at Dolby with a strange reverence in her

eyes, exhaling a deep sigh of relief, saying, "At last, dearest one, at last."

The first smile Bluefeather—or anyone else—had seen, crept across Dolby's face with the words, "Yes. Yes. The fulfillment. The finality is near."

She answered considerately, "Only the finish of one magnificent step. It is really endless."

Dolby answered, "You are correct, precious one. It is in fact, perpetuity. No recorded beginning . . . and no end."

Bluefeather said to himself with his mind-voice, *As for me, old dumb-butt Bluefeather, I'm growing speechless, mute as a mummy.*

SEVENTEEN

SHERRY DROVE BLUEFEATHER BACK INTO TOWN AS THE
sun was beginning to warm the east side of the scattered
homes of Meanwhile. People were already up and stirring
about. Some were shaking the night before from their
sleepy, still half-drunk eyes, while others were starting to
cook breakfast over open fires and in the trailers and
campers.

"Don't get impatient now, Blue. We'll contact you a
few days ahead of the expedition," Sherry said.

"I'll be getting ready, nonetheless, as fast as possible.
Say two weeks. By the way, thanks for . . ."

"Forget it. We're on. All the way."

Sally and Charlie were just getting out of his pickup
camper, which was parked by the hotel. Bluefeather
didn't waste any time. He handed Sally the key to his
room so she could clean up and told Charlie to wait. He
went over and pounded on Marsha's door until he woke
her. He told her to pack her things—they had business
to attend to. He asked Charlie where Flo and Harvey
were. Charlie pointed to Flo's motel room.

"Good. Now you guys all stay here and finish your playing today. Then, Charlie, you get after those maps. Harvey
can take the girls home tomorrow. Say, get plenty of olive

greens, climbing boots, bedrolls, the whole bit, just like we were going into the wilderness for months. Don't need any food or weapons though. We've got plenty of both." At Charlie's quizzical look, he explained, "Look, ol' pardner, we're goin' after a big score. The biggest ever. You're just gonna have to trust me. Call in every day at Rugers'. I gotta know where you are all the time."

"Well hell, couldn't you just give me a hint at what's up, Blue?"

"Not now. Anyway, you probably wouldn't believe it," Bluefeather said, shaking his head. "I want all of Tilton's floor plans. Then I'll explain. Marsha and I have to get on out and talk to Willy. And then I've got to get hold of Pack."

Bluefeather and Marsha were about a mile from Willy's when he finished telling her where he had been and everything he had seen at Dolby's. She sat silently around several curves. A doe and fawn bounced across the road and vanished into the timber.

"My God, Blue. What you have told me will alter human history. Earthly history, as well, I suppose. I'm completely dumbfounded."

"We'll probably get the bullion, too," he said.

"What does it matter now, after what you've just told me?"

"It matters even more to me. It's, well, shit, Marsha, it's just part of what we set out to do. It's our job. Our duty."

"No. No, it's not. We started out to find the Mouton 1880. That's all."

"Yeah, maybe. You gotta remember Korbell did make a strong point about the bullion. I know that wasn't part of the deal with him, but it has become our deal. Ours."

"Well . . ." and she shook her head, dismayed to a degree.

They drove to the front of Willy's house. Old Brown

was on the porch but did not come to meet them as he usually did. He looked awful. One of his ears was shredded, and he had several scattered cuts.

Bluefeather yelled for Willy and got no answer. They entered the house. Willy sat there on the couch with a glass of whiskey in his hand and a bottle on the floor within reach. They had left Willy at home a wreck and he hadn't improved in their absence. He looked like he had been kicked by a mule and crapped on by an elephant.

"What in hell happened to you, Willy?"

Willy stared at his drink like old Dolby and finally choked out, "The lion. The lion killed Toby and Jumper and made off with a calf."

It was another brain-shaker. They had come here to tell Willy about their monumental challenge and now this. Right here, in the woods with his dogs, was Willy's world. They would just have to forget the other fantastic, subterranean one right now and take care of his.

"When did all this happen?"

"Jist 'fore dawn. The racket of the fightin' woke me up. I got the gun, but it was already too late. I done buried the dogs. Jist finished 'while ago. Forgot, goddamn it. I jist forgot to pen 'em up."

Bluefeather checked the .30-30. It was loaded. He got a holding leash for Old Brown.

"Marsha, if you want to go with me, we have to move out now." She nodded "yes." He handed her the 357 Magnum. "The lion will be full of calf meat and bushed up somewhere. We gotta get after him while his belly is full. It'll slow him down."

Willy stood up, weaving, silent tears washing over his blunt, drawn face. "I'm ready."

"No, you're not, ol' pardner. You're gonna stay here. It won't take long."

They left him standing there, making feeble protests. Bluefeather knew damn well Willy had suffered all the killing he could take in his condition. Besides, Willy had an admiration and deep feeling for the very creature that was destroying his livestock.

Bluefeather ran the cotton rope through the iron ring on Old Brown's collar and held the two ends in his hand. This way he could control the dog until he was ready to turn him loose by simply dropping one end of the rope. Release would be instantaneous, and one second might decide success or failure with the obviously survivalist cat.

In spite of the pain from his mauling, Old Brown was pulling hard ahead of Bluefeather on the rope, excited and anxious. He was a hunting dog and that's what he was doing with all he had. He led them to the spot of the previous night's battle. The grass was torn up in spots and bits of bloody hair were scattered about. They followed, with little trouble, the signs of the calf being dragged to the creek. There the lion had turned north, looking for a place to cross with his kill.

Bluefeather said, "The old dickens still has plenty of power left. That calf had to weigh around two hundred pounds—but he's lost most of his speed."

Marsha was amazed at the crippled lion's strength. She said, "You have to admire him, no matter what."

"Yeah. Just like us. He's making a living, the only way he knows how," Bluefeather contributed with a slight grin.

They found where the lion had crossed. The wet blood left a visible trail. Then, on a rise in a small circle of short brush, they found where he had fed. He had picked a spot so he could escape in any direction if interrupted.

Bluefeather whispered, "The cache won't be too far from here."

It was, however, over a half a mile uphill before they found the calf's remains. The cat had dropped it in a vacant badger hole and half covered it with dirt and sticks.

Bluefeather scooped the covering off and they saw that

the cat had eaten a good third of the meat. Some of the bones were stripped relatively clean. The oldster had been desperately hungry. Without any interference, he could have loafed around and fattened up for several days.

The man, the woman and the dog followed the lion's tracks, observing that the right hind foot twisted to the side from the old injury. This slowed him.

Old Brown strained harder against the rope as the scent became stronger. Bluefeather admired both the dog and lion very much at that moment. Both were doing the best they could under difficult conditions.

Suddenly, Bluefeather saw that they were a lot higher up in flat rocks and boulders than he had noticed. Then Old Brown became confused about the scent on the rocks. Because of the bad leg, Bluefeather surmised that the old lion had made an erratic climb, looking for a safe lair in which to sleep and digest his huge breakfast. Old Brown moved back and forth, once giving Bluefeather a glance like, "Hey you, a little help is in order."

Now they were stalled because of the rocky terrain directly in front of them. Bluefeather motioned to Marsha and softly told her to circle out to the left to look for a patch of soft earth so they could pick up the tracks again. He would do the same with Old Brown, to the right. He also warned her to be very careful. The lion would not be charmed at having a rare meal disturbed.

She nodded and holstered the 357. As Bluefeather and Old Brown scrambled through the rocks and brush he had a sudden regret of having let Marsha go off alone.

Then Old Brown lunged against the rope so hard he almost jerked Bluefeather off the rocky slope. The dog bellowed. Bluefeather turned one end of the rope loose and Old Brown was gone. Bluefeather wadded up the rope, jammed it in his belt, crawling, climbing, and running when he could, after the hound's cries. The dog was out of sight now as the slope got steeper and the rocks bigger. Bluefeather could tell by the intensity of the bay-ing that Old Brown was on a hot trail. The lion was mov-ing on up, just ahead of them. The sounds were as clear and full of information as a telegrapher's message.

Bluefeather forgot everything in existence but his hunt. He was tearing through brush and clawing recklessly over the rocks without thought of injury. At this moment, he lusted to be there when Old Brown treed the lion, more than anything in the world. It had always been so with man.

Then he saw a flash of Old Brown through some cedars and looked on up where the heavily limping lion was leap-ing off a rock and moving higher into the massive boul-ders. It was becoming very steep here. Bluefeather was slipping and falling now and then, grabbing at the jagged stones with his free hand. By training and nature, he pro-tected the rifle beyond himself.

Now the sound came, terrible, clear and beautiful. Old Brown had treed the lion. Bluefeather stopped and looked up, but could not see either one of the animals. One thing was obvious: there was no tree there. The lion's run had been stopped by a bluff, and there he was, making his stand. Bluefeather could tell by Old Brown's sounds that he was frantically trying to get at the cat. If he did, he was dead.

Bluefeather caught a glimpse of Marsha higher up on the other side of the confrontation. It was all coming to-gether like the instruments ending a Wagner symphony.

His mind blurred but his body's adrenaline pushed him on. On up, up. Now he was on a little promontory. He saw them. Old Brown was leaping back and forth, trying to get a foothold up the ledge where the enemy was backed against a bluff. The lion moved to the edge and made a swipe at Old Brown, just missing.

Bluefeather yelled. The lion backed up again. Blue-feather still had to climb down a few yards before climbing back up. He was crawling on his stomach, slipping, digging his feet at pebbled rocks, using elbows and clutching for any kind of hold with his free hand. At last he struggled to an angle where he could get a shot. He raised the rifle as he levered a shell into the chamber.

Then he saw a blur on the rocks above the lion. It was Marsha. She slipped, letting out a cry. The 357 dropped down by the lion. She hung by her fingers a few yards above him. Old Brown was filling the mountains with his voice of the kill. All eternity collided in an instant. Marsha's fingers were losing their grip. If she fell, it would be right on top of the lion. Mountain lions seldom attack humans. In all known history, only a few instances exist where they have. In most cases they had been wounded or cornered, just as in this tragic moment.

Now Marsha was holding on with one hand, clawing desperately with the other. Old Brown had, by chance, found a foothold and was moving awkwardly almost to the edge of the shelf. Bluefeather was near enough to see the saliva in the mouth of the overheated lion.

Bluefeather took all this in at one glance as the big cat turned to face him, his fangs revealed under his stretched-back lips.

Bluefeather centered the gun sight between the yellow-brown eyes. For one unmeasureable piece of time, he stared into the soul of the universe. He pulled the trigger and said, "Forgive me, brother." Death was instantaneous.

Marsha dropped on top of the lion's limp body, thereby saving broken bones. Old Brown scratched over the ledge and chewed at the lion in victory. Bluefeather crawled on over and held Marsha to him without words. Only the growling of the dog interrupted the silence. No birds sang, as yet. All lizards and other earthlings were frozen, still listening.

Then Bluefeather grasped that it was over and lay down

on the shelf, panting heavily. He held Marsha to him. He could feel their hearts pounding the blood of life through their slowly relaxing bodies.

He caressed her hair against her neck and held her cheek, damp with soundless tears, against his. Then she moved her head and her mouth sought his. They kissed in a mist of tenderness and warmth-giving that enveloped them as a golden protective shroud. She removed her clothes without haste and spread them on the rocks by the lion and laid her naked body upon them. He removed his own clothes and eased between her thighs. There was no waiting, no tricks, no games, as their bodies joined with the delicious commitment of love. Yes, love. There on the rocky side of the mountain, by the body of the valiant lion and the exhausted hound, they gave all they had to each other.

Bluefeather slept. When he awakened one of his arms was under her head, her face turned to him, and her enormous blue eyes studied him. She smiled so slightly it almost wasn't there. With the tips of one skinned finger, she touched his lips. Then she stretched back, her breasts catching the late sun. He touched a nipple and it stood up stiff. He touched the other and then closed his hand on its firm smoothness.

This time there was the ineluctable pleasure of their separate parts. At the last moment, she let out a cry of pleasure that echoed across the hills into the sky, part of all and of him.

They came to a creek. He took the bloody lion hide from his shoulder. He could not let all of this majestic creature go to the vultures. Willy must have it to admire just as he had when it lived. Marsha, Bluefeather and Old Brown knelt together and drank the cold liquid gift of mountain snows.

EIGHTEEN

SINCE BLUEFEATHER WAS AFRAID TO TALK ON THE phone to Korbell about his current knowledge and pressing needs, he was pleased and surprised when the man agreed to come to Willy's place.

He came sweeping in with three large helicopters. The multiple roar made the cattle run, the mules circle, heads high, and birds fly from tree to tree in clattering panic.

All the present Ruger household and the heroic Mr. Brown hound joined Korbell and his retinue where they landed in the meadow.

Before the country bunch could offer any amenities, a large portable table was assembled and set with fine linens and exquisite silver. There was also a bounty of food—including Bluefeather's favorite, wild quail. There were at least six people working on the lunch setup. About a half dozen armed, security personnel stood about, professionally studying the landscape for they knew not what.

Bluefeather recognized Fontaine, Marsha's adopted brother, the one he had first seen at Korbell's guard tower—the one who had a deep scar completely cutting his face in half at a forty-five-degree angle. The seven footer was obviously in charge of this tiny army. He reminded Bluefeather of the arrogant SS officers they had captured at Brest, France. Bluefeather felt Fontaine was just as dangerous.

Korbell was dressed all in white, including tie and shoes, which emphasized the sleekness of his silver hair. His thin, butcher-knife face was accentuated by a perfect golden tan. The adopted wife, Elena, wore a formal black dress that matched her hair and eyes, giving them tremendous punch. His adopted assistant Nedra was also dressed formally in a burnt orange, exquisitely fashioned cocktail dress with Aztec designs.

At first, Bluefeather was puzzled by the formality of dress and dining. But somehow he knew this was part of Korbell's smooth intimidation. However, he reasoned, the man with skillful utility would again expertly, in fact, exquisitely, mix business and pleasure—just as Korbell had told him when they first met.

Amid plentiful small talk, everyone was introduced with enough smiles to hypnotize Satan.

Nedra poured Chateau Lafitte '53 and they feasted as they visited. It was pleasant, indeed, here in the meadow with a soft breeze teasing the warm air, stirring the vegetation that reflected emerald green in the noonday sun. The purple shadows under the trees and the blue-violet haze of the mountain canyons served up a background worthy of the table's bounty that all so eagerly consumed.

Marsha slipped Old Brown several bites under the table. Nedra had arranged the place settings so that Bluefeather was next to Korbell, who naturally sat as head of the table.

Korbell raised his glass of fine wine and said, "May we dine with pleasure, work with total dedication, and win with relish." All raised their glasses at Korbell's movement and drank to his thoughts. He sounded so sincere, Bluefeather felt guilty when his mind-voice broke in with an unsolicited warning, *If that man asked me for a loan, I'm dead certain he'd insist on a cashier's check.*

Now Korbell turned his head slightly toward Blue-feather and said, "I assume you have a lead on the Mouton Rothschild, Mr. Fellini."

"No, not yet. Something far greater."

"Indeed. Well, now, knowing the depth of my feeling for the rare wine, I can only consider that you have made a discovery at least equal to the conquering of gravity."

Bluefeather strained to catch some sarcasm in his voice but could not. The man sounded as sincere as the ringing of church bells. Bluefeather was having some difficulty following up on his end of the conversation. He knew that Dancing Bear was somewhere near, having a little fun at Bluefeather's expense, because they were all now sitting at a table that was approximately forty feet in the air. No one appeared to give this fact the attention Bluefeather felt it deserved. The entire group dined and chatted as if they were on solid ground. Bluefeather moved his feet up and down in the pure, thin mountain air. There was no question he was aloft in spite of the others absolutely ignoring the spatial situation that was so obvious to him.

"If you don't mind, we'll have a private talk after lunch," Bluefeather said to Korbell.

"Of course, Mr. Fellini."

What Bluefeather really desperately desired was a conversation with his guiding spirit. He strained mightily, trying to project his mind-voice to the dancing trickster. For once it worked!

There he was, down in the meadow, dancing with one of Willy's mules. He believed it was a waltz. 'Round and 'round they went. The Jenny mule followed gracefully, flawlessly. The music was being presented by the Zia Creek. It suddenly changed into a fancy-stepping foxtrot. The mule was leading Dancing Bear.

Now he looked up at Bluefeather, grinning like a chicken-stealing fox and said, "Oh dear brudder Blue-feather Fellini, it is very good to see you again. How you likin' this dance I do here in grass with my friend the mule? Huh?"

"Two well-matched asses, I'd say," so spoke Bluefeather, not knowing where the words came from. At this Dancing Bear and the mule stepped swiftly, perfectly, together, finishing exactly when the music did. They both turned to him and kneeled, bowing three times in faultless unison. Bluefeather shook his head three times. It changed nothing. The sun punched a hole between two clouds and spotlighted the pines, piñons and cedar trees that clapped and waved their branches wildly in appreciation.

Bluefeather had to take three quick swallows of Chateau Lafitte '53 to keep from choking.

Dancing Bear, obviously thinking that Bluefeather was triple toasting his performance, said gleefully, "Thank you. Thank you. I appreciate you like my dance so much. I do another good 'un for you. I do tree dance for sure."

Dancing Bear tried doing a Texas two-step with a sixty-foot ponderosa pine but soon said, "Too tall, dat tree."

Dancing Bear was directing the nearest rock bluff—where Bluefeather had killed the lion—in some kind of symphony. Slim slags of stone slipped loose from the bluff's efforts to match its music with the lightning action of Dancing Bear's arms. The pines remained motionless, and their cousins the piñons only applauded lightly out of courtesy. Bluefeather knew, suddenly, that Dancing Bear had blasted his brains with these apparitions for a purpose, but he wasn't going to show his gratitude until after the hoped-for revelation.

In an instant, he was on a limb of a dead pine next to an exultant Indian spirit guide. He was grinning as if he had just sold a shovelful of fresh horseshit for the price of platinum.

"Dat's enough dancing for dis day."

"That's enough dancing for a full year, and don't you

start using that cockeyed Indian dialect on me, again. That's for the tourists. You hear?"

Dancing Bear ignored his subject's insolence and said, "Now, dear brudder Blue, I ready to give you plenty good guidance."

"It's about time you showed some responsibility to me. I've got an extremely dangerous and daring venture to perform. There's never been one like it in the history of the world."

"Whooo-eee," said Dancing Bear, "that's a big one, alright. The world she been goin' on pretty long time."

"I'm telling you, Bear, this is so important you may have to ask the Authority for advice on how to give advice."

Dancing Bear jumped upright on the limb and sailed over on top of a big orange bluff. He sat there with his chin in his hand, like Rodin's sculpture, thinking hard. Then he zipped right back on the limb.

"I talk with Authority. He tell me that I done had about a hunnert years to learn, so I gotta do advice for you by my ownself."

"Well, as deadly and provident as the final adventure is, I may just have to go over your head, old friend."

Bluefeather looked down at the dining table; there sat his other self right where he had left it, taking another drink of the fancy wine. He could tell from way up here on the pine limb that he had overindulged in that wonderful stuff.

"Listen, Bear, you've got to stay with us all the time when we do the subterranean. We can't pull this off without your help. The last discovery we reveal down there will have to be kept in total secrecy until the hour we move underground. It would scare and muddle our associates' minds out of reason. I'm not telling anyone but you and Marsha. Anyway, there's plenty of wonders to work on until we're ready for the finals."

"How long, dear brudder, before you do this great thing?"

"I think we can have everything ready in about ten days to two weeks."

"That's gonna crowd your friend Dancing Bear. I got to go to Canada and help my trapper buddy. His wife leave him and run off with police that mount. Then I got to go to Andes for to see my Inca friend. He got himself a big dose of screaming clap, and he give it to five of his six wives."

"He's got six wives?"

"No. No. He don't got any. None wives. These are his amigos' wives. That's the reason he need help so very much. Savvy?"

Bluefeather nodded that he understood, but the wild Indian dancer was still avoiding a full commitment.

"You notice today, dear brudder Blue, how I use both Spanish and English? Authority make me learn nineteen languages. Only one I don't know is Ethiopian. I go there tomorrow for conference on how to make money. Some folks still eatin' buzzards for beef and drinkin' muddy water for milk. That not good for Dancin' Bear, Bluefeather Fellini or wide, wide world."

Bluefeather was beginning to wonder how he could possibly compete with all the problems Dancing Bear had to solve when his ragged thoughts were interrupted by, "Problems. Problems. When white men discover this country, Indians were runnin' it. No taxes. No debt. Women did most of the work. Indian men hunt and fish all the time. White man dumb enough to think he could improve a system like that?"

Bluefeather burst out laughing and so did Dancing Bear. In fact, Bluefeather almost fell out of the tree, forgetting for a moment he was a temporary spirit. He grabbed Dancing Bear just in time, reminding him who he was. At that he just rolled over and over in the air, spinning like a floating top, both hands on his belly, trying to stop his Indian sense of mirth. Laughter has no accent.

Dancing Bear finally controlled himself, soberly asking Bluefeather if he would like a special dance before he left for Canada. "Maybe Lithuanian? Huh? Huh?"

The young adventurer told him "no" in several different tongues that he had just invented. He repeated one last time his need for help and advice.

"Hokay. Okay. You got help. Sure as I tell you truth. Sure as moon make blue-colored nights. Sure as long-lasting rain make long-lasting grass. Sure as cactus spine make hole in skin. Sure as winter make frozen water. Sure as pretty red woman make you jump and . . . and . . ."

Bluefeather had to stop him right there or otherwise he would leap from the limb, hoping to get a clean but fatal break in his neck. He yelled desperately, "Enough. Enough of hearing about you watering rare orchids with skunk piss. Just give me one pure word of advice. Just one."

"Go!" said Dancing Bear and danced off across the sky on his moccasined toes like a mad choreographer of ballet.

Bluefeather discovered his numbed self walking along Zia Creek with Korbell. Four of Korbell's security people followed discreetly with their automatic weapons held ready for action toward he knew not what. Bluefeather was playing poker with a professional devil, but at least he was a charming one.

He said, "Mister Korbell, if it would be possible for you to accept my word about the significance of this discovery without my spelling it out, I would be forever grateful."

Korbell took two Havanas out of his leather case and handed one to Bluefeather. Even though he had finally conquered the vile smoking habit, he could not turn down Korbell or resist lighting up with him.

"I shall respect your wish, and I must say, I respect you for undertaking what must be a great risk and challenge."

"Thank you, sir. Yes, it is all I say it is and much, much more."

Korbell replied to Bluefeather, "There are a lot more 'never beens' than 'has beens' let me tell you."

Bluefeather took about three more steps before he got the man's meaning. The words made Bluefeather realize that Korbell had as many levels as the Grand Canyon, and one would only forget this at great peril.

"Is my daughter contributing her share to your efforts?"

"Marsha is first cabin all the way. Thanks for providing her presence."

"Ah. That is good to hear, Mr. Fellini. Yes. Uh . . ." He stopped walking, and his companions did likewise. He turned, looking straight into Bluefeather's eyes, saying softly as a snake slithering over silk, "You know of course that love—love is giving up something?"

Before Bluefeather could answer, Korbell looked at his heavy gold watch and said they must depart, turned quickly on his feet as deftly as a tennis champion and strode back toward the choppers.

Bluefeather followed. The good-byes were swift, without waste or hesitation. The thank-yous were accepted and waved off. They were gone, falling into formation up in Dancing Bear's realm, clacking out of sight over the horizon as if they had crashed through the wall into eternity.

Bluefeather's bunch was all alone again. It was suddenly, sweetly quiet. They walked back to the house before they conversed again. Marsha held his arm all the way across the pasture—not possessively, but affectionately. The gesture felt good to Bluefeather and, even better, comfortable.

NINETEEN

TINA AND TRANQUILINO HAD CERTAINLY KEPT BLUE-
feather's place up in style. The mules were solid and
healthy from a balance of grain, grass and exercise. Bluefeather and Marsha petted and conversed with Miss Mary
and Nancy, bringing them up to date as they would long-
lost relatives. The mules listened and moved their ears.
The trees, grass, bushes and even the vegetable garden
were watered and fertilized and growing happily.

Marsha picked Big Boy tomatoes, cucumbers, squash,
green beans and lettuce from the garden. She made a
huge fresh salad with wine vinegar and olive oil dressing.
Bluefeather made up a big pot of his grandmother Fellini's special sauce to pour over the pasta. It took a lot of
careful time, but in the end the Marsha Korbell and Bluefeather Fellini repast would have pleased even the rulers
of the Vatican.

"I'm bragging, of course, but this salad is heavenly."

"I'm bragging, of course, but this sauce was inspired in
heaven."

They both laughed and acted fun-silly for awhile.

"I think you must be missing your family right now,
aren't you?"

"Grandmother Fellini's sauce caused it. And this Italian wine we're having has created a certain nostalgia."

She had been reading his mind a lot lately. She was at it again, saying, "You must take me to meet them soon."

They were both quiet for a moment. Then he said, "Yes, soon."

"I'll surely be happy when we've finished with it," she said. "The trip—the job, I mean. I love to work in a garden. Well, I mean I would like working in a garden of my own."

He just pulled her up close and let her know he understood and knew what she meant. It was a nice feeling all the way around for both of them. So they just left the table and climbed into bed as if they only had ten minutes to make love before the world came to an end.

For a few moments afterward, Bluefeather did not much care if the globe was finished. There was nothing to look forward to better than this. After they had showered and changed into fresh clothes, another form of adrenaline started to flow. They dropped by Tranquilino and Tina's for a visit and to bring their caretakers' pay up to date.

Tranquilino refused to accept it, but Tina was more practical—there were three children to get through school. She let Bluefeather slip the money into her apron pocket. She put it in a cigar box full of knickknacks. The Luceros would have an extra feast or two out of this, and Tranquilino would never know how it happened. Their children were in Socorro with the grandparents for their last visit before school started.

Marsha and Tina got along as if they had been friends since childhood. While they visited, Tranquilino and Bluefeather slipped out to the barn. He could tell Tranquilino wanted to talk in private.

"Hey, amigo Blue, you got one good girl there, so don't

you let her jump the pasture fence, huh? What you think, huh?"

"I think you're right as rainwater, Tranc, but she's the kind of woman that can't be fenced in unless she builds her own corral. Savvy?"

"Ahhh, *sí, sí* for sure, I do. Just help her build it, okay? Tina and me, we sure like to have one more good neighbor."

They chatted on about rain, crops, who was in trouble, who was making money, who was getting married, having affairs and getting divorced.

Then Bluefeather got the 357 Magnum pistol and the Remington 30.06 rifle and took Marsha out to the shooting range south of town. He asked her if she had any experience shooting.

She replied, "A little."

He put her on a hundred-and-fifty-yard target. It was small—very small. She shot a tiny pattern, six shots all touching or in the black center of the paper target. After seeing this, Bluefeather prudently decided not to risk showing her his own abilities. She knew he had fired thousands of rounds in the war, anyway. They moved on to the pistol range. Bluefeather was only average at best with the small arms. He decided to shoot first and get his embarrassment, if any, over with. He put in the ear plugs and drilled the small target seventy-five feet away dead center.

Knowing this was pure luck, he handed her the 357 pistol before she found out, and said, "Your turn."

Marsha held the weapon out in front in both hands. She blasted away the second he had hooked the ear plugs over her thick auburn hair that glistened in the mile-high sun like burning wire.

She shot a three-inch pattern with the remaining four bullets. Then she looked at him with her head tilted over in her puppy dog way and smiled with her eyes, saying, "Will that do, Master Fellini?"

"That's all right for now," he said, proud as a first-time daddy. "You'll do until something better comes along. It's none of my business, I guess, but where did you learn to shoot like that?"

She answered, "Korbell. That's one of the qualifications one must fulfill to be adopted by him."

Since he had varied emotions about eventually being adopted himself by Korbell, he didn't pursue it. They went home and got "spiffed up" for an evening out.

They drove down Rio Grande Boulevard, turning left on Central to the Sunset Club. The club had a large dance floor and a fine, popular band that was playing "Amapola" as they entered. There was a huge dining area that offered space enough for privacy to visit while enjoying a meal, the music and other action in the background. Politicians, promoters, ranchers and local businesspeople were the main customers. The steaks and all the Mexican food was superb.

They chose a table in a far corner and were on their second glass of house wine when Bluefeather finally overcame his childhood training not to ask questions and quizzed her about how she had been adopted by Korbell.

"Well, my parents were killed in an airplane crash when I was fifteen, and I went to live with my aunt and uncle in Los Angeles. At seventeen, I won a scholarship to USC in communications. My sophomore year in college, I was at the top of my class when I was interviewed by one of Korbell's people. The next thing I knew I was meeting Korbell and Nedra in a suite at the Beverly Hills Hotel. I was shocked that he would propose adopting me right then and there, with the understanding that after graduation I could take a position in one of his companies—or directly with him. It's very difficult to explain, Blue, how he can influence people. It sounds self-serving, I know, but his whole empire has been based from the beginning on acquiring the best talent in the world. When he decides, there is no hesitation. Just like he did with you. Remember?"

"I don't think anyone can criticize his approach to that. The record is there for all to observe," he answered.

"It wasn't that easy. My aunt and uncle wanted to adopt me as well."

"So do I. Right this minute."

"All right, now. You wanted to know about Korbell, so no more unsolicited remarks, okay?"

"Yeah. Okay."

Marsha continued to explain, "Finally, after checking out his company, the quality and attitude of his main people, my uncle—who is a banker—and my aunt—who is a horsewoman—reluctantly agreed. So, I chose to work for the main man himself as a combination publicist and troubleshooter. And that's the story of my little life."

Bluefeather knew that was a small portion, but he decided not to ask any more questions. What in hell did he care anyway, as long as she felt about him as he did for her? Besides, if they survived the trip into the earth together, there could never be anything else to question. Never.

He said, half-jokingly, "Maybe he'll adopt me if I deliver what he wants."

"Oh, no. That would never do." At Bluefeather's questioning stare, she continued, "You see, my darling, we'd be brother and sister then, and I don't believe in incest."

"In that case, I'll never be a son of Korbell's."

"In that case," she returned, "I have something to give you. I've been waiting for the right moment." She reached into the soft leather handbag hanging on the back of her chair and removed a flat package wrapped tightly in colorful paper. She handed it to Bluefeather with a nervous smile.

His heart was pounding from the suddenly surging blood of anticipation. Marsha did not pass out gifts, of any kind, lightly. He struggled to remove the paper without letting her see his shaking hands. It was a book. A large book. There on the front was a photo of himself, his head held high, looking off toward Taos Mountain. The angle was dramatic and so was the effect on Bluefeather. The photograph showed him wrapped in a blanket, Taos Pueblo style.

Bluefeather was really taken aback. "My God, I was just a little kid," he said, looking at the lettering on the dust jacket of the book that said, "Bluefeather," and at the bottom, "Photos and Text by Lorrie Friedman."

He looked through the book, being instantly teleported back to that time of beginnings, of his mentor Grinder, and his love for Lorrie and the lands and spirits surrounding his half-home, the Taos Pueblo. It was shocking to know that Lorrie had taken so many shots he had been unaware of. There were those up Twining Canyon he remembered, but there were many on Taos Plaza and at the pueblo with his grandparents, Stump Jumper and others of his clan that he had been unaware of until now. His stomach was tingling delicately from nerves throbbing from old, warm memories and ancient nostalgia. On the back of the dust jacket was a photo of Lorrie. She was as beautiful as he remembered her. He read underneath that she now lived in Connecticut with her husband and twin daughters. The tears dewed his large, black eyes as he cast them with scattered emotions at a waiting Marsha.

"Thank you. I don't know how to . . ." He swallowed twice and sniffed, then went on, "Where on earth did this come from?"

"From the publisher, in New York, in 1946, the year you returned from the war. It's selfish of me, but I hoped you were unaware of its existence—that it would be a surprise that pleased you."

"I wonder how I missed it. Of course, I missed most everything in forty-six, except drinking, laughing and raising hell. Hey, forgive my numbness. I do thank you for it with all my heart. I had no pictures of old Grinder except in my mind, and those tend to get fuzzier as the years pass. Come to think of it, that's the only kind I have of Lorrie. She was always promising me copies, but never gave them."

"Well, she has now. There you are and there she is on the back of the book. It's obvious from the photos she took that she loved you very much."

"I suppose I did her, too, at the time. Yes, yes, I surely did love her as much as I knew how. It all seems so very long ago."

"What happened, Blue?" Then she quickly reversed, "No. Forget I asked that. It's none of my business."

"No. Really. It's all right. Her mother wanted to bind us together by buying me, that's all. It wasn't Lorrie's fault. None of it was. The blame must be with me and her mother, Candi. That was one powerful and beautiful woman. Now that I think of it, your adopted mother, Elena, reminds me of her." He stroked the book, "I shall treasure it always . . . not just because of the photos of me . . ."

"Oh, I know."

He thumbed quickly, embarrassedly, through the book again, stopping only to look at Grinder and himself standing with the burro Tony in his Taos home pasture. He could visualize Lorrie behind her camera, moving, squatting, seeking the perfect light and angle. He could hear her lilting laughter and see her warm eyes looking into his, enjoying a mutual reaction of joy. Then he closed the book saying, "That was a very special thing for a very special lady to do. Where did you find it? A rare bookstore?"

"No. I stole it out of Korbell's collection."

"Thanks again to a lovely lady, who is not only special but very daring and brave as well."

Bluefeather felt grand all of a sudden. The nostalgia of the past was gone, replaced by the splendor of his lady now and the grandiose escapades they were about to share. They lifted their wineglasses in a silent, but understood, toast.

"Say, Marsha, I've been wanting to ask you a crazy question."

"It would be rather childish for us to hold anything back now, wouldn't it?"

"Yeah. Sure . . . well, is Korbell magic?"

She laughed out through her perfect teeth, "A lot of people seem to think he is when they're dealing with him, but he is not a Merlin, if that's what you mean."

"Never mind. You answered my stupid question. One more. Did you come to bed with me the first night I spent at Korbell's castle?"

"Good heavens, whatever made you dream up something like that? Not that it wouldn't have been a good idea."

"Oh. I don't know. Maybe I had more drinks than I realized."

After a thoughtful moment, they turned the subject back to Dolby. He told her about seeing the room of gold.

"Where is it hidden?"

"Under the house, in a huge concrete vault. The door must be four feet thick. Sherry said they had spent the silver bullion, and about a tenth of the gold, on fixtures underneath in the . . ."

"My God, Blue, do you realize there was over forty million in gold when it was only twenty dollars an ounce?"

"Yeah. I tried to figure up what it would be worth today and make a projection twenty years into the future. It was too much."

Marsha's wide, blue eyes became more so. She said,

"I'm just now beginning to realize what we're really in for. Wars between entire nations have been fought for less than that."

"Yeah, that's true, but beyond the uncountable riches and altering the concepts of world society with the knowledge we're going to attempt to verify—we, you, me, Pack, all of us, will be changed forever, as well."

Bluefeather worried a moment. He wondered if Pack, much less all the others who would accompany them, could accept the reality of a world so different from their own. Even seeing it on film had rattled his own senses like multiple lightning bolts striking his body all at once. He had time now to adjust his mind to the vast differences of this new world and its creatures. His friends would not.

Marsha said, "Yes. Well, while we still have time, let us order dinner."

They had enchiladas. The red chile sauce was perfectly balanced in flavor and heat. They had another bottle of wine, but part of the taste was lost because no matter how they tried now, thoughts of the phenomenal experience shortly to come kept intruding.

Then it hit him. He had to get Pack out of the mental hospital at Las Vegas, New Mexico.

He explained to Marsha, "He's the most sane crazy person one is ever likely to meet. I knew him in the war and we partied some afterward. He ran guns to Latin America in every revolution he believed in, and if he didn't believe in it, he supplied guns to the defenders. Pack is one of those men who go on long-lost weekends that sometimes turn into years when they are unable to find work that has a chance to save the world."

"What's he in for now?"

"Oh, he has many ways of going on 'vacation.' That's what he calls going to a mental institution. He usually throws something, or someone, through a plate glass window to get the attention of the straitjacket crew. This last time he showed more class. He was discovered sitting on the curb in front of La Fonda de Santa Fe, nude except for one item."

Marsha looked at him now with the tilted head and a quizzical gleam in her blue, magic eyes. She pushed a thick strand of hair from her face. Seeing her like this made it hard for him to carry on about Pack.

"Well? What was the item?" she prompted.

"He had a red wool sock on his dinger. That's all."

"That should do it," she said, laughing.

Bluefeather didn't think Pack's last "entry fee" was that funny, but he was caught up in her glee and made as much happy noise as she did. Surprisingly, she picked up her glass of burgundy and said, "To Pack. How do we acquire his services?"

"I can't. But your father—Korbell—can get him out."

"I'll call him then."

"He'll never talk to you, Marsha, about using his influence like this on the phone."

"Yes, he will. I know how to talk to him in code."

The last would have certainly surprised Bluefeather a few months ago, but now he accepted it as the norm. "Go ahead then, if you don't mind."

She stood up, saying softly, "When do you want Pack out?"

"Oh, tomorrow would be just fine," he said casually, half joking. Then he thought to himself, "We've been accomplishing the impossible by joining up with Sherry Rousset and Dolby, so why not ask for more miracles?"

Marsha walked away to the pay phone in the entryway. There wasn't a man or woman in the place who didn't stop eating, drinking or talking to watch her smooth, thoroughbred walk. Class.

He poured a little more of the dark red in his glass and thought about how good it would be to see Pack again, although his old friend's impatience for action would be a strain.

Marsha returned with all the patrons' heads following her in the opposite direction as if they were watching a slow-motion tennis game. She sat down matter-of-factly, unaware of the halt in conversational ideas, maybe permanent changes in the flow of people's lives, that she had innocently created by merely passing by.

"Done," she said. "Two P.M. tomorrow at the main office in Las Vegas. Say, it's off the subject, but I'd like to know: How did Dolby come by Tilton's silver and gold? That is, if you feel free to share it with me."

"I suppose it's okay. Sherry said it was too late now to worry anyway. We four have to trust one another whether we like it or not. There's no choice now. The story goes: contrary to what all of us have heard, Tilton was not taking care of his partner, Dolby. In fact, he had cut him completely out of his will. Sherry swears that Dolby has no idea why, to this day. The fact that he had spent twenty-five totally loyal years of his life in the service of Tilton's wishes and wealth made Dolby's actions at least justifiable to himself. The reasons for Tilton still being listed as missing are all clear in Dolby's mind. He knew there was no record of Tilton's fingerprints. So he just cut off his head and took it with him when he left that Silver City hotel by the fire escape."

"My God, Blue, what earthly reason could he give for committing such a barbaric act?"

"Not barbaric at all . . . in his way of thinking. It was simply the right thing to do. No fingerprints, and along with the missing head, dental records would be useless. He took clothing, jewelry and everything but the nude torso. There was no one around to say the remains were Tilton's. After that Dolby . . ."

She cut him off there with, "I believe you've answered

all the questions I care to know, darling. I'd as soon leave it there. Could we go home now?"

The last question caused Bluefeather to almost dislocate his elbow waving at the waiter for the tab, and by nature he was most often a shy man.

TWENTY

BLUEFEATHER DROVE ALONE THROUGH LAS VEGAS, New Mexico, hunting the street that led *to La Casa del Locos*, as the local Latinos called the mental institution, with some fondness.

The mighty Sangre de Cristo Range sheared the sky west toward Santa Fe and north to Taos. The massive architectural clouds piled up, creating spots of shadows so deep that the terrain mostly vanished under the cloak. But there were portions of the landscape and the town where the sun splashed shoutingly down, revealing intense patches of green and yellow like falling gold dust.

Scores of the old frontier buildings still stood, some with repairs just beginning, others being historically maintained to give a frontier aura unsurpassed in America. Just north of town was the famous old Montezuma Castle. Its earlier occupants had ranged from Jesse James to Theodore Roosevelt.

Las Vegas caused Bluefeather to feel as if he had one-half of himself in the Old West of Billy the Kid, Wyatt Earp, Doc Holliday and many more of their ilk who had once inflicted the town with their persons. Then too, the old issues of the *Las Vegas Optic* revealed such prominent names of the past as Flyspeck Sam, Cockeyed Frank and the Dodge City Gang, who once ruled the town under the tutelage of one Hoodoo Brown.

Bluefeather slowed down and looked at a one-story building facing the old town plaza, where General Stephen Watts Kearney had taken possession of the territory of New Mexico for the United States. He enjoyed looking at the century-old Plaza Hotel—now restored to its former glory.

Ruts of the Santa Fe Trail could still be found outside town, yet here he was, Bluefeather Fellini, driving to pick up Sergeant Pack, a modern-day warrior, from the institution and go on a trek of dimensions far, far beyond the local history of Las Vegas, New Mexico. Yet, it seemed to the young man that this was the perfect place to launch an expedition of such wondrous—though deadly—potential.

He had wanted Marsha to share the day with him, but she had politely and wisely refused, saying she felt he and Pack should have some time alone. She also felt it would probably be good politics if she returned home for a short stay while he and Pack prepared for their inestimable travels into what might be the infinite. The subterranean journey could possibly be "forever" for the entities already there as well as for those en route.

PART TWO

~

THE CAVERN OF
WONDROUS MARVELS AND
THE SECRET RIVER OF RICHES

TWENTY-ONE

IT WAS THE TIME TO TAKE GREAT AND SPECTACULAR risks. As Bluefeather drove Pack into the edge of old Santa Fe, Pack broke a twenty-minute silence with, "What happened, Blue? Those people at 'The Institute of Incapacities' were going to offer me a manager's position if you hadn't shown up."

"Korbell called. That's all."

"Not the Korbell who owns the world?"

"That's the one, old pardner. He doesn't own it all yet. Our friend Dolby is way ahead of him."

"That's some going. How'n hell did you wind up involved with both of them? My God, that's like having dinner with Churchill and Napoleon."

"One introduction was on purpose and the other was planned luck."

Bluefeather had answered most of Pack's questions and explained all the details by the time they were seated in Maria's Mexican Kitchen on Cerrillos Road, having a drink before partaking of Maria's famous enchiladas.

Bluefeather ordered a margarita from Gilbert Lopez, Maria's husband. Gilbert handled the bar orders and did most of the visiting while Maria cooked the meals and oversaw the kitchen. Bluefeather enjoyed looking at the

Alfred Morang murals on the walls. The oil paints were so thick and bright it reminded him of some childhood dream.

Pack said, "Gimme a liter of the cheapest red wine you've got." At Gilbert's puzzled look, Pack went on seriously, "Ain't any need to be poor, when you can be rich for two dollars."

This would have been beyond most bartenders, but not Gilbert. He laughed and joined right in. "Makes sense to me. For four dollars you'll probably not only be rich but be a free guest of the city—the part with the crossed iron windows," he said, chuckling.

Bluefeather raised his margarita to Pack's glass of wine. These would probably be the last drinks they would have for a long time. Neither one had ever drunk alcohol during the battle of work or the work of battle. They knew they could die quicker that way.

"Here's to the world and all that's in it, Pack, and the old days and old ways we survived together."

"Yeah, Blue, yeah." Pack thought a minute and then grinned out, "Hey world, there's no way out, so let's just plunge right on in."

Bluefeather was amazed again at Pack's almost common appearance. He was about six two or three but didn't strike one as being of that height, because sitting, standing, running or walking, he always slumped a little, as if it was just too much bother to straighten up all the way. His small blue eyes were faded and always seemed a little extra damp, as if he could cry or laugh himself to tears instantly. He never quite did either one that Bluefeather was aware of.

There was a perpetual, almost imperceptible, smile on his face. In the intensity of battle and death, Bluefeather had never seen him without it. It was as if he was constantly on the verge of caring deeply about something, but never quite making it.

Bluefeather had always been amazed by the physical power of the thin body that showed no musculature at all. Pack looked soft, easy, even weak. At the thought of this, Bluefeather laughed, and then choked it hurriedly back, for this man before him could be so mean he cast a shadow over the sun, and so gentle he could turn dog turds into tulips. No one could pin down what his thoughts, conversation or actions might be about anything but battle. There, he was as dependable as a grandmother's love.

Bluefeather suddenly felt comfortable and confident having him along on the great venture. They started naming off acquaintances that would fit well in the expedition. People whom they could trust with their lives and, even more difficult, keep what they saw inside their heads. Hard choices. They had talked an hour and the only person Bluefeather had come up with was his neighbor, Tranquilino; and then he decided he could not bring this upon his friend. Tranquilino had too many children and other dependents.

"What do you think about Felix Hadley?" Blue asked.

"He's a talker."

"Oh, well, then old Gene Smedler? He's a hell of a fist-fighter."

"Aw, he don't like dogs."

Bluefeather finally named three miners and one cowboy he had known. He gave the names and last known addresses to Pack—who had made a few bar napkin notes himself.

Bluefeather handed him a sheaf of folded hundreds and said, "Use this to gather 'em up. If you can find them."

They agreed to rendezvous at Willy's in ten days or less. With the business talk out of the way for the moment, they talked of other random things, such as Marsha. Bluefeather had told Marsha about Pack and how their friendship was cemented with blood as the binder.

Bluefeather had gone to the pay phone and had tried to call her several times. Now he wanted Marsha to meet Pack, but he couldn't get past a strange voice on the phone, explaining that Marsha was unavailable but would he please leave his name and number. Anger and disappointment moved through him at the same time, but he subdued them and continued drinking and visiting with Pack.

After Maria's delicious enchiladas, Pack discussed the three wives he'd had since the war. "How lucky we all were—no offspring had to suffer through the split-ups," he said by way of a minor explanation. "You see, Blue, I never knew how to pick out a new suit either. I was proud when people asked me how much it cost. I'm so dumb I always thought it showed my good taste." Pack sat silently a moment, staring at the almost empty liter, then continued speaking so quietly from his soft, unlined face through his thin lips that Bluefeather had to lean forward in a strain to hear: "The battles with the wives were never really worthy wars." And that would end the discussion of Pack's marital difficulties from now on.

Bluefeather was having more and more trouble with his annoyance and puzzlement at not being able to get a phone call through to Marsha. To his surprise, he had a momentary cold feeling of being deserted, but of course it couldn't be—she had risked her life in the dangerous old tunnels with him. She had backed him to the limit in the barroom fight. She had loved him with all he could have ever hoped for, physically and mentally. And most important of all, they had had much fun and laughed at many ridiculous things together. No, it was just a temporary mistake. She simply had not expected him to call so soon. Or maybe Korbell had her tending to one of the chores he had adopted her to do. This thought didn't help him at all. Korbell had chores around the world. For a fleeting moment, a little pain of loss stabbed him under the breastbone and spread into his stomach.

Then the thoughts of the subterranean expedition came again. The solid wealth and opiate power of the stacked bars of gold in Dolby's vault grew even heavier and larger before his mind-vision. In spite of his past dispersions of the metal and his vows to defeat its sorcery of seduction, he could not help but feel exhilarated.

He suddenly felt as much an imposter as all the pretend Indians beginning to infiltrate the Southwest. He had made a vow, unthinkable to break, at Miss Mary's tomb, that he would never let gold even start to possess him again. He blinked his eyes, and his mind-vision, hard. The craving for the yellow metal vanished and the one for Marsha returned. It surprised him how the two longings had been so closely allied in the spectacle of his mind-picture.

He came back to his outer self, hearing Pack talking on. He was saying, ". . . By working him over with the hammer handle I had saved him from the wrath of his returning peers." Bluefeather let that one slip on past, but when Pack added, "Somebody hung the sun up for a stop-light and then turned it green, so, it's time for everybody to get going!"

Bluefeather decided that Pack's rare conversation was as erratic and puzzling as Dancing Bear's. He decided it was also time for a nightcap. He ordered a double brandy and explained to Gilbert, so he wouldn't have to worry, that it was a nightcap, for sure.

Pack said, "Hey Gilbert, I desperately need a cyanide and root beer." For an instant, even Gilbert was thrown off, but there was enough of a grin on Pack's face to actually be visible in the dim restaurant candlelight. "But I'll take a brandy with ol' Blue, instead." While Gilbert poured the brandies, Pack continued, "Now don't let's ever forget . . ."

"Forget what, Pack?" asked Bluefeather.

"Oh . . . that all the world's clever schemers and plotters have great advantage over the few dreamers and lovers of beauty."

"Understood, sergeant. If the 'accumulators' abuse our trust, we shall send them to the far beyond."

"With pleasure—and with skill."

Maria came out of the kitchen with her tired, lovely face expressing gratitude for their business before she said it. Gilbert took the money, dawdling over it, making change slowly, as he finally said, "You guys don't wait so long to come back."

"Thanks, Gilbert, and thank you Maria, for the usual great meal."

"Likewise and double," said Pack.

As they stepped out the door, Bluefeather spoke to the night: "A single coyote's howl circles the earth forever like cobalt rays and touches everything." So for that very reason he tilted his head back slightly and howled at the Santa Fe half-moon.

Pack clapped his soft, long-fingered hands silently together twice and did a tiny, lazy, two-step that would have made Dancing Bear close his eyes in shame and groan in misery.

Since Pack had lost his apartment soon after he placed the red sock over his privates, Bluefeather got them a double room at La Posada. They slept.

When Bluefeather stumbled up the next morning, Pack was sitting up in bed trying to drink a glass of water. His hangover drooped all the way off the bed onto the carpet. He did, however, speak with considerable valor. "What we need is people of every color, type, and mixed blood for our little venture. Thoroughbreds don't much like this kind of continuous rough goin'."

Bluefeather said, through a bale of cotton in his mouth, "Agreed. Go get 'em."

They shaved, showered and had breakfast—huevos rancheros with really hot chile and tortillas—in the dining room.

"This is the only medicine that'll cure a hangover . . . and you can enjoy it at the same time," Bluefeather said. Pack agreed with wholehearted appetite as he attacked the food with a purpose. "This stuff here will cure fleas, sinus problems and evil thoughts."

They ate the rest of the fiery meal in silence, planning and preparing for, as Pack had said, "The great, big, audacious quest."

TWENTY-TWO

BLUEFEATHER HAD BEEN BACK AT WILLY'S PLACE TWO days when Charlie Waters showed up. After the hellos and an ardent kiss from Sally, he told Bluefeather he had all the maps there had ever been on Tilton's properties. The two men excused themselves and went to the bunkhouse to look them over. The whole Ruger family had asked Bluefeather about Marsha, and now Charlie was doing the same thing.

"She's got some chores to do for Korbell. She'll be here in a day or so."

He couldn't get his mind on studying the maps, even though he had something important, not quite revealed yet, on his brain relating to them. Instead, he decided to risk confiding somewhat in Charlie—not enough to scare him, but enough to grasp what his attitude was about what Dancing Bear had first named "the subterranean journey." It was enough to make Charlie's face radiate questions.

"Okay, Charlie, you're in. Sally can't go. She has to stay here with Flo and help her look after the place. Okay?"

"I understand that, and I'm damned relieved. I'd be worrying about her every minute."

Bluefeather didn't tell him how true the statement would be.

They went back to the house and he used Willy's porch phone. This time he said, "Look, Miss Whoever-you-are, I'm at Willy's place. Got it? Willy Ruger's place. Have her call me here today. You hear? Today."

"I'll convey your message, sir."

He was relieved he hadn't brought Nancy and Miss Mary. He walked out to the corral to talk to the other mules, feeling selfish, because they would all have to go. He went back to the phone and called again and again, first for adoptees Marsha, Nedra, Elena, and finally for Korbell, the adopter himself. He couldn't reach anyone but the message person.

He had to struggle with himself to stay out of his jeep. He wanted to race and ram right through Korbell's mighty iron gateway, blasting anybody who tried to stop him. Instead, he took off walking swiftly through the meadow, across Zia Creek and climbed up on the first rock ledge he reached. He leaned back, breathing more from anger and anxiety than exertion. He rubbed at the thin scar across his nose and pondered the questions. What the hell kind of mess was he in? What had happened to her? Why had she deserted him after all they had shared together?

Bluefeather was in a quandary—one he had asked for. He now had to work for Dolby for a chance to fulfill Korbell's search for the wine. It was an extremely tight place to be in. He was just now learning how deadly the competition was between the two men, and now more pressure was added by Marsha's vanishing act. Such strained loyalties.

He still felt his obligation to find the wine for Korbell, if at all possible. After all, the wine deal had saved his home in Corrales, his jeep and his phone. Ah hell, Korbell had just plain saved him in every way, financially. He had even given him his only adopted daughter as an assistant and she had become his lover. No. She was more, much more, than that. She was his love. He knew. He knew because of the dull, seemingly incurable ache he had in his center.

Had they planned it this way all the time? Bluefeather wondered if she had deceived him and had told Korbell what he had asked her not to divulge. For a moment, he hated Korbell so hard he considered ways of putting him to sleep in a marble orchard.

Were they already plotting to move on Dolby and Sherry's domain—one that Korbell, with all his shrewdness, power and will could not have even dreamed existed? Not unless, of course, Marsha had broken her vow of silence. This was unforgivable to Bluefeather's Italian genes. Deceit must not matter now, though. No matter how his heart hurt. He had made an agreement with Dolby far beyond all other deals. That one he had to keep regardless of anyone or anything else in the entire world.

His thoughts turned to the spirit world and he began looking around for Dancing Bear. He listened to the softly whistling wind for the sound of his guiding spirit's flute. Dancing Bear didn't come. He strained to see any angle, light or shadow of Marsha's face, but all was just a blur. He could not conjure up Dancing Bear, and he could not visualize Marsha. The two who were closest to him were out of his imagining reach.

He leaned back against the rock, staring into the sky at an eagle circling, making unseen tracks in the air like the ectoplasm of souls. He watched until the powerful bird glided out of sight behind the first mountain, the circles appearing smaller as the distance increased.

He walked back without speaking to the mules or the dog and entered the house. Flo and Sally were fixing supper and Charlie was drinking coffee and listening to Willy. Bluefeather got a cup and sat down on the sunken couch next to Willy, who started trying to cheer him up.

"Heritage? It's here, right here, Charlie. My old daddy said, 'We're all remnants of history. You just can't see it anymore.' Now I'm finally beginning to see it. It's just like my old daddy said, but it don't do me much good, yet. Now in just a few days we may be making history, but how in hell are we gonna know? What seems like history one minute may be a little, dying dust devil the next."

Bluefeather appreciated Willy trying to help out. "Willy, I think you're on the right track," he said. Bluefeather felt better, and remained so through most of the fine country supper. But he just couldn't make his part of the conversation move. So he got up saying, " 'Night everybody. If I get a phone call, wake me up no matter what time it is."

He heard Charlie come in from walking Sally in the woods about midnight. Then he went into a tossing, dreaming, but never-remembered sleep.

The silent sun woke him up with the first beam that changed the color of the top half of New Mexico. He was out of the bunkhouse and into the kitchen in a few steps. He had just made a pot of coffee when Sally came in, rubbing her face and pushing the hair back. They would have a chance to visit alone for a brief spell.

"Blue, I want to thank you for trusting Charlie enough to include him on our . . . your venture. He's a good person. I'm sure he'll prove to be an asset."

Bluefeather said, "I hope you understand why you and your mother can't go with us. And I know you wouldn't want to leave Flo here by herself. She just couldn't take care of everything here on the place without your help."

"Sure, I'm fine about it, don't worry. And mom is, too. Anyway, she's getting along real good with Harvey Dix, so she hadn't even thought about going with you all. He'll be out to see her regularly. Of course, she wants me to get a veterinary degree so badly she'd do most anything to help. God bless her."

"We've all got plans to get your education taken care of, Sally, but Charlie may have other ideas."

Sally's face turned a little red, and she took a quick swallow of coffee to hide it.

"Say Blue, forgive me for getting so personal, but I can't help it. Is anything wrong between you and Marsha?"

"Not that I know of. Why do you ask?"

"Well, you've been itchy ever since you got back and, well, I know she's really plumb nuts in love with you."

"How do you know anyway? Did she tell you that?"

"A woman can tell about another woman that way."

Bluefeather could not bring himself to share his anxieties about Marsha and Korbell possibly double crossing him, nor could he force himself to express his sense of loss. He had to force it down and away. There were things more important even than the love between a man and a woman. Even more than that of this man, Bluefeather, and that woman, Marsha, no matter what the depth of their dedication and instinctual feeling toward one another. What awaited at the end of the trek was more, far more, important than anything he could ever have imagined. Even with such heavyweights as Korbell, Sherry and Dolby, along with Pack, Marsha, Charlie and the Rugers—who were bright, tough and finalists—any way he looked at it, he, Bluefeather Fellini, had somehow become the catalyst and the glue. He was it. Without his total commitment the whole venture would crash and crumble into a disaster of formidable, maybe everlasting, consequences. Bluefeather had so many thoughts he could hardly keep them in his mouth.

Flo came in, followed soon by Charlie and Willy. Flo fixed a breakfast so huge it seemed wasteful for people who lived on the edge at least half the time, but it was the last they would have as a family alone for a long time.

Wordlessly, quietly pleased with her labors, Flo set the table with milk gravy, sourdough biscuits, fresh-gathered eggs, hand-cured bacon, homemade butter and jams. She refilled each coffee cup before it was empty. It was her personal gesture, and though everyone made polite complaints about getting fat, being foundered and never having to eat again, Flo relished the rapid disappearance of the last breakfast. It was her unspoken contribution to the eminent subterranean journey.

TWENTY-THREE

THE MEN AND WOMEN OF ADVENTURE ARRIVED ONE and two at a time by pickup truck mainly—a couple in cars. Pack had not wanted the route to the Ruger's to look like a military movement. He was a quarter of a mile up the road, checking the potpourri of mercenaries in. He came back and reported to Bluefeather as he would a company commander. Bluefeather was amused at their reversed roles, since he never figured he was anything but a "get-by" soldier.

They were all in camouflage clothing. They arrived with a minimum of equipment—a small bedroll, packs and a few personal supplies. No surplus. The encampment hid their personal vehicles in, and behind, the barn. Those left out in the open were covered with camouflage nets. The trucks would arrive the following morning. The ex-sergeant of infantry had delivered expertly as expected.

Bluefeather had never considered anything else from Pack but a premium performance. He made his last possible phone call to Marsha from the Ruger's place. His mind must now be on the men, women and equipment. Bluefeather explained to Pack that he would rather not be introduced to the group until they were at Dolby's, where the chain of command would be explained explicitly. Pack understood.

No one slept much that night. Bluefeather stayed at the house with his friends. Pack was with the "chosen ones" beside a campfire near the forest. There were sounds of quiet laughter, a song or two and then the silence of the individual dreams and thoughts intermingled with the talk of night birds and coyotes.

Just after daybreak the two trucks arrived. One canvas-covered truck would haul only people, and the other would carry Willy's mules. The elderly drivers from Dolby's headquarters caused a slight side casting of eyes from the younger, uninitiated troops, but there were no comments. They had all been regimented in various battles and high-risk endeavors before.

Bluefeather waited, watching carefully, until all was loaded. All the other friends and family close to Flo and Sally had told them good-bye.

Then Bluefeather went to Flo and Sally and hugged them. He said, "Flo, you and Sally being here taking care of things is going to be as important to us as anything anyone could do. Maybe more so. I'll look after your loved ones the best I know how," Bluefeather assured them.

"I know that, Blue. Don't worry about us, darlin'. I know bein' conceived or born or simply climbin' a tree is all part of the risk of this life."

He could feel her heart beating hard against their two chests as he said, "See you 'round the corner, Flo. Love you."

"Love you too."

He hugged Sally and said, "Take care of your mama, you hear? Love you both."

He turned and walked to the waiting truck loaded with men and women ready to gamble their lives. He crawled in the front with the driver. Unlike the war, when he could not make himself cry, his eyes were blurred as he glanced back from the large rearview mirror on the truck and saw Flo and Sally waving good-bye until they were out of sight. The trucks ground away until the forest and bluffs absorbed all their sounds.

TWENTY-FOUR

PACK WAS TRAINING HIS TROOPS IN HAND SIGNALS.
Willy and Dolby's old mule keeper were readying the animals and the packs. Bluefeather was in the great room
below and beyond the house in conference with Dolby
and Sherry.

Sherry pointed a stick at a map, saying, "Okay. Now,
Blue, here we have way stations for going and coming
pack trains to pass. Each station has protective shelter
with water and food for several days." She indicated the
stations in blue. "The three main points, or posts, are in
red. Here is a scale map for you and one for Sergeant
Pack. They are absolutely water- and fireproof."

Dolby sat up as straight as a broom handle. He crooked
his eyes sideways under eyebrows that were thick and long
enough to have been fertilized and irrigated. He said,
"And the Lady Marsha? She is to arrive today?"

"Today or tomorrow," Blue answered, hiding his concern.

"And if she doesn't?"

"I think it will mean that she has been forcefully de-
tained or . . . that she has joined against us."

Dolby said, "Correct. I'm pleased that you have an
open mind."

"In case Marsha has divulged any information to Korbell . . . I suppose . . ."

Dolby interrupted and finished the sentence, "It will present an attainable difficulty—a contingency we have prepared for."

"On the other hand, Mr. Dolby, when Marsha arrives, as I believe she will, we should be secure. You have sufficient armed resources above ground to protect your interests below, and besides, Korbell surely wouldn't risk jeopardizing the life of his only daughter."

"All settled then, Mr. Blue. Let's just hope she shows."

"Yes," said Sherry. "I predict she will."

Bluefeather could feel the large, slanted, African eyes boring into him, studying him for he knew not what. He wondered how this woman, Sherry, could be so certain Marsha would show up. There were less than thirty-six hours left until they moved underground. He felt like a traitor to himself, but he believed that Korbell and the huge, scar-faced Fontaine and his force would be waiting for them when they returned from below. If, of course . . . well, he must not think like that.

From where he stood, Bluefeather could see, through a crack in a doorway, several smocked old men working in the large laboratory that had been empty of people when he had been down here before.

Sherry observed Bluefeather looking and explained, "That is where we process the minerals—some from the star material—break them down with chemicals and separate the different structures with heat. There is another huge, blind vault under the northwest corner floor. It is almost full of the precious and invaluable products. That is just one more critical reason we have to move now."

Dolby joined in, "We are starving our souls with an abundance of riches, Mr. Blue. You do totally understand the criticality of the urgency to proceed so that a final decision can be made?"

"Mr. Dolby, I don't know what to add to the knowledge you have just shared with me, but I've already committed my life to you and your truly majestic dream."

"So you have, my boy. So you have," Dolby said. "Well now, Sherry, will you proceed ahead of us to see that a proper last supper is served? Also see that Mr. Pack is invited. I need a few more moments of discussion with our commander."

Bluefeather wondered at this phraseology relating to the military. Why not "our boss" or "our leader" or "our control?" Why "our commander?"

Sherry was gone by the time he closed this thought and turned to face Dolby—a now standing old, old man. His look was far away again, just as it had been before they became associates. Dolby spoke in a monotone as he slowly opened the door to the vault.

He said, "You could live in a tomb the entirety of your life, Mr. Blue, covered with the strongest sun block lotion. You could be buried on a moonless night and the sun would still make grass grow over your grave. You could be sealed a thousand feet inside an arctic glacier, and only a few million years afterward the sun would finally melt it and you would wash into the open to be touched by its life-giving beams. Whole civilizations exist in a grain of sand washed by the great blazing orb."

The massive door on the vault moved slowly, ever so slowly, open. The monologue continued, "You must remember that the force of the sun has been everywhere in one aeon or another. Everywhere—with no exceptions where things breathe, until . . . until, well, until now."

The door was open and again Bluefeather stared at the little Fort Knox of mined, extracted, melted, rectangularly formed cords of gold. Their dull yellow edges did indeed reflect the artificial lights as if they were suns. He stared at scores of millions and millions of dollars' worth of re-flected, yellow suns, hand-formed in the laboratory.

"You must remember," Dolby continued, "no matter the difficulty, that the treasure you gaze upon is nothing, absolutely nothing, compared to the other rewards of your task."

Bluefeather could not answer all of this. He did not understand it anyway. Oh, he understood how his heart served notice of his mind's greed at the sight, how it was difficult to keep Dolby from seeing his chest rise as his lungs expanded, searching for more air.

Then he did manage to speak: "I have already conquered that urge, Mr. Dolby. Long ago."

He knew it was a lie. Dolby knew it was a lie. He was still in battle against the yellow-yearning, and at this moment the golden swords of color were piercing his resolve, his word, his faith and his promises to Miss Mary near Harmony Creek long years before.

The aged servants served the meal in movements so smooth they were hardly visible or noticeable. The talk was of the business ahead and below, but it now had an almost celebratory tone.

Dolby, the only one drinking anything alcoholic, sipped at a glass of ruby red wine as delicately as he did his bourbon, saying, "Of course, Mr. Blue, if your research fulfills our promise, our dreams, then the fun, and then the worldwide entertainment, I might add, will begin."

"I admit the difficulty of keeping our minds locked in the present," Bluefeather agreed.

Sherry said, "I always favor beginnings as much as finishing. I suppose it is simply the anticipation."

Pack listened to her so carefully one would have thought she had written the Bible. Bluefeather was startled at the obvious and instant fascination Pack had shown with Sherry. He had hardly glanced at anyone else, and it was very doubtful if he tasted the tender veal and steamed vegetables at all. He had as much as admitted to

Bluefeather that his other marriages had been more or less an attempt to fill up a space of boredom. But now, right here, Pack the warrior had finally fallen. Bluefeather felt that "stricken" would be the proper word to describe Pack's emotions.

"My God," he thought, "we are involved in one of the few great escapades left for humankind and my sergeant has a stabbing case of quixotic love."

It caused his temples to throb in tune with the motors and other vibrations of the Dolby compound. As they had dinner, huge dynamos and engines pumped electric power and water far below the surface. Old men and a few old women were dining. Others tended the machinery of power, and some, with their failing eyes, were at guard posts, protectively studying the surrounding terrain, their hands near warning buttons and automatic weapons.

The gracious, patient mules ate high-grade hay and oats, awaiting their return to the strange winding up and down trails below. They could be counted on as solidly as a cathedral cross made of mahogany. The dogs circled and listened in their enclosures. Phones and radios were constantly checked and spoken over, maintaining constant contact between the nether and outer worlds. Yes, a decrepit but proficient and powerful force did actually create a tiny, but steady, oscillation of the floors and walls of the building and the surrounding earth. Bluefeather could feel it in his feet as it moved up his body, right on out his fingertips.

The meal was done.

Dolby said, "If all you see is black and white and grey, then those are your colors." His eyes now looked backward into his head.

The three of them were on their way to fulfill his awesome visions. Not one of them existed for any other reason now—if at all.

TWENTY-FIVE

THE MULES WERE PACKED. BATTERIES AND BIG HAND lights were issued to all. Two flamethrowers, the automatic rifles, the handguns, and a razor-sharp machete for each had been issued. After several conferences with Sherry, which Pack had conveniently arranged, it was decided that hand grenades would be taken, but not issued, as yet.

Now the troops, so to speak, were lined up in a casual manner like guerilla soldiers. Sherry and Bluefeather stood a few yards out in front of the line as Pack faced down it and spoke.

"Men, women, these are your leaders," Pack said. "In case of the need for action of any kind, to protect our endeavors, I report to Commander Fellini. You report to me. Miss Sherry's position is one of total adviser to Commander Fellini. Understood?"

"Yes sir!" they all shouted.

Pack moved down the erratic line. "This is Moosha. He's from Africa. I fought with him in a small revolution there." The ebony African stood rigid and implacable. His powerful body radiated an energy of force.

Pack continued, "This is Hector Garcia of Las Cruces,

New Mexico. He worked with your commander, Mr. Fellini, in a minor smuggling operation."

Hector grinned at the words, his short wire-like body anxious to move out.

"This is George Tack Won," Pack said. "He is a professional ambusher of political plunder from Indonesia. We're friends. This is Jimmy D. Ratchett, a former pro football player who went wrong in the sports booking business. Now he's in the cooking business. He'll be our chef. If you don't like the food, don't you dare tell him."

They all looked at the two hundred and fifty pounder and had a little laugh.

There were six more of Pack's friends: Kowalski, Kubeck, O'Malley, Davis, Dunning and Osaka.

"All friends of mine," Pack smiled as he said it.

Bluefeather whispered to Sherry without turning his head, "It seems like the crazy bastard has the United Nations as an ally, but rest assured, that is an illusion. He has simply chosen the best, that's all."

She smiled with her wondrous, raven-colored eyes only.

Then Pack introduced the last three swiftly: "Jody, Estrella and Charlene. These ladies are professional entertainers from Las Vegas, Nevada. Early in their careers they worked the streets enough to become proficient in the use of knives and guns. Besides their expertise in protection, they will be available for entertainment appointments at proper times, and through me."

Bluefeather spoke softly to Sherry again, "Our warrior, army organizer and special employee is now a blasted pimp."

He was surprised when Sherry said, "Great foresight. Napoleon was aware of and made use of these needs."

For just this one moment, he felt more Italian than he ever had in his life. Here was "his" family standing around him, ready to die if he asked them to. He felt a surge of power that the Florentine Medicis must have sensed as

they developed their papal and art connections in the
Florentine Renaissance. He felt as tall as Giotto's tower
in the heart of Florence. He was Romulus, the mythical
and efficient ruler of ancient Rome. He was as dauntless
as Garibaldi, who had twice come back from exile to free
his country in the nineteenth century. He was a poet of
the scope of Dante and a painter and sculptor equal to
Michelangelo. He could still the explosions of Mount Ve-
suvius. He could outsail Columbus and sing along with
the great Caruso. Then, just as suddenly, he was plain
Bluefeather. His history was here among these men and
women of all bloods and soils.

Pack brought him all the way back to the eminent instant, saying, "Now our commander has a few words to
say. Hear him well."

Bluefeather said, "Men, women, associates, we are em-
barking on an adventure that could change the thinking
of the world's inhabitants. A remote chance, I admit, but
possible. We are the chosen. You have already made a
blood oath to Pack. Let me say, now, that it is too late to
pull out. We're all in it to a finality of either riches and
glory for all, or we die in the effort. Are there any questions?"

There was a wild shout of excitement from the entire
group.

"Well," Bluefeather continued, "then we'll now . . ."

The increasing "clack clack" of a helicopter stopped his
words and thoughts. It came in high above the bluffs to
the north. Instinctively, Pack's section spread out and
aimed guns, awaiting orders.

Bluefeather shouted, "Hold fire."

Pack repeated it.

Sherry turned and hand signalled the guard towers to
do the same. A figure plummeted from the machine's side
and then the little parachute jerked the large one open.
It drifted toward them and would have made a precise

landing, but a gust of wind caused a slight stagger, just enough to roll the figure. The face under a cream-colored felt hat, of a Riviera style, tied down with a cord, rose to look up into the barrels of many guns. The figure scrambled to its feet while others gathered up the parachute. The blue, seven-seas eyes stared straight at Bluefeather.

The fashion model face uttered serious words, "Reporting for any duty, sir." Then it broke into various grins ranging from exultant to pitiful. It was Marsha, the only adopted daughter of Korbell the Mighty, and once, a short time back, the lover of confused Commander Bluefeather Fellini. She had her own private .45 automatic side arm, a sheathed dagger, a pack that contained a deflated bedroll, personal necessities and a World War II carbine with extra ammunition.

The entire section now numbered eighteen eager and capable bodies. They moved to the mule entrance, where Willy would join Dolby's associates on the twelve-animal pack train.

Marsha walked expressionless now, behind Bluefeather. Sherry's face had an "I told you so" smile. Bluefeather's mouth was dry. He swallowed over and over what seemed like chips of sandpaper, but he would truly expire before he would let anyone know of both his torment and relief.

The great gate—disguised as a cedar-covered rock wall—swung open. The entire section, the mules and the youngest of Dolby's animal tenders (who was probably sixty-five) entered the gateway to the earthen deep. The electricity sealed the gate behind them so solidly and faultlessly that the avaricious eyes of a tax collector or the hungry ones of a young eagle would never have known it existed. They had disappeared from the sustaining world of the sun.

TWENTY-SIX

THE CAVE ENTRANCE WAS CEMENTED FOR ABOUT A hundred yards. Soft electric lights protruded from sunken sockets. The mules' hooves made echoes bounce from the walls. Everyone felt more natural when the concrete ended and they entered rooms that widened and narrowed for about a quarter of a mile. In places, they needed a couple of hand lights to guide them.

Just as they were getting excited about what might confront them around each turn of the human-constructed trail, they hit a large irregular opening with diffused sunlight shining through cracks in the earth above.

Sherry reached into another indentation and pushed a button. A large beam of light emanated about the cave room and revealed a clean, emerald pond perhaps forty yards across. The intake of breath was audible from all. It was a huge liquid jewel. Back from it was a way station with camping facilities, corrals for the mules, electric plugs for additional light, water faucets and stainless metal sinks, hidden chemical toilets and wooden tables and chairs to seat at least twenty-five people.

It was a pleasant shock to all when Sherry's message was passed on from Bluefeather to Pack that all could go for a swim in the pool and enjoy a stopover of many hours.

The packs were unloaded, the animals cared for. Hector Garcia stripped off all his clothes and dived into the precious pool. Soon everyone followed. The naked, variously hued skins of the men and women of The Section flashed under and around the lighted liquid like porpoises shouting and splashing water on one another with the abandonment of children.

They had not broken even a mild sweat, as yet, and here they were in paradise. What was all this talk of life-risking situations, anyway?

Sherry slung a small leather pouch over her shoulder and led Bluefeather, Marsha and Pack on a private excursion. Hector Garcia, now Bluefeather's corporal, would be in charge during their absence. Willy stayed behind with the old man, Gordon, and his mule packers, taking care of the animals.

After an undetermined, but certainly not great, distance they turned off to the right into a side cave. There Sherry switched on another series of lights. Before she had a chance to point them out, Bluefeather's half-Indian eyes had seen the petroglyphs chipped into the cavern walls. There were pictures of deer, mountain goats, dancers, hunters, medicine men and women and other designs he did not recognize.

"These images were made by the lost Mimbres tribe. As you probably know, their pueblos were scattered over wide ranges of southwestern New Mexico and southeastern Arizona. Hundreds of pueblo locations still exist and not one piece of viable evidence is available as to what might have caused their disappearance many hundreds of years ago. There are, of course, the usual drought-famine-war-evacuation theories, but until now, the late fifties, none have been validated."

Sherry noticed her companions' special curiosity at one carving of a rabbit—a circle with twenty-three points seemed to be dropping off a hind foot—so she tried to explain it in laymen's language. "To the Mimbres, the rabbit is the man in the moon. In other words, it is a space creature. In approximately eleven hundred A.D., a royal Chinese astrologer recorded that he observed a star exploding that formed the crab nebula, millions of light-years from our earth. The constellation, as you know it, is called Taurus. The Chinese said that the supernova was visible for twenty-three days. That circle falling from the rabbit's foot has twenty-three rays. Count them."

They did and there were certainly twenty-three.

Sherry continued, "I've found a book with the same drawing that dates to about eleven hundred A.D. What I'm saying is, the Mimbres Indians saw, and recorded, the forming of the supernova. So we must not sell the observational abilities and intelligence of any creature short. Ever. Especially those we shall soon be meeting."

They studied all the carved drawings, entranced. Sherry continued, "I know how intriguing they are, but I'm impatient to show you . . . well, come on. Follow me."

They did, and after awhile they came to a rocked-in wall of sandstone rocks fitted together with perfection, except where one side had collapsed or been knocked out. The debris had long ago been stacked neatly to the side by Dolby's people. They all tiptoed unnecessarily through the opening. Then it became so dark they all had to use their hand lights.

Sherry stopped. She asked them all to turn off their lights when they reached her side and to link hands. She moved ahead, leading them along the left wall. In the dark, measurable distance vanishes, and any measurement of time is distorted beyond human comprehension. Their muffled footsteps and breathing were hardly heard.

Then Sherry stopped. "Wait just a moment, please. Ah, here. Now ease forward beside me. There. No, up a step. Here, let me place you. Now." She flipped a switch.

The light shocked the pupils of their eyes and revealed

a large, auditorium-sized room filled with people—dried, mummified, Indian people. They sat around in seven separate circles as if having a hunting or root gathering pow-wow. Bluefeather momentarily expected heads to turn toward them, but then realized that the entrance was cut off with layers of heavy glass. The window was several sheets wide, and in front were chairs with sealed binoculars embedded at different eye levels and angles. There was one sliding partition for cameras.

"The last of the Mimbres tribes," Sherry said. Then she opened a large cabinet door and pulled out, for each, a small oxygen bottle attached to a breathing mask. She helped them put them on. She said, "Come," as she opened the heavily glassed door with a large key that she pulled from her leather pouch. "No one is allowed in except on special occasions, and then only with masks. Our breath, you know? It corrodes ancient things." Then she led them through three airtight doors, assuring that no human breath or outer air could follow them into the room of historical wonders.

Bluefeather was honored beyond expression. Walking carefully, fearfully, behind Sherry, they entered the first circle of the dead, looking themselves like space beings. The air had been so dry there that the animal skin breeches still hung on the bodies, and placed by each one was painted pottery, shell, turquoise and bone jewelry. Hide drums were still intact. Bows, arrows, tomahawks, spears were laid out alongside others.

At first Bluefeather almost fainted from the fear that he might be desecrating this ancient spot of his possible ancient kin. But soon the enthralment of discovery eased his concern. He shone his light around the circle into the dried, hollowed eyes, and the lights and shadows made the Mimbres heads seem to see at one moment, move their head slightly at another and eternally grin through the dried lips stretched back, revealing ground-down, short and often missing teeth.

Sherry seemed to be tuned to their minds as she said, "They're all *viejas*—the old ones. After years of study I now believe that these were the ones who were too old to migrate and were brought here near the pool, which had to be a sacred place, for them to die in dignity. I'm certain, for now, in my mind at least, that all the others migrated south. I'll get to that evidence later."

Their voices were muffled by the masks, but the more they conversed, the better their hearing adjusted.

Marsha asked, "Is it possible that the Mayans contributed to their disappearance?"

Sherry answered the best she could. "Yes. It is entirely possible that the Mayans deceived and destroyed them, but considering the evidence in this room, I'd rather think they were enticed south and assimilated into the cultures of other tribes."

There were great clay jars called *ollas* scattered about, corn grinders and water jars—some with clay handles, others with rawhide. The quality of preservation was the most dramatic any of them had ever seen.

Bluefeather looked into the jars, saying, "Well, Sherry, the corn seed in these *ollas* is very small and drought stricken. They probably had to move somewhere. Huh?"

"We only know one thing for sure . . . they vanished forever from their home area."

Bluefeather felt a hand touch and hold his arm. It was Marsha. He stepped away so that her arm dropped back to her side. He felt guilty at his continued reticence at Marsha's possible deceit. She was here, but he still couldn't help his feelings. However, the wonders of the Mimbres remained.

They visited each circle and Bluefeather made silent chants and prayers in each. It was impossible not to visualize crackling ceremonial fires, dances, songs. Timeless time.

Sherry pointed up with her hand light, enhancing the beams of the floodlight, at the walls for over a hundred yards where there were richly colored paintings mixed in with the line carvings. All the Mimbres pots and jars were in black and white, making the colored ones stand out. This pointed to the presence of other tribes. Some of the designs were definitely Mayan.

One painting was, as Sherry explained, of a Mayan pot, and on the floor just below the painting sat its model. There was sequence writing and an alphabet in use as well here. On one pot was a figure of a howler monkey that could only come from knowledge of the jungles far to the south. This vision, in part, explained to Bluefeather why, as far north as his own Taos Pueblo, the shamans still sought and used parrot feathers in their ceremonies. There were no indigenous parrots in the land of the Mimbres or the Taos. They had come in the form of trade from the jungles far to the south.

Then they spent several hours studying primitive, but somehow explicit, cave wall carvings of what Sherry believed was, at least in goodly portion, the last history of the Mimbres. It was obvious, too—because of the Mayan symbols intermingled with the Mimbres'—that they had made the long perilous journey back and forth from the Mexican jungles to the New Mexico high desert, trading in apparent friendship. There was one outstanding painting in reds, umbers and blacks of the Mimbres sharing a deer kill with a figure from a different tribe. Sherry believed he could only be a Mayan. The richness of the colors gathered from oxidized iron and copper and many natural plants was dazzling. Even though here and there a chip had fallen, the record was brilliantly intact and just as important to the ancient Mimbres and Mayans as the Dead Sea Scrolls were to the Jews. When they had sealed the dry, ceremonial cave of darkness with rocks, no doubt the ancient laborers felt they had left their old ones, plus their painted records and all their belongings for use in another world, safe for their gods.

Bluefeather felt that Sherry and Dolby had done a priceless job in protecting the valuable find. Now, as Sherry pointed out the positions of the old women next to their men, it was apparent that the women had outlived the men, even back then. Some of the male figures were accompanied by one to three elderly females.

When everyone's awe finally subsided to simple elation, they dared ask Sherry questions.

Marsha led it off: "How did they die sitting up like this? They look as if they'd just walked in and squatted down for a ceremony."

"It took us three years in the lab to test the relaxant of peyote and the poison of the loco weed that killed them. The combination was probably painless and they died with visions before their eyes and in their minds, but the cause of their lifelike attitudes has escaped us. I sometimes feel that was done spiritually, though I have no idea how, as yet. Someday I intend to discover the answer."

Pack could hardly speak for his perpetual examination of Sherry's classic African beauty, but he forced out, "Maybe they just went to sleep along with their visions. What do you think, Miss . . . Miss . . . ?"

"Please call me Sherry from now on, Pack."

"Yeah. Yeah. Sure. What do you think, Sherry?"

"It sounds as reasonable as anything I've come up with."

Pack grinned, pleased at this faint praise.

Bluefeather knew now that Sherry could already have become world famous and the winner of many anthropological awards and generous grants for her voluminous notes and theories about this discovery. He could not imagine the courage, the patience, it had taken to go on studying all these long years while subduing the terrible desire to share her massive historical find with her colleagues. A hell of a woman here. Pack might be foolish, but he was correct in his admiration of Sherry. Deserved. All of it.

Bluefeather did not ask her a question, but his statement was directed to her. "I'm beginning to feel at home down here. Right now I don't know the living from the dead."

Hours had passed in seconds here. Finally, with reluctance, Sherry led them out of the sanitariums. They all turned, still staring back, seeing their own private, different visions. Bluefeather heard a chant old as wind and an accompanying flute playing somewhere inside the gathering of the ancients.

Sherry turned off the floodlight, and in that moment before the first hand light was thumbed on, all of the figures inside the sanctified room and those by the triple glass shared a second of eternity.

TWENTY-SEVEN

THEY LEFT THE PEACE OF WAY STATION ONE, THE EM-
erald pool and the haunting rock hall of mummies and
headed along the trail down, ever down. Sometimes the
path was wide and safe through tunnels; at other times it
narrowed and even the mules hugged near the wall as
they moved. Now, Bluefeather's concern increased at how
his command could handle what they would soon witness.
He wondered if even he could take the massive change
in thinking, feeling, the acceptance that would be required. They were all, every one, proven in battles of
some kind or other, but what they were about to see
would be mind-altering if they were not stronger, by far,
than they had ever been before or would ever have to be
again. Well, for now there were acceptable wonders to
enjoy. Later?

Stalactites hung from the roofs of the large rooms,
formed there over hundreds of thousands of years from
moisture dripping through the massive deposit of limestone. The stalagmites growing up from the cavern's floors
were just as impressive. When the two joined together
they formed columns. They were of every shape and color
according to the mineral content of a particular portion
of the host limestone.

Bluefeather marveled, as they all did. Occasionally, Sherry would switch on one of the recessed buttons and floodlight a particular majestic formation for them. There were mineral curtains ten stories high, flowing down in places as if once a mighty wind had penetrated even the billions of tons of stone and frozen them forever in a graceful flow. In places pagodas towered above the group so high in rippled patterns like melted matter that the entire pack train appeared minute. Specks. Sometimes there would be dry spaces, but mostly, now, one could hear the infinite drip of water eternally changing the underworld to ever more beautiful and uncountable designs.

They came upon a dripping spring of fresh water that ran into a side cave. Since there was a way station nearby where they could pen the mules, Sherry led The Section into the dark dampness. Their hand lights revealed creatures slick, hairless and blind from living in the total blackness so long. There were sightless salamanders and crayfish smelling out a rare blind beetle that survived on fungi.

In several pools there were white fish about three inches long. Sherry had to shine the light close to point out the tiny suggestion of eyes still remaining since their evolution. There were translucent cave worms and a pure white beetle-like creature with long, ever-moving tentacles of delicate feeling, hunting its prey with the same deadly efficiency as a jungle leopard but with different senses. There were little white frogs, not much bigger than a thumbnail. It was difficult to discern that some of their backs were clutched by young ones no larger than a match head. It was a cave of the blind and the white.

Sherry asked everyone to switch off their lights and then imagine the miracle of how these creatures had adapted to the total darkness. The silence, except for their shallow breathing and the "drip, drip, drip," only empha-

sized the wonder of things moving, killing, eating, defe-
cating and mating in an inky world all their own.

Sherry said, "Even now the whole of the cave and the
pools are crawling with life." She waited a couple of beats
and then switched on her light and revealed three pearly
fish swimming slowly about. One darted forward and swallowed a tiny transparent shrimp. They were all humbled
at Sherry's demonstration.

By the end of the next day, they had reached Way Station Six. The Section, and even the mules, were tired
enough to crave a rest, but Sherry took Pack, Marsha and
Bluefeather into another cave.

The creatures here were three, maybe four, times
larger. It was disturbing, and Pack had to know, "What
could possibly cause this change in size in such a short
distance?"

"Well, we're in farther than it seems. But this growth is
unique in the recorded world of caves. The mineral content
of the limestone, and consequently the water, is very high,
and the deposits get richer the deeper we go. Maybe—
maybe, I repeat—that could be part of the answer."

One white beetle, its tentacles wiggling out ahead—
ceaselessly moving, searching for prey or predator—
seemed to be transfiguring into a different creature than
those above.

Everyone crouched down to study it when Marsha
grabbed Bluefeather's arm again, leaning forward excitedly,
"Look. Look. It's transparent. My God, you can see the
heart beating, actually pumping blood through its veins."

It was a difficult to believe their eyes, but nonetheless,
there it was right before them: a critter that defied all
traditional thinking. Bluefeather did not move his arm until Marsha removed her hand.

When they got back to the way station, Ratchett had

started preparing powdered eggs, fruit and biscuits. It was a good meal and he was pleased to please.

They all rested now except Sherry and Bluefeather, who walked down the trail a ways to a dry shelf and sat with one hand light for illumination.

"Blue, it would be prudent if you advised Pack to alert The Section from here on. There are a couple of points of extreme danger between the next two way stations. Sometimes they are totally without mishap, and on other occasions, permanent harm has been done." She explained about the wind and the flying beasts. "The wind we call simply 'The Unholy' and we have no control over the flying beasts except our preparedness."

Bluefeather hesitated, then blurted out, "Unfortunately, Pack has fallen so in love with you, he's not his usual deadly, efficient self."

"Yes, I noticed. However, when you alert him to the upcoming hazards, I'm sure another form of adrenaline will take over his mind and body."

Bluefeather couldn't think of an apt reply to such a perceptive statement.

They went back to the camp and crawled into their bedrolls. Sherry left on one partially hidden light that shone so softly it could not disturb sleep. Bluefeather's eyes soon adjusted to it and, just before pulling his head all the way into the bedroll, he saw the face peeking out of the cloth cocoon next to him less than a yard away. It was Marsha staring at him with eyes deep and dark blue as the deep Atlantic, but even in this cavern far below the earth, the slight artificial light created rings like the ripples on a pool in her orbs. She did not blink, nor did Bluefeather, until they closed their eyes for the night. Both could see things under their clamped lids. Things they hurt and craved for but couldn't bring themselves to reveal openly.

They arose at Sherry's waking call. For now, only she

could guess at the hours to move and the hours to sleep. A different rest cycle existed here. A definite one would have to be settled on later, deeper.

Gordon rode out ahead of the mules, following the leaders, Bluefeather, Marsha and Hector Garcia.

Pack walked in the middle of the hoofed and booted train to better control both ends. Moosha brought up the rear with the rest of The Section scattered from front to back. The mules' tie-ropes had been undone and every animal had a personal trooper leading it. It was the best formation Pack could figure out for the movement of the operation, having never faced such threats before. It was difficult for any of them, except Sherry, to believe there was any danger.

She had temporarily switched on enough lights to reveal the enormous circling rhythms of the caves. There were circles in circles in archways—blue-whites, creams, orange, brown flowstone like shiny marble rivers. Some had grown so large they cut off certain cave entrances.

Pack realized this surfeit of dazzling beauty could be, and was becoming, dangerously hypnotic. One could look on and on until the eyes were dead and never see the end of originally shaped formations and unlimited subtleties of color. He walked up and down the line from Bluefeather to Moosha, keeping everyone alert, and a good thing too.

Sherry was tuned to the noise first, since she had heard it so many times in the past. But before she could comment, Bluefeather noticed the low growl like a tiger on the other side of a hill. It slowly grew louder until all could hear and begin to feel a slight suction pulling their clothing.

The mules' ears and nostrils were working and their hooves clicked against the floor quicker and more erratically. They pulled now and then nervously at their halter ropes and their eyes rolled around, showing more of the white.

The roar came now in almost solid sound at times with a deep bass underlying tone, pierced occasionally by stabbing needle sounds that screamed in a high tenor through the deepening roar. The mules, flicking their large ears with twitching pain, were skittish and wanted to break and run from the unknown forces pulling at them.

The lead mule tender, Gordon, had dismounted now and was holding the animal's reins up close to the bit and walking on the left side, which was on the down side of the wind. It was more dangerous for the humans on this side, for the mules could bolt and shove them off into the numerous stone crevasses filled with up-jutting spear points of stalagmites. However, to control the animals from the windward side would be futile. No one can hold a mule if it decides to break free. The presence of comforting, warm flesh pushing against them was absolutely requisite here.

Now they were nearing the great tunnels to each side that wound throughout to some lost and hidden openings far apart, forming an enormous tilted chimney with mighty powers of suction. It was, in fact, the world's largest, longest flue.

Gordon fell and his mule whirled, slipping, stepping over him, somehow without treading on him. His shirt had ripped as he had fallen, and it was sucked downwind into blackness so swiftly it could have been shot from a cannon. The dark brown animal was loose, stumbling, trying to flee ahead, almost falling off into the dark emptiness with nothing but flesh-smashing and spearing stone at the bottom.

Marsha tried to lift Gordon, but the wind pulled her over and away from him. She started to slide toward the crevice. She dug in with her fingertips, seeking an indentation to halt her slide to doom.

Bluefeather reached with one hand and grasped Marsha's wrist. He gripped Gordon's belt and dragged both of them to a pagoda column, which split the wind. He yelled for them to stay put. Then he forced his way into the opening again, leaning into the moaning blast and taking short steps sideways. As each person and each mule came to him, he grabbed and shoved them along the path until they were in the area of the columns.

The wind screamed around these uneven stone posts with a sound of horrendous agony, but the people and the mules could now keep their feet, even while sliding and taking halted steps in the air at times. Eternity is eternity. One can live only a single eternity technically, but all members of Bluefeather's section had lived them before, and again this day. This hour. This moment.

Pack had held the middle of the train on course by pure human will and that strange resource of strength that came to his lax muscles in time of action.

At last, Moosha was ushered on past as Bluefeather struggled in the invisible fury to Marsha and the shirtless old man, Gordon, looking as weak as a straw blown from the top of a weathered haystack.

Then there was the time of the blur, like a full-blown barroom brawl. They came out of the haze safely. Now they struggled forward with eagerness, for each few yards they could feel the force of the The Unholy subside as well as its nerve-ripping devilish voice.

The path widened and slopes became gentler again. The flailing fingers of The Unholy reached out for them futilely now and it seemed to be crying with sad regret.

All were safe but O'Malley's mule. It had gone over, trying to claw at the steepening roll of stones with all four hooves. Helpless. Gone.

As everyone checked their person, the remaining mules, the packs and each other, an air of survived togetherness caused them to shake hands and strongly embrace in relief.

Sherry consoled them with, "Anyway, when it doesn't kill, it serves to cleanse the dull, musty air from the entire cavern. Although frightfully dangerous, it is a necessary safety vent." She explained further to all, how weather conditions on the surface of each opening in the outer world evidently made the force of the air either a spring-like breeze or a hurricane-force wind. She said, "Someday we'll probably understand the unpredictable winds completely, but for now, we must move on."

They did, stepping alive and lively, on to the comfort of Way Station Seven. Suddenly, the full realization that they were safe became apparent and no one wanted to do more than drink a lot of water and rest. In the morning the soreness and stiffness would reveal at each step that The Unholy had actually tried to blow their flesh free from their bones and their minds out of their skulls. They felt lucky. They were.

TWENTY-EIGHT

They were awakened from exhausted slumber by anxious shouting and the "clop clop" of hooves of an upward-bound mule train, or what was left of it.

The leader, Verner, wore the same bluish black soft cloth uniform as all the other Olders. He would talk only to Sherry. He told her that they had been attacked by the screechers at the worst possible place along the ledge above Needle Canyon.

They had broken about even in the battle. Verner, himself, had finally fired enough lead from his .45 automatic tommy gun to down one screecher into the canyon and had wounded two others. They had lost a loaded mule, a handler and had three more packers wounded.

Pack, always in the forefront to tend the injured, along with Hector Garcia, who had been a combat medic with the 36th Infantry Division in Italy, immediately examined the wounds and treated them with efficient care. They were painful injuries, but the two Olders would survive. One had his left shoulder muscle ripped through as if a madman had swung a razor-sharp hay hook through it. The other was luckier. He was raked from his waist all the way up the back. Two ribs were revealed slightly, but no crucial tendons or muscles had been severed—painful, but survivable. Way Station Seven was as busy as any combat command post for awhile. Even in the excitement of the unexpected arrival of the damaged mule train, the muscles of The Section felt as if they had been mashed by a ten-ton vice. The power of The Unholy would be felt for days, but now others had to be cared for. They, too, might soon have to face the screechers.

Three of the mules with flesh rakes were doctored by Willy and Gordon, the latter so infirm that he was mostly in the way. It was decided to take the walking wounded on back down with them, where there was an infirmary. Finally, everything was attended; man and beast and the battered mule train would proceed on up with the precious concentrations of ore. The upward-bound would, of course, wait until The Unholy was in a period of relative quiet, no matter how long it took.

Sherry called a meeting of the leaders into the phone and radio room of the way station compound. Sherry, Bluefeather, Pack, Hector, Moosha and old Verner met over coffee uselessly prepared the night before and now reheated.

"First, I'd like to relay Commander Fellini's compliments on your individual bravery and self-control at The Unholy, Sherry said. "It was a particularly hard blow, but usually our losses are much greater when we've been trapped this way."

"Luck," said Pack. "Pure luck."

"Nevertheless, my congratulations, as well," Sherry said, shooting a swift glance at Pack.

Bluefeather had noticed that in contrast to Pack's constant gaze upon the entire physical being of Sherry, she never looked directly at him.

Sherry continued, "Before I proceed fully, I must explain once again that my opinions, although backed up with several degrees and considerable experience, are expressed in layman's terms. I shall always use layman's terms with you. Only inferred guesses are possible. It's the best any of us can do when we're working in the frame of scores of millions of years."

"The screechers, as you might have gathered by now, appear to be half bird and half mammal. They do fly, but they also leap along the earth in great bounds. I do not know if they have moved up from the floor of this cavern—an area of the most fertile grounds and waters imaginable, as you will eventually see—or whether their genes are driving them upward in a belated return to the outer world. I don't know if they're progressing up or down. They may have migrated down aeons ago and slowly have metamorphosed into this new form. We do know this: their attacks on the trains are so erratic that they're totally unpredictable with a single exception. After one of them has been wounded, they apparently carry a grudge for awhile, and they do like the meat of mules." She went on to explain, "The screechers, in some amazing way, although as blind as the salamanders we have just studied, find their way back to the River of Radiance for hunting. They have been seen flying back with fish weighing a hundred or more pounds."

Pack asked, "Shall I break out the flamethrower?"

"I leave it up to you, but if they do attack, it always seems to come by surprise. I imagine lighter weapons would be more practical."

This made sense to Pack, and anyway he would have taken her word about the creation of all thought without question.

Bluefeather said, "I believe a full meal will help us think."

Hector said, "When did we eat last? Maybe we could have a couple of screechers for dinner, huh?"

Sherry smiled, "We tried it once. They tasted like I imagine buzzards would. Not too appetizing."

Moosha said, "Sergeant Pack and I once ate buzzard."

"Not by choice, Moosha. That wasn't the only strange thing we ate on that little venture on . . . ah, hell, forget that one." He bounded up from the bench. Suddenly, his usual little misty grey eyes jammed with excited lights and his naturally slumped and lazy-appearing body had turned into long muscles of spring steel. Battle might be done. It was catching.

In awhile they were on the trail with the wounded, guns fully loaded, sharp, holstered machetes flopping against thighs and hearts singing with their blood suddenly surging with the chemicals of warriors.

Pack said to himself, "By God, this is going to be thrilling." All his warring and warning nerves vibrated in anticipation. Hector and Moosha's adrenaline had reacted the same as Pack's.

Sherry thought, *These crazy people don't realize we have far greater things to accomplish than killing screechers, but I'm glad they're ready. Ready? Hell, they're eager.*

Marsha thought, *Oh, dear God, protect everyone, protect Blue—and even myself, if you will. I've got to try to explain things to him before something happens to us.*

Bluefeather's mind-voice cut in, *We've gotta get on past this area of danger if we have to kill every screecher and its kin in the entire cavern. We've got honored promises to fulfill and—and I'd like to somehow be alone with Marsha. We've got to have an understanding, a truth, about Korbell and—us.*

The rest of The Section was charged up like sparks from broken high lines. The threat of possible imminent death gives life an intensity of fear and buoyancy like nothing else.

Since there was no hiding from the enemy, they were free to talk if they so desired.

Willy, looking over the multitudes of caverns that Sherry kept switch-lighting ahead of them and darkening behind, said, "This here makes Carlsbad Caverns and Mammoth Caves look like prairie dog holes."

Charlie Waters thought of Sally, *I'm here, and I'm glad you're there.* Then he said aloud to the others, "This would make one hell of an orchestra pit."

"Or a hay barn."

"Or a bomb shelter."

"A way station for the gods."

"A great place for the world to end."

"Or begin."

And then Sherry motioned for Bluefeather to stop The Section. There was a covered box of switches. She opened it and pulled several. Ahead and far down into the canyon of needles it was lit up. The canyon gleamed here and there, looking like pearly, ice cream-filled bowls many yards wide. Between them were the sharp formations that gave the canyon its name. Hundreds of pointed stalagmitesstabbed upward, threatening anyone or anything that fell into the enticement of the milky surface of the seductive, deadly translucence.

Bluefeather adjusted his binoculars as Sherry had. All shifted about, seeking a position to focus in closer on the canyon.

They saw three of the great screechers feeding on the remains of the mule carcass. It was obvious now that they had been named properly from the shrill sounds they uttered. Their beaks must have been over a yard long and they hopped about like giant African vultures with their wings constantly spreading and folding. When they stretched their wings all the way out, three long, fish-hooked, lion-like claws dropped down from each tip. There was a straighter, sharper one on the edge of each elbow-like appendage. Similar claws came out of large pads on their feet, giving them a powerful grasp and a base from which to launch their awkward but effective ground leap. Their color was white with patterned ripples of pink through it. Each had a large knob on its head that was its main sonar reflector. Even with the help of field glasses, the blind indentations of their receding eye sockets were so small they were barely visible.

The birds had the amazing ability to pick at the remaining scraps of flesh on the mule's bones with both the beak and the deft, clawed hands at the tips of their eight-foot wings. Even more astounding to all viewers was the fact that the extensive wings smoothly folded inward so that the outer hands could deliver the flesh to the beak with ease. The screechers were equipped with five appurtenances or, in their case, five extremely useful weapons.

The mule had fallen and was pierced by several needles, but the screechers had pulled and torn at the carcass until it was completely askew. They flung the bones in random directions with a jerk of their huge heads. They alternately hopped above the needles to touch the sides of their heads several times to their own dead—in a ritual of grief or beyond—then returned each time to rip viciously at the mule's carcass in both hunger and apparent anger.

Sherry said to Pack, Marsha and Bluefeather, "It does seem as if they have the beginning of recognizable anger and grief, doesn't it?"

Before anyone could give more than a thought to her combined statement and question, one of the screechers acted out her prophecy. The creature flapped its wings up and down, holding itself in place like a hovering hawk. A needle pierced the buttocks up through the area of the privates of a fallen mule tender. The screecher dropped down, clamping its beak on the human body and jerked it up and free from the rock spear. The shrieks the screecher made were so loud, shrill and piercing that The Section wanted to go deaf. In fact, Jody, Charlene and Osaka did clamp their hands hard over their ears. Others started to do the same and then forgot it as they observed, stunned, the screecher screaming in what sounded like horrendous delight as it flew high above the canyon floor with its victim.

Its two companions circled underneath, their sounds just as loud, and even more excited. The massive one purposely dropped the body, while another, with its sonar in perfect pitch, soared and grabbed the limp, bloody carcass and flapped upward like the other. Then it, too, dropped the lifeless form, continuing the game. They tossed the body in the air like children playing with a ball. Their cries were pitched to the volume of a thousand mad people in a tin building, echoing back and forth in the caverns so that it sounded as though a screecher was sequestered in every recess of the seemingly limitless limestone. The now nude cadaver was shredded and red. Finally, they dropped it onto a needle that pierced what was left of the chest and neck. It hung there halfway down the point with strings of flesh like a rag doll ripped into strips by a mad dog.

The mules, skittish and frightened as holed rabbits at the touch of a badger's claws, were somehow controlled, but The Section was in a rage, as the screechers had been, at the defilement of one of their own. They charged forward, closing in to fire, but when they were close enough for vengeance, the screechers had disappeared. They all swung about with their weapons ready. Bluefeather and Pack, having once before gone mad at Brest, France, performing heroic acts because of a sudden mutilation of one of their own, reacted like the rest of The Section, but now there was no visible enemy to kill.

Now it was silent. They stood. They waited.

Pack spaced his armed people about, facing both ways where one great cavern was above them and one below. On beyond the canyon of needles, he and Bluefeather stood in the middle, surveying the dark silence of the far-reaching space. They each grasped the nozzle of a flame-thrower.

The silence became the enemy. They thought it was truly insulting. Then from above came the screech. It was so far away it sounded like the cry of a red-tailed hawk in a high wind. Another cry came, and yet another, from above. Then they were screeching from below. Now their great, blind bodies moved forward from both sides. Their sonar control overcame their blindness with extremely sensitive sound echoes. The extraordinary large and receptive scent openings on each side of their beaks made them even more frightening. There were no eyes to blind with a spray of bullets or flame. None of these tactics would work here. Only solid death would do.

Nearer, louder came the painful sounds. Crescendoing.

Bluefeather shouted, "Hold your position until they're in a clear beam of light. Their shrieks are one of their main weapons. You hear? You understand?" He raised his voice now to be heard above the enemy. "Ignore their little, baby screams. Aim where the throat joins the breast."

The screaming stopped with shocking suddenness, but Bluefeather could hear the mighty wings whoosh as they displaced air. He said softly, "It's a trick. Here they come."

Pack had trouble holding his fire. His washy, blue eyes were filling his sight with flashes of crimson. "There!" he cried.

Bluefeather yelled at the same instant. "There the bastards are!"

The attacking birds' sonar might have been slightly disoriented by the spread-out explosion of bullets and their huge scent glands thrown awry by the smell of gunpowder, but their heat indicators worked perfectly. The screechers were surprisingly aware of the searching blazes and veered away without even nearing the burning flare.

Pack and Bluefeather resecured the flamethrowers on their backs and picked up their semiautomatic rifles.

The screechers arced again swiftly into the light from the front and the back. The spread-out troops stayed kneeling while they fired, leaving space above for Pack and Bluefeather to blast away. The ones with the mules needed both hands to control the animals. They were the most vulnerable. But for now the screechers' heads smelled and felt the sound-shattering explosion of the shells and headed into the barrage. The terrible noise of the mighty birds and the loud echoing clatter of the weapons created a maelstrom of frenzied action and sound.

Bluefeather saw one screecher circle high and come down in a straight angle at him. He pulled off three shots straight into the circular indentation of the thorax just above the huge breastbone. The creature twisted and flopped, crashing into a pagoda-style pole, fluttering in a wad, missing Moosha by inches. It tumbled on over the ledge and down into the needles, sticking there like Christ on the cross.

Another had been wounded about fifty yards away and had fallen, but now came leaping at them twenty or thirty feet at a time.

Bluefeather slapped another clip in the M-2 and fired, trying for the vulnerable spot. He could see bullets tearing into the creature, crippling it, but on it came. Then it made a huge leap, a strangling cry and rolled over in a desperate attempt to control its forward direction. Now its flopping was accompanied by gurgles instead of screams. It managed to thrash its way within about ten feet of the troops when the blood poured out of the blueish veins as big as water pipes that were clearly visible on the surface of its thin-skinned body. The bird's blood coursed down the satin-smooth rocks, making little rivers and richly colored designs. A beautiful death.

Pack and the group on the other side of the ledge had

maintained such heavy and accurate fire under his orders that four screechers were blasted down into the needles: two pierced dead, two crawling and flopping about, crippled.

Then a different call came. It was one of retreat. It sounded as if the screechers consoled one another for their losses.

Bluefeather knew now that the screechers were valiant—caring deeply for one another—but not foolish. They were like the Comanches—if out-gunned, retreat for another day's battle.

He started back to the mules as Pack and Hector commenced caring for the injured men. He was within forty steps, and was thrilled to see that they had held the caravan of frightened mules and the two wounded Olders all together and safe, when he heard the noise below. A screecher, too full of holes to fly, was nevertheless determinedly limping up the more gradual slope here toward the group.

Bluefeather pulled the trigger on the M-2. It was empty. He jerked out his side arm and fired, feeling the weapon kick in his hands as he could see the heavy Magnum shells jolt and slow the screecher, but it strained on up, slipping back a tiny bit at the very edge of the canyon.

The mules were squealing and bolting now as the creature clawed to the edge, struggling to make its final attack. Bluefeather jerked out his machete and leaped at the creature, cutting at the knob, slicing it in half. Then as one clawed hand of a wing tip reached for Marsha, Bluefeather smashed the blade down, splitting the wing. He swung now with a force that was actually beyond his normal strength. The wing dropped, but the one claw held the edge while the other reached out, weaving back and forth, searching for flesh.

Bluefeather ducked under the flailing to his knees and chopped down with a prodigious swing, almost severing the clawed foot that clung to the edge. The screecher tumbled down now, bouncing, flouncing, making feeble grabs at the slick wall with its remaining usable appurtenances, then fell into darkness. One last feeble sound came up, then was sucked back into its body in final silence.

It was over.

The mules were scattered up and down the trail; all but one was safe. Pack had three men wounded from wing claws. O'Malley, who had lost the mule, had a rip in his left chest muscle. The top of Moosha's head had been raked to the skull. He would have a permanent part now. Kowalski's side was sliced open to his entrails. He was in serious condition.

Bluefeather gathered together all mules and people, while Pack and Hector patched up the wounded, giving antibiotics and even sewing up some. They gave Kowalski morphine.

Then Bluefeather found a cave with a narrow entrance that widened inside to form a room big enough to accommodate all. Fortunately, there was a clear pool of water here. Pack set up two guards at the entrance. Willy, Gordon and Charlie unpacked the mules and rigged a rope into a calvary-type picket line. They watered and fed them oats. There would be no hay here.

Hector was making the injured comfortable by blowing up their air mattresses and covering them with blankets and coats borrowed from others for extra warmth. Everyone checked their own personal equipment and weapons. Sherry had told them that nobody would know for sure when the screechers would attack.

Ratchett had a portable gas stove going. He heated water to cleanse the wounded and to prepare a meal.

Bluefeather said, "Our compliments again, troop. You

held solid and kept up the fire, otherwise the screechers would be playing catch in midair with us."

This got a few nervous but needed laughs. In spite of Kowalski's serious wounds, some began joking their over-stretched nerves into submission. Willy let out a belch so loud it made the roar of a lion seem timid.

Bluefeather said, "Shhh. Shhh, Willy, you're going to give away our position."

Willy replied, "When I'm hungry and scared my stom-ach talks to me like a used car salesman. Don't be con-cerned, though, because everything is goin' to be grandy dandy from now on."

They all broke up in relief laughter. Even Kowalski grinned in his morphine daze.

Marsha came and sat beside Bluefeather on his bedroll, saying softly, hoping that no one could hear but him, "You dirty bastard. You've saved my life twice in the last two days. It's unfair to make me owe you so much."

Then she went back and got a wash pan from Willy, dipped it in the cold pond and returned to her bedroll. She splashed her face and dampened her red hair, then dried it with a towel. She took a lipstick and tiny mirror out of her bag and put some color on her lips. She began brushing her red hair. Even in the dim light of three Co-leman lamps, the bronze and gold streaks shined.

Bluefeather was trying to get his equipment in order and clean his rifle, but he had seen almost every feminine move Marsha had so deliberately made. She knew it. She suddenly turned her head and gave him a world-class, Korbell adoptee's smile. If there had been any candles around, their flames would have seemed dim compared to its radiance.

In spite of his numb, dull-pained aching of believed deceit, he much desired to motion her outside and go frolicking—if necessary, among the bloody needles—but thought maybe they had better wait. The possessive screechers might resent fornication amid their deceased. He was mostly certain that Sherry would resent them risking antagonizing their worthy opponents so soon.

TWENTY-NINE

BEFORE MOVING OUT THE NEXT MORNING, OR NOON, OR night, Bluefeather asked Sherry if he should give another warning to the group, even though they had held up well through The Unholy and the screechers. She agreed he should.

"Listen up for a moment. You must, do you hear me clearly? You must, this very moment, start adjusting yourselves for many shocks—yet to come—of what you are going to see and experience. Remember, remember well, that you will soon think of it as normal—it is normal for here. *We* are the abnormal here.

They all looked at one another to give reassurances, comfort and to get it.

The march on down into a lower level of the cavern was fearful for a mile or so as they all watched with nerves and senses tingling, waiting for the screechers, but they did not return.

As their nerves relaxed, the wounds, bruises, strained ligaments and muscles made them appear remnants of soldiers retreating from Napoleon's defeat in the Russian motherland. Bluefeather took the lead now, setting a sur-vivable pace. Pack and Hector moved back and forth, talking, joking, consoling those that moved between. Moosha guarded the rear drag.

As they limped out of the cave trail into a great room, they gazed upon a vista that could only have been envisioned by a happy Dante. It welcomed and soothed their tired eyes.

They saw a human-constructed palace of many rooms against a mighty wall. Powerful recessed lights illuminated most of the outstanding features. There were fences of metallic material with dagger-length barbs all about and other mysterious material they did not recognize. There were old people moving about. Some had been waiting for The Section's arrival after receiving the phone message from Dolby's outer world.

The vast limestone room spread up and out farther in some places than the large electric lamps could beam, revealing a world such as no earthly other. There was every conceivable color and variation thereof in the endlessly shaped stone. Stalactites and stalagmites with bases sometimes bigger around than the combined circumference of a hundred redwoods stood taller than a thirty-story building. There were some hanging like huge icicles twirled until the points dropped in the suggestion of giant spirals, gold-hued soda straws and strands of gypsum crystals like clusters of long glass needles. There were drapery formations sizable enough to decorate ten glass buildings.

There were hanging crystals of calcite, chandeliers of aragonite, a wetly gleaming paradise of forms and colors so dazzling that the whole of the room could only be, and was, called God's Castle, and in fact, between two five hundred-foot draperies was a soft orange-colored throne formation that only a god would be worthy of sitting upon.

Beyond, and down through a large opening, was another room that dwarfed this one. Bluefeather had seen this Cavern of Marvels on film at Dolby's home, and he had told Marsha and Pack about it. There was an eerie, soft-glowing light of violets and greens emanating from there. It was not from electricity. This light was . . . well, every mind-voice there was wondering, questioning: *How? How could there be a natural light this deep into the inner world?* And indeed, as if to mystify their mind-voices even more, now and then there would be a soft, red flare through the colored space like lightning reflecting from a far-distant sky. They could hear no thunder. It was soundless.

Later they would understand, but for now Sherry suggested Bluefeather halt the column short of an enormous arched gate and guard tower made of some strange metallic-looking material.

Sherry walked forward to greet several Olders in their grey-rose coveralls. It was the uniform of all the old ones. She talked animatedly, looking back at Bluefeather, gesturing with her arm. The Olders stood holding their weapon barrels cradled across one arm at first, but now carried them casually as one might carry an umbrella on a clear spring day.

Bluefeather could see them nod slowly, now and then looking at The Section.

Then Sherry returned, "Since I have been, and will be for some time, your official guide, please follow me. First, however, I would suggest that you greet the Olders at the entrance with civility and politeness but not in a personal manner. Commander Bluefeather will give you a full briefing later."

After the recent adventures on the down trail and the awe-inspired look at the castle room, it was easily possible for The Section to accept the size and surprising modernization of the castle compound. Once inside the strange metal walls, they saw pools of water surrounded by plants analogous to reeds, branching out into stick-like limbs that forked in straight, angular designs. In some cases they had been trimmed so that the total effect was as circular and varied as the caretaker-designer pleased.

Bluefeather marveled at the soft, violet-green lighting effect that seemed to emanate directly from the obviously living plants. He had been sure, until now, that plants could not live without photosynthesis from the sun, but these weirdly glowing objects certainly contained some kind of life.

There was tiny quartz-like pieces of tectite embedded everywhere in the host rock. The quartz reflected the electric lights, as well as the lights from the strange plants, into little specks, giving an overall effect of one huge partially revealed jewel.

There were walkways throughout the frontal compound from one pool design to another with stone benches of creamy marble flows that had been laboriously secured from some secret place in the immense, rock auditorium.

Some Olders of both sexes and all types of skin tones ranging through black, brown, yellow, pink and white were here, lounging around these delightfully decorated spots, watching their visitors with controlled concentration.

Sherry introduced Willy to Adam and Toliver, the mule keepers. Adam was a veterinarian and separated the wounded mules into padded stalls for treatment. Willy nearly choked when they showed him how to feed the strange, hollow stalks that they had seen glowing in the front grounds to the mules. The animals ate it with relish. Willy was assured by the Olders that all nutrients were plentiful in the plants. They called them the "trees of light."

There were stalls for about fifty mules in all. Even now a team of packers was ready to move out toward the top with the ore sacks full just as another would return with many varied supplies from above.

Kowalski, O'Malley and Hector were taken to the infirmary for immediate treatment. The latter two were stitched, medicated and released, but Kowalski remained in serious condition.

There was a large entryway into God's Castle not unlike a hotel lobby. In fact, the entire structure curved around the natural limestone walls. The foyer was made of different rhythms, colors and textures of rock quarried from some unseen place in the natural auditorium. They were fitted together perfectly like outer world marble, only many times softer and more beautiful. In fact, they would soon find that all the outer halls and entry rooms were constructed of this multitextured material. Obviously, the limestone was available everywhere to finish making the necessary cement.

Some of the natural crystal chandeliers hung about the lobby with lights strategically placed to create a soft glow below and illuminate a sparkling treasure above. There was furniture of heavy oak and cedar from the outer world. It was stained to blend with the pearly grey lustrous sections of cave marble that dominated the other colors. There were large maps in one corner like one might find at the entrance to a national park. They were framed with the cured hollow bushes, trees, vegetation, or whatever they were called that decorated the outside front. It was the same vegetation the mules found so delicious.

Bluefeather was shocked to see four young people. He guessed they were in their mid-twenties. They stood up in a formal row to greet them. The Youngers, two men and two women, smiled by force of will. All bowed. They did not speak until Sherry said, "These are your room engineers. They will help everyone to their habitats and will be on call at all times should you need anything."

Then, as formally as their stance, they said in sequence, "At your service, sir. At your service, ma'am"

Sherry went on to explain that she and Bluefeather

would go ahead first, as they had to confer. It was suggested to the others that they be shown to their rooms. There were bathrooms in each suite and some snacks. They were to wait until their commander gave them further orders.

Sherry was placed in the first room by the stairs. There were elevators, but Sherry explained that they were used by the Olders, who were located on the first floor of the palace for obvious reasons.

Sherry was accompanied into her room by a yellow-skinned young woman with eyes almost as large and certainly as slanted as Sherry's.

A young man with a face as white and fresh as new paint accompanied Bluefeather, saying, "Here sir. I'm experienced. Just sit and rest while I place your things."

All the room furniture here was made from different-sized trees of light. Some had lost the soft lustre and others had only a trace of glow left. The furniture was uniquely comfortable and relaxing.

Bluefeather sat back in a lounge chair for a moment and looked around the room. There were original paintings on the wall, but all abstract. Not a single landscape or certainty to suggest anything from above was there. He got up and patted the huge bed and found it was soft. Across the room was a solid blue wall. As he gazed at it, he realized there were many shades of the outer world sky color so subtlety blended together that it teased the mind and the eye to try and discern the difference. In doing so he dozed off for a moment.

He was awakened by the unnamed young man saying in a voice without accent, "It's all done, sir. Now let me show you the rest of your home."

Home? Bluefeather thought.

There was a large cave-marble bath and shower with real gold fixtures. He had heard about these luxuries but never dreamed he would spend a night with the metal that had haunted his entire life. It was used all around him as plain hardware. There just did not seem to be any way he could escape gold, unless, of course, he was trying to find its natural formation in the desert. Then it became as elusive as waterbugs.

There was a large combination kitchen, containing a refrigerator and an electric cooking unit, and a dining room with eight chairs and a table. Naturally, air-conditioning was not needed, but there was a vent to give circulation. All but the living room and bedroom had been dug from solid limestone, then cemented in with more oddly decorated stones. There were false windows with casements made from some of the larger half logs of the hollow trees of light. And amazingly, stone draperies had been fitted together so perfectly that Bluefeather almost tried to part them before he realized they could only be separated by a jackhammer, and then after doing that, all he would have been able to see was more stone. In any case it was a room unique in all the world and felt soft, restful and secure for the moment.

The young man bowed again, saying, "Instructions are by the phone. When you call, either I, or one of my relief, will be available to you at all times."

Bluefeather showered under the gold spigot, shaved and changed into the soft uniform of God's Castle. However, there was one difference. His was far more rose-colored than pearl grey. He was sure the others of The Section would find theirs the same. They did.

The phone chimed softly. It was Sherry. "Are you ready for the tour and the conference?"

"Ready."

She showed him the large dining halls and the kitchens, where huge freezers hung full of wild fowl, lamb, beef and frozen vegetables imported from all over the outer world.

The tour moved on to a special room where the trees

of light grew. They ranged from some so small and tender that they were sliced as part of a dinner salad to others, just a bit larger, which were bundled for mule fodder. The largest ones were cut to make all sorts of furniture, frames, ladders and design decorations. Bluefeather decided that this tree was a true wonder material. It was food for man and beast, building and art material and, no doubt, when they finally arrived at Way Station Nine where it grew, they would see many other uses for it.

Sherry showed him the entertainment hall with a bar, a bandstand, comfortable chairs and tables of such smooth and creamy stone that it made Bluefeather think of Chinese silk and milk frozen so hard it could never melt. Many lampshades were made of spider web calcite, thin and spiny as strings of cotton candy. Turtle-shaped crystal formations and blue diamond clusters of glass-like rocks formed little jeweled worlds set casually about on tables, serving no use but the greatest of all—beauty. The dance floor was of such amber smoothness that at first Bluefeather walked with short, cautious steps, but soon he found it was smooth without being slick. He did a dance in honor of his spirit guide—a combination waltz, two-step, Cherokee stomp and Taos alley wobble.

Sherry clapped vigorously and joined him for several careless whirls, saying, "More later."

She led him to the conference room, where the decor was a miniature replica of the entertainment room, except one wall was painted so red it seemed to be bleeding. In its very center, all alone, was a blown-up photograph of Dolby when he was a youthful futurist of fifty, but already the eyebrows were beginning to look like cacti and the eyes seemed to tear holes in the photographic paper on which they were processed.

Sherry said, "I have other rooms to show you as we progress, but for now, I want to explain and tell you a few things that were needless to spell out before we reached our present post.

"First, the Olders—they're here because of misdeeds such as murder, fraud and the like. Dolby recruited people desperate to escape life in prison. He lured them in here with luxuries and promises of a life secure from the force of the law. It worked. Once he had them under his spell of wealth and wits, they stayed too long. For many years the great front gates of the 'Outer' have trapped them. There's no escape."

"None have ever returned above ground?"

"None, Blue. Not a single one has ever seen the sun again after entering the caverns."

"These are tough, mean people; surely they've rebelled at some time or other at this . . . this velvet prison?"

"Some did, but he had his old loyal troops you saw above, and they crushed all rebellions until an acceptance set in as you see here now. They are reasonably content, finally, and age has mellowed them. This is home now. Here. They perform their duties slower, but surer, and take more pride than the Youngers. On average, over a year's span, they out-produce the young people by about thirty percent."

"What about the Youngers? Has Dolby just now recruited them?"

"No. They arrived as babies, and some of the women were unknowingly pregnant."

"You mean to tell me, Sherry, that these young men and women have known no other world but this one right here?"

"Yes. That's correct, Blue. Oh, they've overheard talk of an outer world and they see the pack trains come and go, but they've been brainwashed to believe the upper world is full of evil wars and poison air."

"Well?"

"Oh, of course, we know that could be made a truth,

but there is the other side of the mountain still left. There are many things of beauty to try and save. People of dignity and bravery are still scattered about everywhere, Blue. You know that as well as anyone."

"Oh, I know you say a truth, Sherry, but Lord, what a tragedy that these young people have never seen the sun coming up over the Sangre de Cristos or listened to the talk of Twining Creek."

"Well, that's what you were chosen to do—help prove that we have the wealth Dolby believes is here, the wealth to absolutely control this magic world, to show it to the scientists, anthropologists and the thinkers of the earth in freedom, along with the vast knowledge of all life that I know is here. I'm sure you'll soon see this for yourself."

Bluefeather realized now that Sherry was just as mind-controlled as the others in some ways. Sure, she was the one who would save and present it all, if it was within her personal power. He did not doubt a digit that she would give her life to this incredible endeavor one way or another. Then the question crossed his mind: How was a smitten Pack going to approach such a dedicated and flint-willed woman?

"This seems pedantic compared to all the rest, but why haven't the young bred here? I haven't seen any children."

"Oh, they have," she said and laughed with her great eyes and teeth that shined like the light of white suns against the background of her ebony skin. "They surely have, but Dolby felt that birth control, without exception, must be maintained for the work to get done in time."

"In time?"

"His time. He's old. He wants to see the mammoth task to the end." She became defensive now. "Who among us can possibly blame him? It was his discovery, his risks, his money, his mind that brought it to a point where it might, just might, be saved from a grabbing, greedy, stupid world. The knowledge here in these connected caverns opens up old, old worlds and presents the possibilities of new ones far, far into the future. What more can one ask? What more, indeed."

Her usually controlled voice had risen as her eyes had squinted and her lips pulled back like a forest animal ready to defend or attack.

"Look," Bluefeather said, "Look here, I'm with you to the end as I've said before. I just want to know as much as possible so I can contribute the most. I believe, girl. Do you hear ol' Bluefeather? *I believe.*"

"I know you do. I'm too damn defensive, but that's how I've survived all the years of holding back my own growing awareness of what lavish physical and mental rewards await us—await everyone here. God, how I've longed, even craved, to share my notebooks with my colleagues around the world."

"I do understand the agony of that. I had to hide something once . . . long ago. Something I'd—we had—earned."

"You've got to call The Section together, I know, and explain the Olders to them. After they've eaten. I think it best if we time their first sleep. We have found, over the years, that the best average rhythm is ten hours of sleep and twenty awake. And, oh yes, I might as well say it just to you. Only the two of us can share what I'm about to say. Agreed?"

"Agreed."

"If the research of our present expedition doesn't come up to Dolby's expectations, we'll be here forever—just like the rest. He has the early tunnels wired with huge explosive charges. There would be no way out. He can press one button and the return route to the outer world and the light and power and water coming down from it, is gone. 'Boom!' 'Poof!' That quickly. That final." She snapped the fingers on one and then the other hand in time with her words.

Bluefeather felt a shower of icy sleet in his stomach at this terrible and lonely fact Sherry had stated. Then the fires of his ancestral Indian-Italian blood—and as old Grinder had intoned "his separate Bluefeather blood"—scoured the cold away and he felt suddenly ready to face, with all his experience and energy, anything. Anything.

"Then we'll just have to win it all, won't we, dear Sherry?" And he gave her a smile—a Korbell smile that was the equal of her African one. Hell, he might never be adopted by the Korbell powers in this ultimate game, but now, at last, he could smile as grandly as they.

THIRTY

With Bluefeather's help, Sherry had started to get The Section on the twenty-hour-ten-hour rhythm. They lounged about, enjoying the lighted view out in front of God's Castle and the seemingly unending delights of the courtyard. They were fed gourmet food and drinks and spent an hour and a half of their ten-hour sleep rhythm segment in the artificial sun, sauna and exercise room. The wounds and stiffness receded and the vigor of youth and anticipated adventure surged through the entire section.

They had adjusted to the polite reserve of the Olders and the gracious service of the Youngers. Curiosity about many unanswered questions naturally nagged at them, but even that subsided as their bodies rebounded with vitality.

During the next twenty-hour awake period, they were to have what Sherry called a "princely pause." They were to dine and dance just this once as long as they cared to maintain the fun, for after their recovery and careful preparation, they would all depart for Way Station Nine and the River of Radiance in the Cavern of Marvels.

But this day, before the first and final celebration prior to that, Sherry took her command personnel of Bluefeather, Marsha, Pack, Hector and Moosha on a tour of outer space inside inner space.

"It is the time to witness wonders," Sherry said, leading the other five around a sharp curve in the cliffs.

The compound wall curved with the building even after it ended. Then they exited another gate and guard tower and followed a trail for perhaps a mile. They were armed for protection against migrating screechers outside the fortified and weaponized metal fence. Sherry and Bluefeather had high-powered prospector's magnifying glasses. They all carried the short-handled prospector's picks in their belts.

Sherry pointed out the increasing numbers of tiny quartzite flecks and showed them a few heavy dark mineralized chunks of the material that the guard fence was made of—pieces created from the impact explosion.

She explained, "They're much larger than they look from down here. The quartz and its flakes were formed from the remaining heat of the meteorite. We call it a star. For some reason the Olders like to think of it as a fallen star. Maybe it's the memory of other sights and sounds. Maybe it is their genes recollecting; nevertheless, all these are stars."

Now they came to rows of loose chunks of metal forming a sort of fence. A couple of Olders stood guard at a tunnel entrance. They nodded to Sherry as she led her command inside. A portion of the cave wall was rusty, irregular and dark for at least half a mile from its portal. Sherry nodded and spoke to the Olders softly as they passed, "We will return when we've finished our inspection, Grady."

"Yes, ma'am," was all he said. The other tall, bent guard—with a face as grey as old milk, eyes withdrawn and near-blank—nodded a bony head on a turkey-like neck and sat wearily back down on a tree of light chair.

The tunnel floor was level and well lighted, although

Sherry carried a powerful hand light. There were no timbers or reinforcement of any kind here. They walked on solid, shiny, crystallized metal. Now and then she stopped and picked at a loose piece of metal from the tunnel wall and handed it to Bluefeather, the near-geologist, and held her light so he could examine it with his glass.

"I've never seen meteorite rock crystallized like this. The luster is mostly metabolic with fractions of quartzite. This kind of crystallization is unheard of in such a small specimen. I see the hexagonal, isometric, tetrahedrons, on and on."

Sherry held the light steady but lifted her head to explain to the others, "Our labs show heavy concentrations of palladium, iridium, platinum and lesser amounts of nickel and iron. Ordinarily, iron would dominate even a small meteorite—but one of this size . . ." She waved a hand at the solid concentrated metal all around forming the whole tunnel.

They walked on and then suddenly curved out to the left. To the right, facing them, was a much darker, different looking matter.

"Here is the heart of the star. Diamond bits shatter upon it. It was an implosion in the center and explosion on the surface. The core is so dense, we can't mine it except by acid. Look," she said as she pointed down one curving tunnel and then the other. One side of the wall was the dull silvery metal, the same as the tunnel they had seen all the way from the portal to here. The other side of the wall revealed a core dark, even forbidding, in its feeling of heaviness, as if it had closed together forcefully during its long journey from the heavens, preparing to protect itself from the eventual collision. It had actually done so, and consequently survived the impact mostly intact, carving a canyon five miles long before it finally entered the mountain range, with its center still imploding until its long journey had finally stopped right here.

The five section members followed Sherry around the mass, sensing a fearful power within it. Then they heard grinding sounds ahead. Four Youngers were working—two drilling and two carefully sorting what had been blasted earlier.

Bluefeather said, "Of course, they are only working the surface metal free from the concentrated core."

They all nodded in acknowledgment and then Sherry continued her necessary illuminations. She showed them how they used wax to hold sulfuric acid that slowly ate through the core metal. There were fifty of these wax troughs set up against the core about three feet apart, forming squares of the same dimension.

Sherry explained that once the square was cut with acid to a depth of four or five inches, the metal could be peeled with prize bars in relatively even layers. So far, it was the only way they had found to extract it.

Sherry said, "We tested a piece of it above ground with a 105 armor-piercing shell and it bounced off like a dropped needle. Now, allow me to suggest to you that if—and I emphasize *if*—if this kind of implosion had occurred on a huge scale in outer space, it would have left nothing visible to the strongest telescope but a black hole. Though there are several million tons in this meteorite—I mean, star—it's only a miniature replica of what's supposedly occurring at all times in the universe. Now, please understand that only a few people of science have even suggested this theory to date, but here is living, priceless proof before your eyes. It will take the scientific community ten years to get over the shock of this discovery and a thousand years to break it down into its understandable parts."

She went on to explain to The Section's speechless members that there were three heretofore unknown metallic elements that they had already found and no known earthly mineral was even near their hardness.

Bluefeather took Sherry's light and shone it on the core, studying it carefully with his naked eye and then with his glass.

He said, amazed and dumbfounded, "It's made up of hexagonals from the most minute to those wide as a hand. All are hexagons except for some binding substance of many different lusters and apparent multiple gravity."

Beyond his present bewilderment, being a man of minerals his entire life, his mind whizzed, trying to compute even an estimate of the enormous and rare values of wealth contained here. It would stagger a half dozen of the richest and most powerful nations on earth. He must stop these wild thoughts this instant and get his mind back on gold, where it now appeared to greedily belong.

Sherry helped with, "On a more practical side, folks, can you imagine what chemists, metallurgists, designers, engineers, manufacturers of high technology, scientific minds of every kind would give to walk into the center of an imploded, currently unexplainable star?"

"Not to mention plain, wealthy tourists," said Marsha.

"And mercenaries," added Hector.

"And soldiers of good fortune—any fortune," said Pack.

"And me," said Moosha.

"And me, too," Bluefeather agreed.

That was the best they could do with frivolity. The far-distant universe surrounded them. They walked along the tunnel quietly, afraid of God, afraid of sound. Afraid.

Bluefeather said, "Parts of this are what the galaxy is made of—our world, even us. Yes, us—before evolution, before . . ." he couldn't express what he felt any further. It was just too much for a mere human to explain in just one attempt.

Then he had to try again. There might never be another chance. He turned and stared into the blank face of the massive, blackish monolith saying, "Look, look into its void of solidity and see the beginning and the end of yourself."

All looked. All were silent.

Then, a few steps on, outside the star, the artificial lights revealed colors and wondrous formations enough to remove the ponderous, unbearable weight from their beings and they stepped briskly along now, all chattering at once, except Sherry. She smiled inwardly, contentedly.

"The first wonder of the world. The greatest wonder of the world, but what world?" Bluefeather said, as Marsha put her hand on Bluefeather's pointing, waving arm. He covered her hand with his and gave her a smiling look as they walked on. Everyone was talking great sense and nonsense, with no one able to truly hear the messages.

They went to the lab, where the old men showed them how the star metal stopped heavy radiation totally, and on to the infirmary, where they met an old nurse who was as pretty-faced as a twenty-year old. She slowly, with pleasure, moved a little piece of the star metal, far heavier than gold, back and forth in the air above Kowalski's terrible screecher wound. She smiled proudly down at his scar with its flesh almost healed. The old doctor stood back, seeming bored as he watched his nurse and these children of the surface earth exulting over a simple process he had been performing for over two decades.

Sherry said, "It won't make a new liver or a new heart, but it does radiate something that heals cut flesh in a miraculous manner."

They could all see the results.

Kowalski sat up, stepped from the bed, and said, "I heard we're gonna have a princess party."

Sherry corrected, good-humoredly now, "A princely pause."

"Goody. That, too. When do we start?"

"Whenever you're ready."

They all left to prepare for the get-together. Sherry had accurately planned it all, for as each entered the door of the luxurious "homes," the weight of the universe and its metals dissolved and misted away. She had performed proudly with The Section's commanders. Relief untold relaxed her whole being. There were still sixteen hours left of the awake time. Perhaps that would be enough to get in a "kingly" princely pause.

THIRTY-ONE

IT WAS THE TIME FOR RELIEVING CAVERNOUS CON-
cerns. Bluefeather had washed himself clean as decency.
He impulsively phoned Pack's room.

"Hello. This is ol' bother. How're you feelin'? You
ready to party?"

"I feel great. I had a good breakfast and I'm not in jail
yet."

Bluefeather had heard these words before from his old
sergeant, but always welcomed them.

"Meet you in the entertainment room."

"You'll have to hurry to beat me there."

The musicians at God's Castle consisted of four Olders—three men and a woman—and two Youngers—the
Asian girl with the classic eyes who tended Sherry and a
Jewish lad who played the violin. There was a piano, a
clarinet, two violins, a bass fiddle and a drummer. Bluefeather did not exactly identify the specifics of the orchestra. He was just happy to listen. All were.

The bar was open. A sleek, dark, young Apache of fine
temperament, named Alonzo Martinez, was bartender.
Pack and Bluefeather ordered Scotch and water. Everyone gathered in small groups, excitedly enjoying the soft
music of Strauss waltzes in the background. The softness

of the lighting, combined with the jeweled spots of natural chandeliers and strategically placed lamps and other cave-grown decorations, created an ambience that both soothed and excited the emotions. They were all *compadres* who had survived The Unholy and the screechers' attack successfully together. That was enough to bond them for the rest of their lives. They had shared great danger together, surviving together. Thereby, they now enjoyed the only true and total love.

After two or three cocktails, Sherry told them to seek out their tables, for dinner would soon be served. Bluefeather, Marsha, Pack, Sherry, Willy and Charlie were seated next to one another at a table.

They were served by two polite old gentlemen who ignored any attempts at light joking, although Bluefeather thought he sensed a longing for new friendships in them. Nevertheless, they served with quiet dignity and efficiency, as all their compatriots seemed to perform their varied tasks.

What a feast it was—pheasant and quail, ham and roast beef topped off with a tree of light salad with tender green onions and spinach leaves. A large tray of assorted cheeses, fruit and fresh bread was placed on each table. The suggestion of candles was provided by sixteen-inch sections of fully glowing trees of light.

They drank. They talked. They ate. Soon they would proceed to the glorious horrors of Way Station Nine. Now they enjoyed.

Pack was the first to dance. He stood in front of Sherry, trying to straighten up his slumping frame in the rose pearl uniform that somehow fit him like a worn-out bedsheet. He held out his soft, killing hands. She took them, rising without looking at him directly. The music changed now. It was original. None present had ever heard it before. It had a slow, but underlying beat of something about to explode. They simply moved with its airy flow and created their own personal, original steps.

Bluefeather could not help watching Sherry and Pack's first tentative steps until she leaned to him and placed her head upon his shoulder. Pack started moving with a slow but irresistible smoothness and strength just as he did in battle. He was a warrior of the dance floor as well as the foxholes. With all of Sherry's brilliance of studied knowledge and experiences, beyond most in this world, she was caught up in Pack's strange spell. They danced seven sets together until the dampness created between their fronts forced a break.

Bluefeather observed that his friend had increased the size of his tiny perpetual smile enough to last a week. Everyone had danced, except Bluefeather. As Hector brought Marsha back to the table, Bluefeather went to her. She looked up at him before she arose. The Korbell smile did not appear. There was a rigidity about her, even though she followed him with expertise.

Then he said, "I've missed this—this holding you."

"You haven't shown it."

"Yeah. Well, you're right, and I'm sorry, but . . ."

She moved with him now and they both forgot, for this moment, here in the ballroom far under the earth, what separated their souls. They were warm, comfortable, with bodies that felt tiny spasms of ecstasy tingling under the surface, longing with a delicious ache for full expression.

As Bluefeather guided her back to her chair, they both had to control their breathing.

Pack was expressing one of his often puzzling statements: "The more ants in the colony, the deeper they have to dig and the greater the size of their beds. Nothing ever vanishes. Nothing. It all goes somewhere."

For the first time, Sherry had her great African-French eyes riveted on Pack. At that moment Bluefeather thought it possible that Pack's far-out statements were as unfathomable as Dolby's. Neither one spoke in riddles to compare with Dancing Bear, but both uttered sensible, occasionally brilliant, thoughts out of context—assuming that the listener understood what came before and after. But it had meaning for Sherry. It related to a decision Dolby would soon be making, using the final efforts of The Section as his arbitrator on the future human habitation of this Cavern of Marvels.

Jody, Charlene and Estrella danced with poise, but in between, they quietly slipped away with the surplus men of The Section, doing their duties in their chosen profession with eager and appreciative partners. They eased tensions and contributed amiably to the contentment of the troops.

Now the Olders served liters of wine made from fermented trees of light extract. All marveled at its delicate balance and body.

Bluefeather said, "Here's to this magic plant. Its uses are endless—wine, food, furniture, candles, mule fodder and no telling what else. The world hunger problem can be permanently solved with this honorable growth."

Glasses of its bounty were raised with shouts and toasts of agreement. Pack leaned over and whispered to Bluefeather, grinning for the first time in his life like an alligator full of ducks, "We're gonna start a new baby boom."

Bluefeather did not or could not answer directly, but he did raise his glass and click it against Pack's, whispering, "A full bowl must be emptied."

Pack's smile went back to its barely visible permanence. His little bluish eyes snapped and gleamed in partial, but strained, understanding of Bluefeather's words.

"Good fortunes for him," thought his longtime friend Bluefeather.

Charlie decided he would sing along with the orchestra, but "Rock of Ages" was somehow out of synch, and he gave it up with a finishing coyote yell. Others from the

dance floor and the tables echoed back shouts that resem-
bled those throated by territorial lions, babies with the
colic, winners of horse races, howler monkeys and losers
of virginity.

It was the time for listening. Bluefeather could not help
this habit he had had since childhood. He looked at the
decor of a distant wall, but did not see. The Section, in
its time of joy, was sharing silly things, which Pack knew
as a good omen of solidarity for a fighting force.

Bluefeather's ears increased their sensitivity as his eyes
dimmed.

"Hey, you don't have to worry about Korbell. He's trying to figure out the secret of thought."

"Figure it out, hell, he ain't even discovered it yet."

"Old One Lion was the best animal instructor I ever
knew. He was so cheap, though. He trained his dogs not
to eat and then they died." He recognized Willy's favorite
story, even though he didn't wish it.

"I really didn't want any conversation from the arrogant
bastard. When I kicked him in the nuts, it knocked all the
dignity out of him."

"This dude says, 'Hey honey, how much for all night?'
And I told him, 'Oh, maybe a thousand.' And he says,
laughing, 'For a thousand, I could buy me one to keep.'
Then I says, 'That might be so, honey, but then you would
have to feed her every day.' Then he laughs and says to
me, 'Okay. Okay. How about a hundred for an hour and
you feed yourself?' And I says, 'It's a done deal, dandy.' "

"Hey, foolish one, there have been many other important things in the world besides Bolsheviks, booze and
books."

"Yeah, I know, but that's all the little cells in my head
could understand."

"Hey, Willy, when you gonna dance with me?"

"When Tack Won turns loose of your thigh, Charlene."

"Oh, he's just warming his hands."

"Well, come on then, 'fore he burns it off . . ."

Bluefeather started seeing again as soon as he recognized his friend Willy's silly talk. He tilted the liter of homemade wine into Marsha's glass and then his. They toasted wordlessly, minds still foolishly shadowboxing.

A sound flowed from the bandstand now that none of The Section had ever heard before. All but one musician were playing flutes carved from the slender growths of the trees of light. The other one used two thin sticks of this same material to beat rectangular drums in strange rhythms.

Bluefeather, having been raised half the time around Taos Indian drums, felt the odd beat and the disturbing, chaotic rhythms from the flutes and the "whack, crack, click, click, boom, toc, toc, toc" from the long drums as part of the rhythm of the caves and its creatures. The slowly rising vibrations entered his blood and joined that of the liquid blended from the same plant that was the players' instruments.

Now they all began to dance. Slowly at first. Then imperceptibly the intensity of the music increased and so did their movements.

Bluefeather whirled Marsha as swiftly as possible, holding her body against his, and then they broke apart. He danced in a complete circle around the edges of the hall, waving his arms above his head. She did the same, whirling on the far side from him. They held a very special eye contact as he yelled at her in tongues from so far back in eroded history that they were naturally unrecognizable but truly felt by all, especially Marsha.

Perspiration soaked all their uniforms to charcoal color. Everyone slowed now as Bluefeather and Marsha continued their steps to the ever-wilder music. Their eyes locked on each other's bodies following the wild cave refrains. The rest of The Section, whether dancing in pairs or singly, slowed to watch.

Willy yelled, trying to echo those louder expressions of Bluefeather. Charlie, Pack and Sherry smiled with gratified personal knowledge. The others were infected with the musk that impregnated the air between the two dancing lovers. Had there ever been such a galvanic dual dance? Now they wove, shook, whirled, moving across the room, coming together with the sweat of flesh and fun. A rousing shout full of many meanings rent the room. At that second they quit all movement and clung together like long-separated souls of sameness. The orchestra suddenly stopped. It was time for the ten-hour sleep period. Everyone knew it. Everyone left.

"My God, I've missed you," Bluefeather said.

Marsha responded, "I've hurt for you so, I thought I'd perish."

"Don't ever leave me again. Never. Never. Never."

"Now. Now. Now?"

"Yes. Yes. Yes."

"Oh. Oh."

"Oh."

In the residual flush of the dance of splendor and the night of the princely pause they made love—Bluefeather Fellini and Marsha Korbell.

THIRTY-TWO

BLUEFEATHER HAD BREAKFAST READY FOR HER AT THE beginning of the awake time. They had danced and loved away any possible hangover. It was known only to Sherry that the last wine was of very low alcohol content, but so delicious one felt inebriated and exhilarated anyway.

Bluefeather had scrambled some fresh eggs with chopped ham and green chile. There was toast, jelly, orange juice and lots of hot coffee.

They ate and gossiped about the wondrous night.

All over God's Castle, section members were awakening from the sleep period. They all knew they had two more such times free to heal, rest, relax and adjust to the new sleeping-working schedule—to do whatever they needed most before training began for the final segment of their venture.

Bluefeather and Marsha made love again with no words intelligible except to longtime lovers. They lay in the bed, staring up at the ceiling, shoulders touching, until their breathing subsided. All their flesh and bones felt so relaxed that they were sure they could never be coaxed to move again.

Slowly, Bluefeather's mind-voice ticked at him: *This is wonderful lust of love, but what about her unexplained absence before the formidable undertaking? What excuse could there be for her neglectful silence—not even a phone call—when we had already shared laughter, love and survived disasters of life and death? What? What?*

Bluefeather showered, put on his clean uniform and opened the door out on the balcony as silently as possible. He looked across the barely lighted front gardens. The trees of light glowed little residues of illumination in spots. The distant environs of the cavern melted the soft light into a darkness far beyond any he had ever seen on the surface. He heard the distant, traveling calls of sonar location between screechers. The almost loving sounds moved on through the suet blackness toward the glow above the River of Radiance. The birds were going hunting.

The slowly diminishing talk between the massive creatures of both earth and air left him suddenly forlorn. It was all so very old. Such timeless mysteries of the aeons had transpired here that he felt for a moment he had never been conceived or gifted with thought. Infinitesimal. He listened for the far, far sound of distant planets for an explanation, but he couldn't hear them audibly.

He physically shook his body. He stretched the strength of the muscles in his arms and an unrestricted feeling of power and optimism suddenly permeated his being. As if on signal, the clocks of cavern time switched on the abundant electric lights and the inspiring distant sight of God's throne gave credence to his living self. Regardless of the dangers or restrictions, he decided to visit and touch the throne during this twenty-hour period. His mind was afire with the sudden shining scheme.

Then he felt Marsha's arm in his and her head leaning possessively into his shoulder. For just an instant, the awesome lighting spectacle causing the swift alteration of his feeling and her touch was everything. One.

Then the primitive parts of his humanness transcended

the eternal, and he pulled loose, stepping back from her, saying, "You sold me out to Korbell, didn't you? You broke a sacred vow and revealed our mission to the bastard. You told him our secrets, didn't you? Even after he, himself, had agreed that my knowledge of the bullion was all I needed to tell him for now. You told him about it all, didn't you?"

With eyes like round turquoise, she tried to interject, "Blue, oh, Blue, for God's sake. Listen to me. It's all going to . . ."

"Don't lie to me, Marsha. I know. I can tell. You've done it. Don't the lives of your lover and friends, the knowledge of the ages mean more to you than . . . than . . . ?"

Before he could say Korbell, she turned with sudden resentment, saying, "You have a right to be upset, I guess, but I don't have to explain or excuse Korbell to you or anyone else."

"The hell you don't. He no longer amounts to a fart. All his real estate, money, power and political briberies are nothing. Nothing. They don't even amount to a whisper in the center of a hurricane, not a single splinter in the Amazon Forest compared to the offerings of this great cavern. Don't you understand the difference? Can't you see . . . see what's important? What's lasting? What's falsely temporary? Well, can't you?"

"Don't sell me short like that, you unreasonable bastard. I've given you all I have to give and more."

"Well then, answer me, just answer me, Marsha. Now. You can't blame me for insisting . . . before we leave for the river. You owe it to me, just as everyone in The Section owes loyalty to one another. It's our survival—and the survival of all this." He swept his arm in an arc, pointing at what he felt was the obvious.

"All right. Yes. I did lead you on, reporting to him how highly I felt about you and your abilities. I did tell Korbell what you told me. He cajoled me. He intimidated me with kindness, the loyalty to family and all that crap. Then he threatened me with every known torture. His daughter? Can you believe it? His only adopted daughter? Do you care about that? Do you care about me? Or do you just care about yourself, Bluefeather Fellini?"

"Did that son of a bitch abuse you? Tell me? Huh? Huh?"

"No. They drugged me and I suppose pulled it out of me."

"You don't know, for Christsake? You don't know for sure exactly what you told them?"

"I think I know. Of course I know, because they didn't bother me anymore. Just the opposite. I was coddled, pampered and had full cooperation and offers of anything I wished. So I asked for the helicopter to fly me to you."

"Bullshit, Marsha. You're here to spy for him. He'd never let you come back, knowing you'd let it slip out one way or the other. You were leading me on and setting me up all that time with the Godchucks in Cerrillos and Santa Fe, weren't you?"

"I've told you the truth, you bull-headed jerk. That's the best I can do."

"Well, that's pretty damned good. Do you think I believe for one second that you're on our side? What kind of fool do you take me for, anyway?"

"A big one. The biggest one I've ever known," she screamed, "except for myself. I'm not only a fool, but a blind one at that, to have ever believed in you."

"You believing in me? Now doesn't that frost the governor's balls. Hah."

"You go to hell, Bluefeather Fellini, and stay there until you grow horns out your rear." She charged the door and slammed it heavy as a dropped anvil.

He turned, looking outward again and ground his teeth, breathing like an exhausted marathon runner and gasped out, "Dumb. Dumb. Dumb." But he wasn't sure whom or what he was describing.

Then he made up his mind, at least all of it that would allow him access. He would somehow believe in her until proof solid as the star core was revealed. He must. He wanted to take back the harsh tone of his last words to her, but those words could never be returned to his tongue. He would have to show her some way how much he cared, so that his anger would be ignored and eventually forgotten.

Marsha was in her room furiously combing at her hair. Then she slowed the motion and wished she had somehow muted the anger in her voice. In truth, he really had the right to at least question her loyalty. She had expected him to feel it—not have to hear it. She took a shower, soaping more than needed.

THIRTY-THREE

OVER SHERRY'S PROTESTATIONS, BLUEFEATHER FINALLY got permission to go to the throne alone. She insisted he take hand grenades as well as his semiautomatic, a machete and a handgun. The exhilaration of the trip caused his worried war with Marsha to subside for now.

The endlessly changing beauty of multiple-colored formations and crystallizations would have caused the best of the Great Spirit's helpers to skip a week of work in rapture. There was a ridge of rock animals—suggestions of lions, elephants and horses—all walking through deep cake frosting in a combination of perpetual motion and never-ending stillness.

He saw the room full of great rock horns, in shapes that suggested all those ancient musical instruments that signaled battles, crownings and celebrations from great occasions of the past. He could hear their trumpeting across hills and through the streets and archways of history.

Dazzling jewels gleamed under his hand-carried light that only angels would be allowed to wear. Then he came to the hill of pearls. There were thousands, from small as a pinhead to the circumference of a grapefruit. For thousands of centuries, the ceiling above had dripped the calcite just right to form perfectly smooth, opaque ovals of indescribable colors—hints of soft tan, a touch of violet under his hand light. Some had a tiny suggestion of white blended into grey-blue green. They all had been formed around a seed blown down here, or a speck of foreign rock, or even a tiny particle of an insect's bone. They lay in slight indentations, like stone birds' nests, and had been formed by the dripping over unmeasurable time.

Bluefeather, without conscious thought, picked one up and put it in his pocket for Marsha. Even this minute removal of the minuscule pearl caused him to feel like he had committed a sacrilege against the insides of Mother Earth. Fifty yards on past the field of pearls, he found the hill of sea urchins. Their rounded forms bristled with short, sharp stalactites of a yellowish orange similar in color to the coat of a golden palomino stallion.

Then he came to a natural flow bridge like those in some national parks in Utah and Arizona. He had cautiously crossed and was now settled on conquering the hypnotic variety of views and getting on to the great throne itself.

His hunter's blood caused him to hear the unmistakable "whoosh whoosh" of the screechers' huge wings. He froze his movement, then slowly turned toward the sound so there would be no noticeable sudden action to be picked up by the land-air creatures' sensitivity. There were three of them between him and the searching lights of God's Castle. Two of them carried a fish of perhaps a hundred pounds in their claws. The third one had either dined at the River of Radiance or intended to share with its companions, for it carried nothing.

Bluefeather held his breath in fearful obedience as they air-lumbered past. He turned his head with them, eyes locked on the follower. They were just past when the last one circled away as the leaders moved on up and out of sight. It came circling slowly above Bluefeather with the knobby antenna atop its head moving, searching for him. The edges of the bridge seemed to be slightly distorting the returning echoes, but the screecher knew something alien was there. It made a low dip, then swerved back up to a half circle. A paralyzing sound emitted from its throat that seemed to send waves of unseen wire, piercing the air, flesh, stone, everything.

Bluefeather knew the searcher had honed in very close on his hidden spot. It was just him and the screecher now. The outer world, the galaxies of stars, the universe and the Cavern of Marvels did not exist. Only the two of them and infinity were real. There was nothing else. His heart made noises that a deaf-mute could have heard—so it felt and sounded, to him.

Now the screecher, with wings spread and sloped to stop his flight, landed on a prominence, tilting its sightless head from one side to the other with the beak bigger and sharper than a factory bellows. It listened, seeing with the echoes the exact forms all around, smelling Bluefeather's exact shape, as well. Silence. More silence. A forever silence. Then the head slanted with the receptor knob directed straight ahead. Bluefeather knew that the silence of Pharaoh's tomb was being split apart by echoing emissions sent back to the screecher that were beyond his own hearing but clear as cathedral bells to the bird-animal.

Bluefeather waited for that immeasurable, instinctive movement between the hunter and its prey that decides which attacks first, which lives. He jerked the pin from a grenade, counting off as the bird crouched to launch its leaping charge. He hurled it in an arc at the bird as it arose. It was just hitting the cave floor to spring forward again when the grenade dropped, exploding under its breast, knocking it over and crippling one wing. The screecher struggled upright, nevertheless, with the weight of the dragging wing slowing it and clawed closer and closer to Bluefeather.

He jerked his finger on the trigger of the rifle as swiftly and smoothly as all his years of training and nature had taught him. The bullets pierced the sunken area just above the protruding, foot-thick breastbone in the spot where the neck joined it. It slowed. It stopped. Then came on anyway.

He desperately, but with precision, jammed another clip in the rifle and concentrated on the antenna knob. He missed the first shot because of the screecher's movement, but now he could feel out through space right with the bullet as it thudded into and through flesh.

The screecher was only a couple of short, jumping jerks away from him now, but he had thrown its radar system off and it leapt on past him, one huge claw raking at the top of the rock formation under which Bluefeather threw himself. Then it turned, wobbling out of balance, pecking with its beak in space toward him. It reached for him with one claw, using the other foot and the unharmed wing, with its own retractable swords, to make a final launch and devour him like a bug.

Bluefeather grabbed for another ammunition clip, rolling down a slope just as the screecher leaped, dropping on the exact spot Bluefeather had just vacated. He lost the clip in his tumbling fall but leaped up, pulling out the razor-sharp machete. The screecher slipped sideways, awkwardly, incapacitated from its many wounds, down toward him. Bluefeather leaped as far as his legs could possibly take him to avoid being mashed into a smear by the two-ton brute.

He was struck by only a glancing blow from the screecher's good wing. Even so, the contact knocked him a good six feet sideways, but his surging body chemicals of conflict enabled him to recover and charge on top of the fluttering beast's back. He started slashing and stabbing with vicious abandon and even after it was still and dead, he stood on its back and stabbed, over and over, with the bloody machete, until the realization of certain survival caused him to stop and fall down on the soft, helpless wing of the screecher until he could breathe and think clearly again. Close.

He reached out, his chest still heaving, and patted the velvet-soft wing, gasping out, "I'm so very sorry. Please forgive me, my dear, blind brother."

As he walked through the glazed underworld toward the throne, the high from battling with the screecher subsided. His mind-voice spoke to him, *Is this entity you just killed a beginning thinker like mankind once was? Is it being driven by a genetic force away from the watered field of stones to seek the outer world? Of course, it couldn't survive there a day. Someone would kill it, just as you have, whether it be self-defense or not. It is not even settled whether it becomes an animal of the ground or a fowl of the air. It will take scores upon scores of thousands of years yet, before that is decided. Ponder on it some, Bluefeather. You are supposed to be the creature of thought and reason, so start living up to your abilities, your gifts, your privileges, you foolish man.*

Ponder he did, but then the elegance of the surroundings overwhelmed thought with feelings of reverence. So he knelt his blood-splattered body on a smooth parapet and said aloud, "Ah, Great Spirit, I'm doing the best I know how toward fulfilling my commitments to those two villainous forces of efficient greed, Dolby and Korbell. I ask you, oh Great One—and smart one, too—what are the limits of my obligations to these causes? Illuminate my thinking brain. Enlighten my soul, oh Great Tutor. Kick my dumb ass into righteous and proper obedience. I am lost on the subject of those two satanic bastards. Help me find the invisible path of nobility. Then make me run up and down that son of a . . . son of a saint, until my ability to cogitate is no longer impaired and my butt is so tired it's bouncing off my boot heels. You got it down correctly, oh Splendid One? Be sure of it now. Please."

He felt better as he walked between the two immense calcite curtains filled with enough oxidized iron to give them an orangish lustre the same as the remarkable throne. He was there.

He slowly raised his head, absorbing the beauty by degrees so he would be sure of containing it. Up. Up. Up. His eyes moved right on up to the seat of the throne of God's Castle. What was that way up there?

He turned and carefully walked backward so he would have a better angle of vision. He turned and tilted his head and eyes upward again. "What is that speck defiling the seat of the great one? Is it a fly turd?" he questioned. "Is it the droppings of a sickly mouse? Huh? What is that tiny pile up there that stinks like all the sewers of Bombay, all the garbage of New York City and the combined flatulence from all the beans ever raised and eaten in the whole states of New Mexico, Oklahoma and West Texas? What is it, I repeat?"

"Dear brudder, it is Dancing Bear, your friend and spirit guide." Dancing Bear kicked his soft leather moccasins back and forth where they hung over the throne so small and fragile-looking. Bluefeather had to take a look with his binoculars to be certain he was there.

"What are you doing on that throne, you smarmy pretender? How could you be so presumptuous as to think you're the Authority? Come down from there for your chastisement. Remember my last begging words to you? Huh? I asked with all humility for your constant help in this . . ." he waved an arm all around, "this world of caves and monstrous events, and now, you show up, playing at being the Authority. The next thing I know you will be setting at His desk, feet up, smoking His cigars."

"He don't smoke."

"Well you'll be reading His mail then."

"He don't get no mail. He get important news on the TP."

"No. No. No. Tell me you lie, tell me my ears are deceiving me. Authority just can't get his communication from all the people of the universe on the TV."

"No. No. No. Like you say, dear brudder, No, no, no again. He gets messages from TP—T like in tap dance and P like in pardner. That means telepathic. Now you savvy?"

"Telepathic, huh? Well that makes more sense to me."

"That's what I'm here for, dear brudder."

"What's that again?"

Dancing Bear stood up and leapt out on the curtain, sliding down its rippling curves on the seat of his leather breeches, yelling, "Wheee, Wahhaaa, hey yehhh and whoa now." He pushed upright on his feet and did a Balinese dance, waving and undulating his arms and hands, jerking his head from side to side like his neck was out of socket, bending his knees and pointing his feet sideways. Then he bounded up on top of a column about six feet from Bluefeather, crouching there on one foot, saying proudly, "I learn that one in Bali."

"I could tell. I could tell."

"Now, dear brudder, now what can your kind helper and friend forever do for you?"

"Well, friend forever, I got lots of chores that could use plenty of help. Let me count the ways, as the poet person said. First of all I have a broken heart. I busted up with Marsha—well . . . we had a terrible fight—I guess we broke up. I'm pretty sure Korbell has washed her brain plumb out of her head. I got Dolby setting up there on top the outer world trying to decide whether to open this entire damn Cavern of Marvels up to the scientists and tourists and thereby get richer than all the world's banks combined and nearly as famous as Alexander the Great and Shakespeare. Again, he might decide to blast the whole thing shut for that 'forever' you just mentioned, leaving us down here so long the word 'forever' is meaningless. On top of all that, I've got many friends to worry about and the screechers and the goddamned fallen, collapsed star and a palace full of olden coots to boot. Now, Mr. Bear, let me tell you that I've spoken of only the beginning. The River of Radiance has got more wonders yet to behold and conquer than seven thousand erupting volcanoes, on a world bigger than the sky, composed of twenty-four-carat gold, redwood trees, strawberry plants and poison ivy . . ."

"Wheee whooo-eee. You got perty near close to 'bout half my problems. We got to have a talk."

"Wait just a damn minute. That isn't even half of it."

"Well then, we got to have a bi-i-i-g talk."

"Yeah, I suppose so. I don't have any idea what Korbell has planned for us."

Dancing Bear perched on the other foot now, squinted his eyes and tried his best to look worried, saying, "Now, that is a big worry right there, dear brudder Blue. My most profound sympathies are offered."

"Bear, old buddy, spirit guide and forever friend, it is not sympathy I gotta have, it is wisdom I crave. Wisdom of the ages. Wisdom of the Great Spirit, wisdom from the Great Dancing Bear."

"You beginning to sound just like me, so maybe some good judgment has possessed you. I say to you sometimes this truth, dear brudder, the cement is still wet. Nothing is set for sure yet. Maybe you know many answers when someone else makes their decisions. Huh? Huh? Maybe . . . ?"

"Oh, dear Authority, please enlighten your servile associate before I'm doomed. He talks into vapors and thinks with his head in a bucket of worms. Help this poor, lost spirit."

Bluefeather sat down on the bottom of the cave awhile,

staring between his feet. "You know what, Bear? I'm not getting anything from you but conversation. I've prayed to the Creator and begged his associate, who is a lower-class one for sure, but part of the 'Big Deal' just the same. All I can show for my efforts is a brain slowly spinning into numbness and a heart cold as early morning icicles. Your congeniality is appreciated, but your lack of solid counsel is disheartening. I shall by all that's holy or unholy do whatever it takes by my own damned self." Bluefeather stood. He picked up his rifle and started walking, winding up and down and around toward the distant comforts of his companions, saying back over his shoulder, "Good-bye ol' dancing pardner. It has been interesting knowing you."

Dancing Bear leaped from one stalagmite and pagoda pillar to another, playing his flute, doing war, peace, rain and fertility stomps. He turned somersaults in midair and invented songs and poems in nineteen languages, but Bluefeather Fellini moved on up toward his problematic destiny without glancing even once at the great performer.

THIRTY-FOUR

SHERRY LED BLUEFEATHER THROUGH THE CAVE. EACH had a hand light, although they didn't need them as yet. This cave was dry. No moisture followed the cracks of the surface earth to this lower level.

Then they came to another stone door. Bluefeather wondered what it was with these accumulators—the gatherers of the world's treasures—that impelled them to hide their acquisitions behind iron and steel doors of such magnitude. They all seemed to guard their protective doors with heavily armed little armies as well—only existing in prisons of riches belonging to others. He decided that fear and vanity made up their greed. What else?

He was so accustomed to Sherry, Dolby and Korbell opening these fortress-like entrances that he didn't even watch as she did it. Instead, he noticed how small her waist was and how voluptuous the wide perfect curve of her hips as they slanted back into her strong, graceful legs, moving like perfected machines of flesh under the soft cotton cloth coveralls. No wonder Pack was shell-shocked over this woman of such classic beauty, courage and such dedicated intelligence.

He must stop thinking these compliments to hear, and observe, the message of their sojourn. The cave suddenly

forked so that now there were three openings. They took
the left one. It was a gloomy passage and there was a smell
that Bluefeather recognized instantly. It was very subtle
at first. Then Sherry shone the light along a wall of hand-
dug niches, each about fourteen inches high and seven
feet long. In every one there was a body. Most had a
burial raiment of a canvas-type sheet. The hands were
folded in skeletal exactness over the chest of bones, and
the skulls peered upward at the limestone a few inches
above them, in perpetuity.

"These are the honorable dead. Those who died of natural causes, accidents or attacks from beasts of the cavern.
Sherry stated this as matter-of-factly as a tour guide, and
she swiftly cast her light down the other wall, revealing
the same sort of open tombs, saying, "Just the last few
years, Dolby has allowed burial at the River of Radiance—
which is a form of cremation, as you will soon see."

He had seen so much of death and dying in his young
life that Bluefeather only felt a loneliness here. The bones
were present, still in their burial cloth, but the spirits had
departed. He could feel no vibration or residue of ectoplasm.

The next—the central cave—was different. It was a
shrine for any anthropologist on earth. "This is mine," she
said proudly. There were bones scattered about a room
that had been chosen because it widened suddenly and
was extensive enough to hold the huge remains of creatures unlike any he could imagine. Sherry had completed
the reconstruction of one that was only about four feet
high, but with its tail it must have been thirty feet long.
The head was big as an elephant's and longer than a croc-
odile's. There were only three ample neck vertebrae.
Bluefeather reasoned that if there had been more, it could
never have held up the weight of the elongated head. The
teeth were alligator-like, except much longer, and the
tusks were about the size of an ancient Siberian tiger's.

Noticing his interest, Sherry explained, "This is one of the few carnivorous animals we find at the river."

Bluefeather was a fairly brave man, but the thought of contesting one of these malevolent-looking beasts made the perspiration form on his upper lip, his heart rattle and his rectum pinch down like a python's throat.

She continued, "I have, of course, recorded proper technical names for all the creatures we've been fortunate enough to identify. This one is named in layman's terms, the chomper."

"Apropos as Jack the Ripper."

"Thank you, Blue. Oh, come here."

He followed the path through the deliberately scattered cluster of bones from many species to the outer edges of the extensive room. There was a creature with tiny, almost transparent, bones. In fact, Bluefeather was not sure whether they were bones or hard ligaments, so he asked Sherry about it.

"You've missed your true calling, Blue. These structures are in fact a combination of bone and ligament-like material. In the living animal they are translucent and only become partially opaque after death. This one specimen has taken over a year of my life to get its form laid out properly."

"My Lord, it must be as big as a mastodon."

"Far bigger, and almost as rare."

"Would it be an imposition to ask?"

"Its technical name? No, of course not. We call it the Khyber. If you think of the Khyber Pass and its great battles and intrigue over the centuries, you will possibly understand the why of the name."

For now he did not. Later he would.

"Blue, I could happily—and in fact, do hope to—spend the rest of my life right here, but now we must move on to the third cave." There was hesitation in her voice, but she led him forward almost too energetically.

Then her steps slowed, and she beamed their way totally with the hand light. Bluefeather instantly switched
his on. Now he felt the spiritual turmoil of earthbound
spirits. They were there in the room of killing—of murder. The bodies had been tossed about in piles. These
skeletons lay across one another as if they had been
dropped at random from a rooftop. The skin was dried
and preserved here and there on some of the human chas-
sis.

Sherry just held her light in one place, although there
was a slight quiver to the beam. Bluefeather wandered
around with his spot, seeing the bullet holes in some
skulls. Others had been bashed in from some heavy object; a few heads were completely severed. He could hear
screams and cries for release from somewhere far away,
but he couldn't reach there. Torment. Torment of the
trapped.

He turned his eyes toward her. She was already staring
at him. She read the questions projected from him and
knew she must give some kind of an answer. She sensed
he would not settle for less than a true one.

"These are the rebellious—those who attempted to return to the outer world. Some were rule-breakers who
would have jeopardized all of Dolby's sacrifices and
dreams of contribution to the world of heretofore unknown knowledge, unheard-of wealth and a surplus of
mysteries and revelations from faraway space."

She talked on in a monotone that Bluefeather refused
to acknowledge. It was a speech she had prepared for a
very long time. One she had memorized for whomsoever
was chosen to lead the last expedition before the final
decision was made on the disposition of the Cavern of
Marvels. She was performing the duty she had trained and
prepared for, for so long. But it didn't work with Bluefeather Fellini.

He placed his light on the floor between piles of the

dead, stepping carefully nearer the woman. Her face was
powerfully lighted from below so that the whites of her
eyes and the forms of her living bones under the light
chocolate skin waited for his reaction. She knew she
would have to face him someday, but she dreaded it all
the same. It was, however, going to be now. Here.

"Sherry, oh, Sherry, how do I speak to you of such
things? Can you really believe that these bones lie to us
any more than those left after the Fall of Rome, the Ho-
locaust, or The Crusades? What are the odds, my darling
woman, of Dolby sparing us any more than these—" he
waved his arm around, "these wasted ones here in this
room of rock?"

He waited. She stared on at him, immobile of body,
but her full lips were moving slightly, trying to give voice
to tangled thoughts.

Bluefeather, seeing her hurting from her terrible turmoil, went on, "I know that a trainload of reasons could
be made for this—this taking of lives. It can be, and has
been, said all through recorded history that it means nothing to take the life of a thousand to give greater glory to
a million or to kill a million to benefit a billion, but when
has it ever really happened? Is it any more likely to happen here than at Buchenwald or Devil's Island? Is it?"

"I don't know about those things you speak of. I can't
see the final results defined. But . . . here . . . here I know
only a portion of the good that could come to all the
world, and it is enormous in its ramifications of knowledge
leading to more knowledge, of the whole of the world
realizing how truly miraculous it is that life is marching
on and on, evolving toward individuals—entire societies—
that can think, reason, invent, compose, laugh, love
and . . ."

"Please. Please don't think me rude for interrupting,
but I, too, have already seen all those possibilities you
speak of, and we have yet to enter the really bravura part

of the expedition. I will not cause you to despair again. I will move on with all the energy I've got, letting my actions come from the beliefs that are presented to me."

"I know you will, Blue. You've already proven that." Suddenly, she stepped to him—pressing her head into his chest a moment—then raised her face to his, saying in a voice that was partly from ancestors so far back in time that the generations were unfathomable, "I don't know either, but we must not let these thoughts out of this room. Ever."

Bluefeather touched her tenderly on the cheek with the flats of his fingers, saying, "You can trust everyone in this room to keep the secret with silent tongues, except the two of us, and we don't have any other choice."

"I couldn't have said that much better myself," she smiled.

"I'm sure you could say it much, much, better. However, I'll settle for breaking even on this deal. How about you?"

"Even?" She thought a moment. "Yes, even would be fine," she said. "Even means everyone comes out equal, right?"

"That's about it, but I think the deceiving odds of it happening are about the same as Dolby turning into a missionary and Korbell into an archangel."

They marched along jauntily now, arms linked, heading together toward the palace that Dolby built.

Sherry said, "I feel so goddamned saintly I could lead a church choir."

"I feel somewhat divine my own dumb self," Bluefeather replied.

They chuckled together like two misbegotten cherubs.

THIRTY-FIVE

THE SECTION SHAPED UP FOR THE FINAL PHASE OF THE Dolby expedition. They trained by alternately walking and running two hours each awake period; then they did calisthenics, cleaned weapons, ate gourmet food and mostly enjoyed one another's company.

Pack had taken a shortcut to heaven. He had his dream of Sherry looking at and speaking to him. His section comrades were shaping up, eager and ready. Even Ratchett was extra happy. He had been allowed to study in the gourmet kitchen and help the Olders prepare the meals. The aged and the youthful had their own separate but patterned training methods and areas. They were still helpful, courteous and pleasant at all times, but there was no fraternization between the "inners" and the "outers," with one exception—Shia, the young Asiatic lady, who respected Sherry close to worship and somehow escaped censure for her attendance thereby. In fact, Shia had been accepted as Sherry's assistant by all. The unheard-of order could only have come down from and been approved by Dolby.

Bluefeather only got glimpses of Steinberg, the palace commander. He could be seen standing taller than any down here. He was thin, but appeared in fine physical shape for his age—or any age for that matter. He led the Olders in their exercises with weapons and gave orders to the leader of the Youngers, as well. He wore a beard of iron grey and a mustache that was still as naturally dark as it had been forty years past.

Curiosity did nothing to diminish Bluefeather's astonishment that Steinberg was Dolby's only remaining friend below. They seemed so different at a distance. One thing was for sure: his being down here in charge, and the only one ever allowed above, proved beyond any question that he was an extremely loyal and tough entity.

The Section had adjusted now to the twenty-ten awake and asleep pattern so that it seemed as natural as any schedule they had ever followed above.

Bluefeather checked with the stables. He was amazed over and over at how the cattle, chickens, ducks and geese all seemed to thrive on the mulch feed made from the trees of light. The mules were shiny and alert.

"Hey, Willy, you got your mules ready to take us fishing?"

Willy said. "These mules are overtrained, overfed and underbred."

"Those last words are all that fit you, my dear ol' pardner."

Charlie stopped brushing one long ear and joined in. "Don't listen to the old renegade, Blue. He's been visiting Jody on one shift, then Estrella the next, then Charlene—all in turn."

"That's all I been capable of—just visitin'."

Bluefeather said, grinning, "Well, ol' pardner, I better not hear that the other men are missing their turns because of your greediness. Bad for morale, you know?"

"I'm safe, Blue. Haven't you noticed—all your section boys go around smiling like they just discovered ice cream and cake?"

"I thought it was better than dessert the first time, myself," Charlie added.

"My gosh, is that all you guys think about?" Bluefeather asked, smiling.

"Naw, I think about goin' fishing once in awhile," said Willy. "Hey Blue, they tell me the underground river holds some whoppers."

"Yeah. They're whoppers all right. They never quit bitin'," Bluefeather assured him.

Bluefeather joined in a few more fun and silly remarks before going to make his last call before dinner.

He knocked on Marsha's door and the voice came from just the other side, "Who is it?"

"Blue."

She slowly, wordlessly opened the door. After a moment she pulled it back for him to enter. He walked around the spacious room, then sat down.

"I don't know what's right to say, but I gotta say something," he uttered.

"I think we've already talked enough . . . too much, in fact," she said.

"Yeah, well, I agree."

She had just washed and dried her hair. Now she sat down in front of the dresser mirror with her back to him. She had on a robe and nightgown of peach-colored satin. She could see his face reflected in the mirror. He could see both her face and the back of her auburn hair as she combed it. Her special feminine movements made him warm with desire and a craving to erase all the harsh words and thoughts forever.

He had that feeling of déjà vu that comes from half remembering an almost identical actuality. He knew he had sat like this in torment, wanting her, sometime before, but couldn't peg it exactly. He could smell her from somewhere long ago. It was her true body perfume that teased his memory through his olfactory senses. There was not any use torturing himself further.

"Might as well get to it, Marsha. We go on down into the caverns day after tomorrow. It's the 'Big Do,' you know? A lot of people have died down there attempting to solve and solidify a hold on that world. You have no idea how many," he said softly. "I told you what I saw on the film, but the rest of it—the real thing—is something else altogether, and . . ."

"Well if you're concerned about my dedication to this project . . ."

"Yes, I am concerned about everyone's dedication. One misstep, just one person sloughing off, and the consequences and the loss are too much to contemplate. Do take my word on this."

She put the comb down and walked over to him. Her body lines showed smoothly under the slippery fabric. She stood in front of him with one hand on a hip. Her waist, even with his line of vision, and the faint scent of her perfume so near made it very difficult for him to hear what she was saying. Lesser men had been doomed by these simple gestures. Armies and political careers and kingdoms had fallen to this essence that spoke without words.

"I will obey all commands with the best of my ability and be alert for any danger from any place at all times."

He lifted his body and, reluctantly, his eyes as well, saying, "No one can ask more." He started out of the room, stopped, turned and spoke again. "To try and pull off the imagined impossible is to leave oneself wide open to both great and minuscule forces."

She replied, almost flatly, "It seems the impossible is our motto. We're already experienced at that, aren't we?"

"Yes. Yes, we are, sort of, but it's only a beginning, as we'll all soon see." He was talking at an angle away from her now, fighting to keep from whirling and lunging back to her body.

He went out the door, aching like an abscessed tooth from the pearly floor to the top of his dark-maned head. He said to himself, with his mind-voice, *Bluefeather Fellini, you are one dumb sucker, but you courageously, and at great sacrifice, listened, heard and absorbed every word the woman said, but . . . but it's not relieving that half-raised staff just under your belt buckle now, is it?*

Shut up, shit head, he replied rudely to himself.

THIRTY-SIX

MULES AND HUMAN PACKS WERE LOADED; WEAPONS were cleaned, oiled, prepared. Bluefeather stood behind Pack and Sherry; Marsha and Shia were immediately behind him.

Pack voiced the roll call, "Estrella."

"Here."

"Jody."

"Here."

"Charlene." And on down the list: "Garcia, H.; Waters, C.; Ruger, W.; Moosha, Z.; Tack Won, G.; Ratchett, J.; Dunning, R.; Kowalski, B.; Kubeck, A.; O'Malley, B.; Davis, C.; Fielder, M.; Osaka, M." All answered with a resounding "Here."

Pack said, "Your Commander Fellini will address you."

Bluefeather said, "This next moment we move out on one of the greatest adventures in the history of humankind. Let's go get the job done and celebrate a thousand years. Are you ready?"

There were cheers of such exuberance that Pack immediately strung out the train and started it moving. It would be downhill all the way and only a five-hour trip.

•   •   •

At about the halfway point, a string of screechers moved down parallel with them toward the widening otherworldly light emanating from the river. The entire section stopped, immobile, except for their eyes, which followed the leaping and soaring of the massive creatures. The last one leapt in the air and circled, pointing its knobby antenna toward them. The mules' small hooves shifted around nervously, their ears worked constantly as their eyes rolled. The Section's hands tightened on their weapons, perspiring. A call from a screecher just reaching the River of Radiance was heard, and the beasts sailed on down to seek food in more abundance. Easier breathing returned.

As the panorama of the deep widened, a profound feeling of discovery, of stimulation, of privilege overtook them all. The natural light spreading here thousands of feet underground was so old it transcended the seemingly impossible by such a margin that they rapidly prepared to accept almost any vision. It was a good thing. Rounding a curve in the trail, they could see occasional geysers of fire across miles of steamy water and eerie patches of many-hued greens and blues. The steam clouds were moving violet above, radiating slowly over vibrating rainbows. The musty smell of ancient, heretofore unknown life-forms permeated everything now. The Section would soon adjust to this, too, but for now, every step, every breath, every nerve, every glance, was the very old becoming the very new.

Then the trail widened and Sherry said, "We'll take a short break here. It's only a couple hundred yards on to the elevators."

With the vision and awareness of the ethereal light came primitive sounds of living, loving and death rattles, creating an everlasting symphony of the inexplicable. Bluefeather had heard, and felt, a similar music only on the sides of Taos Mountain.

Hector Garcia said, as if speaking to the keeper of the pearly gates, "*En divina Luz.*"

Someone translated, "The divine light."

Marsha's eyes were as wide as they could be by nature, trying to pull it all in at once. She uttered in awe, "As Charles Darwin said of the Amazon Jungle, 'It is a vast, untidy, hothouse.'"

Someone else muttered in a voice suggesting the sacred, "It's a festival of fire."

Even Willy Ruger only whispered, "Grandy dandy."

Bluefeather said to Sherry so that only she could hear, "I think you had better explain a few things to The Section."

She understood. Sherry was the only one present who had been here before—many times, in fact. But even now on this new pilgrimage, in an attempt at a final penetration of the "Hills of Hell," her own body juices were playing intermezzos of trills.

"May I have your attention, please." Hypnotized eyes slowly turned away from the sight of all sights. She paused a moment, then said, "First, as I've told you before, my suggestions are only theories spoken with my best professional judgment. There seems little doubt that the light scattered all about the river and its environs is that of minute organisms and heavily condensed luminescent bacteria. The occasional increase in illumination comes from the trees of light impregnated with these bacteria. Some of the surface algae as well as the bush-trees also have unexplained qualities of luminosity that flare in nearby locations for several hours after an eruption of fire. It has never been identified like this before, but many scientists suspect there will be such discoveries on the great reefs of the ocean someday.

"The earth we now stand in was supposedly formed about five billion years ago by gases. It is guessed that the first upright animals came from the great rift of Africa some three and a half million years ago. What you are about to witness here is probably just as old, or new—a million or so years, one way or the other."

Sherry stopped a moment, looking across the vast inner panorama of seething elements, searching for a simple way to explain it. "Well . . . you know that Rome fell in A.D. 476. The gap between that seemingly ancient time and this minute is so inconsequential here that the greatest of all scientists would be unable to discern any change in the evolution of the creatures we are about to visit."

"As for trying now to explain this, this . . ." she waved her hand across the River of Radiance, ". . . we'll just have to experience the best we can as we move into the river regions. Let me add one thing more. We gaze upon the living primeval."

The acceptance of Sherry's explanation of the entities of the caverns and lights was surprisingly immediate, but Bluefeather knew from the film he had watched that the wonders and danger they had experienced successfully could be destroyed instantly by what was upcoming.

He added to Sherry's talk, "In any museum of natural history you can see models and reconstructed bones of creatures from a time in the past fully as exotic and natural to their wetlands environment as these we have been seeing and those we are about to encounter. Soon, you will realize they are a properly evolved part of their surrounding elements. All I ask is this: Prepare your minds for openness. I already know your courage. So there is nothing else to ask. Thank you. Let's go see it all."

They moved on now to the elevators. There were two heavy iron ones here under a latticework of steel that went down, surrounding and protecting them. The stone barracks and its compound below were enclosed in a protective arc of steel all the way to the river. Three-foot-long, ice-pick-sharp spikes protruded from every cross section, forming formidable and sometimes deathly bar-

riers to any charging or flying invader. The entire system
was wired to electrify as well, though now it was seldom
used. The primitives had learned the lessons of sharp steel
and electric pain, and had somehow spread the message.
With all of that, the human inhabitants could easily see
out between the spaces of the lattice.

It took three trips for Willy and Charlie to deliver the
packed mules but only one trip for the rest of The Section. There were perhaps twenty Olders as caretakers of
the last outpost and eight or ten Youngers. All had waited
and been trained most of their lives for this final assault
on the river's treasures so fervently protected by fire and
other sweet and devilish things.

They were there. It was millions and millions of years
since their ancestors had crawled out of some ancient surface water probably similar to that just below. Now they
had arrived to fulfill, or fail at, a destiny begun so infinitely
small and so immeasurably long ago.

It had been a hell of a trip for humankind—about three
and a half million years, in fact—and now it would reach
its apex in only a few more days.

Bluefeather could hardly wait to see the end of it. But
first the mules must be put up, fed, watered and brushed.
Each of The Section was assigned small, spare rooms with
running water and a chemical toilet. Dolby might be a
defiler of humans, but he insisted no unnecessary pollut-
ants touch the river or its air. Here, where the wires from
far above ended, they cooked with electricity. Here, too,
the last contact with any sort of so-called civilized world
ended. Outside this iron cobwebbed fortress was the
other mystery, filled with nuances of the incomprehensible.

Sherry, shadowed by Shia, retired for a short time to
write in her notebooks. All the others were unpacked.
After while, Ratchett called them to the outdoor dining
room. They fed on fresh fish, some kind of meat they had

never tasted before and other dishes of vegetables and fruits that were frozen or dried. There was little talk during the first meal here, just low mumbling and stares out through the lattice.

The weather, or temperature, was constant here; even the flares of fire seemed regularly timed. Bluefeather figured the temperature at about seventy degrees here at the outpost. He asked Sherry, and she verified that he was close. The temperature fluctuated only a degree or two, which was caused occasionally by The Unholy taking a cleansing breath for the entire living organism of the cavern. Even so, he figured that quite a rise from the fifty-eight degrees at the Mimbres burial chamber in the Cave of the Dead.

As the last one finished eating, Sherry said to Bluefeather, "Well, let's get the obligatory tour in motion, commander."

She was suddenly all professional anthropologist, getting things that were mundane to her out of the way so the paper and bone chase could continue.

The entire compound was covered by the iron latticework right to the river's edge. Here and there, in proper places, were sliding doors of the same material. It was like an extra-long circus tent except that it was made of latticed iron. She showed them the boat ramp, where they toured the shallow steel craft—the special one they would use for their last voyage, which was encircled in cork all around its middle. They would learn later its purpose. The inside was covered solid with asbestos underneath a rubber matting securing it all in place. There were two gun turrets with double levels fore and aft. The upper level was armed with 20-mm cannon, the lower, more open level, with a 50-caliber machine gun. Two heavy engines powered the craft. They would use only one at a time, saving the spare for an emergency.

The boat crew was the young of both sexes. They stood

by at attention as Sherry explained, "This ship we call *The Columbus* has been tested on all depths of the river. It works. However, it has never been into the area of the Hills of Hell, where we are going, for the simple reason that we can only afford to risk it one time. Our gunners are well trained and we have survived short excursions and attacks from the screechers and the chompers. The ship and crew are as ready as we can make them for the final thrust."

All looked and listened carefully with wonderment. Bluefeather marveled at the labor that had gone into constructing the boat; the heavy pieces of iron hauled down from so far above at such great risk, the engineering, the welding, the motors that had to have been brought below in parts, then reassembled. The petrol that filled the tied-down barrels could only have been hauled in ten-gallon cans at the most. All had arrived and been prepared by force of Dolby's will over his laboring militia and the burdened back of mules.

They followed Sherry on through three gates. Finally, the armed Youngers slid a half-gate, and the river was open before them. Sherry motioned everyone back but Bluefeather.

The Youngers kept automatic weapons ready. But nothing attacked. It was peaceful—this moment.

Bluefeather could hear an inexplicable music, again reminding him that the only other place he had heard such an uncanny sound had been on the side of Taos Mountain. The fact that the mountain was above and far north of these depths puzzled him greatly. Nevertheless, he could swear the source had to be the same.

Sherry motioned the whispering section to silence and produced from her shoulder pack a metallic instrument that could be squeezed so that it was soon making the sound of a dozen castanets. She played it—there was no other word—like little metal drums in a broken but constant rhythm. "Clackety, clack, clack. Clackety, clackety clackety, clack."

Then, after each session, she would pause and stare out across the river. All watched curiously, with little electric signals from their brains teasing countless nerve endings about their bodies.

Bluefeather saw the movement on the water's surface even before Sherry did. Grey-white creatures were sliding into the river at the nearest peninsula. It was too far for him to discern what form they might be, but they entered the water with a singular purpose, he was certain. Then they disappeared under the river's surface.

Sherry continued the clacking sounds with what seemed to Bluefeather a little more urgency now. Her hand must be tiring. After a time that no one could measure, Bluefeather saw the head. Then Sherry saw it. Then the young guards, and at last the entire section, saw one head rise above the water and duck back under instantly. Then another and another performed the same movement with as-yet-indiscernible faces turned toward Sherry's clacking. In unison, all disappeared under the dark blue river for perhaps a full minute. It seemed like hours to The Section, of course.

Bluefeather could sense the tension and radiating nerves in the fine figure of the woman Sherry. He could smell the electricity emanating from the pores of those behind him.

Then. Then a dream of reality, in such perfect harmony they could only be of one mind, rose above the water. These creatures walked on it with arms that had flaps connected from the insides, partway down their bodies. Their arms flailed so fast the flaps appeared like motorized sails, speeding them along the top of the water at least as fast as the most expert of water-skiers.

The Section braced, as the triloids, in perfect synchrony, turned toward the open gate of the iron tent.

Then they came to a halt on the surface and sank down to their shoulders, waists and midlegs at the edge of the river, according to the depth of the water. The greatest of all Bolshoi ballet corps could not have executed the maneuver with more perfection. Their arms hung just to the knees. Their skin flaps were not noticeable now. Their legs were both short and thin so that tendons could be seen underneath the grey-white hairless skin. There was no use for hair here where the sun never shone.

They had tiny waists from which hung brief clothing made from the softened skins of some other cave creatures. A stone knife, with a handle made from trees of light wood, hung from the belt that held up the leather breeches. The knife handles were secured on the stone blades with strips of rawhide and sinew. They had crossed leather suspenders over their chests and shoulders down to the breechcloths. Behind—on each back in a leather, open-ended holster—were short spears made exactly like the knives except the stone points were a little wider and the handles longer.

The triloids' heads were shaped like a short-billed bird's head, about the size of a small human head. Their mouths stretched back from the front perhaps three inches on each side. Their eye sockets were inverted vertically in their head with extra-long eyelids to cover them. The vertical sockets were thin, and only a slit perhaps an eighth to a quarter of an inch is all that was revealed of the eyes. The shape of the orbs projected a feeling of hidden meanings and immense cunning to The Section. The triloids' chests were large and protruding like proud roosters. The females had two large breasts located almost the same as a human's, but each had two nipples.

So, Bluefeather thought, they were placental. Then suddenly, he observed they had reason and thought as well as the mass migration movement and techniques of most birds, fish and grouped land animals in the outer realm.

One female stepped forward to the clacking of Sherry's castanets, clicking her teeth together in return signals. The action proved the existence of a form of thinking and reasoning, because they could converse with a creature from out of their ecosystem. The upper lips lifted and their bottom lips lowered as the teeth clicked sounds of a message in return to Sherry.

Bluefeather thought by now his quotient of surprises was exhausted, but the teeth were all in a solid piece, looking like porcelain bone. The upper and lower teeth could make contact with amazing speed and power to crush all but the largest bones. There was in actuality one single, curved tooth above and one below. However, due to the protruding shape of the mouth, they could also rip with them.

The ears were wide, rounded and as high up on their head as a coyote's. They were flexible and cupped both in front and back, receiving signals from all angles, pouring them into the head.

"Her name is Dolla. The leader of this group," Sherry said softly.

The two females were so natural with one another they could have been having an over-the-fence, backyard conversation. The final proof of intelligence was revealed to Bluefeather when Dolla and Sherry smiled at each other. Each raised a knee and touched them together. The ceremonial movement was the same as a kiss and a hug. The triloids had the magic gift of friendship.

As Dolla raised her knee, Bluefeather noticed her feet. They were very flexible, about five inches wide, and had toes that were partly short claws. Then his eyes went to her hands. They were like her feet, but with longer, retractable claws similar to those of earthly felines. Both male and female had the same. Their jaws, feet and hands were all weapons, so the unarmed knee was a perfect part of the anatomy for a gesture of friendship. These triloids, although not quite as heavy as the humans before them, were armed in five very different ways. The observers had seen that they could swim under water like fish and walk—or rather, run—on it, too.

Dolla and Sherry spoke in their special way again. Then the triloids all turned, following Dolla. They raced upright along the shallow water, up on the banks to some rock bluffs. They climbed them as agilely as squirrels do trees. Powerful, ringed muscles in the bottoms of their feet and hands gripped the bluff as if they were part of it. When each reached a certain height they "showed off" in space, one after the other, their arms spread wide so that the flaps formed a perfect sail-wing. The updraft from hot spots in the river and on the land allowed them to circle, gliding sometimes higher, sometimes lower, on across and beyond the river to become lost in the ever-moving mists. They couldn't exactly fly, but how they could sail.

Sherry turned to The Section, saying, "It took me five years, but we are friends. They've gone home to prepare for our visit later."

Bluefeather knew now why Sherry had included the "tri" in their species name; they were creatures of the water, earth and air. Incredibly appealing and adaptive beings high on the ladder of subterranean evolution.

THIRTY-SEVEN

SHERRY HAD DIRECTED THEM STRAIGHT TO THE CONference room and immediately began to explain: "As you have seen, life has been developing here on the River of Radiance for millions of years. Some of the creatures are still blind from the far back time of total darkness. After the moving earth plates below us opened tiny cracks to its molten core, luminescent light particles formed. Because of that, some—like the triloids—have slowly developed eyesight, weak to be sure, but a much-needed addition to the sonar mind-sight so highly developed in all the creatures here. Our friends, the triloids, have both. Consequently, they have a physical, as well as an intellectual, advantage over all else in this cavern of impossibilities. Of course, the closer to blindness the denizens are, the greater their olfactory abilities. I do believe they can actually smell the outline and movement of any living thing as clearly as we see it with our eyes."

Sherry patiently answered many questions from the group, emphasizing that it would take thousands of minds greater than hers at least a century to even partially explain the beginning and development of the life system here.

She said, "These creatures of the cavern river are not

museum pieces of some long-lost time. This IS their time and place, right here, right now."

Pack did not seem to be bothered so much by the marvels as he was by Sherry's suddenly relentless, professional attitude. Bluefeather could tell Pack took it personally, while he knew himself that it was a focused drive to furnish Dolby his long-pursued dream before it was too late.

She almost brusquely dismissed all but Bluefeather, leading him to a special room high up on the bluff overlooking the river and the smaller caves within the overly monstrous cavern.

The room was long, fairly narrow, with windows that easily slid open. Two large telescopes stared out over the innerscape. There was a comfortable, raised swivel chair in front of each. But what caught Bluefeather's vision first upon entering the room was a five-foot-tall iron rod secured in the floor. The last foot of it appeared to be made of solid gold, and on it perched a gold-plated human skull staring blindly out of its hollow, yellow eye sockets between the telescopes. There was an incongruous wig of scraggly hair sitting atop the smoothness of the gold plating. It was askew and ridiculous looking.

"That's Tilton's head with his own scalp on top. Dolby wants him to look forever, helplessly, out on the richest world ever known," Sherry explained.

"His vengeance would appear to have been artfully completed," said Bluefeather, staring at the partial remains of another accumulator who had, with his evil, instigated considerable early twentieth-century history here in the Southwest. Dolby kept that same acidulous emotion moving around the bone of Tilton's severed head even today. By the Great Spirit, Dolby had not only decapitated Tilton, he had also scalped him as a Comanche might have and had tanned it, for at least some permanency. The seemingly unlimited lengths to which Dolby would go to avenge or control were more extreme than even one with

Bluefeather's experience in mental and bodily violence could fully acknowledge.

"I hope Dolby likes me—I mean, really likes me—especially when it comes to that 'forever' business."

"He does, Blue, just as he does me. As long as we perform and deliver. Delivery, that's what Dolby expects, not excuses. Delivery," she said, as if to herself.

She adjusted a rod connecting the two telescopes so they could look in synch, seeing the same things. First, she slowly moved the telescope upriver through alternately spurting and subsiding geysers of steaming water, on past spear points and needles of burning rock piercing the floor of the cave, building and forming tiny islands as they lit up the caverns in an ever-moving glow.

There were other balls of light, oscillating, dipping, dancing, with no patterns to their movements whatsoever. They were like many UFOs seen in the above land, coming at one with amazing speed, then twisting, turning diagonally or vertically with immense velocity. They were there most of the time, flashing in and out of steam, mist clouds and caverns, circling—sometimes feverishly— 'round and 'round the mighty stalactites and stalagmites. They teased the eye as well as the brain circuits and tantalized the natural timing of all else here. Bluefeather figured they were gas balls squeezed up from plates of earth grinding below. They were an energy of life somehow, as were the fire and metal and other living things that began breathing here in many different manners over the ages. It was a circus of lights celebrated where once the darkness had been supreme and the consequent blindness had created creatures that could only look inward in order to look outward.

Sherry moved the powerful glass past the fiery fissures to the now dead blackish Hills of Hell. There would have been no surprise to either of the two if they had seen devils dancing in delight around suffering sinners.

"There, you see, Blue, do you see the dark Hills of Hell?"

"Yes, I see them. Looks like they've been dead for aeons. Speaking of hell, well, how in the hell do we get there and why?"

"In the boat, of course. There's no other way. Once we brought pieces of a helicopter down here. Took us a year to haul and assemble it. We set up strong radios and relay stations. The two chosen ones flew on over the dark hills and perhaps ten miles beyond before the cave narrowed into blackness and the river vanished over a void."

"We recorded the radio reports on the return trip. They landed on three of the terrible hills—giant fumaroles is what they are, built from cooling minerals of the deep. Anyway, the copilot's voice is recorded as saying that the hills appeared to be burned and condensed down to the most precious of metals. At that announcement, Dolby ordered their return. From their last spoken words, just instants after takeoff, we can only surmise that a Khyber grabbed the chopper and they crashed. You can hear it on the tape. I'll play it for you later. We expect to find the remains of the chopper on the big hill."

Now Bluefeather knew why all had happened before— all the labor and lives sacrificed. It was still the power of riches they were pursuing for Dolby's obsession with greed and conquest. He was suddenly stunned that such a wondrously creative mind and soul as Sherry's could not see it. Her work, her world of knowledge scribbled in the notes, her own foolish dream of believing Dolby, would open and share all this information. Clues to the origin and future of the universe, life and even reason itself would be abandoned to fulfill an evil old man. Bluefeather believed this. He ached because of it with all the pain of the billions of dead creatures over the millions of years of their own hurt to get to here. Right here. Now. This instant. He felt all their hurts at once, and he momentarily blacked out from the unbearable thoughts.

When he gained awareness again, he subjugated all these feelings to the "nowness" of the telescope. He would speak and act later. He must not spoil these minutes, these hours, that Sherry had shared with no one else but Dolby. They saw creatures like miniature dinosaurs that Sherry had named Dinahs. She explained that they laid eggs in concealed places on the edge of small backwater pools, hidden in and around fallen bush-trees. Down here, the Dinahs were food for many—especially the triloids—just as rabbits and squirrels were for the earth animals above.

They witnessed a struggle for the carcass of a horned creature that would have in the outer world appeared to be a cross between a hairless buffalo and a mountain goat. A chomper and a dragon-like animal with six legs, its feet armed with claws like Arabic daggers, rolled and ripped at one another, blood spewing and flowing, until they were solidly covered and slick with it. Both died.

Before Sherry could move the glass, screechers swooshed down and settled their blind selves in the blood and flesh to feast their huge, bellow-like craws full. Even through the constant cacophony of multiple sounds, Bluefeather and Sherry could isolate the shrill and now sometimes choking cries of the massive hopping flyers.

"My God, I keep forgetting what ravenous things they are."

The glass moved on, revealing all kinds of snake-like, alligator-jawed, slithering, lighted, electric eels. The quantity of living, moving things was enormous per square acre. They flourished with a bounty of riches from the fiery center of gravity itself, mixed with the water to make a richness of nutrients and life unparalleled in earthly experience.

Sherry said, as if to a student, "This is no sci-fi comic

book. This is as real as a tyrannosaurus once was or a kangaroo is today."

"Square on, Miss Sherry."

Bluefeather had forgotten Dolby's wickedness now. He had forgotten the flesh and soul of Marsha that he constantly craved. He had even forgotten Sherry. They had become, one or a trillion, of the same grand destiny peeled bare before them to its feral fauna.

He said, "The Great Spirit invented little bacteria and told them to make what they wished."

"Yes. Yes, and here before us are the mighty works they've created."

"We stare at the most lavish cauldron of existent life on earth, without question."

"Yes. Yes. Yes." She answered him as if she were having an orgasm for the whole world.

Then out from the interior of wonderment, the incessant ringing of the last phone finally reached them. It could, of course, only come here, way down here, from Dolby.

Reluctantly, Sherry removed her eyes that had seen so much in the glass, stood up and took a very deep breath that raised and protruded her breasts—pushing them tight against the front of the pinkish grey uniform—turned and zombie-stepped to the instrument linking them to the above land.

Bluefeather was trying to turn loose, to free his being, of the underworld they had just been living in. It seemed like many minutes before he realized that Sherry was talking to him. He could not coordinate his thoughts or her words. She understood. She had been in his condition many times these past years.

Sherry hauled off and slapped the robin piss out of him. At first he was blank again, but then his head cleared in opposite reaction to the blow.

"Blue. Listen, Blue. There's a large man with a scar,"

she made a motion at an angle across her entire face, "hanging around the bar at Meanwhile asking questions about Dolby. The Olders have seen him 'glassing' headquarters. Do you think you might know who he could be?"

"I think so. It sounds like Fontaine."

"Fontaine. Who is he?"

"Fontaine is Korbell's man. His only adopted son, in fact."

"Oh. Then we might have another problem, huh?"

"If Korbell wishes, we've got an oversized problem."

"Dolby's troops will handle anything that comes up. I'm sure of it." She put her hands flat on his chest, looking up into his eyes, "Isn't that right, Blue?"

He knew it was a goddamned lie, but he couldn't help himself. "Dolby can swallow Korbell like Hitler did Poland."

She placed her head against his chest between her hands. He caressed her hair a moment, trying to make the terrible responsibilities she bore a little lighter. Then, inexplicably, she said, "I'm so hungry I could lick the shadow of a cactus tree till it's as shiny as new money."

THIRTY-EIGHT

WHEN THE SECTION CAME OUT OF THE THIRD SLEEP period, they found Sherry in a regimental mode of action. She lined up everyone in the entire compound—the Olders, the Youngers, The Section—and read off the names of those who would go for the underwater walk. Bluefeather headed up the list but was dismayed that Pack was not included in such a dangerous assignment. He eased around and asked Sherry about this privately.

"Look, Sherry, we're going to feel terribly confined in the river cage. I'd like to leave Marsha out of it. I'm afraid worrying about her will weaken my concentration. She can help Pack and the rest get things ready for the Hills of Hell excursion. Okay? Please."

"That's one of the reasons Pack can't go. I should have thought of it myself." Agreeing with his concern, she announced to the group, "Sergeant Pack will remain here in charge. We cannot risk both commanders until the final voyage."

There was no time wasted. They had rehearsed for three days. Now they went under. The iron submarine was nothing but a latticed miniature of the huge protective tent above and around them. It had wheels under the entire oval, mounted below hydraulic systems to fluctuate with any change in the bottom of the river. There were even more iron spear points, thinner and sharper, welded to its outside so that it appeared at a glance to be a large porcupine. There was cork all around a rod underneath to make it lighter in the water. Another rod was welded around the entire inside, standing out about a foot from the shell. It was grooved to make holding it easier. Only hands pushing and pulling here would control its direction going down into the unknown waters. A large steel cable tied to the device would unwind with their descent. It was connected to a powerful electric motor at the tent compound. When the striking of the cable in a coded rhythm occurred, the engine would be reversed and draw the object and its people back to shore. Every few feet on the push rod there hung heavily stitched canvas bags ready to receive the nodules of rich minerals from the floor of the river. There were extra oxygen tanks latched securely inside as well as several dozen spears for the three spear guns in holster-like rigs. The oxygen-fed suits were of the finest heat-resistant material science could devise. There was a water bottle on each of their backs with an attached tube inside, next to their mouths. They only had to turn their heads slightly to suck the water to prevent dehydration from the heat. The circular glass windows they looked out of were ground glass as precious and strong as that of an expensive telescope. There were large battery lights that could be controlled by a switchboard in front of Bluefeather's position.

Bluefeather's section of the crew that Sherry had selected gave him some comfort because they were all top troopers: Hector Garcia, Moosha, Kowalski, George Tack Won, Davis and Osaka.

They entered the river, pushing ahead and downward. The attached steel umbilical cord was slowly unwinding, allowing their penetration toward the river bottom. There were enough concentrations of luminescent microbes to provide sufficient light to move on. The trees of light, which of course had absorbed and concentrated the infinitesimal particles of light, waved very slowly in rhythm with the barely moving water.

The eerie, otherworldly luminosity revealed an abundance of life beyond ordinary comprehension. They soon adjusted to pushing over the wavy terrain in bumps and jerks softened by the water pressure around them. The brilliant colors were at the very least equal to those of the Great Barrier Reef's creatures. They saw striped fish of every shape that looked like swimming rainbows and fish that were so small they were only visible because they swam in such vast numbers. There were mollusk-like crustaceans on the floor and white crabs with a single, perfectly round, black dot in the center of their backs that at first looked like a bullet hole. There were floating things similar to jellyfish, but so transparent they were almost invisible until they moved. A six-foot-long, green and yellow fish with a head like a rhino's and blue teeth—sharp as broken glass and uneven as tornado-ripped timber— dined on the jellied ones constantly.

A ten-foot-long fat fish floated beside them like a large, pink balloon. The odd fish easily coordinated its speed with that of the slowly moving explorers. It had several eyes, forming a perfect hexagon. The change in the density of the luminescence made the eyes appear to be lighted from inside the strange floater. It had a webbed mouth without teeth. Bluefeather surmised that it must filter tiny water creatures very efficiently into its system to be so rotund. He wondered how the pink, tender-looking bulk kept from being eaten by the flat-nosed sharks that were now becoming more numerous, circling the cage with a curious confidence.

Then one shark made a presumptuous lunge at the fat fish. The pink skin suddenly opened hundreds of tiny portholes and shot out a yellow cloud of acidic juices that made the sharks roll over in the mud of the bottom in agony.

Bluefeather and his comrades were all relieved that the gang of flat-noses had dispersed. One of them could easily have shoved its huge frontal object under the craft and caused great destruction. Everyone kept touching his razor-sharp machete. Bluefeather, Moosha and Hector felt the spear guns now and then for comfort, as a baby does it mother's breasts.

The kaleidoscope of swimmers and clingers to the river bottom was so great that the initial astonishment and awe was already becoming the norm. They watched with great care as Bluefeather began picking up a few of the slowly increasing number of nodules and scraping off the rust-like crust to study the heavy metals underneath. Some were mainly of manganese; then he would find a cluster that had malleable metal that could only be an undetermined mixture of silver, platinum and gold.

Increasingly, Bluefeather was realizing what caused Dolby to create such a climate of murderous dedication. Already he had seen rich minerals that could easily be hand-mined, of such quantity that one could purchase any midsized city in the world. He only saved a few of these first samples, handing them to his cohorts and signalling which bags to put them in. He wanted to keep the load as balanced as possible.

Now the loss of the thought of time possessed all of them again. Space as an actuality vanished as well. Time as measured by a mechanical instrument was even more changed here than it was by the infinite sounds and sights of the mighty Cavern of Marvels directly above them. In a few yards it seemed that a decade of years had sneaked by them. In a hundred yards they had breathed and moved through a millennium of time fractures. Sherry had warned them of this hypnotic danger.

Bluefeather signalled them to stop and needlessly inspected the condition of all equipment, and every user, just to break the rhythm of their internal systems and to get the adrenaline of discovery flowing again.

There were areas in the river where no luminescent materials were concentrated, and it seemed as if they had entered the darkness at the center of the great meteorite itself. They automatically pushed harder against the handbar, shoving their feet more strongly against the primal wetness of the floor. The darkness turned to total black, making them feel as if they moved in solid mud. Bluefeather saved the switchboard lights for a dire emergency only. They broke free of this area and the light slowly brightened. There appeared a nicely rounded hill in front of them. As one body now, they all pushed to the side to skirt around it.

Then, Bluefeather, as usual, spotted the vision first. His breath was pulled back into his lungs so hard at the sight he almost became giddy from the increase in oxygen he had pulled into his lungs, and consequently, the blood that rushed to his brain.

A herd of four-legged green fish-horses with purple and orange manes was moving in single file across the hill. The movement caused the stiff manes to wave in the water as if blown by a high desert wind. They had tails that dragged behind them like true wild mustangs of the early Spanish West. Short, incomplete, pointed stripes marked their sides.

All the humans had stopped, mesmerized by the real, but mirage-like, vision they were witnessing. The fish-horses even seemed to have fetlocks until one realized they were connected all the way up their legs to their bellies, translucent as glass beer mugs. It was a soggy dreamscape of bewitchment. The crew was paralyzed with entranced delight.

The spell was silently shattered then, as a one-ton,

twelve-foot-long, saber-toothed monster moved past, jaws chomping in anticipation like massive maws. The three eyes that stuck up above the head like periscopes centered on the remuda of fish-horses. Its white and unevenly black-and-red-patterned sides undulated forward so powerfully that its bulk and power caused the water to move strongly in the cage. Its silence seemed louder than a runaway train. But before the ogre could create successful carnage, the lead fish-horse sent an unseen signal, and the startled adventurers saw the entire herd of horses flow swiftly, efficiently, into one stolid form. The manes and the tails were poisonous barbs, and what had in effect appeared to be short stripes on their sides were daggerlike pins that now protruded in a solid mass of protection as they all together formed the shape of a single giant watery porcupine.

The three-eyed saber-tooth hit the mass and separated it some from the force. As it pulled back from the piercing pain, the fish-horses fell back into a single unit again. The swimming beast bit at the hill below them, trying to rip the entire earth apart from its agony. It shook about in the water, forming foam and unseen ripples, whirling like a dog chasing its tail in an attempt to clamp the monstrous jaws on itself. Failing this, it rolled over and over wildly in the water and then circled a bit before charging straight at the iron-cloistered group. The impact lifted the cage despite the full weight of eight people trying to hold it down. The iron spears shoved into its face and mouth and sent clouds of blood black as motor oil spurting into the water in jets. It came again in such a random, wanton rage that the cage threatened to completely tilt over, but this time the barbs were too much, along with stings from the horses. It turned and erratically vanished into a large, dark hole.

When the cage had tilted, unseen by all, a flat-mouthed shark had swum into the cage and now had Kowalski around the knees of both legs and was shaking him like a goose down pillow. One leg dangled loose from a tendon and the other was ground and cut until it was ready to drop from the upper portion. Davis fired a spear just above the tiny eye of the shark. Its thrashing had knocked several men to their knees, where they held to the iron strips, struggling to get their weapons.

The human blood now mingled with that of the departed saber-toothed beast. Bluefeather swung down with the machete before he realized that that sort of action was only partially effective against the resistance of the water. He stabbed and stabbed into the head and side of the shark as Sherry managed to fire another spear that pinned the shark to the river bottom.

Even when he could hardly see, Bluefeather stabbed on at the lifeless brute. Kowalski, with his lower legs severed and the oxygen gone from his shattered diving suit, floated up to the top of the cage, then slowly sank as the air left the insides of his upper body.

One at a time, Bluefeather checked his crew in the murkiness. Then he saw Davis floating about a foot from the bottom. His glass viewer on his diving suit had been smashed by the shark's tail. He had drowned, and no one had even seen it in the bloody and sudden melee.

This unperceived death struck Bluefeather hard. He felt helplessly deceived, as he had by the two unscathed soldiers he had tried to awaken from their concussion death way back in the Normandy hedgerows. There was no time for guilt here as back there. He wondered, just the same, how much longer he could negate and subdue the awful feelings of losing those he had become so close to—like members of his family now. That's the way wars, no matter how small, had to be fought, if they were to be won. The grief must be saved for later, or all of them would be doomed. He must not become immune to it like Pack.

Bluefeather choked back the tears and banished the numbness in his stomach by pure necessity; he had to make a quick decision. The dead were past his present help. Everyone had signed on this expedition aware that they might die at any moment from unknown forces. It had happened.

After turning on all the battery lights and studying the near waters for any danger and finding none, Bluefeather signalled the men to lift one side of the cage. It took such effort that they all marveled at the strength of the saber-toothed beast. Bluefeather shoved Davis and the remains of Kowalski into the wet forever world. He had a struggle pulling the spears loose from the riverbed, but he finally did and was able to shove the dead shark out. They pushed the cage away from the two bodies that were so very slowly turning, turning in their vast grave.

Now they were numbed against the beauty of the light and darkness blending into the mysteries of uncountable and unfathomable creatures formed here so long ago by chance of time or by the design of gods. Who could say for sure? Who, indeed?

They did not see the fish-horses instantly separate and walk in midwater, forming the same single file as they headed away, above the river's floor. Their legs, now used as fins, headed to some private destination this group would never know about. Ever.

An eyeless worm, a yard around and fifty feet long, came at them but turned away at the last instant, its sonar sensing and reading the sharp steel. It flashed through Bluefeather's mind that for every animal on the surface of the earth, there were a hundred similar forms in the water worlds.

A mighty electric eel struck at them three times, causing jolts to their bodies and minds but no permanent damage, as their heavily treated diving suits gave protection from most of the electric shock. They had never before seen sparks such as were created each time the slick, over-grown, linear creature stabbed itself with the steel. The deviant and enigmatic attacks were like underwater arc welders, until the eel burned and electrocuted itself only to be devoured by a hundred rapacious fish before it could settle to the bottom.

In spite of the rapid series of jolts and disasters, they couldn't help watching in growing awe the actions of the wheel fish. Their forms were perfect circles, perhaps eighteen inches across and very thin in width. There were red and black stripes radiating from their very center, where a golf ball–sized eye looked out from each side. They floated in a seemingly uneven group. Some spun like wheels until all the spoke-like stripes ran together and the fish practically became an invisible blur. Others turned slowly, if at all. But their own personal mass sonar message was there just the same. As a shark moved near them, they all, in one motion, flipped up horizontally, with only their inch-and-half edge visible. This threw the shark's sonar signals, sight and smell into such confused disarray that it circled a couple of times and moved on, seeking simpler pleasures.

The wheel fish moved as erratically again as they had on first sight. Then a mighty demon fish, with rhinoceros-type horns of odd lengths over all the front of its armored body, moved toward them. It had one eye in the moving tube atop its head and another eye circling and searching below. The tube—the size of a stovepipe—was extremely flexible and could turn the eye in any direction, but now they both were aimed, weaving toward the group of wheel fish. A jaw that had nine rows of teeth sharper than ma-chete blades, and almost as long, opened up as wide as the arms on a lounge chair.

The group thought many of the wheel fish were doomed. Then, with amazing speed, they all whirled into vertical positions. Little fins suddenly opened in a circle inside the circle. Teeth like large, sharp diamonds suddenly appeared around their thin edges. Spinning in bunches, they surrounded the massive, horned fish like saw blades, as they did indeed prove to be. One group spun, slicing right through the head of the fish, the armor, hide and bone like a lumber mill saw. One followed another until the victim was almost cut in half lengthwise. Then the other groups whirled in from the sides and the diamond-like teeth sliced the meat into ever smaller pieces. They were river butchers to perfection. Each retracted the teeth now, and the tentacles with little suction cups pulled the smaller shreds of meat into their bodies, swelling the parts around the eye until it was almost invisible. The pieces that were dropped created another free feast for thousands of flashing, diving, smaller fish and other forms of frenzied feeders. The sated wheel fish formed a single line behind an obviously designated leader and circled their way to a ten-foot-high bluff and slowly disappeared into its cracks and crevices. They had precisely served their evolved purpose for now, feeding themselves, and thousands more.

This last underwater show had exhausted everybody. They didn't care now, as they moved on, bent over, testing the nodules that were becoming so thick on the river floor that all walking was difficult. Bluefeather had mined, prospected and studied enough to know that all minerals were formed by magma and gases penetrating fissures in contact with water. Here, so far below the surface and so much nearer the magma, combined with a huge water source flowing interminably, the creating forces had been magnified many, many times. He could barely raise one huge nodule. Even with the lifting effect of the water he had to put it back down.

Then he took a hatchet from his belt and struck at it and became so excited at the yellow revealed that he risked the sharpness of his machete by scraping and cut-

ting at it. The object contained a high percentage of gold.
The battery lights did not distort the color. There were
others that were more silver and platinum. With all his
vows, and the violent deaths of his comrades just behind
them, he felt the old familiar surge of his body juices
exciting, compelling, transforming his whole being at the
thrill of the find. The kill of the hunt after a long chase.
Did it never change? Could it? God. No matter.

Now Bluefeather struggled, controlling his emotions
and actions, as he proceeded professionally, guiding the
crew along the edges of the thousands of visible tons of
nodules and dropping a sample into the canvas bags every
fifteen or twenty steps.

Other uncountable great fishes and entities of phantom
shapes inspected them. A few with teeth made to tear,
rip and chew tested the steel barbs and resentfully backed
away. The bottom-boat moved on, in and out of darkness,
as if it sensed that they were close to completing a mission
of the inconceivable. They turned on the weakening battery lights in the black holes and switched them off as the
glowing microbes gave form and sight to all again.

They passed area after area of fumaroles, where the hot
water spewed out and up through the pipes of blackish
metal and stone, some the size of a water hose, others as
big around as a sewer pipe. At one time or another, they
had helped form the huge mineral deposits of the river
basin. Shrimp and other crustaceans large as rabbits fed
frantically on the sulfides, white crayfish and slow-moving
isopods formed a great food source and there was no telling what else was being emitted from water heated by the
very core of the earth. Some fish, adapted to the three-
hundred-degree temperature next to the fumaroles,
feasted on the shrimp. There were other sulfide-addicted
critters who had developed the ability to turn most of the
poisons into food and life. Some of the wormlike creatures

glowed red with blood formed from the hot sustenance of the fumaroles.

The sweat poured down out of the explorer's bodies and made a squishing feeling around their feet. They conservatively sipped at their limited supply of water.

One geyser fifty feet away shot up with such force it jarred the cage sideways and blinded everything with bubbles. The suddenness of the shock caused George Tack Won to slightly dirty his rubber breeches. Bluefeather and his old buddy Hector just dripped a little more moisture down to their feet. Heavy perspiring caused by the scattered areas of hot water had afforded a considerable reduction in their weight over the last hour. Even the Youngers, who had been trained for this job much longer than Bluefeather's associates, sweated profusely.

Finally, the ore bags were loaded and the crew's energy was depleted. The reserve oxygen tanks were now only a quarter full. It was the time for retreating.

Bluefeather pulled his machete, opened a sliding hatch and whacked the coded signal hard against the cable, and waited. He held his uniformed hand lightly against it, but no signal returned down the cable. They all looked at one another through glass and water. Fear.

Bluefeather repeated the signal against the cable, and again he touched it with his hand. Cold, cold fear. Waiting. Waiting. At last, he felt the tiny tapping that had raced down the steel cord from their life source at the river's edge. It was a living, pumping heart to his hand.

He turned and gave a raised clenched fist of affirmation to his surviving crew and they all gave it back, resisting the urge to celebrate their apparent survival with the natural human gestures of shaking hands, hugging or slapping one another on the back. There were smiles inside the glass apertures of different sizes and shapes, but all with the same meaning—life.

Bluefeather's mind-voice spoke. *Funny how the green*

*pines and sunlight of the outer world, that once were
taken for granted, will now appear as wondrous and new
as the depths of the Cavern of Marvels did a few weeks
back.*

The Great Spirits, or pure luck, had saved one last vi-
sion-gift to partially make up for the loss of their buddies,
Davis and Kowalski. Now they looked over an area like a
farm of fumaroles, which had formed castles of crystals.
They ranged from the size of a cube of sugar to as tall as
church steeples. They were mostly hexagonal, but Bluefeather's trained eye saw many other geometrical arrange-
ments such as tetrahedrons and twin systems of
crystallization. He could not help but play the battery
lights across such artistry from the deep, showing clear
calcite and quartz crystals; others were probably of green
and blue tourmaline and beryl; some were rose and am-
ber-hued.

The totality of their glittering perfection was beyond
the capability of mere eyes to behold properly. One had
to breathe and become mentally suffused with them. The
entire formation could easily be viewed as a small fantasy
city with tilted bridges, streets and buildings—the tallest
being a cubist cathedral.

Long leaf-like crystals of silver and gold grew next to
huge clusters of iron pyrite—no doubt associated with
many other minerals of great value. All the jewels in all
the royal vaults of the world would have looked small and
dull compared to this watery display of beauty in its most
glorious form.

Then the fish-birds came and enhanced this gifted vision even more. They appeared over the fantasy city with
wings moving them like great eagles flying into a wind-
storm. Now the movements of the fish-birds captured the
group's viewpoint with their tantalizing flying swim. They
were about half as large as the screechers, but more

streamlined. Flat tendrils hung from the wide-stretching wingfins, giving the appearance of feathers.

They dived as if from above the Rio Grande Gorge into a group of yellow stripers. They had tongues with barbed points that flashed out and pierced the victims like Comanche spears and jerked them into their open, beak-like mouths. Then they folded the barbs to release the catch into their throats. They swollowed them whole.

As six or seven of the flyers dived, swept up, circled and stopped, like courting scissor-tails, the river turned into a baseball-sized area of fluid motion, creating newly formed bubbles in circles of tinted brightness oscillating in such splendor that The Section was paralyzed.

That was enough, and more, for a final vision of the deep; but they couldn't help watching the rippling psychedelic lights sending flashes of rainbow colors back and forth through the fish-birds' bodies. The chemicals created an incandescence that rushed down to their swishing wing tips, sending a wake of bubbles of every color in existence that slowly diminished behind them, forming a protective diversionary barrier from any possible enemies. It was as if they had been born from the mating of two fumaroles of magma and had retained all the colored flames in their beings.

Then the fish-birds, all in one swoop, water-flew back over the city of crystals, disappearing just as the bubbles blinked to blackness in the void.

Everyone felt enormously blessed, as if they had been truly, tenderly touched by the hand of the Great Spirit. Eyes stared through glass awhile in reverent thanks for the river's gifts. They turned their bodies in unison, upslope. The supreme show had been a special gift that helped ease some of the terrible pain and awareness of their recent tragedies. Bluefeather wept silently, unseen, now, giving thanks that he had left Marsha behind, waiting safely for his return.

The cable slowly rewound, pulling the cage upward. They adjusted to its tilting, sluggish movements, holding onto the iron rail with only one hand, walking freely, but carefully. Very carefully.

Bluefeather jested to himself, *Just another dull day at the office, dear. And how was your day?* But of course, only he could hear his silly satire. He laughed uproariously just the same.

THIRTY-NINE

THEY REHYDRATED. SHERRY WAS SO THRILLED AT THEIR river-crawling success that Bluefeather felt she had forgotten the human cost. He wondered if that part of the Dolbys and Korbells of the world wore off on everyone they touched. If so, the world as he dreamed of it finally being could never exist. Where in the hell had honesty and honor gotten lost? Somewhere. Where? He knew if the day came when a majority of the people had given up their proper portion of truth and dignity for the fragility of greedy gain and vanity, the forests would fall, the air would become rancid and the entire earth would turn to ice and sand, dying of starvation and thirst just as all its inhabitants had before.

He finished his report on the inferred mineral values of the small portion of the river they had covered. He put the assay reports, just returned by mule-back courier from God's Castle, beside them. He clipped them together and started out the door to deliver his findings to Sherry.

He took two steps past Marsha's doorway, turned back and knocked. She opened the door, eyes wide and solemn, waiting wordlessly to hear his verbal approach.

Bluefeather circled the small room a couple of times. He could smell her fragrance with every breath. He tried not to stare at this woman he was in such conflict over, but he could not help himself there. The turquoise robe emphasized the curvature of the body he had enjoyed so much and made her matching eyes seem even bigger and more absorbing. Even her hair showed tints of fire among the autumn auburn he had never seen before. Not to hold her was painful. Not to talk with her of nonsense and laughing matters was numbing; but a sharp knife of doubt had sliced them into separateness.

"Marsha, I'm really pissed."

She stared silently. He waited for a question. It didn't come.

After an uncomfortable awkwardness, he said, "I keep getting this feeling that you not only gave all our venture's secrets to Korbell, but that maybe it's also making it possible for Dolby to use us, our lives, our souls for nothing but a moment of great power before he dies of old age."

"We've been through this before, Mr. Fellini," she said formally, "and it got us exactly nowhere."

"That's because you keep on lying about what you told Korbell."

"I don't like being called a liar. I think my actions make a travesty out of that statement."

"See. See. I told you. You keep avoiding, circling the real issue. You are leaving us vulnerable to these two greedy bastards of evil. They're probably gonna join up and bury us all here just as soon as we prove up the immensity of the wealth."

"They respect, but despise, each other. That should be very obvious. Even worse, they carry vast hidden jealousies. No, they won't join forces. No way that could happen. Anyway, don't blame me for all of that."

"You see these papers?" He waved the reports out toward her. "Entire nations would go to war over this information. And you stand there and deny that Dolby and

Korbell aren't planning to do us in as soon as we make our run at the Hills of Hell? Huh? Well?"

"I'm certainly no clairvoyant. And I haven't denied anything but their partnership. You've been in too many wars. You're losing any semblance of the reasoning you once had. You are letting your imagination run rampant."

"Bullshit, Marsha. My imagination hasn't got anything to do with this. I have seen proof of evils you can't even believe. And this evidence has opened my eyes and mind so that I really know what's possible."

They both breathed heavily now a moment. As their anger subsided, the breathing returned to normal.

"Ah, shitfire," he said, with more regret than ire in his voice. He walked out the door, not looking back, but saying, "I hate these doubts I feel, but dumb-ass me, I love you anyway."

The truth he had failed to admit to himself was suddenly clear. It didn't make any difference about her domination by Korbell. Who would not be intimidated under the conditions? He was arguing to try to find an excuse to cut her out of the final deadly trip. If he survived, he wanted her here waiting for him. It was no use, though. If he cut her out now, she would never speak to him again.

He took the papers to the headquarters room, where Sherry was on the phone. She said, "Don't worry, here's Blue now with the reports. I think you'll be enormously pleased. No, no, I'll call you back in an hour or so. I still think you have plenty of protection. What could he do? He can't bring in army tanks and that's what it would take. Okay. Okay. I'll be back in touch as soon as I read the reports. Okay?" She hung up, saying to Bluefeather, "Dolby's getting concerned at Fontaine's presence. He's thinking about having him hidden."

"Hidden?"

"Forever."

"There's that Dolby word again. It suggests an awfully long time. A longer time than I like to think of. That's one word that doesn't make sense. We all keep using it. Forever! Forever! I wish the dictionary would drop that word."

Sherry's tilted eyes widened even more at this unexpected tirade about a single suggestive word. Nevertheless, she smiled with immense relief in her voice saying, "At last. At last," as she took the papers.

He sat down, then quickly got up and stared out at the river world as she read. No matter what one's emotion, the fact of the sacred cavity's visual and audible existence eased his concern of the upper world. He was becoming—by the day, maybe by the second—pulled into this other world here, far, far below. All his youth he had heard the legends and myths of the underworld from many different Indian nations and pueblos. Here he was in it. A wonderment indeed. For just a moment he was startled that he already felt more at home here than he did above. How could it be? This ancient system down here had already killed some of his best friends and his favorite mule animals. The fact of making the expedition at all had cost him the love of his woman—and they hadn't even started on the deadliest part of the trip yet. Then he knew. This underworld would kill them, just as they might have to kill some of it. But it was honest survival—survival of the fittest; survival of the honest; survival of . . .

He was humming out loud, smiling to himself, when Sherry interrupted his reverie with, "It's mind-shattering, Blue. My God, there's enough riches in the river to buy New Mexico and Colorado."

"Yeah, with Arizona and West Texas thrown in. My dear woman, please be aware that therein lies the joker."

She ignored this, saying, "Dolby is going to be out-of-his-mind thrilled. His dreams, his visions can actually come true now. We could have the power to open these wonders up to the world and protect and share all this for science, for medicine, for knowledge. Just think of it, Blue. The possibilities here in the Carvern of Marvels— this cavern of impossibilities—will leapfrog understanding of the earth, the galaxy, the universe, even ourselves, by millions of years. My mind is exploding with excitement. Have you thought about it?"

"Oh, I've sure been thinking about it, all right. That's for sure. I've certainly been thinking overtime, Sherry."

At that moment, his heart had overcome his desire for the greatest of all adventures. He would have given it all up to be back at Corrales fixing his grandmother Fellini's sauce for a pasta and wine dinner with Marsha. Then he eradicated these warming thoughts. He had to.

Sherry's scientific mind was racing on beyond his temporal thoughts. She said, "The schools and pools of positive facts here will prove and disprove theorems by a thousandfold."

She had suffered the silence of her knowledge, so carefully recorded in her many notebooks, so long that Bluefeather could not bring himself to interfere with her very natural enthusiasm.

He started to tell her that none of this gracious and glorious gift to the outer world was planned by the powerful ones above. There would only be, in the final faceoff, just another use of power for more power, until there was no force left with which to destroy. They, the little group of them, could save it—give her dreams a chance— if they were aware and stayed open to the truth. If, of course, they survived the next and final journey of the expedition. The Section had already taken the risks and paid the price—some of it terrible, some of it glorious. Only they—as a solid, dedicated unit of love and rever-

ence for earth, for flesh, for guilelessness—could save it.
It would be their choice. It always was. Choice.

He talked on with her in the most hopeful terms he
could dredge up, and being a natural-born optimist himself, he was soon, even if temporarily, laughing and planning great and momentous occurrences, right alongside
her.

"Well, Blue, none of it would have happened if Dolby
hadn't had the wisdom to choose you as the leader."

"I'm flattered, but I've always hoped it was you who
really convinced him."

"Well . . . I think maybe I had a tiny bit of influence.
Maybe," she said.

"Tomorrow we go visit the triloids?"

"Yes."

"Is it really necessary, Sherry? I would feel better if we
launched our excursion to the Hills of Hell now. Too
much anticipation, like that of making love, can take the
edge off The Section. Waiting too long can create a mental dullness in the best of soldiers—and a big increase in
causalities."

"I understand what you're saying, but believe me when
I tell you, all of us will enjoy it, and the visit is a critical
part of our venture. Critical."

"Good enough for me then."

"Fine. We'll depart after the next sleep period."

He started to leave and then stopped, "Uh, say, Sherry,
I know . . . I know you'll think this a strange request,
but . . . see these nodules here?" He had selected the
richest of the lot and had set aside about four hundred
pounds of them. "I'd like for you to have one of your men
load these in the leather panniers on a couple of mules
and have them camp above the elevators until we're on
our way back to God's Castle. Okay?"

She looked at him strangely, but then figured that it

was somehow part of his geological work and said, "You've got it. It's done."

"Thank you. Dream well."

"How can I miss? Dear Blue, you've given me whole worlds of dreams and reality."

FORTY

BLUEFEATHER WAS ADMITTED INTO PACK'S ROOM AND instantly saw that eternal wisp of a smile was completely gone from his pale face for the first time he could remember. He had come here positively exploding with something he had to tell someone, and his old friend Pack had been chosen. But Pack was already mumbling things that he strained to hear.

"I don't know about that Sherry woman. Ever since we got down here she has been as cold as four-day-old oatmeal. Looks right through me like a dose of salts."

"Hey, old pard', she does the same to me—to everyone—unless she's giving specific instructions. In her mind she is carrying the future of our planet on her already weary back."

Pack sat back down and continued his ceaseless cleaning of the weapons of war. "I s'pose you're right, but . . ."

"Listen, soon as we get back from the Hills of Hell and return to God's Castle, you're going to see a regular Sherry. That woman is gonna pour her happiness all over you like icing on a wedding cake. She just prepares for battle just like you do, huh? That's why you like her. She's a female version of Sergeant Pack."

The little delicate smile was back now, "Aw, shit. She's ten times smarter'n me."

"You think for a whistle that I like what's happened to me and Marsha? Hell, I wanted to leave her with Flo and Sally. But if I had she wouldn't have been waiting for me there or anywhere else. Patience, Pack. That's the way for you. When we complete Sherry's dreams, she'll turn them all back to you. I swear it."

The little hint of a smile returned to Pack's thin lips. His slumped shoulders lifted some. He said, "Okay. That sounds reasonable to me, Fellini."

Bluefeather had done his duty to Sherry and Pack; now he had to rid himself of a heavy inner load of constant concern that wouldn't be a worry at all for his friend.

"Pack, listen to me. Listen close and careful."

Pack stopped wiping the surplus oil from the rifle and carefully rearranged the six grenades in a hexagonal shape on his bed, listening hard.

"I finally figured out why we keep on doing these crazy, dangerous things," Bluefeather continued. "All addiction is plain memory, whether it be the first high from booze, sex or your first shot fired in war. You can never forget that adrenaline rush when you pan your first color of gold. The swift surge of thrills is imprinted for a lifetime, many lifetimes. The instant dreams of luxury in all things, opulence and glory become possible. The dream and the memories continue. At the time the memory genes remind you of past thrills and highs, they are conveniently skipping the struggles, the sacrifices, and only fill your blood with past resplendency and pleasures—especially those dreams attached to the idolized yellow metal. Goddamn it, Pack, that's it. I know where the fever and loss of control comes from. It has taken me my whole ignorant life to figure out such a simple thing. Now ain't that something, ol' pardner?"

"Yessir, Blue, that is one hell of a something."

Bluefeather Fellini was so happy that he pounded his friend on the back so hard that Pack's throat momentarily jarred shut.

"It's sleep time now, sergeant." He started for the door, then said, "Oh yeah, I almost forgot. I've arranged to provide enough of the river minerals to take care of us, just in case—close to four hundred pounds of about eighty-five percent gold. Not bad, huh? Just thought you might like to know that, after my speech and . . . before you go to sleep." He left, stepping with bounces.

Pack stared at the closed door, picked up his rifle and aimed it at the heart of anything.

FORTY-ONE

THE BOAT CREW OF THE YOUNGERS WAS READY AND, surprisingly, anxious. Guns were cleaned, polished, loaded in the turrets, and all The Section was armed, just as they would be on the final charge down the River of Radiance. The trip across to visit the triloids would be a rehearsal. Barrels of gasoline were latched in place. Ammunition and extra grenades were in a gun box. It was welded onto the bottom of the boat and had secure latches that could be easily opened with the knowledge that had been imparted to all. The two flamethrowers were also secured, ready to be unhooked. They would not be needed on this day, so they remained in place. Sherry stood upon an ammunition box.

"Attention, please. Attention. We're going to visit a pueblo of our neighbors, the triloids. We've been invited to their territory. I know how tempting it is to compare certain traits of theirs with ours. Chimpanzees, dogs and wolves have some actions similar to humans', but they are not us. Neither are the triloids. They are their own entities and we must respectfully treat them so." She motioned to the motor man. "Crank it up."

He started one of the large engines, leaving the other in reserve. The boat quivered a little like a racehorse in the starting gate. Everyone took swivel seats and dropped the simple safety belts over their laps. They could, if need be, be instantly removed. A group of Olders waved them away from the dock. They had visited the triloids with Sherry before.

The boat trip had the thrill of a first hayride or the first unpacking of goodies for a family picnic. Since the river moved as slowly as cooling molasses, the ride across was a smooth joy. Everyone opened up and chatted about the majesty of the great multilighted cavern and the dark blue river. They made curious gossip about the triliods. All was festive.

They saw the head and arcing back of what could only be called a monster. It circled the boat fifty or so yards out. Its head and corrugated-appearing neck arched out of the water to stare at them. Then it went under except for the undulations of its spine, creating strong waves that began to rock the boat as it continued circling.

The gunners in the two turrets kept it in their sights most of the time. Their first flash of fear had now turned into intense interest.

Sherry soothed them by explaining, "We call it Nessie after the legend of the Loch Ness monster."

She had no sooner said this than the huge creature turned away in a spray, heading with amazing speed down the river until all that was left was the wake.

Two-thirds of the way across, Bluefeather saw some triloids waiting on shore, pointing at the boat and communicating with one another in obvious pleasurable anticipation. Several sailed above with spears, looking all around protectively.

Sherry said, pointing, "They are on the watch for screechers."

Then they were there.

After Sherry clacked her odd castanet in greeting to Dolla and was jaw clacked in return, the crewmen leapt down and secured the boat to a tree-bush. They would have to stay with the boat. Sherry was taking no chances of any kind this near the end of the long, long struggle and wait.

The triloids stood in a row. Sherry directed The Section to do the same. She and Dolla raised their left knee, then their right, to touch in greeting. The other triloids and The Section understood the official greeting gesture, and all did likewise.

This over, Sherry and Dolla walked along an ancient trail, wide as a road, like two neighbors heading for a shopping trip together. They were preceded by spear warriors, while sailing warriors protected them from above. The Section automatically fell in a column of fours with Bluefeather, Garcia, Moosha and Marsha leading. Pack and another chosen three brought up the rear guard.

There were ponds formed by the river inlets and trees of light grew in patches around them along with bush-trees. Here and there, where the path led them by the edge of dampness, algae had crawled out and taken hold in uneven patches on the limestone, providing a grazing source for the plentiful Dinahs that darted now and then from one source of cover to another. At times the trees and the luminous concentration of the microbes thinned so that a space of near darkness formed in the thick, damp fog. This was no problem, for they simply followed the glowing handles of the triloids' knives and spear shafts. It was not unlike the great candle-bearing processions of the Old Mexico Indians.

Pack said, "I feel like I'm in a dust storm somewhere near Texas." The easy, sometimes senseless, banter of soldiers marching to a rest period before battle rippled back and forth through The Section.

As they walked in the middle of the darkest air hole, a UFO or gas bubble, as Bluefeather guessed it, whizzed silently toward them. It stopped right above them, illuminating every nearby stalactite or stalagmite, revealing the creases in the rock pagodas and outer cavern walls and dimming the other distant light sources to nothing.

There was a slight increase in the teeth clacks of the triloids, who had been born to this phenomena and had accepted it, countless generations back, as commonplace. The Section, however, stopped, transfixed, shading their eyes, yet attempting to see into the great ball of light. Then it zoomed sideways at such speed their sight could not follow. When their vision did catch up with the gleam, it was whirling and dancing a mile away.

They moved on now in a slight trance. Bluefeather was feeling and hearing the cadences of the caverns: the animals; the fish that also crawled on land; the screechers; the Dinahs; the pursuers; the captured; the spewing of thousands of steaming geysers, some with spouts as small as a pencil, others as big around as ice-skating rinks; shafts of molten rock spurting up from fissures and breaking into droplets as they returned to water and earth, building little islands one place, causing holes to sink at another. He was hearing the sounds of a virgin jungle.

Bluefeather fully realized now that the world inside and out made constant music. Everywhere. Great composers simply heard it cleaner, more clearly and rearranged what was there for all the rest. Always.

The clacking sounds increased in intensity. They were there. A two-hundred-yard-high face of limestone cliff fronted them in a half arc. There were homes of holes all over its face, starting about seventy feet up. They had been partially porched in and had unlighted river reeds tied together with dried sinew as a combination door and window. Some had rock ledge perches. Others were constructed from the river reeds, similar to a huge eagle's nest. Guards watched from properly spaced perches. The rest of the triloids, perhaps a hundred or more, waited.

When Dolla clacked a signal, they moved forward en masse.

Some females were suckling from one to four babies, who hung on their mothers with claws that surprisingly seemed to give no pain. There were young ones who followed right next to both the fathers and mothers with much shorter, but imitative, steps. Then there were those The Section would call teenagers, walking to the rear.

Now they lined up in a half circle and all but the babies raised first the right leg and then the left knee out prominently in greeting. The Section was a little late in its movements, but fulfilled the ceremonial gesture anyway. The triloids seemed satisfied.

Now each of those from the outer world was led to be seated in a partial circle and the triloids finished filling it in. In the middle were cooking pits with river reeds as fuel. There were spits made from thin rocks, and on them some of the triloids turned huge fish and many Dinahs. There were multiple metate-like bowls at which some sat slicing the cut saplings of trees of light, then grinding them with another, smaller hand-rock into a flour—a process not unlike that used by the ancient Anasazi grinders of corn. The powder was mixed with water, crab meat and other delicacies that not even Sherry recognized.

Sherry walked over to The Section accompanied by Dolla and her teen daughter, Reesha. Then they were joined by Dolla's mate, the father, whom Sherry had named Odad.

Sherry went on with her explanation. "Today we have been invited to Reesha's wedding. Soon the members from another pueblito will arrive with the groom."

The feast was about ready. The triloids' guests were all nearby, hidden, awaiting the signal to be asked to present their son to be wed.

Bluefeather was personally thrilled to know there were fourteen pueblitos scattered up and down the river. The

triloids lived peacefully in their own territories, similar to
the pueblo nations of the Rio Grande. Certainly half of
him felt at home here by blood and instinct, and the rest
by genial invitation.

He looked at the Dolby Youngers so eagerly absorbing
the visit. It was as new to them as it was to him. Steinberg
had trained his militia well. They obeyed orders instantly
and efficiently. A sudden pang grabbed Bluefeather's
throat when he realized he would never get to know their
minds, or souls, or dreams. Dolby had already arranged
that. His eyes moved to The Section. Only Pack was aware
of their loves, desires, families and childhood. There had
been no time for him to know them outside battle. Maybe
later. Maybe.

His sight jumped to Marsha and he moved down next
to her, squeezing her hand. She squeezed back so lightly
he almost missed the pressure.

Then his mind-voice plugged in: *Why, we could live
here with the triloids, Marsha and I. We sure could. Let
the rest of them go on and risk their lives, while Sherry
fulfills old Dolby's ambitions. Marsha and I could survive
here on our own skills*—and those learned from the triloids. We could live and love and laugh and mate, like
we're supposed to. The mind-voice fell silent and he came
back to the reality of the near-unreal.

It was the time of the wedding. Dolla clacked her teeth
a certain way. Four triloids, two old males and two even
older females, moved into the circle with drums of rawhide stretched around stems from the magical trees. Their
drumsticks glowed from the microbes, and the ends were
leather-wrapped in such a way as to create perfect per-
cussion.

They sat in a square and suddenly, at an unseen signal,
simultaneously pounded a powerful rhythm on the drums.
Out from the crevasses of the bluffs, and up from behind
indentations in the earth, out of ponds of reeds, the guest

triloids suddenly arose, watching as the young male left their company and moved out toward the opening circle where Reesha now stood alone, waiting. The host triloids widened the circle smoothly to allow all the visitors to enter it, creating one twice as large.

The young groom, whom Sherry called Metza, moved to the very front of Reesha. They lifted and touched knees one at a time, stepped back a yard, then advanced and repeated the greeting thrice. The drums suddenly stopped. Metza clacked his teeth at Reesha. Then again. Again. Now she answered. His sounds of conversation became louder, faster. So did hers, lagging just behind his.

Then he started a sort of shuffling dance, circling her, moving first one hand and then the other out toward her midsection, each time getting an inch closer to touching her. He circled more and more, faster. Now his hands touched her, and touched her, and touched her, all over. Her clacking became shallow and fast as her breasts were moving in and out. Suddenly, she dropped to her hands and knees as the drums began pounding, pounding blood rhythms. He circled now on his hands and knees. It seemed impossible, but the drums increased in volume. The others, both human and triloid, stared—mesmerized.

Metza circled swiftly now and then mounted her from behind like a dog, a stallion or a bull, and he pumped away with the rhythm of the drums. To the shock of the above-grounders, the two young triloids were making their first love. They rolled on the ground, holding each other close, their flaps pulled and wrapped in such a way that they appeared to be a huge, round baseball.

They rolled in circles that became more erratic with each pounding sequence of the drums. Then the grey-white ball almost stopped—whirled jerkily, swiftly, three or four times—and then the two fell apart as the drums reached a crescendo at such speed that it was one beat.

They unfolded and lay side by side, their breaths heaving mightily. They were wed. No one paid them any more attention. They could wander around the compound within safe limits doing anything they wished, totally ignored. Later, when the visit was over, Metza would lead Reesha, following his tribe, to the new cave home he had built for her on down the river in his territory.

The drums played softly now, accompanied by some others beating a rhythm with the sticks cut from the endlessly useful trees of light. They drank slightly fermented juice from a tube of the same. The fermented plant gave them a mild sensation of mellowness no matter how little or how much they drank. Everyone lined up and sliced their own meat onto plates of woven reeds. From the metate dishes they dined on food of many varied textures and shapes. It was a feast of difference—a wedding feast, a friendship feast—but a feast, nevertheless.

At first, Bluefeather had been taken aback by the fact that the triloids cooked their food, but, of course, with their obvious reasoning powers and fire rising and falling over all the basin, they could hardly have escaped discovering its delights.

Suddenly, such practical thoughts became unimportant as he had a desperate urge to grab Marsha and dance in wild circles and take her to the mating mat with him as Metza and Reesha had done. He controlled this powerful drive by forcing his thinking in the direction of Taos Mountain and all the secret canyons he knew surrounding it with deer, bear, bobcats and squirrels. Its own song came to him for a moment, above that of the cave, and soothed him, quieting his lust and making him feel foolish for having thoughts of actions that might have appeared impolite to his hosts. He wondered what all the rest were feeling. Partly the same as him, he was sure.

They were all rescued from their varied musings by Sherry and Dolla, who took them on a tour. The triloids had their own fish farms with gates to hold and control them in the pools around inlets from the main river. Then they were shown the waterfall that came out of a cavern upon the bluff and formed a deep fresh waterhole. They had dammed it up with rock work.

There were a bunch of young triloids waiting on a ledge high above the water for a signal from Dolla. She clacked her teeth and raised an arm, swinging it down hard by her side. The entire section, except for Sherry, gasped as three young triloids raced, leaping off the high ledge, rolling up into round balls, plunging down at the speed of gravity's pull. Then their ball-like roundness rolled over and over in the air. When it looked like they would strike the surface of the pool with such force that they were in peril of being splattered into bits across the landscape, they unwound. The folds under their spread arms caught the air, and they sailed off in circles without ever having touched the water.

One by one they circled back up like well-guided kites to the proper altitude, rolled into balls again and plunged into the pool, resurfacing swiftly and water-walking right out on the bank. They stood in line and raised their knees in unison to their guests, who started to clap but then realized that Sherry was imitating Dolla, raising her knees in swift applause and slapping a hand on each. Everyone followed this example, trying to be proper.

The teens smiled with what could have been taken as a snarl if The Section had not already seen Dolla do the same at their first meeting. Then Dolla tilted her head back, looking way up on the precipice, and gave her signal again. This time a dozen of the young raced and leaped off the edge, spreading their wind flaps. They sailed along the same air drafts as the others had, in a flying ballet— in and out, up and down, in a gorgeous harmony of slow bird movement. They circled lower and lower above the pond. One by one they formed a ball and dove into the pond. Each stayed under water until all had joined them.

Then the ripples subsided so that the surface of the pond was almost smooth. "Boom!" All twelve of them came out of the water at once. Flapping their way on the surface of the pond in curving single file, they moved faster in a bubbling, frothing race around the pond, doing figure eights and double figure eights, leapfrogging one another with foaming speed.

Charlie Waters said, "If I could dance like that I'd own Broadway."

Hector Garcia intoned, "Such a *baile* would fill Bernalillo County with tourists from around the world. No?"

Willy said, "I wouldn't travel this far to see it, but I'd pay a lot for a ticket if the show was put on close to home."

The ex-football player–chef, Jimmy D. Ratchett, said, "The Superdome would fall down from the applause."

Bluefeather could tell by these and other remarks that the watery dance was a stunning success and much needed relief for the troops. It was a show such as no one above, and not many here below, had ever seen.

Shortly, Bluefeather would find out that Sherry had made a bargain for the triloids to follow them into the Hills of Hell, giving whatever support they could. So they also were putting out extra effort to entertain and to enjoy, for the tomorrow of all their tomorrows was near.

The dozen young leapt up out of the edge of the pool in perfect synchrony, coming down softly on the cavern floor with their flaps folding just as they touched stone, rolling, all together, right over in front of Dolla, Sherry and The Section, unwinding and standing up at the same time, lifting their knees to form a perfect chorus line.

This time The Section lost control. The recognition of such a performance could not be held back. They clapped and yelled, "Bravo! Bravo! Bravo!" raising fisted hands in the air and making bent-over side motions with arms of excited approval.

Bluefeather thought of the purity and rareness of this welcome given and performed for strange creatures from another world above them, who had intruded on their domain. Incomprehensible beauty. Pureness.

They had shared with them an intimate wedding, a feast, a performance of life-risking action and had volunteered to follow them to hell. Totality.

It was time to return to the boat. There was nothing left to receive from the triloids without great embarrassment. Fortunately, for the hosts, the triloids didn't have that last word in their clacking, clattering vocabulary, as yet. They had never done anything to warrant its invention.

FORTY-TWO

BLUEFEATHER LAY BACK ON THE COUCH AND TRIED TO put things in order before going to bed. They would leave for the hills right after the sleep time, which was going on now for most of The Section, as well as the Olders and Youngers, but his sleep did not come. Then it struck him—it was the Mouton '80. That's how Korbell had trapped him. Step by step the man had taken control of his life so smoothly Bluefeather had almost failed to notice.

The Mouton '80 had done the trick, all right. It sounded so reasonable for a man of such wealth and power, who could buy almost anything, to crave what he couldn't find, or have. Nothing unusual there. He was willing to pay good money for skilled services. He had even assigned his adopted daughter, Marsha, to assist Bluefeather in order to make the deal seem true. Korbell had shrewdly figured that Bluefeather's friends, the Rugers, would eventually lead him to the contact with Dolby. They had.

Then Korbell had relied on Dolby and Sherry to recognize a good hired hand. Being both a soldier and near-geologist, Bluefeather would fit all their plans. Marsha, his love, had been there all the time, giving to him—or giving for Korbell? That was the mainline question not answered with any definity yet. Korbell had probably known all along that Dolby had beheaded Tilton and taken the gold bullion. It was the accursed yellow metal that Korbell had wanted all the time.

It was difficult to cogitate upon, but Marsha had to have told her father of the filmed images here below, and—as a nation covets a strategic seaport or energy source, a farm or timber belt—his natural powers of acquisition and greed had taken over.

Marsha? Marsha? Marsha? Had she been the manipulator all the time? It could be nothing else. The wine search had been forgotten too easily by the both of them. The original deal had been subordinated. However, if this was one-hundred-percent true, why did he worry so with a nagging presentiment that something terrible was going to happen to Marsha on this next trip? Why did his fleeting dreams almost reveal the cause of his feeling of dread for her? Why? Why? Why? Again and again.

Now he was working for both Dolby and Korbell—two respectful enemies—and innocent people were dying. Well, in spite of Korbell or Dolby or Marsha, he was going to fulfill his obligations to Sherry and the surviving section now or he would burn and sink in the River of Radiance— that river of riches, river of revelations. He would pursue the Tilton maps that Charlie Waters had acquired for him. He would search every inch of every building and he would find the wine and fulfill his word. Then, and only then, would he decide whether to kill the two greedy bastards or not.

If The Section pulled off the last phase of the expedition successfully, one or the other, or both, of the world-class accumulators could control the largest, most precious and rare mineral deposits in the world. The winner would be able to swing money and stock markets at his will. He could, at the movement of a finger or the uttering on one word, "yes" or "no," make kings from paupers and vice versa. Then, of course, other accumulators would start plotting and planning, and in a decade, a century, whatever, take it away from him. By so doing, the avaricious cycle of the powerful, the rich, the imprisoned, the tortured, the beheaded and disemboweled would start all over again. Endlessly.

From the other viewpoint, Sherry's, the galaxies could be studied right here in the cave of "the star." The whole of the creation of old worlds, giving clues to the new, was here to be studied and the knowledge applied to those above and beyond. In the blackness of the center of the fallen meteorite, great curative powers, plus every metal of the earth—and several as yet unidentified—had been concentrated in the great kettle of fire and water intersecting here.

The plants called the trees of light were a miracle of creation and bounteous giving just by themselves. The wonders of the life-forms here would have to be totally respected and protected or they would soon deteriorate and suffocate, as those on the surface were rapidly doing. There was the possibility of vast knowledge for the youth of the entire world here. Wonderment. That's what they could commonly share—that necessity of all young things without which they become half blind and half dead and so inwardly directed that they create only half lives for themselves. Wonderment. Yes, wonderment was abundant here. Awaiting—making it the greatest of all gifts or the greatest of all sins—its destruction.

However it went, Bluefeather was going into the Hills of Hell and would return to face Korbell with the whereabouts of the wine. He laughed, alone and aloud, at himself. His mind had leapt from the priceless rocks of heaven and earth to twenty cases of wine—and he was guilty of equalizing them. The grand questions became practical and singular after all. Still, one had to have both.

With this thought he decided it was time for a half-vision. It did not come easily or clearly; it was more like the mists of the Cavern of Marvels.

Dancing Bear sashayed toward him, but he knew this only by the movement of his head and hands, for his lower body was in fog. He was doing some of his favorite dances—a nameless Greek step, segueing into a Scottish fling, a Cherokee stomp, a Taos round and a Russian tippy toe. Although the moccasins were lost in the low mist, Bluefeather could not miss the motions he had seen a hundred times.

Bluefeather whispered, "Iceland. Do Icelandic for me."

Dancing Bear only smiled and Hawaiian hip shook and New Orleans tap danced himself into Marsha, who smiled until all he could see were her teeth. Then she receded into Miss Mary, who first waved at him in greeting and then beckoned him to come with her into the filminess. Miss Mary. Oh God. Then he was thankful that guitarists Ramon Hernandez and Antonio Mendoza played a duet just for him. Could it be? Yes it was. "La Golondrina." Then they did an old Italian classic in such harmony as to be one.

He now caught swift glimpses in the clouds and there he saw the Friedmans of a Taos summer—both mother and daughter—and old Grinder yelled at him from the fog above the fading music, "Get the idee? Get the idee?"

His two mules were clearer than all else. They were contentedly eating oats there at home in Corrales, looking up now and then, watching for his return.

He came out of his half-vision just as he was saying, "I'll see you in awhile, little darlings."

They switched their tails and moved their ears back and forth, hearing something from somewhere. He slept.

FORTY-THREE

IT WAS THE TIME TO ATTACK BEYOND THE BEYOND—
even farther, if needed. At the departure, Sherry had said,
simply, "This is no sci-fi film we're going to attend; it's
real. Real as homemade fudge."

All listened, all heard, all understood. At first it was
easy. The boat purred along the smooth waters with no
threat from the water or air. Sherry instructed the mo-
torman to slow down and pull over next to a nearly sheer
bluff that joined the river where it became narrower for
a quarter mile or so. He stopped the boat. She pointed
out watermarks etched into the stone of different ages
with different lines and colors. There were ice ages, great
droughts, years of heavy snows and rains, tales told as in
the rings of redwood trees. Here was the history of the
upper and lower earth for aeons—a geological map.

Sherry had long ago photographed and catalogued this
Morse code from the far and near past. These water messages on rocks could tell why and when great herds of
animals and pueblos of Indians had migrated. There
would be fossils and sediments of large lakes and seabeds
above to match these linear messages down here—a bul-
letin board from the long ago.

Sherry had done some work on its ancient signs, but

she would need help from the world's scientific minds even to get a start on the massive information stored everywhere one gazed, stepped or breathed.

They moved on through the narrows and into a wide area where there were many side shallows. Sherry pointed out the triloids moving on the ground, parallel with them. At times they climbed the endless formations with their muscled palms and foot soles, leaping free and sailing in circles, always staying protectively even with the progress of the boat.

It seemed that every mile or so the number of steam geysers and the amount of magma increased, as did the light, noise and heat. The triloids were having to move forward with more and more effort, even though they were still a good distance from the spewing, erratic, half ring of fiery geysers that protected the entrance to the dead—the reportedly gold-rich Hills of Hell.

Bluefeather's eyes were first on the danger. He spotted seven or eight wide water wakes moving toward them. Even so, he had almost been too late. The heavy chomper came leaping and diving over the edge of the boat and grabbed the two-inch pipe railing, biting it in half as Pack let loose a burst of M-2 lead right into its nostrils. Several chompers were now attacking all sides of the low-slung ship, rocking it down to the cork rim, encircling its entire outer shell.

Bluefeather yelled for the people in front of him to hit the deck. He let loose a blast into the open throat of the huge-jawed chomper that had chewed a piece of the boat edge loose as a rat might the cardboard around a box of cheese. The gun mounts were useless now. There was too much chaos, and personnel movement, to fire such high-caliber weapons this close in.

Pack emptied another clip into the short neck where it joined the great chest. He had found the weak spot—the same as on the screechers. The beast fell slowly backward,

claws hanging till the last on the ship rim. Blood spewed
in the air like a lawn spray from its dying bellows.

Bluefeather had just slapped another clip in his rifle
when Jimmy D. Ratchett let loose a burst with his .45
tommy gun, shooting enough off the top of its head to
reveal its brain. Moosha sank his razored machete into
the opening, plunging it back and forth until the chomper
slid away to end its day.

Bluefeather whirled to look for Marsha. She, Sherry
and Willy had all emptied clips into one of the attackers
without seeming to slow him down. It had snapped the
railing like a toothpick and bit a bolted-down swivel chair
into junk. It turned on Bluefeather as it opened its jaws
again.

Marsha took a terrible gamble on all their lives. She
made an instinctive, lightning decision as she jerked the
pin from a grenade, screaming, "Hit the deck," and all
that were standing did. As the animal opened those terrible jaws of teeth—bigger, sharper by far than those of
the largest of the Australian whites—Marsha hurled the
grenade down its throat with all her strength. The creature instinctively, and with great good fortune, swallowed.
A couple more steps and the beast would have crushed
or bitten some of them in half.

The grenade lifted a hump in the brute's heavy frame
and blew holes in its sides. Streams of blood gushed out
the wounds, along with its guts. The overly heavy head
dropped, and it clawed weakly with its front legs a few
times. Then a death sigh of "war lost" was emitted. It was
still.

The gun turrets were firing now at those that had failed
to make it to the boat's rim. The 50-caliber machine guns
and 20-mm cannon turned them into rolling tails and
heads that splashed water and blood. Their yellow-white,
perforated bellies turned upward and thrashed wildly
about, over and over, until the boat pulled away, leaving

a thousand smaller, sharp-toothed fish and other swimmers dining well. It took most of The Section to lift the
dead chomper and roll it over the edge of the boat.

Only Moosha and Willy were injured. A couple small
pieces of the grenade shrapnel had exited the chomper,
striking Moosha along the ribs, breaking the skin but not
penetrating the bone. Willy had received a metal sliver in
his bicep. Pack and a couple of the Youngers gave immediate first aid. They did a good clean job of it.

The temperature of the air and water was getting hotter. Now little bits of mist, almost steam, lifted here and
there, even from areas of the river where there were no
geysers or bottom fumaroles. They were now in a vast
humidifier.

Bluefeather checked with everyone to be sure of no
more injuries. When he came to Marsha, he said, quietly,
"Thanks. Thanks from all of us. That was magnificent."

"I didn't even think. I just did it," she said fearfully.

"There was no time for anything but action, little darling," he said without forethought, but he was actually still
possessed with the premonition of something terrible happening to her. He couldn't let his concern show to the
others, not a particle. None. Especially Marsha. The
slightest nervousness revealed could lead to disaster for
all.

Sherry kneeled on the ammo magazine, watching all
around. Shia stood, rifle ready, as close as possible to
Sherry at all times. Unlike the rest, Sherry was all she
cared about.

Then everyone went on full alert. Bluefeather and Pack
took over, posting guards in proper positions. Bluefeather
assigned the young female first aides the job of filling and
refilling canteens so that no one would dehydrate in the
huge cooker. The sweat poured from them so that they
looked like users of country club steam baths fully clothed

or denizens of a Navajo sweat lodge. The canteens were emptied and refilled twice in a brief period.

They now traveled in torrid unpleasantness. The rubber-covered asbestos and the titanium steel hull held together and kept them from seriously burning, though. The ship worked.

The Youngers in the gun turrets raised the steel flaps and took more drinking water than anyone else. The great plumes of smoke from the gas and magma fire geysers both darkened and lightened places in the cavern up ahead, but they could still see relatively well, at least for awhile.

The Section forced its collective nervous system to prepare for the upcoming passage through the Ring of Fire. Adrenaline charged everyone up again. It was a good thing, for soon Sherry heard the loud and worried "clack-clack" from their friends, the triloids, penetrate the fogs to her ears, warning of the screechers.

Sherry shouted to all, "Screechers. One o'clock high."

Five of the massive, air-ground creatures were following above, along river updrafts, which were strong enough to keep their hollow bones floating with only an occasional flap of the wings for guidance. They floated easily, conserving most of their energy and strength. Their ear-numbing shrieks shafted the air and the heads of the boaters like millions of minute needles. The occupants' hearts pounded from this assault of sound the same as they would have from exploding bombs.

To the amazement and relief of all on the boat, a score or so of the sailing triloids attacked their number one enemy first. The triloids angled in from all sides on the leading bird. Hurling spears into its bulk, then arcing out and back to jerk the weapons free, they circled until they were in range again. Some of the projectiles sank a foot deep into the screechers' bodies.

One especially daring triloid landed right on the lead

screecher's back and stabbed up and down into its flesh, but another screecher swept down, grabbing and crushing the brave triloid and dropped its formlessness into the river. Other triloids were hooked on the scimitar claws at the ends of the screechers' wings and were ripped apart like swords slicing jellyfish, falling in their own spray of red to feed the millions of odd-sized jaws waiting below. They were losing members, perhaps seven or eight already. They zoomed in and out, around and up under the mammoth screechers.

The boaters were shouting encouragement. They suffered every wound of the triloids and exulted with each piercing of a spear into the enemy.

The screechers were so busy trying to fight the constant stabbing circles of the little grey-white enemy—attacking with the ferocity of killer bees—that they had broken formation and no longer considered them mere pests to be slashed from the air like biting flies. The birds were angered, pained and losing life fluids—although not enough to cripple one as yet. Nevertheless, as accurate and exact as their sonar, scent glands and mind-vision were, there were just too many moving objects coming at them from too many angles. It became impossible for them to keep the formidable weapons of wing and feet claws and the slicing, crushing beaks in proper killing mode. Their attack on the humans had been disorganized.

Now one of them lost control of a wing and circled off toward the shore. All the triloids, sensing an actual kill, followed it like vengeful wasps. The message of memory had been passed among them. Here on this boat were the true intruders. The attack of the triloids, while injurious and unexpected, was nevertheless part of the nature of their domain. The uncounted creatures of the water and air were part of the allness in this vast habitat, but those on the boat were foreign splinters.

The triloids were victorious. All the screechers but one

were now being dined on and assimilated into the food chain by the thousands of smaller water creatures.

The last one splashed so near the ship, the shocked waves of water almost capsized the boat, throwing everyone crashing into each other and battering everyone against chains and the sides of the boat.

Kubeck, struck by Ratchett's heavily tossed body, was knocked overboard to the feeders and only had time to raise one arm and yell for help twice before he disappeared. His hurtling body had saved Ratchett's life.

A part of the screecher's wing had struck the engine mount so hard that it had bent the frame of the boat.

The survivors crawled up out of the sloshing deck water. They could feel the ship shaking as the engine pushed its unevenness against the water's constant bulk. It was barely moving.

Bluefeather ordered them to activate the other engine. With both propellers now shoving, the craft moved somewhat faster, although constantly shuddering, trying to alter its course. The boatmen were struggling mightily to keep it moving in the general direction of the Ring of Fire. They succeeded.

Pack said, "Hey, you guys, get it back together like we were when we left port. There ain't been any shrapnel here. Just flying bird guts."

Those unhurt or only lightly wounded did a celebratory dance of victory and then a more somber one, of respect, for the vanquished. The latter action was cut short when Dolla made a Sergeant Pack–type speech of her own, with different sounds but the same meaning. They would have to reorganize, winding their way in the air above the intermittent and erratically blazing fire line; otherwise, they would rapidly bake to a nice brown on the hot banks of the river.

The seriously wounded were stabbed in the heart and rolled into the water. This was a rule of battle the triloids had followed for epochs. All who were capable fought on. All unable, died quickly. This kept the forces intact to win. No sympathy. No regrets. They survived their constant wars healthy, intact, or they would never have survived at all. Venerable. Dolla ordered the able-bodied to the walls and pillars of stalactites and stalagmites, where they hung like large, pale bats.

Sherry was looking ahead at varied geysers with daring exuding from her eyes and stance. She, above them all, had waited to enter this deadly approach so long that the dangers seemed secondhand now. To the others, the geysers, the smoke, the rising and falling mists, the constant roar of the most powerful forces of earth—fire and water—were fearful and enticing at once. Nevertheless, as the mists became heavier, hotter, and the magma flares ever brighter and louder, their fears tilted to the greatest opiate of all—the enveloping intoxication of possible instant life, or death. The ancient hairline of the ultimate thrill was upon them.

Bluefeather signalled the directions with arm movements to the waiting motormen. No verbal instructions were possible. The burning gases and the boiling spouts of water coming up from the molten center of the earth were as loud as an exploding volcano. They moved into the fiery, watery abyss. No return tickets at this point.

Several dropped from the heat as if struck by an invisible, invincible force applied by the gods. The standing leapt about, keeping the faces of the fallen out of the bottom water, where they would have drowned. Marsha swayed upright beside Bluefeather, then moved on to help the fallen. The center of hell surrounded them below, above, and on all sides—churning, burning, roaring with the voice of all the forces of life, death and doom, of birth and rebirth.

They had been in the vortex of Hades for timeless time. A coven of craven witches brewed mixtures of devils all around them. The Section's ability to regulate reason was gone, though they were sane. Their senses of direction had been scattered, but they moved on. They remained ready to live or die as the call came. Bluefeather held their direction together and now his voice could be heard. It seemed remote, planets away, but was recognized as the voice of their commander in the sound receivers of their brains. Louder, clearer.

"Now left. Now right. More. Now straight ahead. Hold it there. Straight on, troops. Forward!"

They were in a lake of placid water before they knew it. The great fumaroles that had formed the dead Hills of Hell had dammed the river enough to create a lake. It drained out a narrow opening on one side, a mile or so beyond the island that in itself formed a holding dam. None of the natural inhabitants of this deep place cared a damn about gold. All they wanted to do was eat, any way they could, and reproduce their own kind.

The remaining section members came out of the necessary daze slowly. Their breathing returned. Bluefeather ordered the motors at half power to ease the jolting of the bent ship. Eyes began to clear and little smiles broke through the grime-coated faces.

Sherry crawled up by Bluefeather on the shattered gun turret. She looked across the smooth surface of the lake and at quiet dark hills, hugging him silently from the side. The motion conveyed her thanks and the depth of her feelings with no need for words.

They had made it. Unbelievable. True.

FORTY-FOUR

IT WAS SO PEACEFUL PUT-PUTTING ACROSS THE LAKE
that for awhile a lethargy settled on them. Even such experienced warriors as Pack and Bluefeather moved about
the boat as if they had been dining on opium for a decade.
The cuts, bruises and fears were all numbed for a spell.
The din of the peerless line of fire and water in conflict
with itself receded behind them, so they ignored its existence. The subsiding of their lifesaving adrenaline and
electrified thinking of battle, followed by the confusion of
the fiery fissures, left them in a peculiar and pensive
mood. Tranquil. The only surprise came when they casually swept their eyes across the new, yet ancient, landscape and discovered that the triloids had beaten them
there. They waited with obvious patience—guards strategically posted on various low rises. The triloids' appearance ahead of them was almost instantly accepted as
normal.

They tied the boat to an upswung rock and slowly dis-
embarked. Bluefeather, Pack and Sherry eased back into
a cautious command mode, checking all equipment, including the saws, axes and the large canvas ore bags made
to fit on a special backpack. All weapons were loaded,
clips filled, grenades secured. The flamethrowers were

unloaded from the craft but not back-slung as yet. Long drinks of water were taken and canteens refilled.

Then Bluefeather positioned different members of The Section on the moonscape shore so that a watch could be kept and still leave someone to visit. Besides, the triloids occupied higher ground and would front any danger if it existed. Nothing threatened them for now. Nothing at all.

They sat on the rocks and had a lunch of hard energy candy that had melted together into a slab but was now broken into servings by good-humored Chef Ratchett. Sherry was becoming extremely anxious to finish the final journey but knew they would need the nourishment and subsequent renewed strength to climb and work the hard metallic hills.

Bluefeather took two pieces of the candy and eased over and sat next to Marsha, handing her a chunk. She took it, smiling her great smile through the grime of the day. Bluefeather's heart turned to newborn magma. The successful trip together, through the torrid line of fizzing fissures, and the survival of the battles had erased all sins against one another—no matter what they had believed or imagined. Vanished. Gone. Never to matter again.

He touched the back of her now blackish hair as if it were new silk and said as simply and sincerely as sunshine, "I sure do love you a whole bunch."

Her Korbell smile would have lighted a Yankee Stadium night game with enough left over for New Year's fireworks.

"I love you too. About this much." She started with the palms of her hands about three inches apart and then spread them slowly until her arms were spread as wide as possible. Then she flung them around him. They held one another closely, warmly and hard.

Bluefeather saw Sherry stand and order a Younger to sack up all the lunch waste and put it back on the boat. He knew it was time for her final lap.

Pack and Ratchett put on the flamethrowers. Everyone took positions as Pack designated. Nothing was in sight or sound to hinder them, but back at God's Castle they had trained and prepared for any eventuality. Sticking closely to the prior plans had gotten them to this last destination.

They climbed up the hills toward the triloids, who moved much faster and had taken up positions far ahead of them around the sides of the large hills. They were glued there comfortably with their powerful suction muscles.

At the beginning of the slope of the largest hill, Bluefeather made his first cut with the axe. He chopped through the dark, burned crust that crunched under their feet with the sound of cinders. His axe cut into the mostly malleable metal, revealing spots and streaks of yellow and silver dominating the harder and widely varied colors of other rare metals. The long, long time of intense heat had boiled and melted the weaker metals—such as iron—away, leaving only this surface crust to cover the massive volume of unfathomable richness underneath.

Bluefeather ordered George Tack Won to slice a linear chunk out with the diamond-surfaced chain saw. Won pulled the cord and the gas motor started on the second yank.

The metal was very heavy. The Youngers, with their packs, were sent back and forth from the cuts, carrying the precious metals to the boat. Pack watched the triloid guards for any danger signals as Bluefeather worked. Bluefeather and Willy measured the distance between cuts with a long, steel tape. Bluefeather recorded them all in a wax-wrapped notebook.

Clock hours passed and even the relative coolness became hot as they marched on from one totally barren hill to the other, cutting, measuring, carrying the heavy samples again and again to the boat. The richness varied. They had now sampled out about a square mile of metal with obvious depths in places above the river, ranging from a few feet to three hundred.

Bluefeather, Willy and the carriers were exhausted. Now Bluefeather paused and really looked at the landscape here for the first time. Not a blade of grass, not a sprout of a weed or a cactus or a seedling of any kind— not even algae from the lake's edge—showed life here. Where once hellish fires had flamed and cooked, there was only a crust of burned iron and underneath enough wealth to control the flesh of most of the world and the forests, bushes and grasses that covered it. He was too tired to analyze any of the results of their current labor, even for a moment. But Willy did.

Willy said, sitting down and leaning back against a small, dead fumarole, "You know, this stuff looks like it's over half malleable metal to me. So, if all we did was mine this an inch deep, there would be enough reserves to buy Germany, Japan, Roosha and all the Hawaiian Islands. Don't you reckon, Blue?"

"I hear you, old pardner, and as soon as we can stand up, I'm going to call it finished."

"Good. I'd give half this Island of Gold for six bottles of cold beer."

"When did you switch from whiskey?"

"Oh, about the middle of that goddamned firestorm. I figured a change would do me good."

"Makes a world full of sense to me."

The two old buddies were just on the verge of silly-happy when the unmistakable warning of the triloids' clatter came clicking out across the dead, black hills. Everyone who was sitting leapt up. Those standing crouched. All were looking and listening for the cause of the triloids' warning.

It was so huge and nearly colorless that everyone but the triloids missed it. The object of their notification was so much bigger than any creature the humans had ever imagined, it was at first indefinable.

Bluefeather's superior eyesight saw it looming up over the hills into the sky of the cave. It was translucent and only shadows of light gave it any form at all. In fact, most portions of the as-yet-formless body were transparent. Then he saw the red, throbbing thing inside it. His eyes tracked the thin lines of red fluid pumping throughout the body. That pump was its heart and the liquid its blood. It had no eyes, but it had all the other senses of the cavern's blind ones. It had, in fact, begun to take on a nameless shape something like forty transparent elephants metamorphosed into one. It had two mighty bluish white trunks at least fifty feet long with a mouth at each end that widely opened and closed, over and over. It had glassy, but tactile, arms, similar to a giant octopus, along each side. In between these were tentacles that swiftly rolled up into balls, then flung themselves open, reaching out twice the distance beyond the mouths of trunks. Its main body was almost like a huge, transparent, rectangle of a box, but with rounded corners.

Willy whispered in awe, "That thing's big enough to use the moon for a volleyball."

Charlie Waters gasped, "We are in dung of great depth."

No one seemed to hear them. All eyes went to the boat, where the remaining cannon and 50 calibers were, but there was no way to reach them now. The Khyber beast had that area easily covered with writhing, searching protuberances.

Simultaneously, it seemed everyone heard and felt the triloids change their warning sounds. A look, far back downhill, revealed another Khyber crawling onto land with its hundred legs moving in impossible cohesion. There was total pause of everyone and everything. No triloid, no human, no Khyber moved. It lasted less than a gasp of air but seemed like the length of a three-day blizzard.

The first movement came from the triloids. En masse they leapt into the air and attacked, circling high above, then plummeting down to within a few yards of the Khyber. They stretched out their underarm folds to brake just on the surface of the now moving, bluish white mountain of molecules. Their spears, knives and four-inch claws appeared useless. However, as with their charges at the screechers, they had slowed the Khyber's attack by diverting its attention.

Bluefeather and Pack scattered their troops and attacked. They had no other choice. Without the boat they were—every one of them—doomed.

Now all recognized the beating, red heart and poured round after round of bullets into the transparent body until the lead looked like flakes of pepper in mashed potatoes, but none of the slugs could penetrate deep enough to reach its heart.

A tentacle reached into the air and plucked a triloid like an apple from a tree. With an amazingly swift, accurate movement, the Khyber tossed it into the nearest octopus mouth. The discernible triloid was sucked down the long trunk into another tunnel to the clearly visible stomach and, before their stunned eyes, was swiftly digested into juice.

Moosha and Hector remembered Marsha's action with the grenade. Each pulled a pin, holding the hand trigger closed as they charged the octopus's mouths. For just a moment it looked as if they had a chance to wound the Khyber, but the tentacles snaked out and encircled them so swiftly that they were jerked loose from the grenades. Both grenades fell, exploding in midair, doing little more damage than the hundreds of bullets the Khyber had now absorbed.

Moosha dropped down one trunk-tube and Hector

down the other, right into the stomach. Both were melted by the acids and mixed invisibly with those of the vanished triloid.

Bluefeather and Pack started firing rifle grenades. The Khyber was jarred and torn enough to make it hesitate. Fielder and two of the Youngers made a run for the ship's guns. They were almost there when the Khyber shifted in what seemed like slow motion because of its massive bulk. Its tentacles swished out like living bullwhip sinews and captured them, curling the bodies back and into the tube for the same visible fate.

Almost as shocking to Bluefeather as the liquid deaths was the fact that Sherry suddenly knelt down, opened her notebook and started writing. Shia knelt in front of her, offering her body first as Sherry wrote: "The Khybers are soft-bodied fauna organisms without shell, teeth or bone. It appears that they are halfway evolved in the development from soft tissue to bone. Considering their size, this is an amazing discovery."

Bluefeather had a flashing thought, *My God, in the face of imminent death Sherry is momentarily ignoring everything to record a few lines for a posterity that is in extreme doubt.*

Sherry secured the notebook and stood up to join Shia and the rest in the desperate situation. By now, seven of The Section had been savaged in less than a minute. Three more triloids were hurled inward. The stomach juices had become so thickened with the plenitude of other bodies that the victims now kicked about like small children playing in a wading pool before they dissolved into shapelessness.

About half the triloids were making dives on the other advancing Khyber, delaying it temporarily. Some of the grenades from the launcher had shattered and slowed the tentacles.

Now Osaka's last grenade was attached to the rifle

launcher. He advanced. The crippled tentacles searched
for him and came within inches. When he saw the Khyber
move the other undamaged mouth, spreading wide to
suck him in, he fired and fell. The grenade entered the
opening with much force. The grasping mouth dipped to
suck him up. Osaka was lifted several feet from the
ground as the grenade exploded. The grenade burst the
transparent flesh open just behind the trunk-mouth, and
blood flowed down like bayou rain. Osaka was dropped—
jolted, but intact—on the iron crust.

Pack dashed forward with the flamethrower now and
burned the tentacles from around the mouth. The scent
of seared blood filled all the survivors' nostrils. Even
though the Khyber had workable arms left, it stopped a
moment. Somehow its mind-voice was telling it for the
first time ever that it was no longer invincible.

Jimmy D. Ratchett had gambled with the grenade instead of the flamethrower and lost. He joined the multiple
liquid bodies in the stomach of the Khyber. O'Malley had
hurled grenades and charged, firing his rifle to the last
empty clip, and had been crushed into a little flat roll by
a flailing, impaired tentacle.

Bluefeather saw that in spite of the triloids' valiant agitation of the companion Khyber, it kept on advancing,
narrowing the terrible vise.

A female Younger was the first and only one to crack.
She did so in style, charging, screaming at the beast, slicing with her razored machete in one hand and firing her
handgun with the other. Surprisingly, she didn't have a
wasted death. The Khyber was so awkward with the injured tentacles that it fumbled attempting to tuck her into
its remaining usable mouth. She emptied the handgun
into the more sensitive parts of the interior and cut and
sliced with the machete all the way to the stomach acids.

Major damage was done to the nerves of the beast.
Pack sensed this and struggled forward again with the

flamethrower, cooking the ends of the tentacles and burning most of them from the Khyber's remaining mouth. It was weakened but still held them at bay with its crippled but wildly flailing tentacles.

The triloids had occasionally fought the Khybers back from their personal territories throughout the millenniums. Now they sensed the weakness and the chance. One raced up to the very top of the dominant Hills of Hell and leaped upon a thermal, circling as high as it would carry him. Then at a selected point, it dropped, wrapping itself into a ball. It plunged for the Khyber as fast as gravity could propel it, penetrating deep into the creature, jarring itself dead only three or four yards from the Khyber's heart. Another followed and another. All missed the heart and were lodged there, looking like tiny balls of cotton from where the humans watched.

Then a triloid raced up the side of the highest hill. Its suction muscles worked in perfect rhythm to hold but let it gain speed. It got a much greater leap than the others had. The thermal gave a boost as well and lifted it up, up, up on its outstretched flaps until it was very high. It circled, aiming its tiny body at the colossus. Then it rolled up and the living cannonball plummeted down, down, faster and faster, entering the same wound pioneered and dearly paid for by its predecessors at a slightly different angle. The sacrificial triloid ripped through the already weakened flesh and struck all the way to the heart of the beast, bursting it apart. Its oozing redness spread rapidly in the cavity around it.

Sherry, Bluefeather, Marsha, Charlie Waters, Willy and Osaka raced toward the ship. Pack held back a moment. His flamethrower was still burning nerves in the few floundering tentacles.

Bluefeather grasped Marsha's waist and hoisted her up. They all made it on board, falling over the railing in heaps. Willy started the motors. Bluefeather headed for the re-

maining 20 mm and fired four direct line shells into what
was left of the quivering heart of the Khyber. Pack fell on
board so tired he could barely keep his head out of the
water.

The ship moved away, desperately trying to escape the
last throes of the mammoth creature. Sherry leaped upon
the ammo box. She took the castanet from her bag, clapping it together over and over on its fulcrum with
astounding sound. The remaining triloids heard and retreated from the other, enormously energized Khyber.
The fatally wounded behemoth's hundred legs all crumbled under its weight. With feeble movements of its dis-
tressed extremities, the Khyber slowly sank sideways until
the gravity of its main body gained speed and slumped in
a mass of huge waste, slipping on its own slickness into
the lake. It created another wave, but the boat was too
far away to be in danger.

To the survivors' surprise, their part of the lake became
so peaceful-looking it was almost holy. At the dying Khyber, though, the water frothed with creatures that had
risen from the river's depths to tackle the biggest bait of
all. The other Khyber stopped there, helplessly seeing its
mate being eaten by creatures so small a hundred would
not make a taste. Even so, their tiny working jaws had
turned the lake a darker color of blue by far—a reddish
blue. The living Khyber's transparent body emitted little
sounds of despair, like a rabbit's last muffled squeal as a
bobcat breaks its neck. Then in a sliding, lumbering movement, it turned back to seek out the dark void of the far
unknown part of the cavern—its home—where no human
had ever gazed.

They were the conquerors—those who had made it to
the ship. They had prevailed where others, and other
things, had perished. After such an awesome adventure
no one was wise enough to judge what the reaction would
be of those remaining alive.

Sherry said, "It just occurred to me: we never did see the remains of the helicopter. Do you suppose the Khybers swallowed it?"

"Wouldn't surprise me none," Willy said. "I believe those critters could swallow a whole penitentiary, barbwire and all, without even belching."

Bluefeather gave instructions: "Willy, turn her left, right over there. I picked us out an opening through the fire when we were making our highest measurement on Khyber Island."

Willy said, "Done."

Marsha said to Bluefeather, "I guess this sounds frivolous right now, but god, I would love a meal, a bath and about twelve hours' sleep."

"Well, there's plenty of hot water for the bath. Have at it," Bluefeather said with a grin, motioning to the rings of fire.

"This particular hot water isn't exactly what I had in mind. And come to think of it, forget the sleep part, too. I might miss something."

Charlie agreed, "You got that right." He took a deep swallow of water from the canteen, emptying it.

They went on with the necessary, silly, survival talk as Bluefeather directed Willy and the boat to relative safety. Then they all became very, very quiet, not even hearing or feeling the motors turn the propellers that shoved the boat jerkily, steadily toward the compound—much heavier with gold, much lighter with loving flesh, than it had started out. All the molecules of their beings longed for peace now. It was the time of repose.

FORTY-FIVE

THEY WERE DRINKING WATER AND COOLING DOWN NOW after safely negotiating the melting heat line. Willy kept the motor at low rev to prevent the bent boat from shaking them any more than necessary. On the banks and in the air, the triloids followed, parallel. They had lost fifteen percent of their numbers but were staying with the remaining section all the way.

Pack had taken over the one unbroken 50-caliber turret. Bluefeather counted the survivors over and over. No matter how he tried to stretch it, there were only eleven of them left. He inspected Marsha with loving eyes and counted her a hundred times. The premonition was wrong, it seemed. He gave silent thanks to all the Authorities that had ever been.

He named them off once more: Marsha, Sherry, Shia, Pack, Willy, Osaka, Charlie, three Youngers and himself. That added up to eleven. No more. All must be kept on the alert or none would return to report the astounding results of the costly victory.

He recognized the narrows coming up. Nothing had bothered them on the ingoing trip until they had been well past this point. Everyone relaxed several degrees now. The triloids were out of vision, blocked by the solid walls arcing here into a stone tent as big as ten circus coverings above their heads.

The river widened again. Even at this slow progress they were only a couple of hours from the lower base camp. They passed the easily identifiable spot where the water-etched lines of ancient history had given Sherry so much priceless information for her notebooks.

Then Bluefeather saw them coming from the port side. Giant, undulating white worms with pointed, hardened noses.

He yelled, "Pack, three o'clock," and automatically reached for a grenade. There were none. All had been used against the Khyber.

Pack turned the 50 into the Nessie. It churned wildly as some of the en-masse attackers were shot into shreds. There was an early effect this time, but those that came on struck the ship with such force that their snouts penetrated the hull and rocked the boat. Where the metal had previously only been impacted, now holes were punched all the way in. Fortunately, the worms were not physically equipped to make it over the edge of the boat unless it listed much lower.

All but Pack thought, *Would there forever be one last war—on and on until nothing is left? Nothing?* Pack, the war-lover, loved on. But his lust for battle was unknowingly tempered some now by his love for Sherry.

Osaka sliced his machete down on the heads of worms that got through the steel and asbestos, then kicked their remains back into the river.

The Section had damaged the worms enough to stop them. They had lost no more of The Section, but now the *Columbus* was taking water so fast that all hands were using buckets instead of guns. They didn't have to worry about the worms anymore. A group of chompers had started feeding and fighting with the pieces of worms that wiggled and stabbed on with their saber-snouts even after the large-jawed beasts bit them in half.

The triloids came in formation now, water-walking with all their speed, but they could see the worms' battle with the humans was finished. The two kinds of water beasts fought one another in a frenzy of killing and feeding that overwhelmed any possible interest in human or triloid presence. The triloids stood on the water, their bent-over figures kept afloat by the whirling of their arms and the winglike flaps.

Dolla clacked at Sherry, but she could not stop the bucket brigade to look for her castanet. They were in very real danger of sinking.

Bluefeather had to risk The Section, the ship and its treasure now. He shouted for Willy to give both motors all the power they could produce even if it shook the ship apart. Slow sinking would have the same final result, anyway.

As the motors revved, Sherry painfully clacked a message to Dolla with her own teeth. At first Dolla was so surprised she missed it, but not for long. She led the rest of her tribe swiftly ahead.

The *Columbus* was vibrating so hard that the occupants were not only sure it would split into shreds, they also felt their brains were being bruised against their skulls.

The water was sloshing almost up to their knees now, but they kept on bailing in strength-draining desperation. The triloids joined the struggle now as Sherry had asked. They were pushing behind and pulling in front of the crippled boat in a last effort to get it into its shallow dock.

The Olders and the Youngers at the compound had been waiting in shifts with telescopes aimed down the river. They had witnessed the attack of the giant worms and the subsequent nearly fatal damage to the ship. They acted now.

The cable had been unhooked from the submersible

unit and made ready to attach to the injured *Columbus*. Several of the Youngers, standing chest deep in front of the deck, hooked the cable to the ship. The powerful motors now assisted the two boat motors, and the craft was pulled three-quarters into dry dock. Only a moment ago The Section had been bailing water with arms so stiff, pained and exhausted that each lift of the container had been like chopping wood with bones cracked and split from compound breaks.

Now they steadied themselves, getting some control of their breathing, and watched the water drain out the holes made by the charging worms. Everything critical to the success of the expedition was now retrievable. The iron-webbed gate was closed over the entrance and they were finally safe.

Sherry retrieved her castanet and went to speak with Dolla and her tribe through the webbing. After all these years, she had never learned how to signal "thank you." Even if she had, the triloids would probably have failed to comprehend such a gesture. Friendship and loyalty were total with them, so the meaning of the signal would not have been understood. In lieu of this, she gave as close an approximation to saying "the trip was fun, and we'll have to do it again sometime." Sherry gave a huge, forced smile with only her face. Her heart did smile, but she was too weak to be sure it was projected to her friends.

Dolla returned a smile even bigger—because the size of her mouth stretched around her face and away from her large, solid teeth. It was magnificent, this gesture, this smile. All the other triloids imitated her.

Then with the invisible signal of birds and fish and triloids, they all turned in unison and breezed their way across the river toward home—a home tens of hundreds of thousands of years old.

Sherry stood, instinctively putting the castanet away,

and allowed a few tiny tears of love and gratitude to escape from the corners of her eyes. Shia watched her every
move and imitated her tears just as the triloids had Dolla's
smile. Then they wiped their eyes and joined in the effort
to unload weapons and mineral samples of much richness.

It was not the time for celebration until the garden of
treasures was secure in its proper place. Then she would
call all the survivors together—The Section, the Olders
and Youngers—and properly compliment them on their
sacrifices and successes. That done, she would phone their
victory to Dolby. Afterward, they could rest and heal before The Section's victorious return to the surface with
riches and knowledge enough for many worlds.

Bluefeather pitched right in with all the rest helping to
carry the heavy mineral samples. It was all soon displayed
in the conference room. He was already planning many
things, but he felt good that he had had the foresight to
ask Sherry to have two mule-loads of the river nodules
waiting above. One thing for sure—the gold in the nodules was solid and real. He would die to see that his surviving friends got to share the comfort of a little financial
security. He did not, in any form, trust Dolby or Korbell
to pay them what they deserved for their bloody striving.
He made silent prayers for them to be fair for once if for
no other reasons than to save more complications leading
to more casualties.

He prayed hard for those persons with so much greed
that they became bloodhounds of gold. He knew that he,
too, was infected with the yellow virus, but by admitting
his illness he had been able to keep it mostly controlled.
The trouble with praying for accumulators like Dolby and
Korbell was that they were unthinking and blind to any
defect within themselves. It was always others, they believed, who were flawed and should be used up, then destroyed. Bluefeather knew what he was facing to get his
friends through this and safely out of the widely spread

fences of folly the two powers would try to herd them into. He was ready to wrap it up, and he did not have to doubt the dedication of his surviving companions. These people were fulcrums of friendship.

He brightened at the certain feeling that he and Marsha could live long lives, enjoying Corrales while they made their minds up about what they really wanted to do. Of course, he still had to find the Mouton '80, but he was sure that the diagrams of Tilton's building plans would reveal the undiscovered hiding place without too many problems.

At this he quit praying, giving many complimentary thoughts instead, and went to clean, oil and reload his weapons—again.

FORTY-SIX

SHERRY CALLED EVERY CITIZEN OF THE COMPOUND TO
the meeting. Bluefeather had expected her to be full of
smiles and commendations for the survivors of the killing
trek. Instead, there was a solemnness about her as she
said right off, "I know you deserve a rest and a celebration. You know it, too. However, I've decided we'll gather
our wills together and move on up to God's Castle so we'll
have the proper luxurious amenities for the victory pag-
eant." She forced a quick smile and then ordered all the
samples loaded on mules.

Everyone was armed with full packs. The Youngers
would go with The Section. Bluefeather requested that
Willy, the mules and the two mule keepers, Adam and
Tolliver, go ahead and wait above with the gold nodules.
The Olders would follow at their own pace. All the rest
would force-march ahead to fittingly prepare for the ceremony.

There were none who did not sense something out of
kilter. Sherry's attitude and orders seemed unnatural, considering the situation and the exhaustion of the returnees.
No less afflicted were those who had waited at the compound without sleep during a seemingly endless spell of
wrenching anxiety. Their fate hung with those on the front

lines. Now they were all to be marched away without even a few grams of rest from their last murderous journey. A slight dose of relaxant was essential for those whose mightily strained muscles were already stiffening. Nevertheless, they obeyed without complaint and made ready to ascend to the next level on the elevators.

The line moved with Bluefeather leading it. Behind him were Marsha and Charlie. Sherry moved back and forth from Bluefeather to the Youngers, in constant motion. Willy and the two mule packers trailed behind the Youngers with the heavily loaded mule train. Willy resented this extra weight on the mules but had tried to see that it was balanced equally among all. Pack guarded the rear. Osaka walked to the side as the flank guard. The Olders moved at the only pace they had—slow.

In spite of the near-exhaustion suffered in many forms, they kept a wary lookout for the screechers. The unpredictable power of these ground-air creatures was deeply imprinted in the genes of all.

Now that Sherry was sure that her gold samples, her notebooks and her associates were all moving forward in the best possible shape, she walked up beside Bluefeather and whispered, "The phone line was dead to Dolby's." That's all. Then she continued her edgy walking up and down the line.

The entire progression was slowing. Muscles could no longer be sped up by the force of will alone. Willy's chest felt like two boulders were pressing on each side. He said nothing, but felt much. Bluefeather was able to maintain the pace without too much exertion, because everyone else was lagging. It was the same with Pack in the rear. It felt as if there was extra heavy leather on their boots and as if the seams of their trousers were surely sewed together with lead thread. The packs with the blankets, shovels, the battery lights, the personal items had all fallen in love with gravity and pulled downward. Slow clock hours. Slower cave hours. Slower mind hours.

The lead mule heard it first. He stopped and raised his head, all muscles tensed as his ears worked back and forth, distilling the sound. It was gunfire.

Then everyone heard it. There could be no mistake. It was not Steinberg directing target practice. It was the sound of a small war. There were no mortars, of course, their being useless because of the terrain. There was no noise of artillery, but Bluefeather and Pack recognized the exploding sounds of intermittent grenades and hand-held rocket launcher projectiles. They had heard them often, long ago in France and Germany. There was also the "crack, crack, crack" of semiautomatic rifle fire and the heavier, faster rattle of a 45 Thompson. It didn't matter. An M-2 rifle bullet could kill one just as dead as any 150-mm artillery shell or hydrogen bomb. Death played no favorites. A rock, a spear point, a bullet, a bomb were all the same to death. The means was meaningless. The results certain.

Bluefeather knew someone had to take total charge instantly. It should have been Pack, he supposed, but somehow he felt the responsibility of it all was rightfully on him now. He halted the column and told them to take protective cover even though the battle was obviously farther on at God's Castle.

He moved forward at a trot now to reconnoiter alone. He climbed a large gypsum slope, seeking a high point. Static muscles were forgotten, but not war. Damn. He had really had his share. No use regretting, no use worrying. There was another one to face now. Even so, damn. He fell belly-down, knowing that when he raised his head he would gaze upon its craven face again. It was harder to do this time than ever before. No matter. It was there in front of him.

He rose up reluctantly. He could make out bodies inside the star-metal walls—many bodies—but the sounds and most of the movements were on beyond. This surprised him. The castle occupants had obviously attacked "out" from the protection of the strong, solid fence. He focused his binoculars on the castle courtyard. Around the bulwarks of the fortress fence the bodies were clustered heavier.

He saw where the three girls—Jody, Estrella and Charlene—lay dead, almost side by side. No doubt they had been hit by the same burst of bullets, having never been taught to disperse. He tried to take a guess at the number killed and the number still fighting. Numbers—love was like numbers, full of addition and subtraction. There was never a meaningful evenness in either. Being even or getting even was neither winning nor losing; winding up even is impossible in love or war or life.

The gun turrets had been knocked out by fire through the portholes. He could see the movements of the castle brigade around the dropping and rising massive fingers and abutments of the lighted cavern along with other, endless, smoother, varied formations. The brigade circled, fell, climbed, leapt, fought and died.

There was old Steinberg, his tall greyness limping heavily but giving orders and firing, in charge of his battered troops with a wounded flair. The elegance of a true command filled the viewing glass.

Now Bluefeather's ears adjusted to the sounds and realized that nearly every bullet was ricocheting—most of them many times—so that one shot sounded like a dozen coming from all angles. Gradually, as he watched, the entire picture came to him. The ricochets, the grenades and the shoulder-held bazooka shells had all been helpless against the strength of the star-metal fortifications. When fired over the top or the powerful fence into the rock abutments and ceilings, they had been able to decimate Steinberg's forces. The castle and all its research facilities, its hidden and protected knowledge of the Cavern of Marvels, the Star Cave, the Cave of Bones and so much more, would have been lost to attrition if Steinberg and his forces had stayed in place.

Steinberg had no choice but to attack. Bluefeather could see where the scattered bodies of a squad had moved outside the half circle of the fortress wall to draw fire so Steinberg's remaining force could attack through the great archway of the main gate. It had worked—at great cost, of course, as evidenced by the scattered bodies strung out in a zigzagged line. The squad had offered its flesh so the main group could reach outer cover and return the fire on a more flexible front.

Bluefeather had no doubt that everyone in and out of the courtyard, the Olders and the Youngers, had been committed to the engagement of forces. All those who were not lifeless were now fighting in the rocky formations. He focused the glass closer on Steinberg and saw him take another ricochet in his left side. He reeled back and straightened, still able to fire and shout encouragement.

From this angle, Bluefeather could see a little movement of the enemy as well. Then he recognized the figure, the movement, of Fontaine, even though he couldn't glass close enough to see the scar that angled across his entire face. It was not necessary. The man's powerful athletic mobility was unmistakable. He raced with three men to the cover of a large pagoda, motioning two others to different forms of protection. One from each group fell from the firing. One was still. The other crawled on toward cover. Movement.

It was impossible for Bluefeather to figure the number of combined fighters left to either Steinberg or Fontaine. But the latter's presence confirmed that Korbell had attacked Dolby's domain. There was probably no one left alive above to answer Sherry when she phoned. Of course, that was the worry she had denied all the previous weeks, hoping within prayerful hope that her suspicions were unfounded, right up until the first mule heard the shooting. At least now the uncertainty was over.

The map of the entire battle was there before Bluefeather to read. The story was as clear as if he had been in the middle of it all. Clearer. Much clearer. His picture-mind rolled the war past at high speed, in color, with full sound effects. The only things this part of his brain failed to show him of the immediate past was the pain and the shocked screams before the body systems were nonexistent.

He would have liked to believe that Steinberg could have held out and won without them, but the bodies kept falling on his side. Steinberg's ranks were thinning faster than Fontaine's. He had been surprise-attacked, and the first gunpowder war between humans here below had taken a terrible, early toll. He now fought with a mixture of the Olders and a few surviving Youngers.

No, The Section couldn't wait. Fontaine might take the castle and he would not care about the damage. If he got holed up there with its large armory and food supplies, Bluefeather's small force could never dislodge him. The last thought was all the analysis he would give for or against joining the bloody fracas.

Bluefeather leapt up and slid his way down from the gypsum hill and ran back to his waiting friends and loved ones.

"Willy," Bluefeather shouted in a whisper, "you and the keepers stay behind us with the mules. Be as quiet as possible. Surprise is our greatest weapon." Now he had become like Sherry. So many had died for the cargo in the mule packs that they must save it, along with themselves.

All moved at double time now, and as silently as possible, following Bluefeather to the rise he had just left.

Everyone of the command staff was ordered to glass the situation as Bluefeather explained it.

"Sherry, the Youngers will never stay organized except under your command. Take them in the back gate, through the compound and out the front gate to support Steinberg. The rest of us will circle right and come in on the flank. I saw Fontaine. They are Korbell's men. Move out. Now."

Marsha said quietly, "Oh, my God. Oh dear God." Nobody heard her. She moved up beside Bluefeather and no matter how he climbed, slid, twisted, rolled or turned, she stayed right with him like a shadow of flesh.

Sherry, Shia and the Youngers did not have nearly as much trouble. Their way down undulated in smooth surfaces with only an occasional pointed stalagmite to circle. There was no direct gunfire as they moved through the red-spattered compound. It was difficult for a few of the Youngers to follow her because they saw the bodies of their parents and all recognized friends, even in the eternal blue fog of beginning battle. But on they moved behind Dolby's right arm, Sherry, following her to their death, if need be.

Bluefeather's section obeyed his every move, every signal, as a single mind—almost as well as the triloids. They moved forward, crouching when he crouched, stopping and listening when he did, racing or slowing as he did. They moved unseen to scattered positions selected by Bluefeather and made ready to fire. He sent word down the line for all to select targets of opportunity for one mass firing. Then they would be on their own until a new victory was won. Yes, another. They waited for his signal. He held back, for they could all see Sherry and her Youngers advancing from one pillar to another in uneven fashion. Some fell forward against the stone floor of the cavern as Fontaine's men increased the firing on the fresh, young, moving meat.

At last the fourteen or fifteen survivors of God's Castle had joined the wildly erratic line of Steinberg's remaining force. Sherry's group moved up on the left flank and Bluefeather's was ready on the right. It would be a three-pronged attack.

Bluefeather dropped his raised arm, shouting, "Fire! Kill the invaders! Fire! Fire!"

They did—circling, ducking, dodging into the new three-pronged battle of erupting frenzy. Bluefeather caught a glance of a dark blue uniform moving low, forward toward Steinberg's position. He mind-sighted and fired. The figure doubled up, arching its back, then kicked with both feet, falling flat and dead.

Bluefeather had lost track of his section except for Pack and Osaka, who were on each side of him. They were firing, crawling, rising, looking and firing again, just as he was, and all around the ricochets became frenzied like the drums of a rock band, like the whine of breaking guitar strings, like a wail of insane thoughts flashing through a brain and bouncing off one part of the skull to another. The invisible diagrams that the ricochets drew between cavern walls and ancient pagodas would have destroyed all known geometrical concepts and caused the makers of spider webs to fight in frustration.

Now three of Fontaine's men dashed successfully across an opening to a large pagoda. Bluefeather and someone else fired, but too late. The three were at a protected angle to easily exterminate several of Steinberg's fighters. They did. Bluefeather watched them fall. Because of the ceaseless singing, zinging hive of bullets bouncing from stone to stone until they were expended or embedded in soft spots of limestone, no one knew from whence their death came.

Bluefeather saw Osaka charge through an undulation of rocks very near them. Osaka pulled the pin from a grenade and rose to throw it, absorbing several rounds in his chest. He fell on the dropped grenade, already dead. The grenade didn't give a damn. It exploded anyway, scattering pieces of Osaka about the surrounding terrain. One piece of bone struck Bluefeather on the cheek; another stuck to the top of his left shoulder. He brushed its warmness away, pulled the pin from his own grenade and played billiards. He hurled it at a stalactite just past the stalagmite Fontaine's little group was fortressed behind. It was a good bank shot and certainly counted more than most. The grenade bounced left and back behind and exploded with extreme beauty. It blew one gutted enemy out to the side. Another was slapped up against the stone like a doll made of cheesecloth. Half of his upper head and one hand was missing. Since there was not enough left to identify of the third one, Bluefeather let his picture-mind work in slow motion as portions of the body drift-floated apart like a dropped, overripe watermelon. Now, as all three fighting organisms closed on the enemy, it became only the ageless, twenty-yard circle for each combatant to call home. There was no more world than that for now. Anywhere.

Bluefeather rolled over some rocks and fell on top of a dark blue uniform. The blue clothes covered a living body. It tried to shove the barrel of a rifle in his belly, but Bluefeather grabbed it, twisted, jerked it loose and threw it aside. In continuous movement, he gouged so hard with his thumbs at the man's eyes that one burst like a grape and the other popped, dangling across his cheek. Then he battered the blind head until the back skull bones were chips inside the mushy head. He bashed all the memory out of him. He gathered his rifle and moved on, firing at everything that moved and some things that didn't.

Bluefeather had forgotten his oldest and best friend, Sergeant Pack. He had forgotten his love, Marsha. That was what moments of war do to people's minds. Now his thoughts and feelings turned just as suddenly the other way. Where were they? They had to be alive, those two; no matter what, they must survive beyond all. The cavern and its treasures of gold and knowledge were instantly worthless to him. Only those two were in his immediate thoughts. That's all the time that mattered, whether measured by earthly or unearthly standards. Oh, Great Spirit— oh, Dancing Bear, my spirit guide, take me to them so I can love and protect those two. Before his prayers were finished he had fallen behind a rock formation where Pack fired and jerked back down to reload on one edge and Marsha crouched on the other, just finishing reloading.

He sat down right by her. The bullets sang less now, because there were far fewer fingers left to pull the triggers. There was even one of those sudden battle lulls that happen without explanation. It was the oddest war ever fought. More than half of the front lines were old men and women. Reversed.

Bluefeather and Marsha looked directly into each other's eyes and saw there something of such a craving for perpetuating life that wordlessly they fell together, removing and separating enough clothing so that their love, through their flesh, joined in the ancient movements creating future. The continuum. It was violent in its fleshly moist tenderness. It was a desperate seeking of all the senses of one another. A joining of renewal. Their bodies lustfully, but loving, drove hard together, increasing in intensity as Pack gave covering fire next to them. They were coming to the indescribably delicious finish of abandonment together.

Then Bluefeather lay atop his love, both spent to perspiring limpness. The instant after the grand finale, she had sighed two words, "Oh, Blue."

He moved his lips over to kiss her eyes. The first one was wet, full of tears. He moved his damp lips over to kiss the other lid, but the eye was open. He raised his head to look into both her wondrous blue irises that had thrilled him so much so many times. Only one was visible. It stared up blankly. The other socket was empty except for a pool of blood with a tiny stream running out the corner. A couple of drops, the size of a lemon seed, dripped from his mouth to the delicate crease above her chin and splashed into little red patterns on her pale dead face. A ricochet had struck her straight on, entering the socket and then the inner skull. She had never felt it. Marsha had died from a bullet sent here by Korbell, her own father.

Bluefeather stared, paralyzed, stricken. The old scar across his nose burned with a cutting pain he had never felt before. Then he rolled from her, took three grenades from her belt and screamed at Pack. "They killed Marsha. The bastards killed her."

Pack recognized now the madman Bluefeather had once seen in him years before at Brest, France. Pack grabbed for him too late and followed after his friend's madness, just as Bluefeather had once followed him. They both fired at every edge of rock visible and were separated from each other by these same rocks. Bluefeather screamed oaths, both silently and aloud. Every survivor on Steinberg's side heard and understood. Bluefeather hurled the grenades in a magical manner. Each one floated or drove just right to encircle, reach behind and shatter the enemy.

The madness had given him the force of not caring. There was absolutely no fear. It was subdued beyond belief by the raging of his temporary derangement. He hurled all the grenades with deadly and efficient effect, emptied all his ammunition clips, pulled his machete and could find nothing to slice or stab.

He saw Fontaine and another man vanish into the edge of the dim light at full retreat. His reason slowly returned. There was no firing, no sound now that he could hear above his own heavy breathing.

He stumbled around a pillar and fell over Pack's prone figure. He reached out a hand, crawling to the body, feeling for, and finding, an erratic pulse. He pulled himself to a sitting position and took Pack's head in his lap. The bullets had got him in the lungs. He knew. He could hear the inner rattle of Pack's diminishing breath.

He rubbed the side of Pack's ashen face and rocked back and forth like an abandoned child with Pack's head cradled in his lap. His old friend opened his eyes slightly. There was the tiny little grin on his thin, white lips he had seen so many times in battles and barrooms.

The lips moved slightly and Bluefeather bent his head to hear, "Did we win, Blue, ol' pardner?"

"Yeah, we beat 'em good, sergeant. We beat 'em real good."

Pack was so still, Bluefeather thought he was gone. Then he strained but heard the last whisper Pack would ever make, "Take care of Sherry, Blue. I loved her, you know?"

"I will, Pack. Don't you worry about . . ."

Pack's head rolled over. Bluefeather got up on his hands and knees, straightened Pack out, placed his hands over his chest and touched his eyelids closed. He stood up, saluted him and turned away. One cannot weep in battle, for one cannot see to shoot with accuracy.

Bluefeather walked and walked among the dead, looking for Marsha, circling back on himself. He found the still body of Dunning nearby. There was no use moving around now. He sat down on a stone rise and yelled, "It's me. I am here. Here by the orange-stained pagoda. It is me. Bluefeather Fellini." He waited and yelled again. "They're all gone. The Korbells are all gone. It's me, I say, Bluefeather Fellini, from Raton, and Taos and Corrales, New Mexico, by way of the rest of the world and a great portion of the landscapes of heaven and hell. Now, if there are any friends or enemies left, you know who I am."

He heard the movement behind him. Even now he expected a bullet in his spine, but no powder exploded. He heard a voice say, "Blue? Blue, is it you? It's me. Charlie, I'm . . . I'm here, Blue, alive."

"I'm Blue. Here. Right here."

Charlie came and sat by his side. His head and arms dropped forward. Then Sherry and Shia moved in front of them silently. Sherry's eyes, which were big enough to see many worlds, stared—frozen in position in her head. She knelt in front of the two and put her head down against a leg of each and hugged them with both arms. Shia knelt behind her, her Oriental face pale as ivory. She reached out hesitantly with one hand and lightly, automatically patted Sherry between the shoulders.

Bluefeather pushed their hair silently out of their faces and tenderly rubbed their cheeks and temples for a long while before he realized that Charlie felt no more.

Then he gently rose up and said softly, "Stay here, Sherry. Don't move until I return."

He walked away in full control now. He passed over many bodies, some several times, until he found Marsha. She must have a tomb safe from the screechers, for they would, by nature, clean the cavern, and by desire, dine on the remains of the now vanquished enemy. He accepted this as inevitable for all but Marsha, his Marsha.

Then he searched about until he spotted a crevice. He gathered her up and eased her tenderly down into it without looking at her face. He pulled over two sloughed sections of limestone and dropped them to seal the crevice. He removed his pack and took the perfectly cylindrical rock-pearl and placed it on top of the tiny tomb. He had saved it, intending to have a silver necklace made for her after they returned to their adobe home at Corrales.

He took a pocketknife from his trousers and, with a

strenuous effort, crudely carved: "Marsha—who died with love."

He didn't date it, for dates were meaningless in the context of caverns and caring. As he walked away his mind-voice spoke soothingly to him. *It is part of the over-allness that we finally bury the ones we love or they us.*

Then he heard a mule bray, and another in the same direction. He spotted the orange-stained pagoda and said to the waiting Sherry, "Did you hear them? The mules called from way over there."

She had heard. So they moved toward the sound that did not come again, shouting unintelligible things so that the mules and Willy and Adam and Tolliver could hear their approach. The trio had forgotten the war, but Willy hadn't. He had a rifle fully loaded, dead centered on them as they rounded the stalagmite carelessly, for they had forgotten fear in their silent grief.

Willy stood up, grinning with monumental relief saying, "Well, I'll be damned. My two best friends are here . . . and a new one. Say, ain't that keen?"

They all embraced and then admired the pack train, whole and healthy, even if Adam and Tolliver had died from the strain—one of heart attack and the other from a stroke.

Willy laughed, "Hard to believe, but the old farts never knew that every single one of the thousands of bullets missed 'em. Now ain't that a puzzle to ponder?"

FORTY-SEVEN

THE REMAINS OF THE SECTION MOVED WITH THE MULE train safely past the deep, climbing cave of screechers. Bluefeather knew why. He had heard their signal cries moving through the multiple caverns; the screechers were finding their way to the feasts of war. If any of the Olders or the Youngers left behind were alive, they would have very little cleaning up to do.

At each way station, Sherry turned the electric lights off behind them, explaining that it was too much of a strain on the power plant above. Luck moved with them on through The Unholy and past Needle Canyon.

They were safely beyond the place of violent winds when they felt a tug—a suction—pull at them. It was like the cavern had given a great sigh of relief at their leaving and let them move on. They had, many weeks before, given up clock time, but now they had lost the sense of distance. Everything was different with battery lights reflecting in such a small area. The dark swallowed the end of the frail light beam and ate it shorter and shorter as their batteries weakened.

Bluefeather thought, again, *Strange how the sunlight and green trees that once seemed so common will now appear as wondrous and new as the depths of the cavern had only a few weeks before.* He experienced déjà vu. He believed that maybe this same thought had come to him before while deep under the River of Radiance.

They turned off their hand lights now as another set of strong reflection bulbs revealed the endlessly changing formations again.

Just as Sherry moved toward the switch box, the lights were extinguished. The totality of the sudden darkness was a shock to all. Even the mules pulled against their tie-ropes nervously. Sherry turned on her hand light again—as did the others. She moved to the switch box and pulled it up and down several times. No one said it, but everyone knew, without words, that the darkness was permanent. It was a desolate darkness. The power plant had either been shut off from a breakdown, or someone had simply pulled a plug or the wires had been cut. Well, at least now the button that Dolby had hidden to push and blast-seal the caverns was useless.

The small section and the eight mules stepped up their weary pace. If they did not reach the area of the Mimbres before they were without lights, trouble was an insufficient word for the problems they would have to solve. One step off the regular trail and one could wander in the darkness through a thousand miles of both connecting and dead-end caverns. But of course, no one could beat such odds. There were crevasses so deep that a dropped rock could not be heard hitting bottom and uncountable formations sharp and penetrating as daggers. Once they were past the Mimbres Cavern of the Dead there was a chance they could follow the wall on the man-carved trail and make it to the first stone gate. At that thought came another. Would it be open or sealed? Would there be anyone to open it for them? The phone line was dead. If they made it that far, the tunnel could still be their tomb of permanent darkness. There was no going back.

The adrenaline of fear increased in their bodies as the

beams faded from Willy's and Sherry's hand lights. Blue-feather's light was only a rusty little shaft that he led them with. Bluefeather held the lead rope of the front mule. Sherry clasped Bluefeather's belt. Shia kept a hand on top of Sherry's shoulder, constantly grasping and releasing. Behind them all, Willy stumbled along with the last mule's tail in hand.

It was a slow movement, and even in the cooling temperatures the sweat drenched their bodies and began to weaken them beyond the carrying capacity of the dredged-up adrenaline. All had enough sense left to ration the water in their canteens.

When they came to a drip pool, Bluefeather said, "Willy, walk carefully up here to my light." He did. "Now kneel around the pool and get it located with your hands. Okay. I'm turning off the light while you drink and fill our canteens."

The blackness made the amazing guidance systems of many of the blind creatures below seem pure magic. With their fingers in the pool, they had awkward moments tending to such simple chores as Bluefeather had ordered.

"Are you all filled up now?"

"Yes," they chorused.

"Okay. Wash yourselves down." They did so. The cool water and the little rest refreshed them a lot.

Willy felt his way along the mules until he took up the last tail again. Everyone moved clumsily into position, saving the tiny, precious light for one last move forward. All made prayers now to reach the ruins before the batteries died just as dead as the Mimbres mummies.

They edged forward, the mules bunching up and bumping all along the line, then loosening until all the guide ropes, as well as the arms of the survivors, were stretched full length. They were bunching and unbunching over and over again, moving now around a sharp curve. The beam only strained out feebly about six feet in front of Bluefeather, into space, dark and huge.

The shots came as a surprise in a way, even though Bluefeather had figured Fontaine and his comrades had already made it past the Mimbres. It was the miss that was to be honored. The ricocheting whines and wails created a great anger in him at first. He had seen the flash of fire from the muzzles, though, and as he pulled back a step around the curve, he felt both elation and depression. Were Fontaine's lights used up as well as theirs? Or had they simply heard them and attempted a blind ambush in the raven-dark air?

The four were very still, but the delicate shuffling of a mule's hooves made sounds. Bluefeather listened above that, though. The enemy was not moving. His mind-voice gave him lectures that were not easy to hear. *You and Willy are miners. How could you not be prepared with long-lasting carbide lamps?* His other inner-voice answered, *Because we were assured there were several backup generators at the main plant as well as God's Castle. You don't want any more fights no matter how small, do you?* He answered himself quickly, *No, oh, no. I never did.* Then the inner voice said, *I'm truly sorry, you fools, but wars have always existed in the past. Top professional gamblers would give big odds it will remain so in the future.* At this Bluefeather closed off the voice. It was not helping anyway.

He took from his belt the grenades that he had salvaged from the fallen at the battle of God's Castle. If he demolished those who were still trying to maim and kill them, maybe they would have lights to lead them on. It was a chance. Even though a very thin one, it was enough to give him a sudden charge. There was no longer going to be any need to remain silent.

He spoke as if starting a dinner conversation, "You know what, dear friends? Sergeant Pack, the war-lover, once said, 'Life would be miserable, and hardly worth living, without my hand grenades.' "

Bluefeather stepped forward, pulled a pin, hurled a live one and sent the second on its way before the first exploded, laughing so hard he shook and choked right through the explosions.

"Stay put," he whispered, holding the dim light out to his side as far as he could reach to give a misplaced target. He crawled forward on his knees and one elbow, holding a cocked handgun as ready as the awkward movement would allow. He need not have bothered. Fontaine stared up—his entire body ripped with shrapnel. The other man had slid or crawled in a trail of red several yards down a slope.

Bluefeather searched Fontaine for any kind of light. He found none. He scrambled down the slope and could find nothing on the partially disemboweled body there either.

He tried to shout at the others, but his voice was barely above a whisper. He walked back to join them. Now they followed him, locked together again. Just as they reached Fontaine, the battery spent its last tiny charge and all was darkness.

No one spoke for a moment, and then Sherry's usually strong, solid voice, quivering and haunted, sounded, "Blue? Blue, what do we do now?"

"Everyone ease back against the wall, sit down, and rest a few moments. Then we'll try and decide."

Sherry said, "You're right. If we're going to perish, we might as well get our breath back first." Now it was Sherry who became protective of Shia. Her love for Dolby had been decimated by his terrible deceit. And Pack was gone. She pulled Shia to her with a strong hug that spoke silent words in the darkness. She would have been pleased if she could have seen Shia's face upturned, smiling in near worship.

Willy said, "I crawled out of saloons and into my living

room all through my youth. Might as well complete my old age in a familiar position. Don't you folks worry none, I can feel this path all the way to the surface. You think I'm gonna waste all this experience and wisdom? No sirree, I ain't."

In spite of the black shroud surrounding them, they had a small chuckle at Willy's attempt to give hope. They sat down and leaned back. Bluefeather held the lead rope of the mules. It was his job, and the connection to the noble animals gave him comfort.

Bluefeather was straining his entire being trying to come up with an answer for his friends, beyond the remote one—and injurious one—of Willy's crawling them home on solid rock.

The only answer there had ever been to darkness was light. Any childish idiot knew that. He couldn't conjure up the tiniest flicker that could be visualized beyond the interior of his skull. Interminable.

Then there was Dancing Bear, searching and removing a small box of matches and a cigarette lighter from the pockets of the recent corpses. Bluefeather felt like a fool. That would have been enough erratic light to have moved them on a bit.

Bluefeather spoke to Dancing Bear in their own private, unheard dimension, "Well, Bear, it's sure nice to see you. How have you been? How's the spirit business these days? Where have you been? Would you care for a drink of canteen water? Do you happen to have a flashlight on you? If not, do you think it would be forward of me to ask for the loan of the matches and the lighter? How's your assistant Nicole? How's the Authority?"

"Whoa, whoa, dearest brudder. You sound just like me sometimes."

"I thought I'd beat you to it for once so we could get down to some serious conversation about getting us out of here."

"Dear brudder, Nicole is fine, just fine."

"Now that we've got all that settled, Bear, could we cut the clatter just this once, while there's still a once left, and solve the final, and almost certainly fatal, problem?"

"Dearest of all brudders, I have to combine the real and the magic to get you out of here. I just don't have the resources to do it any other way."

"What do you mean by that? I can see you . . . so I follow you and the rest follow me right on to safety. What's so difficult about that?"

"Well, for one thing, it ain't in the rules, dear brudder Blue."

"Now listen, Bear. I know you remember that old cliché about rules being made to be broken."

"Chure, chure, a hunnert times ago. I hear 'em.

"Now, cut out the Indian dialect right now. No more, you hear?

"Okay, okay. Your people know you can't see in the dark like a screecher?"

"Of course."

"Well, my people won't let me carry magic that far. It's the rules. The 'from now on' rules. You gotta help yourselves some. Besides, I can't afford to be breaking no rules right now. I'm up for a promotion to the next."

"Next what?"

"Aw, you know—the next dimension. It's a big leap. I'll have a lot more assistants and won't have to travel so that I'm worn down like a ghost all the time."

"Well?"

"I go before the Authority and the board in just six— maybe nine—days. Gotta work by the book now. I been here about a hunnert . . ."

"All right. All right. What do you suggest?"

"Well, we can't let people who are not ready for it see true miracles performed. You—that's okay, but these people are too risky. They might jeopardize my promotion.

Anybody—fakes, cheats, liars and greedy frauds—could make them believe anything after witnessing a true miracle. We can't have that. It's too easy. Folks gotta have faith in their own strength."

"Lay out the rules. Please."

Dancing Bear was dancing slowly around in a one-yard spot. "This is the dance of the thinkers," he explained, taking the band from his skull, pointing at his heavily furrowed forehead, saying, "See the hard-thinking lines in the front of my head?"

Then he went on dancing the thinking dance. Suddenly, he stopped as accurately as a powwow dancer does on the last beat of the drums. "I got 'er. I got 'er. Here, you take the lighter and the matches. Here's what I been thinkin' this very second, dear brudder. I'm gonna go with my spirit body half in one dimension and half in another. Very dangerous thing, but the sparks from the friction will give you a light to follow. You gotta figure how to do a white man's lie to your friends. Okay?" Then Dancing Bear started dancing harder and wilder than ever before. It was the buffalo dance he performed. Soon there appeared a buffalo head over the top of his skull, its skin flapping down his back.

Bluefeather rose up and announced to his friends, "It's possible that these matches," he shook the two small boxes, "and this lighter . . ." he flared it quickly with his thumb, "can light our way. Because a tiny flare of light every now and then could fatally confuse you, Sherry, I'm gonna insist you hold onto my belt and follow my pull with your eyes closed. Shia, hold onto Sherry and don't let go, no matter what. Willy, you do the same with the mule's tail."

All they had to do was grab hold and they were as ready as they would ever be. Bluefeather had told a truth, but he didn't want his cohorts to have any time to mull it over.

Dancing Bear danced away from them, then poised like

a marathon runner. Bluefeather held the lighter in the air and snapped its flint into a brief light.

Dancing Bear ducked down so that the horns exactly split the different dimensions of time and matter and charged the line of separation at full speed. As he hit the dividing line, he slowed, but struggled valiantly, the friction creating sparks, just as he had said.

The Section followed and, true to the half lie, Bluefeather snapped on the light every so often. It was an unusual sight Bluefeather followed. Half of Dancing Bear was invisible as he worked in parallel dimensions. The single horn left in the sparkling sight, the one leg and one arm and half a body, were a sight Bluefeather could have remembered in the depths of amnesia. Dancing Bear also sawed his head up and down against the invisible line and it showered light like a Fourth of July sparkler.

Sometimes Dancing Bear would run too far ahead, and would yell out in pain, trying to reach the finish line. Bluefeather reminded him that he was the one who had had the idea in the first place and that he must control those urges to run off and stick his searing head in pools of cool water.

The lighter fluid was about used up. Bluefeather could tell this because he now had to thumb the wheel several times to get a flame, but they had made remarkable progress by the time the lighter failed. He started in on the first box of matches. Of course, this slowed them down some, as he found he couldn't strike the little fire sticks while moving without wasting some.

Now Bluefeather was down to the last box of matches and Dancing Bear's smoking buffalo skull sent so much heat into his altered self that he was weaving off line a bit. Sometimes three-quarters of him was visible—other moments only one-quarter. The followers and the mules were totally dependent on Dancing Bear's continuing charge forward as he courageously moved his head up and down against the line of different planes of being. Just the same, it had all been timed like a Shakespearean play.

As Bluefeather struck the last match, there was a loud ripping sound as Dancing Bear strained forward far beyond even his blessed and multiple talents. He fell, weaving wildly and exhausted, and "crashed through" out of sight into the invisible side of his heroic advance.

At that instant they all saw the gorgeous flow of light coming through the open stone doors. They had—Sherry, Shia and Willy with eyes closed—and Bluefeather with his eyes only on the buffalo skull—moved right past the Mimbres area without being aware of it.

The smell of singed buffalo hair vanished from the fresh air that followed the light. The great Dancing Bear vanished with it. Bluefeather thanked him anyway, even though, just as he had insisted, it had taken valiant efforts by all. Dancing Bear could go before the Authority and the promotion board with a clear and hopefully clean conscience.

It was the mule entrance that had been blown open by Fontaine's men, they discovered. The four who now constituted The Section were trying to breathe the sunlight along with the outer air. In spite of the recent struggles, Bluefeather found that not keeping them alert for a possible last battle was one of the great failures of his life. No matter how he warned them that some of the enemy might still be here, they, for the first time, ignored his pleas. At the very last, his ability to command had failed. Or had it? Everyone seemed to know, along with the weary pack mules, that all was safe now. However it came about, Bluefeather's weary brain could not understand, but he joined them in their quietly joyous entry into the new old world.

They were locked in a circle of nineteen guns pointing straight at them from different positions on the rocky foothills and around the corrals—but they instantly became friendly guns. Ten men and nine women slowly rose, lowering their guns, and came forward smiling, walking the circle smaller. They moved faster, now, on their old legs, laughing and closing in to embrace Bluefeather's little bunch.

Then the Olders' story unwrapped a layer at a time.

Korbell's soldiers had caught them by surprise just before daylight, knocking the outer compounds useless by bazooka and machine-gun fire from the outside, reaching the gates by crashing heavy, reinforced trucks through. They had landed other troops by helicopter in the pastures. The battle had been swift, ferocious, and over in a short time.

They, the nineteen, had long ago been trained as "last resort reserves" and had retired by secluded, prearranged passage to the rocks above. Korbell had made the same mistake as Hitler had in Russia and Normandy. He had split his forces, consequently losing the battle of God's Castle and not fully securing the upper compound either. The casualties here had been continuous and heavy on both sides. Korbell's forces had managed to blow the tunnel doors and breach Dolby's lower rooms in order to raid the vault. But the nineteen gunners on the hills had made transporting the gold bars to the helicopters costly indeed.

At last, both sides had called a truce to dispose of the dead. They had been hauled away. Korbell himself had overseen the hauling of the dead and wounded around the other side of a near mountain to an old ghost town with many deep mine shafts. There they had been dropped in and rocks pushed on top of them. There was no other way.

Korbell had disposed of all the dead and living evidence except the nineteen Olders. He knew they would not talk to or contact the social world. They couldn't. Their long-brainwashed minds would see to that. The last phone call out by Fontaine had indicated that Steinberg had counterattacked and driven them back, and then the phone had gone dead. Korbell could not know this, but he had to surmise that the underground battle was a loss, or in such jeopardy, that there was no way he could control it. So he pragmatically settled for the large acquisition of bullion to soothe his losses.

Sherry led the entourage around the buildings to the front gardens, dreading the description of Dolby's death, when a couple of Olders appeared around a hedge, leading Dolby by both arms. He walked in little, short, shuffling steps. Sherry was so joyous at his appearance that she momentarily forgot what he had done to them all and leapt forward, hugging him, kissing his old face and thanking all the gods and their minions in the heavens.

Everyone stood waiting, seeing what Sherry in her enthusiasm and relief had missed. The world that Dolby had often retreated into over the past thirty years was now his permanent abode. His eyes stared inward only. His ears heard only the sounds from whatever his eyes saw inside. He did not recognize Sherry or anyone else in any way. He lived elsewhere. He was dead out here where the sun shined.

When Sherry finally shuddered and saw his true condition, she was suddenly back in control of her remaining and just-beginning destiny.

While Willy and some of the Olders helped unpack the mules, secure their golden burden and water, feed and brush them down, Sherry, Shia and Bluefeather moved down to the lower rooms with a dread tempered by the almost impossible gift of their being alive.

The vault had been blown open. Dolby had obviously not given in to the threats of torture or provided Korbell the combination. For some reason Korbell had left an even dozen gold bars. A gesture. Saying what? Who would ever know for sure what Korbell had in mind? Possibly, it was some kind of weird statement to his only daughter and son if they survived. They hadn't.

Sherry did not puzzle on this as Bluefeather was doing. She leapt in the vault, counting her notebooks of the deep from the last seven years. They had been ignored there right beside the gold—overlooked because of the tens of millions upon millions of dollars' worth of the rectangular yellow. The treasure of all outer-worldly and inner-worldly treasures had been treated as a trifle—no more than a bookkeeper's ancient labors. Worthless.

Sherry had forgotten the note bag still slung over her shoulder. She removed the new notebooks and placed them tenderly atop the still neatly stacked older ones. She stepped out of the vault, pushing its injured door shut, and turned to Bluefeather. Her great, dark eyes wetted with a smile of relief beyond her speaking, beyond most imaginations, but not beyond his. He held her a moment, caressing the beautiful, valorous head so full of inestimable knowledge.

They repaired the damages done by bullets, picked up all the shell casings and disposed of them. Shia worked harder than anyone when she wasn't marveling at the hand-built and God-built surroundings. They were as new and wondrous to her as the Cavern of Marvels had first been to the mesmerized Section. It would take her awhile, but she would adjust to the upper, just as they had to the lower.

Willy stayed on and got all the mules in good shape and patched up the damage to the outbuildings. The power plant was easily restored to service. They had been correct about Fontaine overlooking or ignoring it. Cooks, repairmen, chemists and guards from the Olders soon separated into their own units of service.

Sherry and Bluefeather took Dolby to El Paso, Texas, and put him in a private and highly recommended home so he would be well cared for and could finish whatever time there was left for him to fill up his small, useless space here in the world of humans. For awhile, each time Bluefeather had even a glancing thought of Marsha, or Pack, or Hector, or . . . he wanted to cut the old man open and toss starved rats into the cavity, but these feelings soon dissipated.

Dolby was a voracious murderer, a dreamer of both greedy and noble visions and a complex mixture of acid and roses. He was all of us, only more so. He just turned the wheel one way while others twisted it another. But in the end, he had cared deeply for, and respected, Sherry. He had long ago given her full power of attorney over all his holdings, his many bank accounts, stocks and land, but now his will also showed her as the sole beneficiary.

Bluefeather had to attend a final meeting with Korbell. Korbell knew it and waited with the patience that huge wealth affords. He looked forward to it as much as Blue-feather—almost. But first, Bluefeather, with the help of a couple of Olders, melted down the nodules into small bars, and at Sherry's insistence, all but three of the widely separated samples from the Hills of Hell. She wanted those for further study, as she put it. All told there was enough to pay off Willy's place, send Sally to college—as Bluefeather had sworn would happen—and give Flo and Harvey a good start in any business they desired. His friends, the Rugers, were now provided for. They had earned much more but were overly grateful for—and for a short time even guilty over—what they received. Zia Creek could flow on without interference from bankers or builders at least through their lifetimes. Bluefeather also was left with enough to make him, as country folks say, "fairly well to do."

Now that the compound was running smoothly again, Bluefeather and Sherry sat on the terrace in front of the thirty-foot window, absorbing the green, growing grass, trees, bushes and sunlight. They gazed with delicious delight and appreciation.

Their conversation dodged all around what must be done about the "below" world. They advanced a thought here and there, both pulling them back, afraid, searching for some answer they could settle or believe right between them. It was all up to them now. Just the two of them. Shia and Willy would remain totally loyal and silent unless told otherwise. The decision would be momentous, with chances for terrible destruction or boundless gain. The indecision became destructive stress.

They must decide now.

They agreed that a few of the Olders, and possibly some Youngers, had enough food stored and live chickens, cows, pigs and the bounteous giving of the trees of light to survive quite well. They had known nothing else, anyway.

"Look, Sherry, the system below has survived uncountable aeons without us. It can surely advance without us now—it even might be destroyed with us. Don't you think?"

"I would never let anything permanently injure the lower cave system. We never have."

"I know, but you and Dolby were the sole controllers. There's no way it can be maintained. Look how close Korbell came to taking it. Think about how many died trying to win it and how many died to save it. The percentage rate is astronomical."

"Of course both sides had different goals, Blue, I . . . I well . . ."

"Listen, Sherry, let's admit what's going on around us with the destruction of the forests and poisoning of the rivers. The wolf and grizzly are being pushed back into what few old forests are left and are losing the race of extinction. There is an endless, growing chain of babies— hungry babies, beautiful babies, lovable babies, irresistible babies—crawling across the entire globe, spreading, taking up all available space and finite resources. Babies being conceived, birthed, bathed, fed, fed, fed—cartons, diapers, bottles, cans, cups, glasses, plastics, clothes, toys. For all the surplus babies scrubbed and fattened in one spot, even more will be starved to death in another."

Sherry was so motionless, Bluefeather felt she had quit breathing for a moment, and in truth she had been trying not to hear what he could not hold back. It was beyond his control now, however, and the long-suppressed feelings tumbled out of him in words.

He continued, "Then those babies grow up, Sherry. Their stomachs are bigger, it takes more to fill them, and more trash to wrap the food in and more poison chemicals to make the rapidly dying land produce. Don't you see? It tilts the world and all of nature off balance. It's simply an unthinking mass suicide."

"I know, I know. I can't stand to think of it, and I don't want to hear it anymore."

"But we have to think about this surface earth, dwell on it, in fact, and then act, act, act. And even now we may be too stupidly, greedily late."

"Oh Blue, I know. I'm having selfish thoughts of continuing Dolby's dream—my dream—of sharing it all—the sights, the smells, the notebooks."

There were over eighty thousand privately owned acres of hills, mountains, canyons and forests like earth auditoriums all over the Cavern of Marvels. It was surrounded by national forests, most of it inhospitable even to hunters. Sherry could certainly protect any outside discovery of a crack or hidden cave during her lifetime that might lead the accumulators and desecrators down below.

Bluefeather asked her if these things were not true. Sherry agreed they were. It was her deeded land to protect now. Only she, Bluefeather, Shia and Willy would know during their allotted breathing time.

They both sat in the warm, kissing, ancient sun that would forever be new to them now. Sherry tried to move her mind back to the decision she and Bluefeather had to make, but it kept glancing at, and stumbling over, the glory of the soul that would come from revealing to the world all she alone held inside her head, heart and in the leather-bound pages of her notebooks. Pains came and were fought away at the images of Dolla, the triloids, their river, Dolby, the Star Cave, God's Castle and the smell and feel of Pack. At this instant Bluefeather was missing his friends Charlie, Pack, all the others, even the Youngers, who—except for Shia, alone—had never had a chance to know the difference.

Bluefeather's vision was convoluted with pictures of Marsha's eyes, her hair, her walk, her laugh, her, she, Marsha, Marsha. He saw the never-to-bes they would never have, tempered by the always-ones they had shared. He forced the mind-pictures in fast-sliced images on to the great room of pearls, the iridescent horse-fish, the diving and dancing triloid young and more.

Sherry and Bluefeather were back in the same shared space. They would have to weep and mourn or perish, but for now their mission was untidy, unfinished. Weeping must wait again.

Then he spoke softly aloud, "You know what? Blood and gold and beauty are made from the same chemicals."

Sherry came up out of her reverie of disassembled truths, saying, "What? What did you say, Blue? I'm sorry."

"Oh, nothing really. I was just kinda talking to myself, I guess."

Sherry said, "Would you like a glass of wine?"

"I sure as hell would."

It was served in a full decanter, purple and radiant in the sun that had created the mother grapes of its beginnings. They made a silent toast and sipped, delaying with some pleasure the inevitable agony of final decisions.

Then Bluefeather's mind-voice clicked in from somewhere far away in his head and spoke with authority: *Beware, beware, ye pioneers, for vultures will follow and become fat on your discoveries.* After a moment the voice continued. *Korbell. His heart is as cold and stiff as a Siberian thermometer. Never forget it.*

Sherry spoke aloud now, her voice was as surprising, and suddenly painful, as a paper cut. She said, "I can't. I can't just bury it all, Blue. That's what we'll have to do, isn't it? We'll have to bury it so no one can find it? Well, I can't do it . . . I just can't. Because then . . . then all the years of study . . . knowledge in my little books will be gone, lost. I . . . I . . ."

"I know. Well, I know part of what you are feeling. Just a small part, but . . ."

Her great eyes were so wide and deeply disturbed, searching, that Bluefeather could no longer look into them. Instead, he stared at the blue, misty mesas, all the way to the western horizon.

Then he finally said, "As of right now, the Cavern of Marvels and all its multitude of inhabitants are very much as they were before humans discovered the use of fire. They'll most likely continue to evolve aeons after mankind has destroyed this world . . . and long after the little human empires of wealth and pitiful power have crumbled and vanished. Forgotten. The greatest cities—the mightiest nations—will change boundaries over and over and will probably collapse into piles of matter. This, too, will finally be flattened by the ever-changing heat and cold, wind and rain, and disappear as if these things had never been."

Sherry knew, but was trying to hide from herself, the point that Bluefeather was so desperately struggling to impress upon her. She said, "Blue, I think I know what you are driving at. And I know you are trying to make this easier on both of us. But I . . . I just can't let it go . . . yet. It's like losing my . . . well, my soul. I just can't explain my feelings. I suppose it's even a certain kind of greed . . . not money greed, but greed all the same."

Bluefeather hesitated a full minute. She waited, frightened, knowing he would not give up.

"Well, I sure as hell understand about greed. That cockeyed, yellow metal has haunted my dreams uncounted days and nights, but I fought it, and I think I've won. You're going to have to do the same about the cavern. Oh, God, Sherry, please forgive me . . . the last thing I mean to do is preach or lecture to anyone in this world, much less you. It's just that I'm filled up with all these worries about that wondrous world. I can't help myself."

"But we'll lose everything we've found. It will all be gone. It will all be lost forever. I can't stand the thoughts of it."

"But, darling Sherry, there is a remote chance that all this below could surpass and survive and maybe, in some far-distant time, one or more of its creatures might crawl from a fissure in the earth and out into the sun. You know—just as others came out of the ocean to the land and air and eventually climbed trees. That might be the only chance left." He stopped and looked straight at her before saying, "We do have to bury it. We have no choice, do we?" Then he was quiet.

The desperate effort to convince Sherry to give up the almost limitless knowledge of her life's work pained and drained him. Her eyes looked on through his, out the back of his head. Then she stared straight ahead, motionless, as if in a trance for five or six minutes. Eternity.

Finally, with a start, she blurted out in complete contradiction, "Of course, dear Blue, of course. Let us do our duty and drink to it. What have I been talking about? Who do I think I'm fooling? Not you. Not me."

They had survived hellish wars and pressure together. They had both lost their loves and lovers. Their minds had swiftly become meshed by necessity and now were even more together by respect and love.

"Blue, can you do it so no one outside this compound will ever know?"

"I can do it, but Korbell knows."

They both thought simultaneously that Tilton's gold had been moved to Dolby's vault and now it, along with its evil spirits, had gone on to a new vault with a new master—or slave. They must act. They made a last futile search for Dolby's explosive button. It was not to be found. Maybe it had never been there. The threat was as good as the truth with such an overpowering man.

"Then let's get after it and worry about him after the fact," Bluefeather said as he stood up to phone Willy to come help with the planning. Willy was overjoyed with the decision. It was decided just like that.

Bluefeather had always been naturally good at dynamite blasting. Willy was also an experienced expert. Even so, it took days of drilling to angle and space the holes and measure the powder exactly right. They had to blast the concrete tunnels into rubble so that the next explosions would cover it all. It had to be perfect.

At last it was as ready as it would ever be. One more time they had to be perfect. Just once. It was important to everything that had ever been or ever would be. All the electric lines had been connected to the explosives.

The little group—Bluefeather, Sherry, Shia, Willy and all the Olders—stood about, staring at the box with the plunger raised. All eyes were centered on the plunger.

Bluefeather said, "Sherry, it's your honor."

She looked at him, and then moved without hesitation, knelt and pushed it down. The earth jarred under their feet. The foothill dropped some of its surface in a landslide of the perfection they had sought. The entrance to the underworld was covered and hidden as if Mother Nature had created the rock slide. Maybe she had, actually.

It looked as natural as all the other slides over the entire range. The continuum would be left to the vagaries of chance and the progression of evolution in the cavern far, far below.

They stood silently for several minutes. Then the four went back to the house and sat on the terrace. They stared in appreciation of all the precious greenery of the meadows and mountains, absorbing kisses from the sun playing sweet symphonies of shadows for their grateful eyes.

Bluefeather raised his glass of fine wine and toasted, "As I've said before, here's to the gods, goddamn 'em and bless 'em, too."

Sherry said, "And to their daughters, sons and heirs."

Willy clicked his merry glass against theirs and offered, "Grandy dandy. And here's to dancing, to singing, to love, to growth, for folks cain't have no real fun without 'em all."

They cheered in agreement, laughed and drank their wine with joy. Then, as Willy had suggested, Sherry caught a hand of both Bluefeather and Willy, tugging them up. The three of them danced on the surface of the secured Caverns of Marvels. Shia watched, clapping in rhythm. They danced in small circles, hands on each other's shoulders, smiling, then giggling, then laughing, so that birds and squirrels moved and chattered about in the trees at the happy disturbance.

FORTY-EIGHT

WILLY HAD RETURNED HOME SEVERAL DAYS EARLIER, and now Sherry walked Bluefeather down to his jeep. Neither spoke. There was too much to verbalize.

He opened the door and turned back to her. "I've got a very necessary chore to attend to."

"I know."

"I'll be back to see you—when I finish."

"I'll be looking forward to hearing from you."

They held one another a long moment, feeling their everlasting bond.

"I love you."

"I love you, too."

He climbed into the jeep and drove on out through the new guard gate. She stood looking after him a long time.

He went by the Rugers' and picked up the Tilton property maps that Charlie Waters had gathered for him with such unquestioned dedication. He talked to Sally about how brave Charlie had been and finally managed to get her thinking about school again. He drove on over to Albuquerque and shopped awhile and saw a lawyer before going home to Corrales.

The Tranquilino Lucero family was so happy to see him that they wanted to throw an immediate fiesta. He explained that he had some studying to do and an appointment to keep—then they would celebrate.

He handed Tranquilino two envelopes, one sealed, one open, saying, "Now I gotta have your word and your handshake that you'll accept these envelopes with no hesitation, no apologies and no regrets."

Tranquilino stared at him, at his wife and children, then smiled widely and warmly saying, "Okay. Okay, amigo. Okay. My word and my hand."

They shook hands. It was done.

As Bluefeather left to go see the mules, Nancy and Miss Mary, he could hear the happy cries of the excited family behind him. Tranquilino burst out on the porch to yell at him but remembered his vows and re-entered the house.

In the open envelope was the title to a new Ford pickup truck to be picked up by Tranquilino. He had no idea the truck bed was heaped up past the rim with delicacies of all kinds, educational toys and many books for the whole family, a silver concho belt for the lady of the house and an inflatable boat for Tranquilino to fish in up at Fenton Lake in his beloved Jemez Mountains. More. Yes, more, for Bluefeather had signed the deed to his house and acreage over to the Luceros with one restriction—that he could pitch camp there at any time in the next three years and would have a place for his two mules the same. He felt very good about this. It would give the Luceros enough paid-for land to make a living from without having to give in to the greed of overdevelopment.

Bluefeather was amazed that the mules remembered him. They were sleek, shiny and solid muscled. Tranquilino had obviously fed them well and exercised them properly. Of course, he had only been gone—how long? Nine weeks. Twelve? Fifteen? He couldn't remember, for it seemed, even now as he talked to and petted his long-eared partners, that he had trekked for a thousand generations at least.

"I don't want to leave you, my exquisite ones. Oh no. It breaks my tired heart, but I must fulfill my present destiny. Do you understand, sleek ones?"

They moved their ears, hearing and comprehending every inflection of his voice as before. They watched him with dark, moist eyes made of the essence of stars and loyalty—the latter prized above all by the half Taos Indian and half Raton, New Mexico, Italian—now meshed, as old Grinder had demanded, into just simply Bluefeather. Now he could weep, here with his familiars. He sobbed and shook so that his ribs were near breaking and his lungs bursting. He wept for Marsha, for Pack, for all who had perished and even for the dream itself. He finally wept for its success and failure and even a little for himself. The weeping was over at last. The silent grieving would be slower to withdraw, but it would—mostly.

He acquired a suite of rooms at the Hilton in downtown Albuquerque and stayed there four days and nights—all alone. He used room service only, so as to study Tilton's maps undisturbed. He would stay put as long as it took. That is the way he was. But at midnight of the fourth day he was satisfied. With his picture-mind, he saw Tilton's golden skull staring across the River of Radiance and said aloud, "Thank you, Mr. Tilton. All small favors are deeply appreciated."

He picked up the phone and called Korbell. With a little explanation as to who he was, Bluefeather was put through to him.

"Ahhh, Mr. Fellini, no less, the midnight caller. I've been expecting your call. The timing is perfect. I often stay up until two or three in the morning, studying and enjoying the silence and . . . my collection."

Bluefeather didn't ask him what collection, since he owned some part of the world somewhere, and a bit of everything in it, along with about fifty million dollars' worth of Tilton's metal.

"When shall we meet? I have information that might lead us toward closing our original deal."

"Ah, yes. The Mouton '80."

Bluefeather was enjoying Korbell's cautious cleverness on the phone, as if he didn't have every means to discover a phone tap.

"Yes, the eighty-eight."

Bluefeather wondered if the man had gotten his double entrendre about the Mouton 1880 and the deadly German eighty-eight shells they had both once been so very close to.

"Afternoon after next. Three o'clock. I have some old friends from various parts of the planet arriving for a small soiree. Informal, of course."

Bluefeather held the phone a moment, looking at it after the other end was dead. He could see the "Korbell smile that spoke" all the way to where he sat.

FORTY-NINE

IT WAS THE TIME FOR ROUNDING UP LOOSE ENDS AND
tying them together. The guards shook Bluefeather down
at the gate to Korbell's retreat. They seemed surprised he
was clean. Nedra smiled and complimented him on his
health, his sport jacket and his general attitude all the way
to meet Korbell. The man with the silver hair and the
silver voice left a little covey of worldly citizens, greeted
Bluefeather with enthusiasm and introduced him to men
and women from London, Bombay, Tokyo, Paris, Hous-
ton and Bogota. There were others he met and to whom
he said the "Happy to . . . honored to . . . pleased to meet
you" party gargle.

Korbell spoke their languages flawlessly, with natural-
ness, with each guest, except for the oil men from Hous-
ton. He slightly overdid that particular foreign accent.
Bluefeather covered for him there, since he had the
southwestern, geological drawl down to its beefsteak, pork
chops and red-eye gravy. He liked it.

Even with the Scotch in his hand and the huge patio
with the small pool in his vision—things were a little
blurred. Bluefeather wasn't here to focus his mind-camera
on these people so practiced, planned and perfectly casual
in all ways. The dress, the conversations hinting at power

and wealth were barely, but strongly, suggested among those who really had it. The worshipped power was presented, along with an attitude of responsible respectability, as smoothly as an Old Vic play. Only here, their stage and the masks were real. The rest was the play itself. All the actors wore masks of opaque illusions. Magic was made by little tricks of cleverness. Sincerity was acquired by the purchase price—lovely appearances in expensive disguise.

Bluefeather even gave Korbell a complimentary thought. Korbell recognized all this, but he was not aware that Bluefeather had seen him glance over his adopted wife Elena's shoulder at him. Korbell had long ago won all the other games, including the games played here. Bluefeather was the only prey left.

Bluefeather walked along the hors d'oeuvres table filled with every imaginable delicacy. He picked at the food, setting his drink down carefully, untouched. He never drank alcohol when he worked. Right now he was very busy indeed. He moved a china plate in deliberate misdirection—an eye-fooling trick he had learned in his card playing days from Nancy of Tonopah—and stuck a carving knife in the back of his belt under his jacket. He moved on around the table and with the same smooth motion placed a bread knife in the inside wallet pocket of his jacket for extra insurance. Then he took a few nibbles of shrimp and waited. He was trying to make himself invisible until Korbell could separate himself from his guests.

When the mariachi band started up and all eyes and ears were drawn in their direction for a moment, Korbell moved to Bluefeather, saying, "Come with me, Mr. Fellini. We have things to discuss in private, do we not?"

"Indeed we do, Mr. Korbell." He didn't emphasize the "mister," but got it slipped in anyway.

They moved easily through three rooms to a hallway. Korbell opened a door, switched on a light and led Bluefeather down two turns of circular concrete stairs underground. Then he touched an iron door. It swung open, moving as smoothly as a snake on Italian marble, revealing a vast wine cellar. Even Bluefeather's awareness of Korbell's hobby had not prepared him for this.

Korbell marched him grandly around, pointing out and describing different bottles of rare vintages. He often picked up a special bottle to read the impressive label.

Bluefeather's perception of the bottles and of Korbell fused. He could no longer waste any faked interest on what they both knew was a formality—a hollow one at that. Then, at the very back northwest corner, Korbell reached under and between two bottles on the second shelf and pushed a hidden latch. The shelves swung outward, revealing a solid-looking wall. Then Korbell easily pushed the great stone door open. The massive two-foot-thick block had been cut so mathematically, so flawlessly, that Einstein would have published a paper on its precision.

Bluefeather noticed that Korbell left this door open. There was a huge, hidden room unmasked before them. It was full of treasures on shelves and in glass cases— treasures from around the world. Bluefeather saw Ming vases, Egyptian mummies in solid gold uniforms, a nugget that must have weighed five hundred pounds from a Brazilian placer mine and a diamond the size of a prizefighter's fist. Surrounding it were piles and clusters of smaller blue, white and yellow diamonds of all sizes and cuts. There were old, old Mayan and Aztec masks—objects of a unique, and sometimes tragic, beauty. There was a Rembrandt painting of a golden-lit lady, dazzling to behold. Renoirs of dancing light and moving shadows. An El Greco figure, twisted, long, lean, elongated, so it seemed to stretch up past the picture frame to the ceiling.

Korbell proudly, profusely, eloquently described the

value, the place of origin and even his acquisition of the
mostly stolen goods.

It was not lost on Bluefeather that the accumulator
seemed to enjoy incriminating himself to Bluefeather. On
and on it went—the riches cut, carved and painted so long
ago by great artists and craftsmen who were now all
worm-eaten dust.

Korbell's chest was rising and falling in exhalation. Now
at last they came to the corner shelves, where a waist-high
narrow table fronted them. The shelves were all replete
with the same vintage wine bottles. To the side was a very
old-fashioned but elegant washbasin with solid gold handles and pipes and a glass case full of wineglasses above
it.

Korbell stopped between the case and the table,
reached in and took out two glasses. He placed one in
front of each of them. He moved around a moment, then,
leaning over, pushed a plush chair, sending it rolling away
toward a couch. All the furniture was on rollers to move
easily over the smooth, tiled floor of a neutral color with
a tiny unobtrusive pattern.

"I come here, Mr. Fellini, and sip my wine. You see, I
enjoy sitting here and gazing at many of the greatest treasures and artifacts in the world. I take great pleasure in
knowing they are all mine and I am the only one in this
world left alive, except you, who knows about this room's
existence. Selfish to the extreme, huh, Mr. Fellini?"

"I would agree with your last judgment totally."

Bluefeather knew now what was coming. Korbell never
intended him to leave the cellar alive. He couldn't allow
it, now. Not after his admissions.

"Don't you find it a revelatory irony that Tilton invented this room, and these marvelous doors, just for me?
For me, Mr. Fellini. None of us, not one, ever knows in
the end whom we have really been working for during
our lifetime."

Bluefeather had finally seen that exact same truth on Charlie's maps two nights before at a minute to midnight, but Korbell—with all his knowledge—was not aware of this.

"I agree with you in totality, and if and when you ever find out, it's probably too late to change it," Bluefeather said, studying Korbell, sensing the slight bulge cleverly hidden under his armpit. He didn't believe that that was how Korbell meant to kill him, though. The gun was only protection against his guest. Korbell would surely have a more subtle method.

Now, as Korbell reached to the shelf for the wine bottle, his face was a vibrant pink, his eyes turned to shiny pearls and his smile was one of near orgasm. He set the bottle on the table ceremoniously and wiped it carefully, lovingly, with a white silk handkerchief. Then he turned the wine label toward Bluefeather, staring at him in what could only appear as a form of gloating glee.

Bluefeather calmly read aloud, "Mouton 1880."

"Forty cases of it, courtesy of Mr. Tilton. Of course there are a few bottles I've sipped while perusing my . . . my little cache."

Bluefeather had known that the wine could be no other place than here. One of Tilton's architectural drawings revealed the front cellar and the one where they now stood. He must not let Korbell know this yet, for he intended to kill him some way soon.

"You sly rascal, you," Bluefeather grinned. "You've had the wine here ever since you bought the place. Tilton had already hidden it here before he finished the upper house. Pretty slick." Bluefeather reached over playfully and tapped Korbell on the shoulder, but let his hand swiftly feel the gun. It was there all right. He had to watch every tiny move now. "You were after the bullion all along, right? Huh?" Bluefeather laughed.

"Of course, Mr. Fellini, and I must say you delivered.

Delivery—that's the word. That's all that matters. Here, let us celebrate our victory with this rare liquid treasure." He expertly removed the old cork, smelled it as his eyeballs rolled up in mock thanks to God and then, as delicately as a mother kisses her new baby, poured them each a glass.

Bluefeather watched for any movement of misdirection, of deceit, as Korbell tilted the bottle with both hands. He could discern none, but a warning coldness tingled on the back of his neck and the once-split nose itched more with joy than anger now. They raised the glasses and stared straight across them at one another.

"To the best of everything, Mr. Fellini, and to the bonus you shall receive momentarily."

"To your dedication, Mr. Korbell, and to a bonus you so abundantly deserve."

They both laughed and then tasted the rare liquid extravagance.

"Ahhh," admired Korbell, savoring a second swallow. "Ahhh."

Bluefeather was taking no chances of Korbell palming poison or flicking it from under his fingernails. One or the other had to be the method of his murder, he figured.

He must get the carving knife out before Korbell could reach his revolver. He was counting on his more youthful, swifter physical movements to beat his opponent.

Bluefeather held the glass at half-toast position as he swung one arm in a gesture that included the tennis court–sized room and said so softly that Korbell would be compelled to strain his hearing, "You killed your only daughter and forced me to kill your only son for the bullion when you already had this room of treasures—and a thousand times more. Why sir? Why, I ask?"

"It wasn't supposed to happen. I underestimated the loyalty and courage of Dolby's people."

"You underestimated your daughter as well."

"Yes, I admit that. We tried every form of bribery and even threats to get the information from her. She was tough. Very tough. Of course, she was tough. I had trained her that way myself."

"Of course."

"Yes. It took a very large and dangerous dose of truth serum to get it out of her."

"Well, here's to your diligence, Mr. Korbell," Bluefeather raised his glass, continuing the toast, "and my many wishes that you enjoy every drop of wine on that shelf and gaze upon nothing but beautiful treasures such as these the rest of your life."

Korbell had just caught on to the satire in Bluefeather's voice, because the pink in his face dissipated into grey and the smile turned down at its edges.

Bluefeather grabbed and swung the half-full bottle of Mouton '80 with extra swift force and speed just as Korbell opened his fingers ever so slightly, preparing to grab his gun. Korbell had miscalculated and given away his position at last. The bottle struck him full on the chin. He fell with a comforting thud, his head bouncing a little on the tastefully tiled floor, adding to his present blankness without permanent injury.

Bluefeather grabbed a bottle with a loose label from the shelf. He quickly finished peeling it off, took a pen from his pocket and wrote on the inside of the label, "Enjoy. Eternally yours, Mr. Fellini."

He set the bottle of Mouton '80 next to the note, moved to the stone door and closed it carefully behind him. Now he had use for the carving knife. He forced the point into the almost invisible crack of the door and drove it as a wedge into the space. He pushed with all his might. It now fit exactly. Then he broke the blade off even with the door and wall. It would never move again. The perfection had been prized away by the knife blade. Now it was a perfect prison. He pushed the wine shelf against it.

The door could not be seen at all now and the recessed latch was invisible. Perpetuity.

Korbell's luxurious entombment had been necessary so that they, the triloids and all their companions, were permanently free of human intervention. The world would not be aware of that action, but now Korbell was hidden underground as well. The public would never know what happened to him, either, but would spend uncounted hours and millions of dollars searching and guessing.

Bluefeather smiled a smile of such brilliance it would have dulled those of the Korbell tribe all the way back to cave frogs.

He walked up and out into the sunlight, visiting, just as casually corrupt as the rest of Korbell's associates. He was enjoying his third Scotch—he was through working, so he could indulge himself a bit. He heard Elena asking several people nearby, and finally him, if they had seen Korbell.

Bluefeather said, "No. I have been enjoying your guests so much, I didn't notice his absence."

"Oh, well, he's always just disappearing like this. Sometimes he's actually gone for days. One never knows if he'll return or not."

"I'm sure that's true," Bluefeather agreed, as he wound around the gardens beyond the patio with the New Mexico mountains swallowing the rays of warm, early fall sun placidly. Content.

A lady in delicate costume came toward him on a curving path. He recognized Nicole, once mistress to Napoleon, poisoned by Josephine.

She smiled and spoke, "Please, monsieur, have pleasant thoughts about me. Am I not worthy?"

"Oh . . . yes . . . you certainly are. What are you doing here, Nicole?"

"Oh, Dancing Bear sent me to substitute again."

"Well, I'll be honest with you, Nicole. I expected Bear here in person to celebrate our victory."

"I'm sure you did, Monsieur Bluefeather, but he asked me to give you this message exact. He said you would understand."

"Of course," he said, mimicking his fallen foe's precise speech.

She quoted Dancing Bear "exact": "Tell Blue that I got the promotion from Authority, but he sends me to the Bahamas to heal. Buffalo who runs a mile uphill with his skull on fire needs a vacation."

"I can certainly understand that—and sympathize."

Nicole reached out, took his hand and they floated over the compound's walls, out over the forest, up onto a little white cloud not much bigger than a king-sized bed. Down below a sheepherder stopped to listen. He would always swear he had heard voices from the sky saying, "Lower. Lower."

"Higher. Higher."

He would spend the rest of his life searching for the meaning.

PART THREE

~

THE TIME OF DECISION:

THE GREAT QUANDARY

AND EMBARKATION

FIFTY

IT WAS THE TIME TO DIE. BLUEFEATHER COULD FEEL all the natural crippling ailments of old age coming on strong. He would beat them at their timeless game. He had lived an extremely active and exciting life. It was not his nature to go bedridden, mind-fogged into the other realm. No, sir. He would go bouncing at his best. He felt especially blessed that he—along with coyotes, Eskimos, turtles and cicadas—knew this.

It might take a few days. Just the same, he felt it was upon him. He had been here long and the thinning legs beneath his body were increasingly uncertain. He must get away from the town. It reached out and surrounded him. He could feel its grasp tightening. He could hear his mind-voice saying, *Come, old Bluefeather, and sit on the porches of my dusty streets in the shade of my trees. Stay and loaf and dream in the sun and warm your worn legs by the log fires of my houses. Stay and die slowly here, looking at the far distant hills of your youth, in the easy time.*

"No!"

First, before dying, he had chores to tend. He sat at the rough, handmade table in his three-room house and wrote his will on a yellow pad. The hands that held the pen looked like twisted oak limbs. He would leave the residence to his amigo, Artesimo Gomez, a prospector like himself. They had drunk the same blood and seen the same lion.

Bluefeather explained in the note about the high-grade silver ore piled in the corner of his bedroom. He had made this heap of rock his retirement. He could hand-crush the ore and retort it down to silver ingots with a few chemicals and a blow torch, as he had need for it. There was enough in the pile to take care of Artesimo for several years—if he was frugal.

Bluefeather thought of leaving his twenty-acre mining claim in the Black Range above the tiny village of Kingston to his godson, Brian Rousset, who had been adopted as an infant by Sherry. Then he changed his mind and decided not even to mention the claim, letting it revert back to the forest service, which had owned it first. He had never patented it, but had simply turned in his yearly assessment.

Near Hillsboro, big copper companies had recently spent scores of millions of dollars core-drilling and building mills, but due to price fluctuations, they had left with nothing but the sad experience. The bonanza-hungry, the greedy, the simple fools, along with the stock promoters, had come and gone all the years Bluefeather had been plugging away here. A few had hit nice pockets of ore on occasion but had raped and ruined most of the tunnels.

He stared at the paper a moment before signing it. His dark eyes glistened out from a face that appeared to be chiseled from the hardest granite in the mountains, but the tiny smile was tender.

Bluefeather fixed himself a large breakfast of sourdough biscuits, sowbelly and sorghum syrup. He ate ravenously and felt elated, younger, much younger. His old legs seemed suddenly solid beneath him. He marveled at how making the ultimate decision of freedom had restored his body and his spirit as well. A small miracle, maybe.

After the Cavern of Marvels expedition and completion, he had drifted south in the Sierra Madres of Old Mexico and then back to the Big Bend country of Texas, without anything but survival deposits. At the border town of Terlingua, he had made a small mercury strike. Then he had worked his way to Globe, Arizona, and panned a nice pocket of placer below a mountain of low-grade ore.

He spent several years wandering with his mules from Prescott, Arizona, down to the Superstition Mountains near Phoenix. Then he moved on over into southern New Mexico. He headquartered at Hillsboro, to be what he felt was an easy half-day's drive from Sherry—near enough to feel her presence but not to bother her. It seemed just the right distance. Any nearer than this and the old haunting of the Cavern of Marvels might have a chance to obsess them again. Anyway, he loved the wonderful diversity of such a small place. Besides, he had finally found the silver deposit—of the exact richness— that he desired.

Hillsboro was inhabited by a few retirees from larger towns and old prospectors, cowboys and artists of various kinds. Bluefeather had decided that this village would be his last hometown.

All his "early life" friends, including most of his family members—at least the ones he knew personally—had long ago "crashed through" to other dimensions. Besides Sherry, Brian, Shia and a few Hillsboro friends who were left from his younger days, he also had Tranquilino's son, Little Tranc, in Corrales. The last few years their visits had become fewer and fewer, but their thoughts of one another were projected many times a day across the mountains.

He had often gone to visit Sherry at what they still called Dolby's Ranch, spending a week or more at times.

Even though it was an easy drive from Hillsboro to Sherry's place, they had both quit driving for themselves now. Nevertheless, they could have if they had wished to concentrate that much. They didn't. Brian was always glad to drive either direction whenever Sherry or Bluefeather wanted to visit. They cared deeply and enjoyed each other's company more than that of anyone else on earth.

Shia had long ago adapted to the upper world, making a fine and trusted companion for Sherry. She insisted on running the household and doing a lot of the cooking herself—which suited Sherry just fine.

Sherry's son, Brian, was now mature and capable of handling the ranch headquarters. Besides being general manager, he was also the gamekeeper. There was an abundance of elk, deer, bear and mountain lion, along with saddle horses, pack mules and donkeys.

Sherry had long ago set up the huge acreage in a trust as a summer camp for the Girl Scouts of America. Before the trust was signed, all trails and campsites, lakes and streams had been designated. One Mimbres ruin—with her help—had been excavated by the University of New Mexico and a small museum of its artifacts and history built near the site. The trust restricted any exploration for minerals or excavations of any kind. It was an unspoiled paradise of the wild for the young Girl Scouts of America.

Bluefeather's life was quiet and uncluttered now. He did have a favorite radio station that was devoted exclusively to classical music. He enjoyed this a lot, but he seldom used his television, read a newspaper or talked on the telephone. All these things were mostly a waste to him, for his active mind was a private and very real television set, turning on, at will, a wild animal show, a mountain storm, Saturday night dances or a mineral strike—and without having to touch a single button. He often thought of his young times, which were now the old times, and knew that these present happenings would soon be the old times, too.

He reread his beloved Jack London. He also read Cervantes, because miners constantly tilted at *unseen* windmills; Balzac, because he once rode a donkey across rough and barren land, for many terrible days of pain to his soft body, to buy a copper mine; and Twain, because he had loved miners and mules and had written about such courage and foolishness as this. The latter trait was sufficient for all-time respect from Bluefeather. Movement. Eternal.

He had, for many years, kept up a correspondence with his kin, but it had slowly dribbled away to nothing as his relations had died or forgotten. He knew they had been hurt at his "apartness" in the early years. He had told himself over and over, as he had wandered in his youth, that Italians had always been heavily family bound and that the Pueblo Indians had their clans hundreds, perhaps thousands, of years old, but he had been gone so long in other worlds that he could not bring himself to gather up his blood ancestry. He couldn't explain this to himself, much less his kin. Bluefeather's parts were all synchronized in HIS world, but they bent the wrong way to fit the dominant one that made up the rest of human existence. He would never forget old Grinder deeming that he was just an American called "Blue."

FIFTY-ONE

BLUEFEATHER HAD LEARNED LONG AGO, THROUGH THE experience of the desert and mountains, that mules are kinder, smarter, more enduring and more affectionate than horses and most other four-legged creatures of the world.

He yelled, "Haaa. Hooo," in greeting to the two brown mules. "Haaa, Nancy. Hooo, Mary." They walked up to him, with their delicate and evenly paced steps, as he poured the oats in a metal trough and stepped back to watch them dine. It always made him feel warm to see working animals enjoying their feed.

He mumbled a few unintelligible things to them and then said, "Ah, yes, my beautiful creatures with wings on top of your heads, eat heartily, for soon we make the final journey together."

They moved their long ears back and forth, acknowledging his familiar voice. Chewing, Mary raised her head and looked at Bluefeather with her wise and tender eyes.

Now he returned to the house and got the three, fist-sized pieces of rose quartz with the wire gold laced throughout like yellow metal worms. One was the rock his father-in-law, Ludwig Schmidt of Breen, Colorado, had first shown him that had started the search for the mine that destroyed their Miss Mary. The second specimen he and Miss Mary had dug from the vein of Ludwig's dream. The third was one he had saved in remembrance of the glory days at Harmony Creek.

He put them into a small canvas bag and walked toward the single business street of Hillsboro. He took his handwritten will along to get the two necessary witness signatures that would make it legal.

First he stopped by the post office and asked for his mail. He was relaxed and joyful at the same time. Sonya Rutledge, who had been here fifty years, looked in his box. She knew, and Bluefeather knew, there was little chance for mail. He thanked her and stood a moment. He wanted to tell her good-bye, but didn't know how.

He said, "Looks like an early fall, Mrs. Rutledge."

She smiled and said it sure did.

"Mrs. Rutledge, would it be too much trouble to ask you to witness my will?"

"Of course not. I'd be happy to help you any way I can, Blue." She signed it after only a swift glance.

He thanked her, bid her a good day and walked on down to Roy's Hillsboro Texaco station. The gas pumps were gone now. It was just a repair garage. Before the pumps had quit paying, he and his friend, Artesimo, would stop here for gas when they drove to Truth or Consequences, the county seat, to fish in Elephant Butte Lake and drink and dance on Saturday nights. All hoped for the gas pumps to return. It was a symbol of survival for this small town and thousands more like it across America.

Bluefeather was pleased to see his two rancher friends, Jimmy Bason and Sterling Roberts, here getting their pickups greased and the oil changed. They were teasing one another about a horse trade.

Sterling said, "Jimmy, you knew that old grey horse you traded me was stone deaf. He don't know 'whoa' from 'go.' "

Bason laughed and said, "Don't be blaming me. I tried to tell you that the horse couldn't hear too good. You checked him out and thought you were stealing him."

Sterling said, "Well, he looks better than he performs."

"Hey, so do you."

Bluefeather had to pass through Bason's F-Cross Ranch to get to his mine. The rancher allowed this without question because he knew that Bluefeather left his camps so neat and clean a coyote would have trouble locating them. Bason was one of those people who would go a mile out of the way to pick up a loose scrap of paper or a soda can. He cared deeply for the land and its animals. He did not take lightly to fools defiling it even in the smallest manner.

Jimmy asked Bluefeather, "Hey, Blue, would you like a Coke before Sterling drinks them all?"

"No thanks, I'm saving room for a beer with Artesimo a little later." Again, he could think of no way to bid his friends farewell, so he just went to the rest room and then back down the street to Sue's Antique Shop to get the second signature on his will.

Sue Bason was Jimmy's ex-wife. She, like the postmistress, had always been especially nice to him, selling his rock specimens when he really needed a little cash. She greeted him when he walked in, although she was busy with a customer.

"What have you been up to these days, Blue?"

"Oh, the same old stuff. Managing to stay out of too much trouble."

"I'll be with you in a minute, Blue."

Sue was a fine watercolorist, and Bluefeather moved about the shop, looking at her paintings while she finished with her business.

When she had completed the sale and they were alone, Bluefeather asked her if she would witness his document. She did. He thanked Sue and presented her with the gold-bearing rock.

She exclaimed, "Oh, Blue, this is truly a beauty. This is real gold, isn't it? How much should we ask for it?"

"No, no, Sue. This one is for you. This one is not for sale. It belongs only to you. It's a memento from my youth."

"I don't know what to say—except, of course, thank you. It's so lovely and . . ." Her eyes, as dark blue as Bluefeather's were black, beamed with pleasure and puzzlement, because the old prospector had already walked out and was angling across the street toward the S-Bar-X Saloon. Sue Bason stared after him and then back at her rock, sewn together by the gods with thick threads of gold.

Bluefeather walked on the flat ground with broad back and powerful arms moving jerkily sideways to keep his balance. Since he had spent most of his life straining over and through mountains of rocks, his slightly bowed legs were unsure on level ground, like an old sailor's.

Bluefeather knew it was almost noon and his friend Artesimo would be halfway through his first beer of the day. Coke Jandro, owner and sometimes dispenser of drinks, was behind the bar. It smelled of spilled whiskey, tobacco and ancient dreams. There was a traveling salesman and a local retiree from Santa Fe sitting at the long bar.

Bluefeather, unlike Artesimo, had quit most of his drinking ten, maybe fifteen years ago. Well, at the annual Apple Festival on Labor Day weekend he had kicked over the wagon, and sometimes on the Fourth of July and Christmas he'd have a few toddies, but, of course, that didn't count as regular drinking. Today, though, he ordered a Mexican beer—Corona. He raised the bottle in a toast: "Here's to Hillsboro, New Mexico, the greatest one-bar, one-church town in the world."

Jandro said, "You're only half right, Blue. The S-Bar-X is Hillsboro's country club and family entertainment center."

Artesimo, or Arty, as his friends called him, said, "Hey, amigo, whatcha do, find the mother lode?"

Bluefeather took a pull at the Corona, wiped his mouth, placed the canvas bag on the bar and stretched the drawstrings open. He said, "See for yourself, feller."

Coke Jandro, the bartender, and Arty Gomez, the prospector, were impressed. They were also instantly curious as to the location of such a find. Finally, Bluefeather broke through their mesmerized state and presented them each with a precious rock. The actual feel and sight of the snaking gold intertwined in the quartz pulled them back from the sudden dreamworld. Reality.

Coke stuttered his thanks. Arty caressed the rock and slapped Bluefeather on the back. The gesture said it all.

He must leave the young friend—the dispenser of relief to the walkers and dreamers of mountains. He must leave his old friend, with whom he had shared the secrets of the earth for so many decades. There was no stopping now. The last great call had possessed him. He must heed. He must.

The bartender set the drinks out saying, "On the house, for sure," and went back to turning in his hands the rose-colored rock containing twisted treasure.

Arty took his prospector's glass out and studied the magnified beauty of his gift.

Now was the right moment. Bluefeather walked to the jukebox and put all his change in it. He punched a mixture of country tunes and popular love songs. He walked out the back door and wound around the old buildings toward his home. The sound of the music faded with each step. The images of his friends blurred. He felt the irresistible pull of the final act.

He walked determinedly to his home. A van was parked there in front. It was Sherry's son, Brian, sitting on his front porch. This was a discord. As much as he loved his godson, he was messing up Bluefeather's life before his imminent death. Brian walked toward him, smiling. They gave each other an embrace.

"Sorry it took me so long, Blue, but I had to wrap up a bunch of things for mother."

Then it dawned on Bluefeather that Brian had called a couple of days ago, saying he would be over to pick him up to drive him for a visit with Sherry.

Bluefeather recovered quickly, saying, "We're always causing you problems, son."

"No problem. Mother had everything in good shape as usual. Just wants to see you. Hey, you're looking ten years younger, Blue. What have you been doing, taking extra-strength vitamins?"

"It's all the dirty, sinful living I've been doing."

They both had a little chuckle.

Bluefeather put his toiletries in a small leather bag, took a change of clothing from the closet and said, "Hey, young'un, we're wasting time standing around here."

Bluefeather always enjoyed the drive to Sherry's. It had both mountains and desert. The van purred smoothly around the curves. Brian was a careful driver and didn't talk so much that he interrupted Bluefeather's musings at "that" mountain, "that" canyon, "that" heavy stand of junipers, all of which he had been on or in.

They rode relaxed, comfortable and caring. Brian was enjoying it as much as the old man. He had always looked up to Bluefeather as a best friend, an uncle and a father. Bluefeather had taken Brian on his first prospecting and fishing trips, his first country dance and had taught him what all the wild animals and plants mean to each other and humankind. He had done more, much more, for him, including kicking his butt a couple of times when he had gotten out of line with his mother.

Shia, with the slanted eyes of mysterious loyalty, served Sherry and Bluefeather out on their favorite terrace. They sipped comfortably, looking across the valley to the long

rows of Girl Scout cabins half hidden by trees. When Shia
served the meal, Brian left the two of them alone to eat
and visit. He went to help his permanent crew winterize
the scouts' compound. The last of the girls had left for
home and school only a couple of weeks ago. Shia, too,
politely vanished back into the house.

It was a delicious meal of pasta and a special Italian
wine. Bluefeather rejoiced that he had given Shia, the
Oriental, his grandmother Fellini's recipe for the greatest
of all pasta sauces. They had benefited often from this
little bit of sharing.

Bluefeather tasted the wine, saying, "Shia hasn't aged
a month in the last twenty years. She's caught that look
of perpetual youth from you, Sherry."

"Ah, you old flatterer. Don't you know I've caught on
to you after all we've shared through the years? But . . .
don't misunderstand, I still love to hear it. And I'm sure
Shia will tremble in delight when I quote your words to
her."

"It's true. It's true or I'd never say it." He changed the
subject. "What is the standing situation on Shia and Bob
Miller? Are they still engaged?"

"Yes. They're actually going to finalize the marriage
next month."

"My gosh, what's the rush? They've only been engaged
nine years."

The Bob Miller in Shia's life was the principal of Meanwhile's high school. He was a widower with a seven-year-
old daughter and ten-year-old son who were in effect, if
not by blood, treated like Sherry's grandchildren. Sherry
adored them and used every excuse, and considerable
cunning, to get Shia to bring them to stay with them every
feasible chance. She even spoke of them as her grandchildren. Bluefeather was happy to feel her happiness at
the upcoming marriage.

Her black eyes beamed as she said, "Brian is getting

pretty 'thick' himself, with a nurse from El Paso. He spends at least two weekends a month down there and they've worn the phone lines to shreds."

"Do you like her?"

"I adore her. She's pretty, practical and, even better, she genuinely loves Brian and she seems to like Shia and me, as well."

They talked on quietly, relaxing in their pleasure of family gossip. For they were all family, cast together from many winds. The night came and chilled them. Inside the great house Shia had prepared a crackling piñon fire in the fireplace to greet them. Soon they were both nodding off and went to bed.

The next morning, Bluefeather hugged Shia and then held Sherry to his breast for a full minute. Each could feel the other's heart beating. They never said good-bye to one another, but the old man could not help glancing back one last time to see the two figures, Sherry and Shia, standing arm in arm, staring after him as Brian drove him away and over the mountains to Hillsboro for the last time. He was a happy old man tinged with a touch of soon-discarded sadness.

As they got out of the van, Brian said, "Come here, Blue, if you please." Bluefeather followed the young man around the vehicle. He opened the back doors and there in a box were four shiny, silvery, metallic cylinders about eighteen inches long and ten inches diameter.

At Bluefeather's puzzled look, Brian said, "Don't ask me what they are. I'm just following mother's orders. There's a sealed envelope in the box. He picked it up and carried it in the house for Bluefeather. They both stared down at the objects on the floor. Then they locked eyes for just an instant, embraced again and embarrassedly, Brian said, "I've got a lot to do, Blue. I'm going on down to El Paso and see my girlfriend, since I'm nearly there anyway. Sorry we can't

have a longer visit. Maybe in a little while you can come
back over and stay longer with us. Huh?"

Bluefeather also felt perplexed at being so impolite that
he didn't insist on Brian staying for coffee, at least.

Brian yelled out the open window of the van, "Be seeing you soon, Blue. Take care now."

"Yes . . . yeah, soon, son."

How could he tell him that he had never been worth
a damn at good-byes anyway? Even as he picked up the
sealed letter and moved to his cluttered desk for an
opener, he felt as if his only son were driving away for
good and he hadn't even protested. This thought vanished
as he both expectantly and fearfully opened the letter. He
put on his over-the-counter reading glasses and sat down
to read:

Dear Blue,

*We have long shared a great glory. It is all contained
in the notebooks in these time capsules. You, of
course, know about the little notebooks that are more
than my blood. I'm told that these capsules will last
millions of years. Dear, dear, Blue, please forgive me
for leaving the awesome responsibility of their destiny in your adroit hands and heart. I weakened at
last. I simply cannot make the final decision regard-
ing their disposition.*

*I've finally been at peace and happy these last few
years except for what's contained in the notebooks and
what it took to fill them. Soon, now, I'll have Shia and
Bob's children as my own grandchildren. It is unfair,
the way you've always taken care of me, to leave the
burden of this knowledge to your judgment alone. I'm
doing it anyway. Whatever you decide will never be
questioned by me. I love you and will do so forever.*

Sherry

He sat staring at the single last page, last words from Sherry Rousset. Then he looked at the containers so shiny, so permanent, containing the most powerful thing in earthy existence—knowledge. Knowledge of riches, of stars, of the beginning of life and maybe the means to stop it from being destroyed or the catalyst to launch its doom. What a pitiful thing that humans were such that this wonder had to be questioned and concealed at all. It had only been a few decades since there had been nine billion passenger pigeons in America. Now there were none. Not one. It caused Bluefeather to ponder seriously where the possible effects of this additional awareness would lead.

Bluefeather said aloud, "Aw, shitfire, why did all these smarts have to come along and mess up a person's life? He had felt, a few hours earlier, the peace of final decision, and now he had been handed a judgment to make that only the Great Spirit should be asked to even contemplate. There was no use dwelling on what might have been. He was into what IS. He and Sherry had certainly done that when they had closed the only known entrance to the Cavern of Marvels with Mr. Nobel's invention. He simply had to decide what in holy hell to do with the most precious of all treasures. His decision alone. Simple? Sure it was.

FIFTY-TWO

IT HAD BEEN JUST A YEAR AGO THAT HIS COMPADRE, Artesimo Gomez, had driven him to Albuquerque. He hadn't been there for twenty-five years and had been filled with both fear and exultation.

Bluefeather had a special purpose for the trip. He wanted to go to a used book store and look for volumes he'd missed by Colette, Joyce Cary and Alberto Moravio. They were among his favorites, now.

Artesimo had been born there in the suburb of Corrales, not far from where Bluefeather had once lived and loved. This had given them a special association. The trip was simply a fine excuse to please his friend and look up Little Tranc.

They stopped at the Owl Bar in the village of San Antonio for one of their famous green chile hamburgers. Each had a bottle of Corona to wash it down properly. They moved on northward on Interstate 40, feeling pretty damn good. Then Bluefeather became disoriented right on the freeway. Everything looked so different to him. Houses and franchises had proliferated in such abundance that the landscape of the old man's memory was shattered. He slid lower and lower in the seat, trying to block out the fearful view. Arty tried to talk him into some form of acceptance, but it didn't work.

When they got to Little Tranc's rambling adobe home in Corrales, Bluefeather finally overcame some of his fear of the city. The Rio Grande River was only a football field away, and the trees of the *bosque* hid everything to the east except the majestic crown of the Sandia Mountains.

He had longed to see his old home next door, but now he had a hard time looking at it. It was the same, but different as well. The house and barns were smaller than he remembered but the trees and bushes much larger. As soon as his mind-vision showed him a glowing Marsha working in the garden, he turned away and never looked again.

They stayed the night. They talked of old times in old familiar spots. A great meal of chile, tortillas and home-made wine in his honor caused Bluefeather to relax. It gave him much pleasure. He was astounded each time at how much Little Tranc and his wife reminded him of Tranquilino and his wife, Tina.

The next morning, he could hardly wait to go to Old Town to start their shopping. Arty noticed Bluefeather shoving his feet almost through the floor of the car and grabbing at the dash with sweating palms as the traffic increased.

He walked stiffly around the Old Town Plaza, sticking so close to Arty that they were constantly tripping and bumping into one another. Bluefeather didn't find his books there, but he was told where he might.

Arty patiently made the drive and, after successfully making his purchases, Bluefeather immediately insisted that they drive around the massive Sandia Mountains. As always, the mountains were his refuge. He could think of nothing else that would ease the terror that was stabbing at his body. The enormity of the apprehension that numbed his mind and soul was indescribable.

Arty drove east on Interstate 40, ever closer to the mountains, and he talked of it to his friend. "Ah, amigo, how fortunate these city dwellers are to have the forests and the coolness so near the city. Ah, yes, it is still untouched higher up."

Bluefeather Fellini was having none of this consolation talk. He saw the tract houses pushing at both sides of the freeway like the pincer movement of a mighty army. "My God," he said, "What has happened to the world since I was here? Only twenty-five years ago there were still large patches of space all around and now it seems that all the people of the world have huddled together and covered all the virgin hills with concrete." He forced words out like the irresistible desire to mask the pain of a throbbing boil. "Turn off, Arty. Turn off here. Drive to the mountain."

Arty said, "I thought you wanted to go all the way around them."

"No, I've changed my mind. Please turn off at the first exit. I want to look at it here . . . here on its western slopes. I prospected here when I was a young man. I slept here on her sides for many nights with the deer and the bear."

Artesimo pulled off at the Tramway exit. In a little while he had wound through an area of beautifully designed homes in the foothills of the Sandias.

"Stop. Stop right here," Bluefeather shouted, his voice loud and quivering.

Gomez pulled over near the end of a cul-de-sac. They could see between the houses and up a canyon for perhaps a quarter of a mile that was still free of development.

"See, way up there? See? That's the way it was. The way it all was, Arty. It was like that all the way up to the tall timber and all the way over the east side to the prairies. See?"

Arty looked and could no longer hide his own feelings

for the benefit of his friend. He sighed and settled back in his seat, letting go of the steering wheel and allowing his gaze to wander with Bluefeather's across the hundreds of houses, streets and the automobiles parked by them and constantly moving to and from them. Then they talked the real truth as real friends must.

Bluefeather said, with a voice that came from thousands of years back, "They are building the city on the only mountain they have. Don't they know that the mountains make all our precious rivers? Don't they care?"

Arty Gomez agreed, "Sad to say the destructive developers are way out ahead of the dutiful defenders of the soil, old amigo."

"*Sí*, my amigo, the promoters are leading the preservationists by many lengths . . . and . . . and the finish line is near. They are shitting in the bears' front yard."

The two old friends sat awhile, silently looking at the brave mountain and its afflictions.

Suddenly, Bluefeather laughed, "Ha, we sit here and preach to one another alone like we were full of wisdom. You know what I think we're full of? Huh? Huh? We should be at Elephant Butte Lake fishing, but first, before we start for home, let's swing by the Indian Cultural Center and see if by chance some of my relatives from the Taos Pueblo might be there exhibiting some work. You never can tell."

Gomez was delighted at the sudden, courageous change in his friend's attitude and drove down from the foothills of the mountain toward the center of the city, toward the Pueblo Indian Cultural Center. They enjoyed the exhibits, but there was nothing there done by Bluefeather's family.

They didn't look back at the mountain then and they didn't look at it as they drove south toward the state's largest lake for some bass fishing and then on home to the wonderfully small, lost little paradise of Hillsboro, New Mexico.

FIFTY-THREE

BLUEFEATHER MOVED OUT IN FRONT OF THE MULES AL-
most straining beyond his reach. The voice of the town
became weaker with each step. With each step he was
nearer his true home—the hills. Up there somewhere was
a secluded spot where he could die as he pleased without
interference from the town. No one could force him to
tell stories that belonged only to him . . . tales that he
alone could understand.

Old Bluefeather had lived as he wanted. Surely then he
could die as he wanted. He had expected a lot from this
world and had done much to return its favors. And all he
asked now was a hidden spot of hard earth on which to
lay his head and depart. What was the use of being buried
in a fenced-in plot, causing trouble and pain? He would
offer his body to the coyotes. They could make a meal of
him and have strength for several hunts. Yes, he would
give himself gladly to those singers of the night who had
been his partners for these many decades. Partners they
were, for they too had scratched their breath and sustenance from these lonely hills. He knew that they were the
true contact between man and the animal world.

He felt no pain. His heart still pumped his blood with
some strength, and though his legs were stiff and very

old, they kept him upright. Still, it was his time, and like a gut-shot wolf he hunted his home. There it was out ahead . . . dry, washed, worn, cruel. It was his. That was the difference.

He stopped after awhile. The mules stopped. They grazed about in the thin patches of grass as Bluefeather looked back. He had made better time than he thought. It was about noon and the paved road splitting the historic village looked narrow and fragile. He could see the trucks. He could hear the trucks. The endless drone that spoke of things he could be no part of. Maybe by nightfall he would be free of their sounds.

He was on the bottom slope of Mount DuBois, named after a noted roper, Frank DuBois, who was also secretary of agriculture for the state of New Mexico. It was five miles northwest of Hillsboro near Percha Creek on Jimmy Bason's F-Cross Ranch. The mountain stood almost alone, like a huge female breast. It was scattered with cedar, juniper and blue grama grass. A good place to camp. He had done so many times before. Just behind it the mountains would become steeper, rougher, and there in the pack was a problem he was trying to forget—Sherry's time capsules. In spite of his efforts against it, his mind wandered back down DuBois mountain to the history of Hillsboro—a minor part of it his own.

For well over a century, Hillsboro had been a running, yelling, stump-jumping town. After the first strike of silver, and then gold, it had roared like a fresh-trapped cougar. From the Bridal Chamber Tunnel alone the miners had taken two and a half million in silver in just one year.

Bluefeather recalled making many pleasurable trips the twenty miles south from Hillsboro to Lake Valley. He would stop just past the Berrenda Four A Ranch sign and move carefully along the east slope of the foothills west of the road until he found the proper spot. He could see the Bridal Chamber mine portal and the railroad bed where miners had actually driven the train inside the tunnel and dug the ore directly into the cars. From his favorite spot he had been able to see the little town and the school and to the right the graveyard on the hill. He could see almost to Skeleton Canyon, where the Apaches had lured a bunch of drunken miners, ambushed and slaughtered them. He would often imagine himself as a youth working in the Bridal Chamber Mine, where the silver ore was so rich it often had to be sawed. He worked, he danced, he fought and loved here just as he had actually done in real life. Silver. It had taken silver to pull him away from the haunting of gold. And the Bridal Chamber was the richest silver mine in the world for a long time. The ghosts of the mine and Lake Valley helped and succored him.

Certainly, many infamous people had lived at Hillsboro. Albert Fall, who had been secretary of the interior in 1921 was one example. He had been mostly responsible for the teapot dome scandal that rocked the nation. And then there was Toppy Johnson's slaughterhouse headquartered on what is now the F-Cross Ranch—so aptly named because of the number of competing rustlers that were butchered there along with the cattle. There was Sadie Orchard, a madam, a dead shot gun woman and owner of a stagecoach line. Sheba Hurst, one of the men who had inspired Mark Twain's *Roughing It,* had come to the area. He was buried a few miles west at the tiny town of Kingston. Later, a Colonel Bradley, who called Hillsboro home, owned horses that won the Kentucky Derby four times. Oh, there had been scores here who made names all across the west and the nation. It was amazing to him still that so many big things had emanated from such a tiny town. Even now, sometimes on a Saturday night, the miners, cowboys, artists and a few adventurous tourists blew a little wild at the welcoming S-Bar-X Saloon and burrito joint.

But all history was done for Bluefeather Fellini. He'd made a little history himself here, but its sight and sound slowly faded away like a soft breeze in a deep canyon. His vision was far over the mountain ahead.

The packs on the mules should have been light, but the metal containers had changed that. Soon he would free them of their burdens and turn them loose. They, too, could roam free and unmolested. But he would need them for awhile yet.

"Haaa, Mary. Hooo, Nancy. Let's move out." The burros raised their heads and followed, their sharp, black hoofs pitching tiny balls of dust at each step.

It had been a damned good and exciting life. That was for sure an understatement. He had enjoyed its various pleasures. The drinks, the tender women, the feasting, the dice tables—they had been his, and more. But it had always been the call of the hills and the search for the days of little wind that had meant the most. It had been but a blink with fog-filled eyes.

Those sunken, black eyes pierced out beyond the sharp, eroded cheekbones to the land ahead. The great red and white mesas' edges cropped up in the distance here and there. On beyond, the high ridges of mountains called like ancient beasts.

He watched the buzzards circle off to the right. Would they find him before the coyotes? He hoped not. It was a chance he would take.

What had started this search of his so long ago? What had kept him at it without fail? Was it the gold? He mumbled to himself. Was it just the gold? He couldn't answer that. He had tried a thousand times to answer that and probably had, but he simply could not remember the result of his questioning. It didn't matter now. He had been young when he started. How old? Just a kid from the mines at Trinidad. It didn't matter. He had been strong then, and he had been strong for years after. He felt strong right now, purposefully so.

Before his first strike he had had other moments. That was for sure. He had dug and panned nine hundred dollars' worth of gold one summer so far past. When a hundred dollars was three months' living. What had the woman said? "We can start a business of our own. You can settle down. You can sleep in a feather bed each and every night. You can possess my body and my heart." Something like that.

How pretty she had made it sound. What was her name? Nancy? Mary? Both? Of course. That's why every burro or mule he'd owned, no matter the sex, had been either Mary or Nancy. His mind was much sharper than this. Why was he forgetting all these things? Did his slow gain in altitude make him grow denser? What did it matter?

He tired now. What used to be foothills suddenly seemed like mighty mountains to his old legs. He hadn't looked back for a long time. He would not look back until the night was upon him. It came swiftly and all at once. He knew that the sky had been filled earlier with gold lights, but he could not make himself look. He could see a good open camping spot above.

Now he shouted words to encourage the mules and himself, "Haaa, Mary. Hooo, Nancy. You listen now with much care because I'm gonna tell you a great truth."

The mules stepped on faster, ears working back and forth as they certainly heard their long-time partner.

"Your great, great grandfather many times over was the burro who carried the Mother of Christ on his back while she carried the Son of God in her belly. Step with pride. Haaa. Hooo." They all three raced the night uphill with inspired strides, painfully bellowing lungs and hard-drumming hearts.

He gathered some wood and built a fire. They were

still some distance from the high timber of the mountains. He was warm from the blaze now. He fried the bacon and took the hard sourdough bread into himself with little taste. It was merely to sustain him until he reached his goal.

He felt, and heard, the whish of the night owl's wings at about the time his old friend gave voice. The coyote sang to Bluefeather. He told in his lonely wail of the Marys and the Nancys, of other warm firesides. He talked to Bluefeather of the things he missed; but even more he spoke to him of the things he had found, those things that only the coyote and Bluefeather could understand. Then again, Bluefeather allowed himself to think of the four metal containers in the panniers filled with Sherry's words of observation, study and soul. He stared and stared. They were right there—imprisoned. Only he could turn them loose to spread across the globe like . . . like what? He didn't dare ask the Great Spirit for help yet. He didn't even call on his representative, Dancing Bear. He, the American called Bluefeather, must make the terrible, or hallowed, decision alone. It was hanging around his neck like log chains.

Now Bluefeather looked and listened downward again. There it still was, the lonesome drone of the mighty trucks. He was not nearly far enough into the hills. It would take another day at least. Maybe two. He could see the tiny, flickering lights from the village below. They looked like a small cluster of earthbound stars.

He had long ago learned that war was hard work, but he had never thought simple dying could be so difficult. Everybody did it. No exceptions.

Bluefeather slept little that night. He lay in his blanket and stared and felt the earth throb beneath him. This earth was his. It was his mother, his father, his brother. It was his love. He craved to have it devour him. But he must live the night out and move on beyond those lights

and noises below. He must decide the undecidable for
Sherry, somehow.

It was the longest night of his life. But occasionally the
coyote kept him company, crying into the darkness from
one valley, then the next, raising his head atop the hills
and voicing his great concern for those who sleep alone
on the high desert mountains.

FIFTY-FOUR

FOR THE FIRST TIME IN YEARS, BLUEFEATHER'S ANCIENT and fading eyes saw the deer before the mules heard it. It was a Coes deer. They are much smaller—a miniature version of the whitetail that also roams the mountains west of Hillsboro. The little deer, not much larger than an average-size dog, poised on an up-slope, looking back at them. Somehow the deer knew the man and his mules would not harm him. He held the elegant pose, as if frozen in a painting, until the trio moved from his sight around a cut bank.

A couple of blue jays flickered across an opening and landed. They stared down from a scrubby pine at the travelers, chattering as if in a heavy discussion with the entire forest about the whys and whats of the menagerie of three moving slowly, but ever higher.

Now the acuteness of Bluefeather's observation lapsed back in dream-walking. His old muscles were relieved for a time from their natural aches by the anesthesia of his mind-pictures of the past.

He saw his parents and the entire family, cousins, uncles, aunts—the Italian family—on a running, playing laughing, eating, drinking picnic near Raton and Dawson. Then he was fly fishing in Taos Pueblo Creek, halfway between the mighty adobe structures and the sacred mountain. The dancing, sparkling water was talking to him, telling where he could catch the fighting, native brown trout. He was filling the banks with them and wishing this was a real, night dream, for catching big trout was a sign of upcoming fine fortune if you saw it in your sleep.

Now he was with the gringo, Grinder, in a Taos lounge. This time there was no fight. They drank beer so cold one could only stay warm by leaping up and dancing, dancing on into warmth, keeping ahead of the coldness of the beer. Then he was eating a huge plate of the finest *chile rellenos* ever made. The smoke from the fireplace only enhanced the taste of the food and the entertainment value of the beer in his blood. A treasure of a time they were having. And then there were Nancy and Mary, and bloody battles, and hot deserts, and cold mountains he walked over and sometimes right through.

When he sensed the slight tensing of the mules at the narrowness of the real trail they were on, the kaleidoscope faded away and he saw and heard the flashing black and white flight of the magpie, and its piercing cry brought him back to his true task of climbing safely upward toward his final adventure.

He felt the ache of bones and the worn muscles tied to them again. He had no choice, it seemed, but to go back to Miss Mary with the hair that had fire in it. At the first perception of her swimming naked in Harmony Creek, he banished it. The time was not ready for these sorts of visions. Later, it would be fine to look back—after he had made his decision about the metal capsules. As he had packed the mules back in Hillsboro for his departure, he had thought of giving the capsules to the archeology department at University of New Mexico or maybe to his old school, New Mexico Tech, at Socorro. He thought maybe he should place them in the archives at UTEP, The University of Texas at El Paso, to be opened in ten, fifty, a hundred or a thousand years. His experiences in the Cavern of Marvels had made known that this much clock time was nothing—not even a single breath. Would humankind have changed enough in that time to deserve and use the priceless information properly? How could he believe it? What should he do? Had ever a man been handed such a terrifying trust? Why did it have to be him? Well, it was him. So? So, he had to resolve the dastardly dilemma somehow in order to "crash through" in peace and possible joy. Bluefeather dropped the forbidding thoughts and decided his old legs needed a rest.

He and the mules came upon the spring. How could he have forgotten the location of such an invaluable source of water here in the high desert mountains? It was only an hour past noon, but he pitched camp, such as it was: simply his blankets, oats for the mules and a little food for himself.

He averted his eyes from the alluring containers for now. Hellsfire, why was he in such a rush to his final passing on? He and his two partners might as well enjoy the early autumn sun and go on tomorrow refreshed and rested. There was an inviting shelf of grass against a rock bluff facing south.

He watered the mules and buckled the *morrals* full of oats over their muzzles. Later, he would let them graze in a little grassy meadow below. He splashed his face. The friendly sun equalized the chill from the spring's cold water. He had a little to eat and for the first time in years got out his old pipe and tobacco.

As he leaned back against the warm rocks and gazed across the seemingly endless, isolated landscape, he lit the pipe and laughed, talking to anything that might be listening,

"I wonder if this tobacco is gonna kill me before I go to meet the Great Spirit." He was surprised at what an instant dizziness the dried plant gave his body after a couple more puffs. He knocked the tobacco out of the pipe and mashed the fire away. That had been his first smoke, except for medicine-making ceremonies, in many years, and it would be his last here on this particular earth.

Bluefeather felt good the way he was so easily and rapidly shedding earthly habits and accoutrements. Things that had seemed so bad—seemed so critically necessary— were truly mostly meaningless after all. He was so relaxed that he dozed with his eyes half closed.

It amazed the old man how, right here, so near the end, his memory-diary was suddenly so vivid again. The gallery that held the portrait of his beloved Miss Mary was always open whenever he wished and followed him about as open as an angel's arms and as intimate as his shadow. He dozed, and she came smiling to him in his dreams, as well. In spite of his reluctant vows. He welcomed her with permanent pleasure.

FIFTY-FIVE

THE OLD MAN WAS BENT LIKE THE HOOK ON A CHAIN hoist as he slumbered astride the mule. The path was narrow and the Nancy mule followed behind, taking careful, even delicate, steps. The drop-off to the left was steep.

Bluefeather Fellini did not purposely start recalling the great world war. The first year after his return, he had cringed at every sudden noise, a few times dropping to the floor or street for cover, getting back up embarrassed and glancing around to see who watched him. He had also spent many nights trying to burrow through the mattress away from the eighty-eight shells of his dreams and the machine guns of his imagination. Just the same, they were as real to him as the taste of his tongue. But soon he gradually put it away, and it only returned a few times during each of his many surviving years.

He felt the mule Mary stop and his senses shifted from the hedgerows of France to the mountains west of Hillsboro as suddenly as his aged brain would allow. In spite of Nancy's care, a part of trail rock cracked at the weight of Blue and Mary. It simply dropped out from under Nancy. Instead of attempting to reach for the earth with her two hooves on the falling side, she had miraculously whirled with one foot solid and pushed herself so she was facing down the slope with her forefeet out in front and her hind legs tucked so far under her belly that her hindquarters were dragging. Without this instant reaction she would probably have tumbled over and over, crippling herself permanently, destroying and scattering the contents of the pack as well. Mary did not bolt but held the trail and turned her head toward the noise just as Bluefeather had. Nancy went on down the slope, dangerously gaining speed until it curved out into a much gentler grade. She still had to run a piece to hold her footing, charging between twin pines. The space was too narrow for her to pass through with the pack on her back. She was jammed there with a very sudden stop.

Bluefeather was looking at her, and then at the slope, trying to find a safe place to crawl down to dislodge her. Then he decided he had better ride down, as it might take the combined strength of both him and Mary to free her. He could see the tops of the canisters gleaming in the sun.

Finally, up ahead, he found a nice round ridge sloping toward Nancy at an angle that was safe to ride. As they moved toward her, Bluefeather saw that she struggled mightily to get on through the trap. No go. She stopped without any movement except her ears. Then, just as they were about to reach her, Nancy solved her own problem. She easily, as if it was the most natural of actions, simply backed out and waited calmly, ready to follow them back up to the trail before they reached her.

Bluefeather looked up into the sky straight as his tired body would allow and said, "Thank you, oh Great One, for the company of your most majestic invention—the mule."

Soon they were back on the trail, moving on upward to Bluefeather's final destination. Damn it. He had, just yesterday, occasionally started thinking way, way back to the

Normandy hedgerows. As unpleasant as it was, he would rather think about the near destruction of the whole world all day long than think a single second on the rocky demise of his beloved Miss Mary of Breen, Colorado.

Now it was taking the images of Miss Mary to draw him away from conjectures about the time tubes. He would think of one of his other loves, the mines, the veins in them, the float rock that often led to their hard-to-get booty.

Three thousand years or so ago, the first humans like him had started mining copper on Cyprus, with the help of what were to become metallurgists. They had mixed different metals to make arms to hunt wild animals for food and to protect their families from pillaging and death from competitors. Finally, printer's type had been made from miner's metals to record the whole movement of the human race—which might not have survived at all without metal swords, spear points and machinery in a land of huge beasts and great natural disasters. The human race had held on precariously. Its ultimate existence, survival and history itself came from minerals. Nor could anyone lay the blame on the diggers for the recent defiling of the earth. Greed had become boss of the mine workers and the whole earth. Greed. Bluefeather was proud to have been a considerate miner. Whether one liked it or not, without the ore diggers, the jaguar would be president of Mexico, Central and South America; the lion would reign as the ruler of all Africa; the wolf would hold, along with a wildly trumpeting elephant, sovereignty over most of Asia; and the grizzly bear would rule unopposed as the monarch of North America.

FIFTY-SIX

THE SHOCK OF THE NEAR LOSS OF MULE NANCY FROM the trail caving in under her had tired old Bluefeather Fellini early this day. For the second time since they had left Hillsboro—seeking the right place to die—he quit in midafternoon and pitched camp. His eyes were hurting in their sockets, trying to stare past Sherry's containers.

He found a reasonably level spot against a bluff facing southwest. He would have the sun here, as well as a breeze. He leaned back. It was the time of half-vision. But today it did not work; he went on past the vision stage into a warm, comfortable sleep with just ordinary dreams.

He was back in Raton, playing hide and seek with two of his friends at the age of six, both joyous and frightened because the next day he was to start school. Of course, his fears would turn out in real life to be unfounded, because his mother had already taught him to read, and that had put him way up on the other students.

As he dreamed of his childhood, he was being carefully observed from a bluff. Across the meadow, scattered with timber of spruce and large ponderosa pines, a mountain lion lay watching him through a thin bush. There was no malice. She was just being cautious, because her den and three cubs were only a short distance around the edge of the bluff. They were at the age of concern for her—big enough to feel adventurous and at the same time small and inexperienced, making them vulnerable to eagles, bears and man.

She licked at one paw, sore from leaping onto a pile of boulders the day before at a three-year-old deer. The deer had felt her presence while she was in midair and had leapt aside so that she only scraped its sides lightly with this sore paw. Having missed, she had whirled in midair to maintain pursuit, jamming the paw into a rock, catapulting down the rough slope after the needed prey. She caught the deer from behind, hurling it over a ten-foot drop. Twisting back violently again, she had dropped down on the young buck's back just as it regained its feet, hooking her claws deep where the shoulders joined the neck, sinking fangs where the skull joined the first vertebra. It was over in a roll.

She feasted and brought her cubs to dine. Then she dragged the carcass up higher and nearer their den, covering it with brush. An hour later, she suckled her cubs and listened to the meat digest in her stomach. The end of her tail switched now and then as she licked her bruises. She had decided the man and his mules presented no danger. She stared now out of curiosity—safe, full and secure about her cubs.

Right around the corner, in a hollow of a great ponderosa pine, a spotted owl had listened to the mules' hooves and had taken a peek, staring from the darkness at the camp. Watching. Just watching.

Farther up on the cliff, forming a half circle of animals around Bluefeather, a red-tailed hawk watched the camp's inhabitants only casually. Its eyes, strong as a telescope, searched for other things. Its head moved as slightly as its feathers that occasionally lifted in the southwestern breeze.

A lizard watched from a four-inch space under a rocky

ledge ten feet from Bluefeather's sleeping body. Yesterday the hawk had dived at it here, missing the lizard by a fraction of an inch as it leapt to safety. The hawk was not dismayed. It simply waited for another chance.

In a smaller, new-growth pine, a tufted-eared grey squirrel peeked from around the trunk of the tree, observing the camp, the hawk and the presence of the lion. Suddenly, it chattered in defiance, the sound breaking across the silent foothills and ledges as a shattering intrusion. The hawk moved its head an unseen bit. The spotted owl lifted a leg and then dropped it. The lion twitched the end of her tail three times in succession. The lizard jerked its eternally tense body around half an inch, and the mules grazed on, flicking one ear each toward the noise.

One part of Bluefeather's mind was hiding a fact from the other. He was delaying the once-relished trip of finality because of the quandary, the duty, of what to do with the containers of precious notebooks.

He woke up refreshed, stood up stiffly, stretched his tightened old muscles, took a drink from the canteen and, before cooking his supper, spoke to the mules.

"Haaa, little darlings, isn't it wonderful to be in the wilderness again? Huh? Huh? Just the three of us all alone?"

They were all three rested and decided to climb another mile before making camp for the night. He felt the nearness of a long-favorite stopping place.

Now the old man looked up ahead expectantly. Yes, that was the rock formation he had anticipated. He wanted to camp here near the rock ruins of an ancient Mimbres hunting campsite because it had a large, bubbling spring. He was sure the waterhole had been active and used way back then, in the time of the Indian tribe's existence. This spot also gave them an almost three-hundred-and-sixty-degree observation point.

He staked the mules so they could reach the water but not disturb the ruin. The outline of the single rock camp house was clear. It had been about half underground and half above to give the maximum protection from both the temperature and any enemy. The upper half had caved in, filling the lower part centuries before. Even so, he could always find pieces of pottery and a few flint objects as the rain and wind revealed them. It would be at least an hour before the sun temporarily yielded its power over to the night.

"Look here, Miss Mary, sweet Nancy. Look here, where they camped and hunted maybe a thousand years before us. There were no motor sounds to make the deer and elk retreat to the most hidden spots. Now, even the bear, mountain lions and coyotes quiver and spend more time watching for intruders than they do hunting for themselves. They didn't have precious pardners like you ladies to help with the burdens of carrying their necessities. No—just their own backs and shoulders. Listen, and you can hear their music, their singing. Hear? Hear? Ahhh haaa. I can feel them as well. Yes, they are here with us, and I can tell they wish us well, for we have no desire to defile their domain."

Old man Bluefeather spotted about an inch of pottery sticking out of the mountain soil. He bent down casually to pick it up. It broke the shallow dirt for about five inches around. He lifted it from the earth, surprised by its size. He carefully hand brushed it and, to his pleasure, saw that the drawing on it was part of a howler monkey. There was no doubt. He had only seen this once before, so long ago, back there in the Mimbres' cave of the dead, with Sherry, Marsha and Pack.

He sat down on the edge of the ruins and stared at the

shard. He slipped into half-vision, seeing many things.
Hearing and feeling The Unholy again and the battle of
the screechers, and now The Section walked sore,
wounded, but with great relief, toward their first look at
God's Castle and all the Olders and Youngers.

FIFTY-SEVEN

IT WAS ALMOST NOON THE NEXT DAY BEFORE THE STIFF-
ness left his legs. He could no longer roam these hills of
home. It only proved how right he was to make this final
decision. Just a little more now and he would be finished—his long, fast run would be over. He walked, nevertheless, leading the mules.

He heard the rattle of a diamondback. He had known
it was there. He felt the lead mule pull on the rope and
turned to look as they tossed their long ears forward and
shied sideways. It lay coiled, black tongue flicking, quivering in tenseness. The rattles were a blur on its tail as it
shook its warning.

"No need for that," Bluefeather muttered. "I'll give you
back your land. I will walk far around you. It is yours.
Take it."

The stoop in his shoulders was great as he climbed on
up through the thickening timber far above the desert
floor. It was now a great effort to put one foot in front of
the other, but on up he moved. He saw the deer and the
bobcat tracks in the soft sand of the washes, and he saw
the fresh droppings of old friend, the coyote, matted with
rabbit hair.

He turned and looked again, taking his ragged, old hat

from his greyed and tangled hair. One more look back. One. It was gone. The village was finally gone from sight. He strained his ears. No sound except the distant calling of a magpie came to him. He was beyond it. But still he felt unsafe. So they moved on up, the three of them.

They topped the high, long mesa and struggled up into the thicker timbers. Bluefeather could feel the blood beating hard in his ears now. His breath rasped through his broken, worn teeth.

Then he found the game trail into the oak brush. It was very steep. The timber thickened. He knew from the "rat-a-tat" of the woodpecker that he was high up. He saw, in the trail, a lion's round track as big as his hand. Yes, he was near his destination, for the lion feared the very thing that was in Bluefeather's heart. He, too, had moved to the outermost reaches. It was just a matter of finding the spot—the right place to return to his earth. But first he would take a last look at his mine. It was near, and there he must make the final decree about the capsules. The mules had recognized the terrain and stepped lively now.

As Bluefeather topped out on the trail, he saw two does and a fawn raise their muzzles from the spring below the High Line Tunnel. They looked at him an entranced moment. Then, in unison, they bounced downhill, vanishing into their world. Bluefeather was pleased that the wild things were sharing the spring he had so laboriously kept clean these many years. Anyway, it had been theirs first.

He unpacked the mules with care before he turned them to the spring. They were very thirsty, but before they drank, they took the time to roll in the dust near the log cabin, shook themselves and moved with deliberate calm to the water and drank patiently, politely. Under similar, exhausted conditions, horses would run to the water and possibly founder or bloat themselves.

The old miner could not resist reading the map of wild animal tracks in the mud around the spring. There were the deer, of course, the rounded paw of a bobcat, the arrowhead-shaped prints of the coyote, the pronged turkey sign, but now there was something new at this altitude—the rooting marks of the wild hogs, the javelina. This shocked Bluefeather. He knew that, for a reason yet unknown, the javelina had been ranging into higher terrain the last few years. According to authorities on the subject, they had remained in the desert areas of northern Mexico, extreme southwest New Mexico and southeast Arizona for many millions of years. Now, suddenly, they were working for a living at a heavily timbered eight thousand seven hundred feet. Unheard of and puzzling. For just a brief moment, Bluefeather knew why they were changing and learning to survive at this height of harsh winters. Then the little seed of knowledge was gone. Haunting. If the time was ever right they would return to lower levels.

No matter, he had to tidy up the mine site. It must be done with an attitude of servility to the place the mountain had so generously loaned him. He went first to his powder box, which he had dug into the earth with the door facing across a wide draw, away from the site, for safety. The dynamite, explosive caps, coiled fuse and hand plungers were all safe and dry. There weren't many real mining individuals left who cared about the land. Now most were violators of the earth's fragile crust. Big, mostly foreign mining companies were strip mining gold all over the Nevada desert now, ripping the fragile soil away from its creatures and poisoning it with leaching cyanide. Soon, he supposed, the corporations' destructive greed would drive them to tear up beautiful Arizona, as well. No matter what, a mechanized world must have copper, lead, zinc, tin, iron and such, but destroying an entire desert for gold to glorify human bodies with jewelry was a sacrilege, in his eyes. There was already enough unused, hidden gold in vaults to accomplish this ten thousand times over.

Then he carried water from the spring and washed and dried the tin dishes, the hand-hewn tables, bunk beds and cabinets. He braced, nailed and tied up the poles and lumber of the little corral and mule shed, tack room and small hay barn. He checked the mining tools in the work shed and arranged them in corners on metal hangers. He fed Mary and Nancy each a half gallon of oats and a block of alfalfa hay.

He gathered up his hard hat with the carbide lamp attached, poured in a little fresh water, let it settle among the carbide for a bit, then flicked the lighter into the gas jet. The flame lit just right. He put the hat on and walked under the portal timbers into the tunnel.

This mine was a mere pinprick on the whole of the mountain, but a lot of Bluefeather's years, flesh and soul had been depleted here. It was a good tunnel and required no timbers once past the slough of the mountain's skin.

He walked on through the silence that heard only his own movements. He stood a moment to appreciate it, as he stared at the seven-foot tunnel face with the tiny vein of quartz weaving through it like a little frozen creek. He tilted his head closer to the vein and strained his eyes to try to see a particle or a thin string of silver. He was not sure, but he thought he saw one.

He straightened up, reached out slowly and touched the spot, saying softly, "Forgive me, old mountain."

Then he turned and walked away from the face of ore for the last time, not looking back. Now it was too late to finish his chores here.

He had no desire for food. He must get to bed, for he had powerful things to do in the morning. Otherworldly duties to attend. Then . . . then on up above to the inexplicable spot of finality.

He stood in the front of the cabin and said, joyfully, "Good morning stately trees. Everlasting blessings on you, precious grass. Dear rocks, may comfort and compassion befall you for aeons. A thousand wishes, sweet mountains that all your trees, bushes and grasses will have wet summers and mild winters. Oh, and the best of mornings to you, Mr. and Mrs. Beetle Bug."

It was the last morning here. The mules were tied to trees. Bluefeather Fellini was almost ready to make his final prayers and Indian medicine. It was a problem of choice: from his Italian blood came a strong Catholic belief; from his maternal side came the Indian conviction; and from inside himself came a third that was simply his. He would do his best to uphold all three. He was an advocate unto himself.

He still had no hunger, but suddenly the nose scar, which was visibly long lost in the roughness of his aged skin, started to itch and burn. The time capsules! For an immeasurable vacuum of a moment, he almost turned back down to the technical world with the idea of calling the media, the geologists, the anthropologists, and the archeologists all together—dumping out, at once, the entire contents of the metal containers. The implications and the temptations were equally enormous. The notion passed.

He spread out his medicine pouch on the ground and knelt by it. He decided to get his personal part of this religious business over with first.

"Oh, dear Lord and Jesus, I sure do thank you for giving me the special privilege of choosing my own time to leave. I realize what a problem this must have been to you since so many folks are probably pestering you to death for the same favor. Anyway, gracious tidings, and thank you very much."

Mary and Nancy watched with curious eyes and tilted ears, sensing something different in their partner's voice and overall demeanor. Mules are like that.

Bluefeather climbed up the tailings pile to the tunnel entrance and nailed a cross he had made on the portal timber. Then he crossed himself and said several Hail Marys and got down to the plan.

"Ah, sweet, thoughtful Saint Anthony of Padua. I know you take care of many problems and give your loving protection to many creatures, but I also know you specialize in burros—or donkeys, if you prefer. Please bless the donkey half of Mary and Nancy that is your special domain. Thank you very much."

Mary and Nancy must have felt the call, because they actually switched their tails and stared at Bluefeather even more attentively.

He crossed himself again and put his fingers and palms together just under his chin in supplication. "Now, my friend, dear Saint James the Greater, I know beyond any possible doubt that you will bless the horse half of my beloved Mary and Nancy. They have been my faithful, hardworking, tender, loving companions for over twenty years. I am forever grateful and beholden to you and thank you very much."

Bluefeather's voice had been rising both in volume and intensity. Just as he finished his thanks, Mary raised her head, opened her mouth and brayed. Nancy did likewise. The loud gasping two-part symphony made Bluefeather know that the blessings he asked for had been presented and properly received. Who could doubt the happy, accepting song of the mules?

He didn't spend quite as much effort on himself, saying to San Raphael the archangel and patron of travelers, "Dear Sir, I ask that you send me whatever direction you wish, and if there are rocks to climb or rivers to swim, please point them out and I shall meet the challenge, knowing you are a benevolent saint who would have much compassion for travelers in the alien dimensions of unfamiliar worlds. May this interloper do justice to your kindness. My deep appreciation for hearing me."

The mules must have known that their part of this particular ceremony was completed, for they dozed contentedly in the midmorning sun.

"Dear St. Francis of Assisi, patron of all animals, birds, peace, reconciler of the family and patron of all needs and all virtues, please join this humble servant in his next, and last, adventure. Thank you very much."

And then to himself, Bluefeather said, as he whacked one heavy hand into the palm of the other, "That ought to do it!"

His own private creed and the Catholic creed had been reverently disposed of. Now he must conscientiously fulfill his duties to his Indian heritage. Then he would be free to seek the ultimate solution. To act.

He took the dry cedar twigs and leaves from his medicine pouch, crumpled them in a prospecting pan and set it on fire. He smothered the flames so they would smoke heavily. He danced about with the smoke from the pan. He chanted softly as he wafted the smoke with an eagle feather over the mules, the outbuildings, the log house, the spring and the tunnel of the mine. He danced back on his worn old legs to the spread-out pouch, took cornmeal and tossed it to the four winds, straight at the earth and then directly upward into the sky. Now all the elements had been fed. He pulled the Earth Spirit from the ground and turned it into a swiftly flying peyote medicine bird. Already it was ripping the sky apart as it neared the domain of the Great Spirit, whose spectra controlled all the earths and all the skies. The message had been delivered.

Now Bluefeather placed the coyote fetish inside a circle of cornmeal with one little opening. He scattered the dried seeds in the circle and he did other things as well. Then he stood and yelled, "Yiiiiii" up into the sky, and his voice boomed as strong as a young Milano opera singer's.

"Oh, Great Spirit, I know that a human's life is made of seconds, and any one of those can be the last breath. I know this thing, Exalted One. How many times have I breathed past the burning fuse? How many times has the mountain held its insides above my humble head without falling on me? Huh? Of course, you know these things, my Ennobled Guide. Yes, for sure. I have been through many, many dangers, and yet, here I am, me, Bluefeather Fellini, mostly in one piece. Thank you again for allowing me to pick my own time and ground. What a lucky man you have made me." Bluefeather was breathing heavily now, but he felt he had played as nearly a cinch with the various gods as a mining man would ever get.

Then the burst of illumination struck. His prayers must have worked. No more uncharacteristic indecision now. He took the time capsules one at a time and set them fifty steps inside the mine, side by silent side. His breath came in gasps, but he paid no mind. He stepped back perhaps forty yards from the mine portal, carefully surveying it, calling on all his engineering skills in his mind's survey. Then he easily hand-drilled holes in the dirt crust and under rocks of all sizes above the tunnel, on up the side of the natural mountain a ways. He armed the dynamite with caps and fuses, his lungs hurting and his hands shaking dangerously from the exertions that would have tested his strength fifty years earlier.

He ignored the pounding in his chest and the pain of old, used-up muscles and ligaments trying to tear. He lit the fuses and slid down. The mules would not mind. They had heard thousands of sticks of dynamite.

The mountain shook all the way under his feet. The dust boiled above and around the portal while Bluefeather waited anxiously for the southwest wind and gravity to reveal its new form. Perfect. It looked exactly like a small natural landslide. He was sure he heard the mountain sigh in relief.

He exclaimed aloud, as he whacked his fist into his palm again, "I'm getting to be a better hider of treasures than I am a finder."

It was no longer up to him. He had done the only thing he knew. He had entombed these priceless objects just as he had other beloved objects in younger years. He had blown the final placement and use of Sherry's little books into the discretionary hands of the High Authority. He was no longer responsible. The odds were heavily against anyone trying to open up the little one-man mine so high in the mountains. If it was ordained, someday, some way, someone would dig here and make the greatest discovery of all history to that date. If not—then that was the way it would and should be.

"Good-bye, friends. Thank you very much."

He folded up his medicine pouch and stuck it inside his overalls. His recent heavenly exertions made him decide to ride Mary to his sacred spot of ground, wherever it was. He got an old McClelland saddle out of the tack shed and, along with a bridle, fit it on the mule. He took the halter from Nancy's head, because she would follow. He led Mary over to the edge of the tailing pile, shuffled his feet up and swung stiffly, but surely, astride her back. Without looking back, he reined her away from the mine site into the wilderness. He loosened the reins and gave Mary her head. She would find his singular spot.

Mary curved her way carefully upward. Far up. Bluefeather was piercingly aware of all their surroundings. He saw where a lion had covered its deer kill with brush. He would not worry about the lions getting the mules. They had instant reflexes and could kick to the side with devastating force, where a horse could only kick forward and backward. Man would take care of them, for they didn't exist without humans to assure the breeding of a donkey and a horse or vice versa. They were mutually dependent in many ways, but the mule's very existence was at the pleasure of humankind. They had paid back in full, millions of times over through the millenniums.

Bluefeather thanked the mules for all the years they had carried the powder, hay, tools, grub and on and on. No matter what the weather or difficulty, they had delivered.

He continued, "Did you know, my precious ones, that George Washington, who is called the father of our country, loved and respected you mules. Huh? Well, it's a fact. When he died he owned over sixty head and willed them to a few special friends and his slaves. See? See how special you girls are?"

The mules responded with increased speed yet sureness of step, one under him, the other right behind. He had a feeling of sublime peace, then exultation. He tilted his stony, weather-etched face back and yelled at the universe.

"Hiiiii yiiiiii, I'm Bluefeather Fellini, the last free man!"

They moved on toward his final departure with elation and relief. He talked to mule Mary now. Her long ears worked back and forth eagerly, recognizing that Bluefeather's voice was meant for her.

"You see, precious one, the other Mary would have made you very proud."

Every now and then the mule rolled her great limpid eyes to the side as if she were trying to see back in time along with him.

It was the time of musing. Bluefeather felt he had been blessed abundantly. He had been born into two cultures that he had loved and that had loved him in return. A fine childhood had been his for sure. The early Taos days with his pueblo family, Grinder, Lorrie and more could only be thought of as a period of divine gifts. The Breen, Tonopah and Corrales eras were laudatory remembrances. Even so, one never knew when an alliance of evil would germinate and alter the surface of the earth with scars, defilement and human horror. Look at pitiful little Adolph Hitler, failed artist and architect, whose growing thirst for vengeance on society, and the power to extract it, could only get him up to the rank of corporal during the First World War. Yet, he had finally gathered around him Heinrich Himmler, a mad mystic, as head of the Third Reich's dreaded police; Joseph Goebbels, a failed writer, to be his head of propaganda and publicity; Hermann Göring, a dope fiend, to lead the economy and later to attempt to bomb the world into servitude or death.

Bluefeather felt good now about having fought this maniacal quartet the best he could. There had never been any war like it, and there never would be again until the very last one—and maybe not even then. Over fifty million people had died and hundreds of millions had been permanently wounded in flesh and soul. Bluefeather knew now, in hindsight, that only one more year of hesitation by the United States in joining the massive retaliation with food, guns and flesh would have absolutely doomed the entire world to slavery. As it was, Hitler had been only about six months away from having atomic energy when he committed suicide in his bunker. The Germans had already invented the jet airplane and had been manufacturing them at the time of their doom. Very soon they would have ruled the skies. He already had rapidly improving missiles to launch against the rest of humanity. Close. Very close for this world that Bluefeather now walked and rode over. The billions of people under forty-nine years of age would not have been here at all. They would never have existed, for their copulation, conception and birth would have been forever altered. Other entities would have existed, but none of those that were here now. None. America alone had committed ten million troops. Only one out of eight had fought on the front lines. America alone had had over eight hundred thousand casualties. Eighty percent of those had been in the infantry. The other twenty percent had been scattered among all the other services. It had cost them three trillion one hundred billion dollars, an uncountable sum in today's currency. And unthinkable, if not impossible, for the future, because too much of the earth's finite resources had already been turned to smoke and dead dust. The Allies had stayed firm and, with a massive will and sacrifice, had given all the world the chance to be free. Amazingly, only a third or so of the world's leaders had chosen the route of democracy that so terribly much had been sacrificed for. The so-called little wars—some more, some less—had never stopped. Even now, as Bluefeather moved upward to seek his well-earned peace, people were butchering each other somewhere in some manner. In Asia, Africa, Central and South America, the Middle East, Mexico, Yugoslavia, all over, groups of various-sized, foggy obsessions were tearing one another into bleeding shreds to make chattels out of the survivors. Little Hitlers still arose in ceaseless succession around the lovely, blue globe.

Well, he and his comrades of the Caverns of Marvels had fought a short decimating battle to save the sanctity of all the natural earth and the beings below. They had won at great cost, with a casualty rate that had been almost a hundred percent. But they had not died in vain, as those in other wars before and after them had. Not yet, anyway. They had allowed the savage and delicate beauty, so many aeons in developing, to progress on in nature. Bluefeather felt content now with their costly decision down there. He had to admit that he had probably learned just one thing of importance in his entire fruitful, fortunate and celebratory life: the greatest mistake of human existence was the still-growing belief that wealth, fame and the power that comes with them are the same as intelligence. This massive, human, judgmental error was rampant.

Then, suddenly, all these memories were behind him—history past. He felt jubilant as his mind-voice pointed out the multitudes of rapturous events he had been so privileged to enjoy in the deserts and over the mountains of Hillsboro and most of the West.

A warmth, like first love and misted sweets, enveloped him. It was the time of times. He must go into his last half-vision now.

He rode eagerly into it. Sure enough, as so often before, the sacred Taos Mountain filled the distant background. He heard the music before he saw the players. Ramon Hernandez came on in a black, silver-fringed costume of both New and Old Mexico. His wide mouth grinned around his face and his dark eyes were full of music and fun. He was followed by his long-ago friend, Antonio Mendoza, whose whole body expressed an attitude of joy as they played a resounding medley of Spanish music and, slowly moving, danced delicately ahead of many followers who were just coming out of the aged mists into view. There was his mother, Morning Star, and father, Valerio, his grandparents and his Chicago cousin, Hog's Head, along with Stump Jumper—all doing little dance steps, smiling, occasionally waving at him with casual friendship. There were his Raton relatives shouting bravos at him. And behind them were mama Anna and papa Tony Marchiondo, proudly pointing to Billy and Johnny and the rest of their sons and daughters, who were dancing along, happily escorting them in the great eternal procession of timeless life. Then his mentor, Grinder the Gringo, chewing and spitting tobacco, shaking his happy head up and down as if approving Bluefeather's life and loves, danced on in the procession. Oh, there were too many. Too many to carefully observe coming in and out of the mists. Lorrie Friedman followed Grinder, sinuously moving her arms at times and at others raising an imaginary camera, taking imaginary pictures of everyone in pantomime. She passed on by, turning, dancing backward, waving at him in a movement of greeting, not good-bye. Dr. Godchuck and his Aunt Tulip dippy-doed and smiled as he twirled his bull prick cane in his smooth hands like a cheerleader—and they both moved just as lively.

Oh, how the music whirled and did its own dance of sounds across the sagebrush and foothills of the most special of mountains. There. There was Nancy of Tonopah, and she was doing a cancan, kicking her lovely legs in rhythm to all the sound of the world of cantinas. Then, then Miss Mary and old Ludwig shuffled gleefully out of the mists, both acknowledging Bluefeather's image with gazes and grins so beautiful that birds started singing along with his old friends' music. Miss Mary blew him a half dozen kisses that turned to white roses and landed between his legs and the leather of the saddle in a perfect bouquet. There was Daniel Wind doing an Osage shuffle, still wearing the steel army helmet that never seemed to fit. Marsha just beamed out of the lowering mists, her hair fiery as the magma of the Cavern of Marvels and her teeth showing strong and bright as the sun on arctic snow. She waved—with her fingers snapping, joyously whirling—to a shuffling Willy Ruger and a tap-dancing Flo. Then Marsha turned her wide, loving eyes toward Bluefeather. At each turn, she tilted her head in its puppy dog way. Oh, how they danced and laughed. Oh, how they smiled and waved. Oh! Then there was Pack, with his silent little smile, motioning for Bluefeather to advance. Hector Garcia followed a few steps behind, obviously inventing new dance steps but becoming more buoyant each yard. They had all casually, almost delicately waved for him to follow. The entire section danced on by, along with other figures, not quiet clear. Ghosts. The ectoplasm of memories, maybe.

Now came ancient relatives dancing from way back in his heritage—strong, purposeful, but radiating warmth and approval as they smiled at him. Turning swiftly in exuberance and stomping his moccasined feet in festive steps came Dancing Bear the spirit guide. Who was that with him? Who was that great dancer of endlessly skilled steps following him? Why, it was Bluefeather Fellini, as a young man of Taos, of Corrales, of many places, and then he turned into old Bluefeather of Hillsboro. The two friends from different dimensions were doing a special dance just for themselves now. It was the laughing dance. They twisted, stepping in time to the undulating stomach-aching, eye-watering mirth. They danced faster and faster around each other, giving one another swift, knowing glances of sidesplitting merriment. They roared. They howled with glee and fun. Then the laughing dance was suddenly done.

Bluefeather was absent, gone, from the procession and was back here in the Hillsboro mountains. Ramon, the entertainer of loving kindness, played on for all who listened, all who followed him, weaving their way through the desert, through the village of Taos and to the pueblo, on up the sides of the magic mountain.

The music and the snaking figures slowly vanished over a rise into the timber. Silence.

Then the sound of the mules' carefully stepping hooves returned. Dancing Bear's early prophesy of Bluefeather's great adventures had come true and had been fulfilled. Old Grinder's recognition of his being "a yearner" had also been correct and verified—all but this last one. He was anxious to get on with it—the dying—for no doubt it would be the greatest adventure yet. Bluefeather had experienced huge helpings of love, war and gold with an almost equal amount of hell and rapture.

They couldn't go much higher on the Black Range.

Sure enough, he found the proper place—a flat area on solid rock.

He dismounted and looked over to the west across the Gila Wilderness, created by President Theodore Roosevelt as the first of its kind in America. Bluefeather felt especially privileged to look upon such rare, grand, protected areas once more before it was all gone. It was perfectly suffused with shades of purples and deep blues.

He then cast a last glance back across the Aldo Leopold Wilderness Area, named after a great conservationist who believed, long before it was fashionable, that the world was a single, living organism, and who had written and preached this endlessly until he died. A lot who heard and read him knew he was a prophet ahead of the time of no return, but all who truly listened would never see the earth the same again. They would come to respect the delicate miracle of a breathing world. And there was the massive 330,000-acre Ladder Ranch, now owned by a world-famous communications couple.

All this area was the ground where the great warriors Geronimo and Chief Victoria and the black buffalo soldiers had roamed. It was all emerald green to him now. He could see as far and wide as his old eyes could search. Without thinking, he felt the insects, the birds, the wild animals, the grasses, the bushes, the trees, the rocks of thousands of square miles of earth. He heard them as well, and there were no vulgar interruptions of grinding steel mechanisms to wound the natural sounds. There was no town. No road.

"It is the rare time of perfection," he thought. "The blessed time."

He unsaddled Mary and took the bridle off. Both mules stared at him, puzzled. He raised his arms and told them to go. Then, seeming to understand, they turned and moved hesitantly away, down through the brush and timber. He hung the saddle from a tree limb with the rein of the bridle.

He slowly, carefully stretched his body out on the flat part of the rock—his back down, his face straight up. He started to fold his arms across his chest but stretched them out by his sides instead. He took his final look at the local sky. The golden element he had sought—then tried to deny—throughout his struggling life was minutely disseminated in an unlimited sky. There would be no more climbing over sandpaper rocks, no digging in the impervious earth, no scalded feet and bleeding, blistered hands. A simple upward glance had provided it all for free. Free.

He closed his eyes and became motionless, as the gold dust drained from the sky and turned into darkness.

The pinks and violets of dawn spread across the morning sky, and later a great shaft of reddish sunlight broke between an opening in the timber and shone on the still, still figure prone there on the rock. The soft, awakening sounds of the daytime creatures were mixed with those of the retiring night hunters. The sun caressed all the eastern slopes of the peaceful Black Range now.

Then the sudden, shattering noise of two fighter jets in training caused the top of the earth to vibrate with a terrible sound—the scream of a thousand doomed and tortured souls—the rending and ripping of miles of metal. As they passed on, vanishing over the mountain horizon beyond the speed of sound, the "chop, chop" of a Forest Service helicopter whirled and whacked its way through the air of the nearest canyon.

A tired coyote registered one more howl of defiance. An eagle screamed at nothing. The blue jays became raucous, and down below them the magpies chattered at one another with high-pitched screeches. A three-hundred-pound black mother bear stood up on her hind legs and roared loudly. Her two cubs squealed like pigs and climbed the nearest pine tree. Several squirrels chattered like little machine guns. Hearing all this from a quarter-mile distance, Mary and Nancy widened their nostrils and snorted and brayed with all the power of their lungs, adding to the crescendo.

Bluefeather was now sitting on the edge of the rock, staring straight out into a blankness. With both hands, he pushed himself up and stumbled stiffly over to untie the saddle and bridle from the limb. Taking the bridle in one hand, he walked downhill into the timber, his steel-toed miner's boots feeling surprisingly lighter with each step, as if they barely touched the ground.

Then he yelled angrily to the forest, "It's too damn noisy to die!"

He followed the tracks of the two mules. All the nearby creatures of the wilderness could hear him calling, "Haaa, Mary. Hooo, Nancy. Haaa, Mary."

ABOUT THE AUTHOR

MAX EVANS has been a painter in oils, a rancher, a cowboy, a mining prospector and speculator, and a trader in arts and antiques. He is the author of sixteen published books, including such western classics as *The Rounders* (made into a film with Henry Fonda and Glenn Ford), *The Hi Lo Country*, *My Pardner*, and *Bobby Jack Smith, You Dirty Coward*. He is the winner of numerous awards, including the Levi Strauss Golden Saddleman Award for lifetime achievement in western literature and the Governor's Award for Excellence in the Arts, New Mexico's highest artistic honor. In addition, *Bluefeather Fellini in the Sacred Realm* was named Best Western Novel of 1994 by the National Cowboy Hall of Fame. Evans lives in Albuquerque, New Mexico, with his wife, the artist Pat Evans.